# THE FIRST DECEPTION

## JACK NOBLE PREQUEL ONE

## L.T. RYAN

LIQUID MIND MEDIA, LLC

For information contact:

ltryan70@gmail.com

http://LTRyan.com

https://www.facebook.com/JackNobleBooks

# THE JACK NOBLE SERIES

*The Recruit (free)*
*The First Deception*
*Noble Beginnings*
*A Deadly Distance*
*Ripple Effect (Bear Logan)*
*Thin Line*
*Noble Intentions*
*When Dead in Greece*
*Noble Retribution*
*Noble Betrayal*
*Never Go Home*
*Beyond Betrayal (Clarissa Abbot)*
*Noble Judgment*
*Never Cry Mercy*
*Deadline*
*End Game*

Receive a free copy of The Recruit by visiting http://ltryan.com/newsletter.

# PART I

# CHAPTER ONE

J ack Noble considered how he had come to be on his knees in the middle of nowhere with a hood over his head and a rifle muzzle jammed into his back.

Seven days ago he was eating dirt. The worn combat boot of a wiry, young Drill Instructor pressed against the back of his head until his nose was no longer capable of drawing a breath of air and his tongue doubled as a mud pie. He coughed up crud for the next thirty-six hours. At least there'd be someone to go after if he ended up with black lung.

Three days ago he was in a fight that almost went to the death with a large prick who went by the nickname Bear, a six-six mountain of a man-child. He supposed that was better than the guy's given name of Riley Logan. The two had been at odds since day one.

Two hours ago they pulled Jack and Bear out of the covered bed of a pickup truck at a piss-covered rest stop somewhere between South Carolina and Virginia. Best guess, at least. No one had lent Noble a map, and the windows had been blackened out.

He passed the time by counting the seconds. Wasn't like he and Bear had all that much to talk about.

Jack spotted three men in a two-tone Bronco parked at the back of the rest stop lot. He didn't like their stares, but he and Bear were with three Marine MPs. No reason to worry, right? He hadn't anticipated there would be a handoff.

Six men jumped and restrained them while they took care of business at the urinals. By the time they were led out of the bathroom, the MPs were gone. The lingering smell of gas from the cranky V-8 was the only remaining clue they had been there.

Noble had spotted the Bronco right away. There must've been another vehicle out there he had missed that accounted for the additional three men. His old man would be pissed.

The blackout hoods went on and were cinched tight, but not before Jack caught a glimpse of the guy on his right. Too bad the guy wore a ski mask. A few body blows as they were tossed inside another vehicle were mixed in with directions not to move unless instructed. The gash over Jack's left eye from the fight earlier in the week with Bear tore open. Warm blood flowed down the side of his nose and settled on his upper lip. He inhaled the sickly-sweet smell.

Now Jack knelt on a patch of gravel that dug into his knees. The air was thick here, saturated with the odor of dead leaves. Sweat covered his body. They made him cross his ankles so he couldn't rise quickly. Heavy plastic zip ties, the kind you might use to keep ductwork from moving, burned like razor wire into the flesh above his wrists. The hood stunk like a Romanian belly dancer's hairy armpit. Not that he knew firsthand. His old man had spent plenty of time in Eastern Europe during the Cold War. Growing up, Jack's room was often described by his father as smelling like the aforementioned armpit. As a kid, he often tried to figure out how his dad had come to gain this knowledge.

Was one of his duties going around village to village, smelling armpits?

Bear was somewhere to Jack's right. The big man choked on every breath, rough and ragged like he'd emerged from ten minutes under water. Had he caught a blow that broke that nose of his? Might be an improvement in the end. Bear hadn't said much during the first leg of the ride with the MPs, only that he was glad they threw them in the back of a pickup with inner tubes to sit on because the bed liner was chewed up and jagged. And he might've mentioned he hated flying. It was the only thing that scared him. Except perhaps being dragged to the middle of nowhere and treated like a captured terrorist, judging by the anxiety attack the big man was in the midst of.

The hell were they doing here? They had been told they were selected for training for a new program. A joint effort, a clandestine group sponsored by the CIA. The Agency wanted young men they could mold into top operators. Guys who for whatever reason weren't going to maximize their talents in their current positions.

Guys like Jack and Bear.

Had it all been a lie?

The two had pissed plenty of people off on Parris Island. Mostly each other. Was that enough to warrant a six-hour drive for an execution?

Sure felt like that was the road they were traveling.

Noble counted the steps as they moved around him, listening for changes in cadence and location of the boots crunching on the loose rocks. One man moved. That was it. The guy circled them, stopping every few steps. No one said a word. Birds, crickets, cicadas. Mostly cicadas. And a goat or two. The woods? A farm, maybe?

"Bigger they are," a man said, "the harder they fall."

Jack tensed his core, glutes and shoulders, leaning a bit

forward to help brace for impact. Someone was about to make a point. At a solid six-two, Noble was bigger than most men. This was how you attacked him.

The sound of a heavy object, likely a rifle's buttstock, slamming into Bear's gut was followed by a swear-laden tirade from someone hovering over them.

Bear grunted and let out a strained breath. He tried to speak, maybe to levy a threat or two, but the words wouldn't come out.

"You'd be wise to fall over, boy." The voice was gravely, and he spoke with a Chicago staccato rhythm.

"Go to hell," Bear said between coughs.

There was a pause for laughter, which died down within five seconds. It went quiet except for a baby goat whining for food. The next blow had the intended effect. It had a much louder crack. Solid on solid. Bear's torso slammed down next to Jack, shaking the ground and sending rocks skidding. For twenty seconds all Jack heard was the big man choking, his body writhing in the gravel as he fought to refill his lungs. Jack knew the horrible feeling all too well. When Bear managed to suck in a solid breath, it sounded like the dead returning to life.

"Get him up and take him over there." Chicago had entrenched himself as the leader of the group. The guy paced a tight circle around Noble.

When would the blow come?

The men to his right strained as they lifted Bear. He offered them no help judging by the sound of his dragging feet.

"So you're the pretty boy, right?" The guy's hot breath penetrated through the hood, hitting Noble's sweaty face. Smelled worse than the cloth surrounding his head. "Ain't you got nothing to say?"

Noble took a deep breath, perhaps his final for a while, and remained quiet.

"See that, men." Knees popped like mini-shotguns being fired as the guy rose. "Pretty boy here has nothing to say to me."

"Trust me, hoss," another guy said. "Saw him at the urinal playing patty cakes with the big one. He's far from pretty."

The guy in front of Jack took two slow and deliberate steps, heel to toe, crunching the ground underfoot. Something snapped. A clasp, perhaps. He slid something out of a sheath or holster.

And then Noble heard the sound he'd been dreading.

The guy racked his pistol's slide several times, clearing it. He slammed a magazine into the grip, gave it a solid pull on the slide, chambering a round.

"They say you're not pretty." Chicago chuckled. "You believe that? Got something to say about it?"

Noble steadied his breath and slowly pushed his wrists outward. The heavy zip ties didn't give a millimeter.

"Don't try it, pretty boy."

"It ain't pretty, hoss. You got that part all wrong."

"Is that right?"

Noble honed in on the guy's location as the man shifted his stance.

"He's All-American. Foosball or some crap like that."

The man knelt down again and spoke near to Jack's face. "An All-American football player? Quarterback, probably. Right? Goddamn prima donnas, all of them. Think you're better than anyone else 'cause you can throw an inflated pigskin. The hell are you doing in my woods? Who the hell thought you'd amount to anything in my woods?"

Noble wondered the same. The decision to forgo his opportunities and join the Marines instead was starting to feel like the wrong call. He'd done it in part out of a sense of duty to his country. It'd been instilled into him from a young age, watching his father serve selflessly. He'd also grown up with the side of his father no one else saw. The relentless pursuit for perfection. Countless punishments for failing to live up to expectations. It created an incessant drive within him. But it came at a price, and he knew it.

There was nothing the old man wanted more than to see the younger Noble lead a professional football team. Misplaced spite can be strong when you're young enough to know everything. Instead of following his father's dream blueprint, Jack enlisted to piss him off.

Two solid thuds to the top of his head sent Jack hunkering down, chin tucked to his chest to keep his face out of the way. A wave of heat overtook him and he began to wonder if he had lost consciousness and hadn't realized it yet. Pain radiated from the top of his head, down his cheeks, neck, and shoulders. He saw bright flashes of colors, despite the black hood. Not a good sign. Chicago had nailed him in just the right spot.

A hand squeezed his shoulder while keeping him upright. Chicago grunted as he knelt down next to Noble. He pictured the guy battleworn and up there in age.

"There's a Winchester 308 aimed at your head. You so much as uncross your legs and the man holding it has been instructed to unload on you. And before you think we're scared of someone hearing the sound of gunfire, we're in the middle of West Virginia on over a thousand acres. There's no one out here."

Noble suppressed the rage rising like bile in his throat. He was restrained to the point of being unable to defend himself. What was he going to do, headbutt the guy? Then what? He'd been taught to think situations through rather than acting on first instinct. He often failed to do so, but right now he couldn't get past what to do after taking the next breath.

The world went quiet over the next several minutes. Even the cicadas silenced their shrill song. He cocked his head like a dog.

Was anyone out there? A slight gust of wind disturbing dead leaves on the forest floor sounded like footsteps all around him. Crickets started up and immediately went silent. Why? It reached the point where every sound required fifteen seconds of analysis.

He resisted the urge to speak. Even a simple *"who's out there?"* would prove him weak.

His exposed arms burned amid the rising heat. The hell was it? There wasn't a crackling fire nearby. Had they doused him with some kind of chemical agent and he hadn't realized it? His arms had been drenched with perspiration for hours now. He might not have felt them putting something on him.

The minutes passed, slow at first, then faster and faster as his thoughts turned into a jumbled mess until he finally zoned out. A meditative state, he supposed. Not something he'd ever strived for.

He had no idea how much time had passed when he stirred at the sound of men approaching. The burning sensation had gone. How long ago? He hadn't even noticed. The men walked around him in pairs, one to each side, four in all. No one said a thing.

Neither did Jack.

Despite the warning, he had uncrossed his legs during his timeout. Even stretched them out to the side. What he hadn't done was taken a seat. He'd kept one knee in the gravel the entire time. His back ached and his hips and shoulders were stiff. But if he had to get up and full-on sprint for half a mile, he could get it done.

"How's the pretty boy feeling this morning?" Chicago chuckled to himself.

Jack felt the comment had grown stale.

"Ain't a pretty boy, hoss. How many times I gotta tell you that?"

There was laughter all around him.

Noble hoped they'd take the hood off before killing him. He had to see if the second voice matched the cartoon caricature of a hog-faced man missing three top teeth that played in his mind every time the guy spoke.

"That's right," Chicago said. "The All-American. Guess we better watch out, lest he tackle us to the ground."

The hood tugged Jack's face downward. The bottom fell open. Light bled through and he noticed the drawstring dangling on two sides, cut in half. A moment later someone yanked the hood off his head. Four intense flashlight beams welcomed him back to the world. They felt like knives penetrating his skull. He clenched his eyelids shut and turned his head. His flinching reaggravated the pain in his knees, which had gone numb hours ago.

A stocky man walked past, stood in front of him. His thick frame blocked the lights. Jack blinked the guy into focus. The sky behind him was pale blue with a hint of orange. The woods were alive with birdsong. The foul odor he'd smelled all night had been replaced with wood smoke.

The man knelt down, looked Jack in the eye. He was probably in his fifties. Grey flecks in his thick stubble. His hairline had receded a few inches and was solid white on the sides, salt and pepper on top. His eyes were dark as coal. His jowls sagged a bit, but not enough to hide the muscles as the guy clenched his teeth.

"Welcome to hell, All-American." A half-smile spread on Chicago's face. There was no joy or welcome in his eyes. "You survived night one. At least sixty-nine more to go and maybe we'll make a spy out of you." He lifted a Bowie knife, presumably the one that had cut the hood's strap.

Jack focused on the sharp blade. It was well taken care of. The insane man behind it split into two blurry images fighting for the same space until Jack made eye contact again. The guy looked beyond Noble and nodded. One of the other men yanked Jack's wrists up, nearly wrenching his shoulders out of socket. He was forced forward, face-first in the gravel. He'd have preferred the dirt.

Jack glanced around, looking for Bear, but was unable to locate him. A few seconds later the zip ties fell to the ground and the weight lifted off his back. He rose, bringing his hands around front. He massaged feeling back into his wrists.

"Now get your ass up, All-American. Chow's in thirty minutes. You better be cleaned up and spit-shined or you don't eat."

# CHAPTER TWO

Two instructors stood in front of Noble and Bear. One tossed them a single bar of soap after they stripped off their dirty and bloodied clothing. Bear snagged it mid-air. Noble didn't ask the big man if he could use it. Each of the instructors held a spray nozzle attached to a long black hose that snaked out of sight. A solid stream of cold water belted them fifteen seconds at a time.

They were given washcloths to dry off with. The small squares of cloth weren't very effective. The instructors handed each man a pair of boxers with instructions to head up the hill and get breakfast.

The morning breeze chilled Jack's damp skin as they followed the dirt road. They first saw the sun when they crested the hilltop. The temperature rose ten degrees. Smoke wafted out of distant trees. The mess hall had to be near.

Their feet and ankles were covered with dirt by the time they entered the woods. Rocks and sticks and who knew what else dug into their soles. They kept moving. Motivated in part by muscles in need of energy, but also fear of suffering through another night like the last.

Bear had tried to talk about it on the trek over. Noble kept his mouth shut and signaled for Bear to do the same. Someone was out there watching their every movement. One step out of line and they'd likely receive a bullet for disobeying orders.

A man in his mid-thirties with a thick brown beard and dressed in a white tank top and gym shorts that were shorter than Jack's boxers greeted them at the door. It wasn't a good look for the guy. Hair stood an inch high off his shoulders and around his upper back.

Inside stood three other guys all wearing nothing but boxer shorts. A table separated them from Noble and Bear. They all looked the same. Dark hair, short beards, stocky and muscled. Couple scars here and there, possibly from knife and bullet wounds. Noble had been around enough Special Forces to know these men had been selected from within the community.

Floorboards creaked with every step Jack and Bear took. The place stunk of bleach and ammonia. The back of Noble's throat burned. How long until they'd pass out from the smell?

The instructor wearing the tank top spoke up. "Once food is served you have one hundred and twenty seconds to consume everything on your plate. What you don't eat is forfeited. You will not eat again for eight hours, so I recommend you do everything in your power to eat every last bite. If you fail to do so, I will person-ally see to it that the contents of your stomach end up on the ground outside. And it better be outside. If you throw up in my personal dining hall, I will waterboard your ass. And then your face. Think about it, gentlemen, it makes sense in the end."

Noble looked down the line. He stood at one end with Bear to his right. A gap the size of a man existed between Bear and the next guy. Why? He realized there had been six at the start of last night's activities. One couldn't hack it.

Tank Top came out of the back room carrying two trays. He disappeared for another thirty seconds. The smell of caffeine beckoned. Tank Top returned with two additional trays of food. He set a tall styrofoam cup filled with sludge that might pass for coffee in front of each man. Then he placed a bowl of tan goo that Jack figured was oatmeal and a plate full of scrambled eggs.

The instructor adjusted his watch, said, "Eat." Then he left the room.

There were no utensils. The men shared nervous glances, waiting for someone to take the lead.

"Time's wasting, boys." Bear grabbed the bowl of oatmeal, put it to his lips, and tipped his head back. Before he finished slamming it down, everyone else had joined in.

The oatmeal was bland. The eggs left unsalted. The coffee cold. Noble finished his meal in a hundred seconds flat. He'd been counting since Tank Top left the room. Seconds after setting his cup down, his stomach began spasming, racked with pain. Had they poisoned the food? He looked for similar signs of discomfort from the others. No one else seemed to have a problem.

They'd poisoned *his* food.

*Think it through, Jack. Why would they do that?*

A couple of deep breaths settled his mind and he pushed the panic back, allowing logic and reasoning a seat at the table. They wouldn't waste below-average chow on a bunch of guys if the plan was to kill them. They'd hang him out to dry and make sure they gained something from it rather than let him go in here.

He'd been under constant stress since leaving Parris Island. They hadn't been fed until now. His stomach only revolted because of this.

Tank Top stormed back into the room and inspected the

plates. Noble couldn't tell if the guy was happy that everyone had heeded his warning. Maybe Tank Top wanted someone to defy him. Give him a reason to lash out. Hell, Noble wanted that, too. A chance to see how serious these guys were with their threats.

"Lace up," Tank Top said. "We're going for a twelve-miler."

The recruit at the other end of the line spoke up. "We don't have any shoes."

"It's an expression, dumb ass. You're running barefoot."

Noble knew it wouldn't be long before he and Tank Top got into it.

The men filed out of the room and were chastised for not cleaning up first. Bear was sent back in while the remaining four did pushups until the big man returned.

The first mile wasn't too bad. They jogged at a moderate pace on a well-worn path through a clearing created by the power company. Splintered poles with power lines attached at the top lined the middle of the path. High grass swayed in the light breeze on either side. The morning sun was at their back. The temperature seemed to climb every couple hundred feet.

Noble kept his stride short and landed on his forefoot. It felt natural and limited the chance of injury.

At about mile two they ducked into the woods, again they ran on a path, but one rife with obstacles. Tank Top had done this many times before. He knew where to step, and what to avoid. It was a chore keeping up with the guy. Every few minutes a recruit shouted or grunted, the result of landing on a root or rock.

By the fifth mile, Jack's soles screamed. They were cut in several places, burning from heel to toe, and blackened with dirt.

They ran through the woods, in grass and mud, and on rocks next to a river bank. The mud had been welcoming, if not concerning, because of the high chance of infection.

By the time they'd run an estimated ten miles, Noble's feet had gone numb. The guy who had spoken up about shoes had collapsed a few miles back. The group took turns supporting him. This seemed to piss Tank Top off to no end. He yelled incessantly about their piss-poor pace.

Noble challenged him on it. "If he doesn't make it, none of us does."

Tank Top kept pushing but eased off a little.

They finished at the site of the early morning deluge. Another cold shower would've been welcome. Instead they were told they had thirty minutes to recoup before range practice.

The group gathered on the shaded side of the building. Bear leaned back against the wall and lowered himself to the ground, massaging his calves on the way down.

"What have we gotten ourselves into?" he said.

Noble shook his head, as much to get rid of the cobwebs as to acknowledge the big man's question. "It's all a game, just like Recruit Training. Remember that."

"Ain't no game ever left me with a gash like this." Bear crossed his leg over his right knee and showed Jack the underside of his foot. A two-inch cut ran down the middle. "I think those bastards hid razor blades out there."

"Wouldn't doubt it." Noble looked past Bear at the other three men. They kept their distance. "Where you guys from?"

They stared back, faces hard, and said nothing.

"Where's the sixth guy?" Jack asked.

Two men continued staring at him. The third looked away. It was his partner who'd washed out the first night.

Noble singled the guy out. "He couldn't hang, huh? Can't blame him for taking the easy way out. I know what was running through my mind last night. This has gotta be tough, even for a Ranger."

It was a stab in the dark. Growing up, he'd known a few of the Army's elite fighting force. This guy had the look about him.

The man nodded as he rose to his feet. His legs wobbled the first few steps. Muscles tightening after their tough run. It didn't matter how conditioned any of them were. Trails worked different muscles than asphalt. Go barefoot, and it was like waking up muscles that hadn't been used in years.

"I'm Spinks." He extended his hand to Noble. "Guy that came with me was weak. It's better he's gone. He'd only cause problems for all of us."

"Noble." He pointed to Bear. "That's Logan."

"Call me Bear."

"You sure about that?" Spinks said. "Cute nicknames aren't gonna be looked at favorably here."

"Let 'em try."

"What's up with those guys?" Noble jutted his chin toward the other two trainees who had retreated further away, engrossed in their own conversation.

Spinks lowered himself onto a log a few feet from Jack. "Only one or two of us will make it through this. No point in getting to know anyone you don't already know. Make sense?"

"Guess so," Noble said.

"Only reason I'm over here is because you guys aren't as big of dicks as they are."

"You don't speak for me." Bear grabbed his crotch.

"You know what I mean." Spinks spit on the ground between them. He looked at Jack and Bear, then at the other two men. "They think they're the top operators, and it's a given they'll make it through this." He shook his head. "You guys look younger, like you ain't been around long. What's your background?"

"We were on Parris Island." Jack studied the guy's face for a reaction. There was none.

Spinks nodded slowly. "If this is anything like Spec Ops training, it's gonna go a little differently than you're used to. Yeah, they're gonna be intimidating. I mean, they gotta break us down a bit for the job we're gonna be assigned to do."

Bear leaned in. "Which is?"

Spinks's eyes narrowed as he studied the man across from him. "Yeah, I'm not sure if you're messing with me, or what. Anyway, chances are they'll tell us to minimize verbal communication from this point forward. They'll be dickheads for a while, probably weeks, but then it'll tone down once we demonstrate we know what we're doing. Don't get me wrong, it's not gonna be easy for us at any point. They'd be doing us no favors by patting us on the butts and ushering us through. Just remember, there's always a method behind the madness."

An explosion ripped through the temporary calm. All five men dove for the ground as a heatwave blew past, rattling trees and sending wildlife scattering. The ringing in Jack's ears left him disoriented as he tried to get his bearings down. He crawled across the leaf-covered ground toward the front of the building. There was a road there, and roads eventually lead out.

Or to dead ends.

He reached the corner, looked up, and saw the old guy standing there laughing. A method behind the madness? This was just pure madness.

"Come on, boys," Chicago said. "Let's go shoot some guns."

# CHAPTER THREE

T wo hours on the range provided a needed break for the recruits. Sleep-deprived, hungry, and sore, they fired an assortment of firearms from standard military-issues such as the Beretta 92FS, M16, and M249 SAW, to more custom and high-end units like the M82A1 heavy sniper rifle, nicknamed the Light Fifty for its .50 caliber load, used by the SEALs. The men were naturals, even with units they had not fired before. To the untrained eye, not a single one fired a miss-shot. To the six trainers watching over them, they'd all screwed up a dozen times, whether they had or not.

Noble had learned Chicago's name after failing to clear a jam fast enough. Another instructor gave it away.

"You let Cribbs see you do that, you'll eat the bullet," said Tank Top, who now had desert-tan long pants and a white t-shirt with sleeves that fit tight against his biceps.

Noble turned to look at the guy. Silver strands stood out in his dark beard in the sunlight. Maybe he was older than Noble had thought. "What's his first name?"

Tank Top's face tightened as he rose and stared downrange. Information was to be withheld from the trainees, and he'd given up one of Cribbs's advantages. "Keep firing, Noble."

Following range training, Tank Top led them on a two-mile run back to the barracks. The session culminated with ninety minutes of pushups, burpees, leg lifts, and wind-sprints. Noble powered through each set, sucking the sweat off his upper lip to wet his dry mouth. Hadn't these guys ever heard of dehydration? They were somewhere in West Virginia in the middle of August. The temperatures soared over ninety by ten in the morning. The humidity had to be encroaching a hundred percent. Every breath they took was half-steam. It should've been mandatory for the men to gulp down a gallon of water every hour or two. Instead there'd only been a couple of sips for the recruits here and there, while the trainers drank freely.

Despite the insatiable thirst, the PT routine was easier than the earlier run. Noble had grown up in Florida. He played sports year-round, and extra conditioning was a way of life when his father was home. This was nothing compared to some of those sessions.

Noble glanced around at the other men, noticed them lagging behind. He was already mid-air, arms extended, while they were just hitting the ground during burpees.

Bear matched Jack's pace the closest, despite his large frame. Presumably because he'd been through similar on Parris Island during Recruit Training. They'd been pulled prematurely, but it was clear that the eight weeks spent there had been good for something.

Noble kept Bear in his periphery. He detested the fact the big man was the only one he could trust now. That wasn't saying much. A short time ago, Bear had been ready to kill him. Crush him through the bottom of a boxing mat.

Maybe all the words and blows thrown prior had been posturing.

Bear caught Jack watching him. His eyebrows knit close together and he threw his hands out as if to say, the hell you looking at. Jack gave him a quick nod, a thumbs up, then matched his pace on the remainder of the exercises.

Cribbs walked over with a rifle slung across his shoulder and joined Tank Top and another trainer. Cribbs leaned back against the barracks building, sipping from a canteen. He wiped water from his lip, then dumped the remaining contents on the ground.

All the men could do was stare.

"That'll be all," Cribbs barked.

The two instructors had been taking turns leading the drills. They backed off and flanked Cribbs.

"You guys tired yet?" Cribbs asked.

No one answered the question. They were exhausted. They'd spent the majority of the day exerting themselves to their physical and mental limits after a breakfast of at most six-hundred calories. If they were lucky enough to keep it down during that first run. That energy had been used up hours ago.

"I said, any of you tired?" Cribbs dared them to speak up. He flipped on a spigot and re-filled his canteen. "If you're thirsty, just say so."

The sight of the water caused Noble's throat to burn. He resisted the urge to lick his lips or try anything else that might result in his mouth watering.

Spinks stepped forward, rubbing the back of his sunburned neck with one hand. His head hung. What was the guy thinking? He'd been through boot, selection, advanced training, and had lived for weeks at a time in the field. He knew how this worked. Begging for water would not work out in his favor, and the guy had to know it.

The right side of Cribbs's mouth twitched. Might be the biggest smile they would see from the guy in their seven weeks at the farm. He unscrewed the canteen's cap and handed the container to Spinks. "You gonna drink that?"

"Yes, sir."

Cribbs eyes lit up. He looked like a mad dog. That was probably his nickname. Mad Dog Cribbs said, "Well, then go ahead. Drink it."

Spinks's lips thinned as he lifted his trembling hands to his face. He closed his eyes, tipped his head back a few inches, then put the canteen to his lips. Water washed over his mouth, trickled from the corners, down his chin, settling into his sweat soaked chest hair. In a few seconds he managed to drain the canteen.

He looked refreshed, but was it worth it?

"Good stuff, isn't it?" Cribbs said. "Comes from the ground under your feet. We don't carry none of that filtered water that all the yuppies are raging about."

Spinks handed the canteen back to the older man, who turned and went back to the spigot. The valve whined as he twisted the handle open. Water rushed into the canteen, thumping against the tin.

Noble could feel it wash over his lips. Taste it pass over his sandpaper-tongue and down his parched throat, taking with it the lumps he couldn't swallow down anymore. Never before had he wanted a mouthful of water so bad. Not even during two-a-day football practices in the Florida heat.

"Who's next?" Cribbs extended the canteen out. "Who else wants some of my fine water?"

The shorter of the other two guys stepped forward. The men hadn't spoken to Noble or Bear. He had no idea what their names were.

"Murphy, right?" Cribbs said, his lip twitching into a smile again.

"Yes, sir."

"You want some of my water, huh?"

"Yes, sir."

"Pretty hot out there today."

"Yes, sir."

Murphy sounded like a groveling robot, willing to play the old guy's game because he couldn't delay his desire any longer.

Cribbs took a step forward so that the canteen was within Murphy's reach. The recruit reached for it. Cribbs dropped the canteen, grabbed ahold of Murphy's wrist, and pulled him in closer. As he reeled Murphy in, Cribbs swept the guy's feet out from under him. Cribbs controlled Murphy's fall so that he landed on his back. All the air in his lungs escaped in one hollow breath. The guy was down, and wouldn't move for another thirty seconds at least. That didn't stop Cribbs from placing his foot on Murphy's throat.

"You see this?" Cribbs said. "The rest of you dumb enough to take a handout from your enemy? The first guy might get away with it, but it only spells death for the rest of you."

Death? What was the end game here?

Noble clenched every muscle he had control over as he stared down Cribbs. It took every ounce of restraint to not go after the man who showed no concern over the beet-red face of the guy on the ground.

Cribbs took note of Noble glaring at him. "Got something to say?"

Noble said nothing.

"Come on, Noble." Cribbs waved him forward. "Or you just a pussy like your old man?" His lip twitched multiple times. "Yeah, I know the old bastard."

The line had been crossed. "Get off him."

Tank Top chuckled as though he'd seen this show before. Every class that came through their little playground had someone stupid like Murphy who'd take a drink. And someone even dumber like Noble, who wouldn't stand for his teammate to take unnecessary punishment.

Cribbs adjusted his foot an inch, then lifted his other off the ground, putting all his weight on Murphy's throat and cutting off air from his lungs. If Cribbs slipped an inch or two, he would crush the guys trachea.

The thread restraining Noble from acting snapped. They could use their psychological and demanding physical tactics all day long. Take it deep into the night for all he cared. But attempted murder wouldn't fly. Jack bounced once on his heels, then lunged forward.

The speed at which Cribbs moved to throw Noble off was astonishing. The other guy might've been on the wrong side of fifty, but he moved like a twenty-year-old. A simple sidestep and a hand on Jack's back sent him stumbling over Murphy, headed for the ground. He planted his right hand and regained his balance with only his knee skidding the ground. He spun on a dime, ready to pounce. Cribbs and the other two instructors were a step ahead of him.

Every move Noble made resulted in them tightening their grip. Tank Top had his back. In a matter of seconds they had his arms pulled back and torqued up high. Noble knew how to escape the move, but then he'd have to turn his back to Cribbs. Of the three, the man seemed the most unhinged.

Cribbs glared at Jack as he kicked Murphy out of the way. Murphy scrambled to his knees, throwing dirt everywhere as he clawed at the ground until he was close enough for Bear and Spinks to help him up.

"You're stupid like your old man," Cribbs said to Jack. "But at least he would've had the sense to stay in line. What do you think would happen if you pulled something like that out in the field? Huh? Every last one of you would be dead!" Drops of spittle smacked Jack in the face. Cribbs's face was a deep red. "You don't belong on my team, Noble. A week, tops. That's what I give you."

Noble held the older man's gaze. His anger hadn't subsided, and if his hands were free, he'd put them to use.

Cribbs must've had the same thought. Without warning, he threw an uppercut into Jack's diaphragm. Noble had prepared for the blow, but it didn't matter. A second and third blow ensured the desired effect had been achieved. Gravity was taking over. The instructors at his back were the only thing holding him up. They hooked his elbows as he collapsed to his knees.

"Take him around back and put him through the paces." Cribbs turned to the remaining recruits. "You can go in the barracks now. Get cleaned up, changed, and come over for dinner. Day two is done."

# CHAPTER FOUR

Douglas Cribbs waited until his men reported the recruits had gone to bed before reaching into the old fridge and pulling out an ice-covered can of Pabst. He peeled back the tab and waited for the head to retreat through the opening. The carbonation mixed with barley and hops filled his nose as he lifted the can to his lips. The first sip went down smooth. Made it too easy to drink too much. That would make for a long night, which in turn would result in tomorrow being an even longer day.

Cribbs grabbed a stepstool, climbed atop it, and felt along the top shelf until he found the pack of Camels. Filtered. Because his sister wouldn't stop fussing at him about smoking the unfiltered ones. He told her all the time it was a miracle he was still kicking. From the early days in Vietnam until they forced him to leave, he survived. From the opening moments of the Cold War as a CIA operative until the wall fell, he survived. He'd made it through some of the worst snafus in history. Things most couldn't imagine. And he'd survived it all. Think he gave a single crap about the negative effects of tobacco?

But she hadn't relented, and seeing as how they were the only family the other had, he gave in to her demands. The smokes still did the trick for him, so if it eased her mind a little, so be it.

With an unlit cigarette dangling from the corner of his mouth, Cribbs dragged a chair out onto the dark front porch. The temperature had dipped into the upper sixties thanks to their position in the mountains. But that offered little respite with the humidity still in the nineties. The earlier thunderstorm didn't help. Only made it more of a struggle for Noble to finish his bonus PT. Cribbs swished a mouthful of beer around and swallowed it hard.

Headlights twinkled through the thick foliage in front of the cabin. A big V-8 rumbled through the woods, grating on the dirt road. The cabin was set further away from the training area than all the other buildings. Mostly for meetings like this one. Also because he generally hated the recruits, and on most days, his instructors. There was a need for secrecy, even with his trainers. They needed to be insulated from those who ran the program. It worked in reverse, too. The program heads from the CIA needed the same separation from the guys on the ground. When they first brought him out to the farm, he thought it was because they were going to ask him to retire and the land would be his hush money. Then they told him he was going to head up a new program. A new kind of agent. Those same people were due for a visit tonight.

Cribbs was not one to take unnecessary chances. He unholstered his Browning 1911 and flipped the safety off. Nine rounds were seven more than he needed.

The light washed over the front of his cabin as the vehicle turned the corner. It stopped, and the engine and headlights cut off, leaving a half-dozen trails floating in Cribbs's vision. Two doors opened, slammed shut. Two sets of shoes crunched through the gravel. The smell of their gas guzzler reached him before they did.

"Cribbs, good to see you." Alexa Steele offered her hand.

He held up his beer and his pistol and shrugged while taking a drag on his cigarette.

"I'll go inside," she said.

"Better stop treating her like that." Randall McKenzie tapped his shoes against the edge of the step. Why the guy wore two-hundred-dollar dress shoes out to this place baffled Cribbs. Every time he came. Maybe he had a set specifically for the visits.

"Screw her." Cribbs planted his elbows against the seat arms and pushed himself up. Old joints popped. He shook his legs out. One day it'd all catch up to him, he was sure of that.

"That'd be a mistake, too." McKenzie looked through the grime-coated screen door and smiled. "She's on the move, and it won't be long before she's a whole lot of people's bosses, and fighting the D.C. folks for more budget money. You'll want to be on her good side."

Cribbs belched. He didn't want to be on any side but the winning one. Steele was not who he'd hitch his wagon to. Even if she was his niece.

"Put the gun away and let's go inside."

"This is a Browning 1911," Cribbs said, leveling the pistol at McKenzie. "Chambered in .45 ACP. It'd tear half your head off if I nicked your ear with a round."

McKenzie smiled in the face of Cribbs's threats. Few, if any, men in a similar position had ever done that to Cribbs. "How much have you had to drink tonight?"

He extended the half-drained can. "This is it, so far."

"Long day?"

Cribbs sighed as he holstered his piece. "You got no idea. These imbeciles you saddled me up with this time. I mean, how far down the drain are you reaching for these guys?"

McKenzie held the screen door open, allowing for a transfer of mosquitos and other bugs. "Let's go inside and talk about it."

Cribbs and the two CIA heads sat at the table. McKenzie took Cribbs up on his offer of a Pabst. Steele stuck with water. They were working. This was not the time for drinking. *Such a damn prude,* Cribbs thought. He couldn't understand how they shared the same DNA. After a few minutes of banter, the conversation turned to the first full day with the recruits.

"Jeremy Gauss," McKenzie said. "How's he doing?"

Cribbs clasped his hands in front of him and shook his head. "Washed out last night."

"Why?" McKenzie asked.

"Couldn't hack it, I guess."

"And what couldn't he hack? What are you doing differently this time?"

Shrugging, Cribbs reached for his beer.

"Douglas, don't take another sip until you answer me." McKenzie had dressed in his big boy undies for this meeting.

"Well, Randy, he found kneeling in the gravel too much for his delicate knees, which apparently he'd only placed on pillows when he got down to suck cock."

"You contemptible prick." McKenzie leveled a loaded index finger at Cribbs. "You only have this position because of your relationship with—"

"Guys!" Steele slammed her hand on the table, barely eliciting a glance from the two men. "Just answer the goddamn questions, Cribbs. And you, Randall, stop egging him on."

Cribbs watched her for a moment trying to ascertain whether she actually cared about the outburst. Nothing would happen between the two men. He knew that. McKenzie knew it. And so did Steele. She wanted to keep the meeting moving so she could hear about her projects. And Cribbs couldn't wait to get to them. He had plenty to say.

"All right," Cribbs said. "All right. Gauss didn't have *it*. He was sitting on his balls in the dirt crying when he thought he was all alone. I debriefed him, and it turned out the guy had cracked before the hood went on. Thought he'd actually fallen into enemy hands and was going to be tortured."

It looked like McKenzie wanted to say something smart, but the guy kept his mouth shut. Wise of him. Instead, he asked about Spinks and the two others.

"Fine, so far. A little beat up, I guess. One passed a test earlier today, the other failed. Had to teach him a little lesson."

McKenzie looked away, presumably because he knew all that entailed.

"What about my guys?" Steele tilted her head as she clamped down on the end of her pen with her front teeth.

Cribbs wasn't thrilled to have a couple green-ass recruits in his midst. And he didn't hold back on letting her know that from the beginning. She had fought him on it, and won. It was the future of the program, she had insisted. Cribbs wanted nothing to do with it moving forward if that was the case.

"Like I suspected," Cribbs said, "They aren't ready for this."

"They wash out last night?" Steele said.

"Nope."

"Problems completing any phase of training today?"

"Nope."

"Then what's the issue?" She sat back in her chair and folded her arms across her chest, a single eyebrow raised while she waited for her uncle to explain himself.

"When I was teaching that Murphy a lesson, your guy, what's his damn name?" Cribbs searched the cabin's exposed rafters for the answer. "Noble. He stuck his foot in a huge pile of excrement."

"Good, we want them to stand up for each other."

"No, we want them to make sound decisions that won't get everyone killed. He goes out in the field and pulls a stunt like that to prove he's macho, they'll all die."

"If it had been one of the others, you'd be praising him to Randall right now." Steele looked between the two men. "And don't give me that look, Cribbs. You know it's true. You hated the idea of this from the very beginning. I heard your points, and there are some valid ones. But this comes down from higher than me. I was only instructed to find the first two recruits to beta this. You've got fresh meat to mold into whatever cut you want. If you can't do it, then it's not my fault, and it's certainly not Noble and Logan's fault, either. This falls squarely on your shoulders. Thirty some years of experience, way more than half in the Agency. That's what you tell everyone. Well, prove you are made of what you espouse and turn those two into *your* kind of men."

Cribbs leaned back in his seat, one hand wrapped around the cold beer, the other flat on the table. He couldn't decide whether to smile or spit. His sister's daughter had finally grown into her own woman.

"I'll try, Alexa. I'll try."

# CHAPTER FIVE

D ay six. Noble had pushed himself further than at any point in his life. Doubts crept in that he might not complete the program. The instructors had singled him out daily. An extra hour of PT, three more miles in the woods with no shoes, and a single meal, if he was lucky. They blamed every single snafu on him. It wasn't entirely limited to Noble. They came down hard on the group, too, blaming Jack for the extra work. The worse the weather, the harsher the punishment.

Temps over ninety? Run five more miles. Steep hill ahead? Sprint, maggots.

He'd do everyone a favor by quitting. Staring up at the dark ceiling, he knew that wasn't the case. They'd pick on someone else. Probably Bear. Jack was surprised they hadn't targeted the big man from the beginning. Lucky for Bear, Noble was the smartest ass in the room.

They rolled out of bed around four-thirty to the sound of AC/DC blasting through twenty-year-old speakers. A lot of fuzz. A lot of screaming about big balls. It got the blood pumping in an anxiety attack sort of way. Every morning it was a different tune. He figured at some point they'd switch to Sesame Street songs, just to mix it up a bit.

Calhoun was the last to get to his feet. The guy had arrived two days ago to take the place of the first-night washout. Tank Top told them they needed six. Company orders. That didn't make sense to Jack. Any one of them could quit the first week. In fact, they'd been encouraged to do so daily. Every extra push-up he performed was met with a *"you ready to quit yet?"* taunt by the instructors.

Noble shook his head at the title given to the guys who carried out Cribbs's wishes. They were glorified bullies who hadn't taught any of the recruits a single thing other than how to push themselves further than they had ever gone before. And that was more a matter of fearing punishment than anything else.

He shuffled across the floor to the head. It took a minute or two to work out the cramps in his feet and lower legs. Judging by the swooshing sound all around him, the others had the same problem.

Noble parked himself in front of a sink next to Bear. The two had managed not to kill one another over the past seventy-two hours. An improvement, for sure. Jack splashed cold water over his face, then took a few large gulps to start hydrating. It smelled like rotten eggs. Tasted like it too.

"Don't know how you do that." Bear spit into the sink.

Noble shrugged. He'd had worse.

"What's in store for us today?" Bear asked.

Noble met his gaze in the mirror. "You can bet on a dozen miles. They went easy on us yesterday keeping it under ten."

Bear pointed at himself and the other guys. "They kept us under ten. How many more did you run?"

"I lost count."

Bear chuckled. "All you gotta do is keep quiet. You know that, right?"

Noble studied the guy's face to see if he was serious. "They're singling me out, Bear. You haven't picked up on that?"

"Seems to me you're going the extra mile to piss them off."

"They're provoking him into it." Calhoun stood in the doorway with a towel draped over his shoulder. "Think about it, man. They wouldn't bring us into something like this without having a solid psych profile, right? Remember all those questions you answered?" He walked behind them and stopped at the sink next to Noble. It was obvious he'd avoided showering the night before. "They know how to push each of our buttons, and you're the guy they want to screw with the most, for whatever reason. Maybe Cribbs doesn't like you and is trying to get you to wash out. And from what I've seen, I can't blame him."

Noble stared at his own reflection. He hadn't always been easy to provoke, unless you knew how. His brother, Sean, was great at it. His father was the master. Someone had figured him out from a simple test and told these guys how to do it?

"He makes a good point," Bear said. "Why don't you try to keep your mouth shut and your hands to yourself today?"

"What can I say? I have a low threshold for idiocy."

Thirty minutes later the six men stood in line for chow. They'd been given an extra sixty seconds to eat today. Might get to taste something for once. Steam rose from the six Styrofoam cups of coffee. The oatmeal was topped with brown sugar and honey. Crystals of salt stood atop the eggs.

Jack's mouth watered. It'd been almost a week since his last full meal. He hadn't consumed a thousand calories in a day since leaving Parris Island. This spread in front of him was nothing short of a feast.

Cribbs burst into the room. He shoved Tank Top aside. He

looked as pissed as Jack had ever seen him. Even the guy's ears were maroon. He walked down the line, glaring at the food on the table.

"Oh, hell no. What the hell is this?" Cribbs grabbed Jack's coffee and tossed it against the wall. It splattered on Calhoun's shoulder. The guy flinched away from the scalding liquid. "Who gave you my damn breakfast, Noble?"

Jack focused on a spot on the wall just above Cribbs's head.

"I asked you a question. I expect an answer."

Jack's eyes didn't waver. His focus started to, though.

Cribbs grabbed the plate of eggs and dumped it out on the table. He leaned over, spat on it. "Go ahead and eat now, Noble."

Noble took a quick glance at the man. Cribbs' cheeks matched his ears. His eyebrows were almost knit together. His upper lip trembled. If this was a test, then Cribbs was a hell of an actor. It seemed the guy walked around like that all day, working himself up for an early retirement due to death by myocardial infarction.

"Didn't you hear me?" Cribbs said.

"You take a bite," Noble said. "I will, too."

Bear shook his head, drawing the angry stare of Cribbs. "You want some, too, boy?"

Bear straightened and said nothing, though Noble spotted the big man balling up his fists.

Cribbs turned his attention back to Jack. "The rest of you, take your food outside and eat. But know that you will never get a meal this good again while you are in my house."

The men grabbed their food and exited the room. The floor reverberated with each step.

After it died down, Cribbs spoke. "You know why I hate you, Noble?"

A dozen smart-ass replies popped into his head. It was second nature, after all. But Noble remembered Calhoun's words earlier and kept his mouth shut. Cribbs wanted him to react a certain way. *Don't give him the satisfaction.*

"You show zero respect," Cribbs said. "And you ain't accomplished a damn thing as far as I'm concerned."

"So you're going extra hard on me," Noble said.

Cribbs narrowed his eyes, as though he couldn't believe Noble had been so incredulous as to speak.

"I want you to quit. That's not some reverse psychology bull, either. I'll leave that for the dickheads at Langley. It is most definitely not in my nature to play mind games with some pissant who hasn't even graduated from boot camp. At the end of the day, what matters most to me, and I am sure the country at large, is that you do not finish this program. Whether that means you walk out with your dick tucked in your poop chute and your head hung in shame, or we wrap your dead body in chains and let you sink to the bottom of the lake, doesn't matter to me."

Noble sucked in his bottom lip, bit it hard, and shook his head.

"You wanna say something?" Cribbs cleared the table with his hand. Egg slid off and fell onto Jack's shoes.

He didn't move. "Got nothing to say."

"What?" Cribbs leaned in closer. If the table weren't there, they'd be touching crotches.

Noble refused to give the guy the courtesy of a *"sir"* and had no intention of doing so.

A broad smile spread over Cribbs's face as he stepped back from the table. He clasped his hands behind his back, puffing out his chest. "I'll tell you what, Mr. Noble." Adding mister was an obvious dig to tell Jack he didn't belong. Cribbs glanced at his watch. "It's your turn to lead the men on a run. Fifteen miles. Better be back in an hour and forty-five minutes starting now. I'd suggest you get going."

Noble hurdled the table and dashed through the door. His

energy-depleted muscles already screamed at him for starting off at a six-minute-mile pace. He couldn't fail. They'd come down hard on him, and harder on the group. He knew where this was headed. "Let's go! Let's go!"

The other men filed in behind him. Tank Top looked at him with one eye cocked, then back at Cribbs, before joining at the tail end of the line.

"Mr. Noble, finish the run at the gym." Cribbs laughed. "I've got a surprise for you today."

# CHAPTER SIX

Calhoun collapsed on the concrete pad that led into the forty-foot wide and twenty-foot high steel shed they called the gym. He dry-heaved while bent over on his hands and knees. The sun cast a tight shadow underneath the guy. The odor of stale sweat surrounded the place. It reminded Noble of his high school wrestling room. How long had the facility been in use? And how often were trainees here? Did they run other clandestine ops through here?

The instructors gathered around the men so the only place they could go was inside. Noble leaned over, his hands on his knees, sucking in wind. He hadn't eaten since four pm the day before. Despite that, his stomach turned and he threw up what little contents there were. Mostly the rotten-egg water he'd sucked down. It tasted even worse coming back up.

"Give us a couple minutes, guys?" Noble said.

"Shut the hell up," Tank Top said. He reached into a bag and started flinging water bottles at the six recruits. "Drink up. You're not getting anymore for a while."

It was a miracle someone hadn't died yet.

Bear tore the cap off and guzzled the bottle down in a couple gulps. At least a third of it washed over his thickening beard and down his chest. He gave Jack a nod, perhaps impressed by how Jack had handled himself just then.

"All right," the instructor said. "Let's get inside."

They filed through in two rows of three. Noble and Bear led the way. Red and grey mats covered most of the room. The weights, benches and squat racks had been moved to the far corner. All the doors and windows were open, allowing a steady breeze to blow through, and more than enough light for the space.

The instructors gathered by the far door while the recruits waited in the middle. They had been ordered not to talk. Calhoun apparently hadn't heard.

"Fight day," he said.

Bear looked back and nodded. Judging by how the big man had enjoyed boxing at Parris Island, he was looking forward to this. Noble wouldn't admit it, but he did too. He was as much in his element on the sparring mat as he was on the football field.

His father had him involved in hand-to-hand combat since he was a little kid. From Taekwondo early in life to instill discipline, to Brazilian Jiu-Jitsu and the Israeli Special Forces fighting form Krav Maga. From the age of four, he'd trained diligently and at times against his will. His older brother, Sean, had served as his main sparring partner. Sean had held the upper hand until Jack turned fifteen. Things were more even then, with Jack even managing to win once in a while. This often provoked an even harsher response from his brother. This taught Jack how to handle a mentally uncentered opponent.

Noble glanced at each of the men and instructors. None were his brother. Bear was the only one he felt a twinge of fear at the thought of fighting. But they'd gone at it a few times on Parris Island, and Noble had bested him.

Cribbs entered the gym wearing a pair of blue shorts. His hands were wrapped with black tape. His defined chest and abs were impressive for a man his age. He'd figured out it wasn't all about biceps and triceps and kept his core strong.

"Today, we're gonna teach you guys how to fight." Cribbs bounced foot-to-foot on the mats like a rabid heavyweight who had gone too long without bloodying a face. It seemed the leader of the camp was in his element on the mat as well. "I've seen your jackets. I know each of you is accomplished in some way." He singled out Bear. "Logan, a national heavyweight class champion in Greco-Roman style wrestling. Says you were recommended to try out for the Olympics."

Bear nodded, said nothing.

"That don't mean a thing here, son. We're not trying to earn points or pin some guy's pussy to the mat. If we are ever close enough to engage in physical combat, somebody's gonna die. You listen to us, it won't be you." Cribbs waved three instructors over. They divided the men up, taking two each.

"Aren't we supposed to have headgear?" Calhoun said.

Cribbs turned around. "What?"

Calhoun repeated his question.

"Come over here." Cribbs waited for Calhoun before continuing. He placed his hand on the recruit's shoulder. "What are you afraid of happening?"

"Sir?" Calhoun teetered back on his heels.

Cribbs shot Noble a glance, smiled, then threw a tight jab at Calhoun's face. The man's head snapped back. Blood trickled from his nose. Again Cribbs looked at Jack as he turned his hands out, palms up. "You think headgear would have prevented that?"

Noble stood firm next to Bear, who muttered, "Don't play his game."

"All right, jerk offs," Tank Top said. "Let's work on some fundamentals."

The session lasted two hours, drilling and repeating. Much of it was instinctive for Jack, though he didn't show it. His training had been highly informal in the sense of belts and competitions. It was practical. Not for show.

They got thirty minutes for lunch and were told to return to the gym after. Maybe the worst of training was over. If so, Noble could get used to days like this. He'd spent most of his free time in life training.

After they ate and rehydrated, the six men jogged a mile back to the gym where Cribbs and the instructors were waiting. They'd been trusted to make it back on their own. A sign that maybe the direction of the program was changing. They'd spent almost a week beating them down, getting them to the point where they were physically and mentally exhausted and ready to quit. Now they would build them up again.

The recruits were divided into three groups once more, but the teaching segment was over. Now it was time to spar. For the next half-hour, Noble and Bear went at it in two-minute rounds with ninety seconds of rest in between. They were an even match using the techniques they'd gone over earlier. When Bear's instincts kicked in and he shifted to his wrestling background, Noble matched him with his BJJ knowledge.

After the final match, Tank Top shook each man's hand. "Good job, guys."

Things were changing. Bear arched an eyebrow as he glanced at Jack. They noticed the same pattern with the instructors and the other two groups. Even Cribbs looked relaxed leaning against a full-sized punching bag.

"Let's mix things up," Cribbs shouted. "Instructors versus recruits."

Every man smiled at that moment. Noble wasn't sure if it was the heavy breeze blowing through, but his skin pricked at the thought of putting Tank Top in a choke hold. Insults had been levied for six days and nights. Now was the recruits' opportunity for payback.

Cribbs held up a finger. "Any of my instructors get hurt, you're gonna pay."

Each match was performed in isolation with the instructors cheering their man on, and the recruits doing the same. When Noble rolled against Tank Top, he went easy on the instructor, who it seemed only knew one way of fighting, which amounted to him on his back trying to pull the other guy into him and then choke him out. In the end, Noble let him win. There'd be more days like this. He'd drop the hammer on him soon enough.

Calhoun didn't get the memo. From the moment Cribbs shouted go, he went for his instructor's throat. Cribbs's face burned red as he watched the beatdown. But he let it go on.

Calhoun had the instructor's back with his right arm wrapped around the guy's throat. The instructor tapped the mat. Calhoun seemed to tighten his grip.

Cribbs took a few steps forward. "Enough."

Calhoun ignored him.

"I said enough." Cribbs stood a few feet away, but kept his cool. "Let him go now."

Calhoun looked back, but didn't release the instructor. It seemed he wouldn't be satisfied until he had rendered the guy unconscious. Made no sense. They'd largely left Calhoun alone since his arrival. Noble and Bear had speculated the guy was a re-roll. Maybe he had a medical issue last time around that prevented him from completing training. He'd finally been given the all-clear to rejoin. If that were the case, the instructors would've already busted his balls and might not feel the need to do so again.

At least before this display of dominance on the mat. This could change their attitude.

Cribbs lowered his shoulder and dove at Calhoun without issuing another warning. He threaded his arm through Calhoun's and pulled him off the instructor. After pinning Calhoun, Cribbs began wailing on him. Three punches to the gut. One to the face. Twice more. Blood flew from Calhoun's mouth and nose. Cribbs hopped up, then started kicking the man on the side. Calhoun grunted between coughs. His face was covered in blood.

What Calhoun had done was not smart, but it didn't deserve a punishment of death by Cribbs's boot.

"Let up, hoss," Tank Top said. "Ain't worth killing him."

Cribbs stopped and stared down at his victim. His chest and shoulders heaved with each breath.

"Dumb bastard," he said. "Should've just stayed home this time." He kicked Calhoun over onto his back, then held out his hand to one of the instructors. "Give me your piece."

Tank Top stepped forward and spoke low. "Sir, I don't think this—"

"I don't need you to think." Cribbs kept his eyes on the bloodied man on the ground. "Give me your god damn pistol."

Tank Top handed it over and stepped back in line.

Cribbs moved toward Calhoun's feet, keeping enough distance so Calhoun couldn't disarm him. "Anything to say?"

The guy didn't respond. The wind died down. No one moved. The room was silent except for the sound of ragged breath as everyone waited to see if Cribbs had gone off the deep end and made the leap from being a hard-ass instructor to murderer.

Noble wiped a thick layer of sweat from his brow. What should he do? He was too far from Cribbs to move unnoticed. Any advance might be met with force, and if that force were to come from the pistol, it wouldn't bode well for Noble's chances of completing the program. He choked down the anger. This would pass in time. It was all part of the show.

Cribbs lowered the weapon. "Get your pathetic self up."

Calhoun propped himself up on his elbows. Two instructors leaned over and pulled him to his feet. A pained expression swept across his face. He was wobbly, but managed to stay upright with a hand on one of the instructor's shoulders.

"Get him checked out. If he needs medical, I'll call Langley." Cribbs headed toward the door with his shoulders slumped and head hanging. He stopped and looked back. "Noble, clean that blood up or it's gonna be mixing with yours."

"Go to hell, you crazy old bastard."

Bear slammed into Jack's side. "What're you doing?"

Cribbs went up to the door and closed it. Metal grating on metal echoed through the gym. "Guys, get all of them out of here. Leave Noble behind. I think it's time for me and him to have a little talk."

# CHAPTER SEVEN

The gym felt like a hollow cave, and Noble shared it with a crazed lunatic. He kept twenty feet between himself and Cribbs. The old bastard had lost his mind. He'd come down hard on Noble in the past, but never had he sent everyone away like this. Tank Top tossed a glance back at Noble. The man's lips were drawn tight, his eyebrows knit close. Had he seen this play out before? Tank Top slid the metal door shut. It banged against the wall.

The large fan in the wall droned on, sucking air out of the gym. It only took a few minutes for the room to feel stifling without fresh air coming in.

"So, what, are we gonna fight now?" Noble said. It wasn't a good idea to talk first, but he was growing weary of the standoff.

Cribbs wiped his face and torso with a fresh towel and tossed it to the side. The towel was covered in brown and red streaks. Grime from Cribbs, blood from Calhoun.

"All right, let's get this over with, then." Noble advanced toward the other man. This was a bad idea. He knew it. Tank Top obviously knew it. Jack saw the man peeking in through a dirt-stained window. At least there'd be a witness if Cribbs drew his pistol again. Without looking at the gun, Noble made a mental note of where it was on Cribbs's person. He had to disarm the guy at once.

Cribbs rolled his shoulders, then whipped his arms back and forth. All for show, Noble figured. The man was already loose. His attack on Calhoun had proven that.

"You sure you're down for this, old man?" Noble wanted to elicit some kind of reaction from his opponent.

Cribbs smiled back at him. "Funny thing about your jacket."

"What's that?"

"I don't see any formal martial arts training, but you looked pretty natural out there sparring."

"Glad to see you took notice."

"That's kinda how I came up, too. Learned in the field, so to speak."

"I learned in a garage. Concrete floor. Sometimes a thin pad so I didn't crack my skull."

"Yeah, your old man didn't have too much upstairs, did he."

Noble clenched his jaw. Sure, he and his father had some issues. What father and son didn't? That didn't mean he'd stand there and let someone else rip on his dad.

They stood five feet apart now. Jack let his arms hang loose at his sides, knees bent, leaning forward slightly. That was his wrestling stance. Let the opponent come to him. The other guy shoots, Noble hooks his arms and comes down on the guy's back.

Cribbs wasn't taking the bait. He stood back, mirroring Noble.

"Not gonna get far if you don't make a move," Noble said.

"Waiting on you, son." Cribbs circled to his left. Noble mirrored him. "Come on, here's my jaw. Just take a swing at it. No one will ever know."

Jack shifted his gaze toward the dirty window and saw Tank Top still there. That was his first mistake. Cribbs moved so quickly that Noble didn't have time to react to the man diving at his knees. He knew the old guy was fast. But this? Cribbs had held back on Calhoun.

Cribbs's shoulder collided with the side of Noble's right knee, sending a spike of pain up to his hip and down to this ankle. The man wrapped his arms around both legs and hugged them in tight. Noble went down on his side. Before he could think about freeing himself, Cribbs was all over his back. The lead instructor wasted no time going for Noble's neck. Jack squeezed his left hand in front of his Adam's apple, leaving a little separation to protect his throat.

"Tap out and you're out of my program," Cribbs said between grunts.

Noble worked his right leg forward until it was pinned under his chest. He did the same with his left. Cribbs forced himself down harder on Noble's back. Noble turned his head enough to see Cribbs' legs extended all the way. The guy was up on his tiptoes.

Perfect.

There wasn't a lot of space to work with, but Noble didn't need much. He dove his head left into the mat. Cribbs had a horrible base at that moment and rolled with him. Jack powered his left hand upward and broke the older man's choke hold. His arm continued up and around the back of Cribbs' head and neck. A moment later they came to rest with Noble on top of the guy secured in a headlock.

"It doesn't have to go any further," Noble said, torquing his body so his weight came down on Cribbs's throat. "You hear me? We can be done right now."

Cribbs reached up and gouged at Noble's face. Jack leaned his head back to keep the man's fingers far from his eyes. He tightened his grip, squeezing harder on Cribbs's neck. The instructor's face reddened as his eyes bugged out. He started wailing on Noble's chest. Jack tightened his core in preparation of a few blows to his abdominal area.

The grating metal sound distracted him for a second. He looked over his shoulder. An intense, knifing beam of sunlight split the room in half. Who was that standing in the opening? Tank Top? Whoever it was didn't make a move or say anything. Were they there to witness, and nothing else? Noble decided to test the observer.

He released his hands, bringing his right fist up in the air and delivered three quick strikes to Cribbs' face. The guy slumped for a moment, and Noble used that time to untie himself from the man and return to a standing base.

Tank Top entered the room and closed the door behind him. He stood there for a few moments, his gaze focused on Cribbs.

Cribbs wiped blood from his upper lip and flung it on the mat.

"He asked for it," Noble said.

Tank Top said nothing as he crossed the room toward them. He knelt down next to Cribbs and said something in too low a voice for Noble to pick up on.

Cribbs nodded, and Tank Top helped him to his feet, then backed off the mat. What was the point of his presence? He was getting to that. Tank Top lifted his shirt and tucked it into his shorts, making it clear that he was armed with his pistol.

Cribbs staggered toward Noble with his hands up like a boxer. "You're gonna regret letting up on me."

Noble shot a glance toward Tank Top. The instructor tipped his head back an inch and placed his right hand on the pistol grip. Didn't take a rocket scientist to figure out what his gesture meant.

With Cribbs less than six feet away, Noble launched at the guy's legs. He twisted his torso and drove his right fist between

Cribbs's knees and up through his groin. Cribbs let out a hollow gasp as Noble's bicep racked his testicles. Noble continued through the move. He powered up through his opponent to a standing position. Cribbs found himself more than six feet in the air for a moment. He rode across Noble's shoulders before tumbling back down to the ground. The sound of the man landing hard on his back ricocheted throughout the gym.

Noble wasn't done.

Cribbs would be neutralized for five to ten seconds. After that he'd regain some composure. The guy hadn't got to his current position by being a pussy.

Tank Top stood there, frozen in place. He hadn't closed his grip around his weapon by the time Noble charged across the mat and was a foot away from impact. Noble's shoulder hit him square in the diaphragm. He reached around and dug his hands in the instructor's hamstrings, lifted him off the ground, and slammed him into the corrugated steel wall. It sounded like a mac truck had collided into the building, had to be loud enough to attract the attention of the others at the camp.

Tank Top remained in place, supported by the wall, racked with pain. Noble caught the guy's chin with a haymaker and he slumped to the ground.

"Goddamn you, Noble."

He looked back and saw Cribbs pushing off his right knee in an attempt to stand.

"You stay down and this is over," Noble said.

Cribbs dragged his left hand across his face. He looked like an insane warrior with the blood smeared all over his face in finger tracks.

Noble took a half-dozen steps forward and stopped at the edge of the mat. His plan was simple. Cribbs was in a rage. He'd charge in a rage. He'd throw punches in a rage. That benefited Noble. A man in a rage was more of a danger to himself than a calm adversary. He made it easy to use his own momentum against him.

Noble took a deep breath and waited for the attack. Cribbs staggered forward a few feet, smiled, and spit a wad of bloody mass that landed halfway between them.

"You're gonna pay for this, you sonofabitch. Should've quit that first night. You know we never had plans on letting you make it through this. You were brought here so we could make an example out of you. If you ain't strong enough, you won't survive. Only way you were getting out of here was in a box."

Noble laughed the old guy's words away. "Think your babble is gonna affect me? You're hurt. You know it. I know it. Best thing for you to do is take a knee and we'll forget this ever happened."

Only neither of them would ever forget it. That's not how these things went. Noble had deconstructed Cribbs's authority. That couldn't be allowed to happen.

Noble glanced back and saw Tank Top unconscious on the floor. Cribbs advanced a few more feet and stopped. The smile on his face broadened. He lifted both arms in the air, index fingers pointed toward the ceiling. He made two quick *come-to-me* gestures, then lowered his stance.

Jack heard the pounding steps and hunched down, readying himself to be hit in the back. He swung his head to the side and saw the two instructors closing in on him. Before he could make a move, he caught Cribbs charging. The guy had produced an extendable metal baton. It was locked and loaded, too. The other instructors hit him fast and hard. Noble didn't go down, which was probably what they wanted. They had his arms pinned back, knocked his legs wide.

Cribbs never stopped charging. He whipped the baton high and brought it down over Jack's head. One blow. That was it. Because that was all it took to render Noble unconscious.

# CHAPTER EIGHT

A dull ache with intermittent sharp pains kept Noble up most of the night. The wound only required a couple of stitches. Turned out Cribbs exercised a little restraint when attempting to brain Jack. And for their part, the instructors stopped Cribbs from doing worse. The guy could have kept wailing away and that would've been all she wrote. Few people knew what was going on out here. Fewer knew who exactly was out there. They could have dug a shallow grave in the woods and no one would be the wiser.

Noble forced himself into a sitting position. The ache intensified for a moment as blood reallocated. He slid off his mattress and shuffled to the bathroom. The floor felt cool and slick. The soft glow of emergency lighting provided more than enough illumination. He cut on the cold water and cupped his hands underneath, dousing his face with the first palmful of sulfur-laden water. A layer of sweat and dried blood washed away. He took a few gulps of the bitter water and then straightened.

The image staring back at him was almost unrecognizable. His hair had grown a bit, and the beard was something new for

Jack. It added some age to his face. But aside from that, the guy staring back at him looked hardened. Older. His eyebrows knit together forming a crease in his forehead. The thought hit him then, one he'd pushed off the entire time they'd been at the camp.

Noble was staring at the face of a killer.

Could that be him? When it came down to it, could he carry out orders he assumed would come from the highest echelons of the Pentagon? Sure, he enlisted in the Marines as a Scout Sniper. That was different, though. That was war. Soldiers knew what they were getting into, whether they fought for their God or Country, or both.

The mission hadn't been laid out by Cribbs or any of the other instructors. That would come with time, he figured. But he wasn't stupid enough to assume they were going through all this at a clandestine facility to learn how to go play patty-cakes in Russian.

Noble didn't notice Bear until the big man had entered the bathroom. Bear walked up to the sink next to him and cut the water on. The guy lived up to his nickname. His beard was twice as thick as Noble's. His hair had grown out twice as much, too. A mat of brown fuzz covered his chest.

"You can squeeze 'em if you want." Bear flexed his pectoral muscles in alternating fashion like a wrestler during a big interview.

"Nah, you're not my type." Noble cupped another handful of water, swished it around his mouth, and spat it in the sink.

"How's the head?"

"Feels about the same as when I ran headfirst into a guy your size trying to score a touchdown on fourth and three."

"You get in?"

"Yeah, they told me later that night at the hospital I did."

Bear chuckled. "So you've always been stupid?"

Noble wiped his face off with a dry towel. He checked it for remaining dirt and blood. "Pretty much."

"You ever think about keeping your mouth shut?"

"Sure, but it's not in my nature. That's all I can figure. Guess it's something I need to work on."

"Damn right. Need to learn that sometimes in life, it's better to bite your tongue and think through a plan rather than charge in leading with the crown of your helmet."

Noble turned to face the big man, leaned his hip against the sink. "Why'd you join up?"

Bear glanced around the room. "They didn't give us much choice in the matter. Remember?"

"Not this place. This is just a crazy twist in our story, man. Why'd you enlist to begin with?"

Bear mirrored Jack's stance and posture. "I just felt a calling, I guess. You remember when they showed those images at the start of Desert Storm?"

"The nighttime bombings? Yeah, sure. That was at the start of football season, we were in the middle of two-a-days."

"Right. Well, that was my start of really following what was going on in this world. Didn't take long to realize how screwed up the place is. Know what I mean?"

Noble nodded, didn't say anything. What was there to say as follow up to that?

"That's when I knew the military was right for me. Was just a matter of figuring out in what capacity. I mean, I could've gone on to the Olympics, but that's secondary to me. I can do that in four years if I still want."

Noble studied Bear's face for a few moments and was left with the feeling there was something more to the story. "That's it? No Commie showed up at your door and stole your ham and cheese when you were little?"

"What more do you need? I felt a burning desire to do something for my country. Isn't that drive enough?" Bear crossed his thick arms over his chest. "What about you? Why'd your smart ass show up at Parris Island? Was it just fate putting you in my way so I could whoop up on you?"

Noble winced at some of their earlier interactions. Bear had gotten the best of him a couple of times. The fact they stood two feet away from each other and no fight had broken out would have seemed impossible a month ago.

"I guess in some ways I was pissed off," Jack said. "Old man rode me hard and had my future mapped out for me. He treated Sean the same way."

"Sean, your brother?"

Noble nodded as his gaze drifted toward the corner of the room. The stretch between leaving for Parris Island and now was the longest he'd gone without talking to his older brother.

"What's he like?" Bear asked.

"About like any older brother, I suppose. Treated me like an jerk most of the time but was the best friend I ever had growing up. I pushed myself harder because of him. Not to be like him, but to beat him. Whether that was sparring martial arts, winning the starting quarterback job over him, relegating him to receiver, or just pissing the old man off the most. I had to win."

"He enlist, too?"

"Nah, he's smarter than me. Took his scholarship to U of F—"

"Florida?"

"Yeah. He redshirted last year, but was supposed to get some real playtime this year. But football's something he does. It's not him. Not his passion. He's in pre-law. Dad drilled it into him as a little kid that's what he'd do."

"Your pop sounds like a lot of fun." Bear smiled at Noble, perhaps genuinely for the first time. "Guess they all are, though."

"Right."

"So I'm guessing this isn't what he had in mind for you?"

"Hell, no," Noble said. "Once it was clear I had some talent, it was all about getting to the pros."

"So you really did shun some big opportunities?" Bear uncrossed his arms and shoved his hands into his shorts pocket. "That tool back at Parris Island mentioned that, but I never believed him. Figured he was trying to rile me up to go after you harder."

"It's true, but it doesn't matter anymore. That kid no longer exists. That life was sacrificed so I can share a moment with your overgrown ass in this shitter of a CIA-sponsored camp in West Virginia that doesn't officially exist."

Bear belted out a round of laughter that probably woke Cribbs from his slumber. If the guy slept at all.

"Maybe I had you all wrong, dude." Bear slapped Noble's shoulder. "I get wanting to piss off your old man, but there's gotta be something else, right?"

Noble took a deep breath as he considered how far he should let the big man in. He had a feeling the two of them would be spending a lot of time together in the coming years, assuming both made it through this training, and survived whatever came next. But being vulnerable to anyone was not in his wheelhouse. Didn't matter whether it was Jessie, his high school sweetheart, or anyone in his immediate family. He didn't open up easily.

But Bear prodded again, and the way he leaned in, it seemed like he wanted to know. They were past the point where the big man would use it against him in some way.

"I was still a kid when it happened," Noble said, speaking slowly as images of that night filled his head. "Our parents were out and the three of us were doing as we did. Molly was the oldest. Four years older than me. As smart as Sean is, and as tough and athletic as I pretend to be, she had it all over us, man. Smart, fast, strong, pretty, and just the kind of person who took life by the balls and twisted tight and clung to them ready to take on whatever was thrown in her direction."

Bear nodded slowly and listened to the story unfold.

"So much of it is a blur now, but I can see that nothing I could have done would've made a difference that night. Those bastards were there for blood, and they were gonna have it. Why her, though? That's the only thought I can't shake. They murdered her in the woods behind our house and I watched it go down. Didn't stop them."

"You were a kid," Bear said. "There were several of them. What could you have done?"

"More." Noble caught a glance of himself in the mirror. The tear that streaked down his cheek was genuine, and he made no move to wipe it away. "I could have done more to save her life, even if it meant losing my own. But I chickened out."

"You froze because it was beyond your capabilities at the time."

"At the time is right."

Bear nodded like a shrink who'd witnessed a breakthrough in his client. "So that's why you enlisted. That's why you're here at this camp. Damn, it was you. All of this was you. I just happened to be in the way and got dragged along for the ride." He dipped his head a couple inches so they were eye to eye and tapped his large fingertip into Noble's chest. "This place is gonna allow you to find your redemption, Jack."

Noble shook his head as his gaze drifted down to the floor. "Not redemption, man. Penance. I owe it to Molly."

Bear reached out with both arms and wrapped his large hands around Noble's shoulders, offering a comforting squeeze. "Look at me, Jack."

Noble looked up into the big man's squinted eyes.

"Keep your mouth shut from here on out. If they want someone to screw with, they can have me now. But you need to stop giving them reasons. I think we've reached the point where things are gonna turn around here, but you need to stop getting in your own damn way with Cribbs and his guys. I guarantee if you stick with me, follow my lead, this ordeal will pass and you'll be on your way to doing right by Molly."

Noble turned toward the mirror and studied himself for a few more moments. Who was that staring back at him? Could the guy in the reflection keep it together long enough to get through training?

Did he have any other choice?

# CHAPTER NINE

The next three weeks went by in a blur. Noble kept in line to the dismay of Cribbs and his band of instructors. Tank Top, who's name turned out to be Bray, goaded him non-stop, but Noble kept his mouth shut and his head down and took everything they threw at him without spitting out the smartass responses that came so naturally to him.

Cribbs gave them Sunday off. The remaining four recruits—Noble, Bear, Spinks, and Calhoun—stayed up late Saturday coming up with plans of waking up early and spending the morning fishing. They overslept two hours and found the temperatures had plummeted overnight into the low thirties. For a Florida boy like Noble, they might as well have been dropped off in the arctic.

Bray came by with a portable television equipped with a seven-inch black-and-white screen. The four men gathered around and watched eleven hours of football. Not a bad way to spend a day off.

The next morning, they were at it again. It was colder than the previous day, but this time Noble had no option to remain inside. Bray ripped into them something fierce over wasting a day off by watching TV. Should have been out working, drilling, shooting. The four am tirade went on for ten minutes, acting like a jolt of caffeine to Noble's system. But it wasn't him who spoke up first.

"Why don't you go fist yourself," Calhoun said.

The other three recruits snapped to attention at the utterance. Had he lost his mind? The guy had been rolled once, and judging by the attitudes of the instructors toward him, was lucky he had been given a second chance. He did something daily that made Noble think the guy didn't want to be there. Why come back at all?

Bray looked right, left, behind him, up to the lingering stars, and down at the frozen ground. "Did someone really just say that to me?" He paced in front of the four trainees, stopped in front of Noble. "What did I just hear?"

Noble stared straight ahead, ignoring the instructor's stare. Bray damn well knew what he heard, and Noble wasn't repeating it.

"I asked you a question, Noble."

"I was busy paying attention, not focusing on what others were doing."

Bray shook his head. "You used to be good for something, Noble. Even if that something was pissing me the hell off." He paced down the line, back again, stopped in front of Bear.

The big man stared down at Bray, a snarl across his face. Nothing had fazed Bear during the training. Want him to do two-hundred pushups? Fine. Make it two-fifty while you're at it. Run twelve miles in the rain? Bear didn't care. He'd stay up all night, do PT until he puked, and go three days with nothing more than a few bottles of water and no sleep, and the guy didn't complain.

"What'd you hear?" Bray said to him.

"A man signing his ticket out of this place."

It was hard to tell by the look on Bear's face whether he spoke about Calhoun or Bray. Apparently Bray agreed, because he didn't linger in front of Bear for too long. He moved in front of Spinks, rolled his eyes, and walked behind Calhoun. The ground crunching under his boots gave way to the silence of night. A stiff breeze rustled through the trees, sending dying leaves spiraling toward the ground.

Bray grabbed a handful of Calhoun's sweatshirt and pulled him back so the man was off balance. "You wanna say that again?"

Calhoun grinned. "Go fist yourself."

Bray struck low and fast, sweeping Calhoun's legs out from underneath him. He landed hard on his side. The frozen ground offered no padding to break his fall. Calhoun rolled over, grunting, and grabbed his ribs. His face turned red as he fought to breathe.

"What was that again?" Bray teed off on Calhoun, kicked him three times at the site of the injury. "What did you want me to do?"

Calhoun clenched his face tight, took a slow breath. His features relaxed. He closed his eyes, exhaled, said, "Go fist yourself."

None of the other recruits could move fast enough to stop Bray's assault on the wounded man. He followed up another steel-toed kick with a diving knee into Calhoun's sternum. Two strikes to Calhoun's face drove the guy's nose left of center and knocked out a tooth.

It was more than Noble could take. He avoided Bear's attempt to stop him and dove on the instructor. Bray toppled over with Noble on his back, locking his arms down and threading his arm around Bray's throat.

Floodlights lit the area up like it was one in the afternoon. The ground crunched under no fewer than three pairs of boots. Bear grabbed Noble by the collar and pulled him off the instructor. Bray collapsed to the ground with his hands on his neck.

"The hell is going on here?" Cribbs stood over Bray, who was up on a knee, head cocked sideways so he could look up. "Well?"

Bray dropped to his hands, head hanging.

Cribbs' gaze shifted to Calhoun, then he turned to Noble and Bear. "Can you two offer any insight?"

Adrenaline coursed through Noble, making him too amped to speak coherently. Bear spoke up.

"Bray went off, went nuts, attacked Calhoun." He left out a couple of details, which Bray was quick to offer up.

"Little prick told me to fist myself." Bray got to his feet and stood bent slightly at the waist. "I had to put him in his place.

Cribbs knelt at Calhoun's side, performed an assessment on the man. They hadn't seen the man look so concerned. Cribbs looked back at another instructor. "Get him to the hospital now. I think he's got a collapsed lung."

One instructor took off in a dead sprint for the van parked nearby while another tended to Calhoun.

Cribbs got in Bray's face. "The hell were you thinking? We're past this point in training. Someone pisses you off, you exhaust them, not beat them. This is twice now with this same guy. Why won't you learn?"

The reason Calhoun was rolled from the previous class became clear. Cribbs was no innocent flower in this mess, but you could reason that what he had done to this point had been to test the men. Bray was a different specimen. It seemed he wanted to hurt the trainees if they pissed him off enough.

The van's headlights washed over the ground. Two instructors lifted Calhoun and put him inside the vehicle, then sped off. He didn't look good, and Noble wondered if the man would make it back to the camp for a third try. He knew his stubbornness would drive him to do it. Hopefully Calhoun had people in his life who could dissuade him from making the mistake again.

Cribbs turned to Noble, Bear and Spinks. "The three of you head back inside. I'll be in to interview you soon." He walked over to Bray, grabbed him by his shirt. "You and me are going to my place."

# CHAPTER TEN

A lexa Steele answered the phone on the third or fourth ring. She wasn't sure which. The blaring phone woke her from the most solid stretch of sleep she'd had in four weeks. Such was life in her position. She had far too many people reaching out to her at all hours for updates, followed by a game of twenty questions.

She licked her lips and cleared her throat and croaked out a dry, "Hello?"

"It's Cribbs."

"OK."

"Aren't you wondering why I'm calling so early?"

She glanced at the clock. Four-thirty. "I'd say it's rather late."

"The hell time you get up, girl?"

Alexa swung her legs over the bed and sat upright. "By five am. And I told you not to call me girl anymore. I don't know why you won't—"

"Yeah, yeah," Cribbs said. "I got it. Sorry, Miss Steele, but in my professional opinion, you should be up and out of bed by now. The world doesn't sleep, and neither do we."

"I got that memo, too." She crossed the room and slid her feet into her slippers. The smell of coffee brewing hit her in the hallway. "So, what's up, Cribbs? Everything OK?"

"Not exactly."

She stopped at the top of the stairs, waiting for him to continue before she descended. Last thing she wanted was a bombshell dropped on her, causing her to trip and roll down a flight. "What do you mean by that?"

"One of the recruits got busted up pretty bad this morning."

While Steele oversaw the program now, she knew there were only two recruits that mattered to her in Cribbs's eye. And of those two, the man hated Noble the most. Probably more than any other trainee he'd ever had the displeasure of laying eyes on. Maybe more than any enemy he'd ever faced. She hurried down the stairs. "What happened to Noble?"

Cribbs exhaled into the phone. "No, not him."

"Logan?" She reached into the cupboard and pulled out a wide coffee mug with the phrase *CIA Agents Do It Under Covers*. It had been a gift from her uncle when she graduated training.

"Calhoun."

Alexa recalled the man. It was his second attempt at training. He had been injured pretty badly the first time with a broken femur. When she had asked for details, Cribbs had been vague. She wouldn't let him get away with the same behavior.

"What happened?"

"Still trying to get to the bottom of that."

"That's ridiculous, Cribbs. You wouldn't be on the phone with me at four in the morning if you didn't know."

"Four-thirty."

"Spit it out, and don't hold back like you did last year when he got hurt." She filled her mug during a long silence. Steam rose and enveloped her hand. When Cribbs still hadn't spoken up, she said, "I'm getting in my car in fifteen minutes and coming out there."

"Now wait a minute, you don't have to go through all that trouble."

She waited a few seconds for him to continue. "Well? Are you going to tell me why?"

"First off, let me state that I'm going to handle this internally. I mean, I'm handling it now."

She turned and leaned back against the counter. She'd known her uncle her whole life, and had come to know who Cribbs really was over the last decade. It wasn't in his nature to pussyfoot around like this. In fact, she couldn't recall a time when he had ever stalled in such a way. "You need to quit babbling on and tell me what is going on, or I'm gonna show up in three hours and put the entire camp on lockdown. And before you think you can call McKenzie to put me in my place, know that he recently told me he's turning the entire thing over to me." She paused and smiled at the thought of Cribbs's anger rising. "That's right, I'm gonna be in charge of all of this. Your interview for this job begins now."

She could practically hear his blood boiling over the line.

"Like I said, Alexa, I'm handling it."

"Handling what, specifically?"

"One of my guys got a little out of hand with Calhoun."

"Which one?" She already knew the answer but asked the question anyway. When Calhoun had been injured the previous year, she questioned him. He stuck with the company line through most of the interrogation, but toward the end, nearly cracked. There was something to the way he looked at her after she listed off the instructors one a time. When she mentioned Bray's name, Calhoun's eyes widened a touch and his pupils dilated quickly. There was a memory there.

Cribbs had gone silent. Had he hung up?

"Hello?" she said. "You there?"

"Yeah, I'm here."

"Well? Which one? Bray?"

Cribbs coughed into the phone a couple times. "Yeah." He spoke low and soft, as though he were defeated and had resigned himself to the fact Steele was about to get far more involved in instructor selection the next go around.

"What'd he do?"

"He lost it. We knew it was a possibility."

"We? Suddenly I'm being blamed for this?"

"I knew. It was all me. I knew the guy might snap, and he did. Thing was, we were past that point. We'd made it to the part of the program where the trainees are doing it all on their own. There was no need for him to react that way."

"I want him detained until I can get someone there to bring him back to Langley. Understood, Cribbs?"

She knew it killed him to tell her yes. But he had no choice.

"What's the damage?" Alexa asked. "To Calhoun, not your guy."

"Broken ribs. Possibly a broken sternum and collapsed lung."

"Jesus," she said. "What are we going to do if he files a lawsuit, or goes to the press about this? Do you even think about that kind of thing when selecting these people to do your dirty work?"

"Now hold it there," Cribbs said. "We are not training girl scouts here. Last I checked, friggin Hezbollah isn't buying cookies from us. I need to turn these worthless recruits into killers capable of blending and operating anywhere at any time. You think any old DI can do that? You think you can do that? I challenge you to come here and lead these men for a day."

"That's not what I'm saying and you know it."

"I don't know what the hell you're saying, because you don't know what the hell you're talking about, *Miss* Steele."

She took a sip of her coffee and set the mug back down in the ring it left behind on the counter. They could go on all morning like this, but it wouldn't do anyone any good. "Have Bray ready to go when our guys get there, or I'll be showing up tonight and making a decision on whether to suspend operations permanently."

The threat was legit, and Cribbs knew it. He also knew that would spell the end of his career with the Agency.

"OK, Steele. He'll be ready to go."

# CHAPTER ELEVEN

The weeks following the Calhoun incident flew by. They were told he'd needed emergency surgery, pulled through, and was recovering on his grandparents's farm in Iowa. Pretty part of the country, from what Noble remembered. They'd driven through the state on the way from Wisconsin to Nebraska on a cross country trip when he was a kid. Lots of rolling hills that gave way to flatland. Farms everywhere.

For Bray's part in the fracas, he received the equivalent to a slap on the wrist. Spent a week on suspension. Came back and spent another week serving food to Noble, Bear, and Spinks. He returned to his work as an instructor, but in a much more subdued capacity. Since his return he hadn't shouted anything but encouragement at the trainees.

In fact, it had been that way all around.

Noble wished he knew what went on behind the scenes. Who did Cribbs report to, and what power did they have over him? He assumed if he made it through training, he'd find out who he was working for. No point in revealing their identity sooner. And there was no way Noble would be thrown into general population. He might go a year or two and not meet any of the geeks slaving away behind tiny computer terminals at Langley.

The three men rose to start their day, threw on their PT gear, and headed outside. They led themselves at this point. No longer did they have to be goaded into a ten mile run through the woods in twenty-degree weather.

They just did it.

Cribbs watched from the porch of the mess hall as they returned. The older man had a smug look on his face. Was he reveling in what his backwards training methods had produced? All three would kill him in his sleep for free. Maybe that's what Cribbs wanted. The camp leader hopped off the porch and met them in front of the stairs.

"Gentlemen," he said with a nod. "Kicking off our last week. How does it feel?"

"Pretty damn good," Spinks said. "Might feel even better if I could get some pancakes to start my day."

Cribbs tipped his head back and laughed. "Tell you what, you three ess-oh-bees have done a hell of a job lately. Head on into the kitchen and whip up whatever you want."

Noble couldn't believe he'd just heard the man say that. For over two months the guy had kicked their asses throughout these woods, and here he was giving them free rein to make whatever they wanted for breakfast? Perhaps it was his distrusting nature taking over, but Noble didn't buy the nice-guy act.

Spinks darted inside with Bear close behind. Noble lingered for a moment, studying Cribbs.

"What is it?" Cribbs said.

"What's the catch?" Noble said.

"Christ, man, I'm showing you guys some leniency."

"I get that. I also get that ain't in your makeup to do so."

Cribbs' smile faded. He squared up to Noble. "Get in there and eat, or we'll have a repeat of our day on the mat together."

Noble paused a moment to soak in a breath of cold air. Even a few weeks ago, his response might've been to step forward, go toe-to-toe with Cribbs. That's what the guy wanted, right? Why not give it to him? But with one week left to get through, he failed to see the point. He broke off eye contact, leapt over the stairs and headed inside and into the kitchen.

Spinks worked a stainless mixing bowl full of flour. Bear watched on. Noble grabbed a mug and filled it with coffee, then moved to the other side of the room to watch.

"Not having anything?" Bear said.

"I'll start with the coffee, then maybe some eggs. And I'd recommend you two do the same."

"The hell you talking about?" Spinks said. "We're in the home stretch. Almost finished."

"I knew a few SEALs growing up," Noble said. "You know what they call the last week of BUD/S?"

Bear pulled the spatula from his mouth and wiped away excess batter clinging to his beard. The look suited him well, and he'd said on more than one occasion he had no plans on ever shaving it off. "Hell Week."

"Right," Noble said. "We heard all about it. So what do you think they've got planned for us here?"

Spinks scooped half-cooked pancakes off the griddle and dumped them in the trash. "Screw you, Noble. Such a damn buzzkill."

The look on Cribbs' face when the three men emerged from the kitchen with plates consisting of four eggs, six strips of bacon, and two pieces of toast was priceless. Noble thought someone had stolen his favorite stuffed animal.

"The hell happened to the pancakes?" Cribbs said.

"There'll be time for that crap when we're done training," Spinks said.

Noble shoved a strip of bacon in his mouth to keep from laughing. This was what happened when a man was taken to the woods, stripped of contact with the outside world and left only with a few people to talk to. He found the slightest off-kilter look hilarious when it was plastered across the face of a man he despised.

"Eat that garbage and get back outside. You've got five minutes." Cribbs kicked the door open and slammed it shut.

"Guess we did our jobs right," Noble said.

"Good call, Jack," Bear said. He'd taken to calling him Jack more in recent weeks.

"I really can't wait for those pancakes," Spinks said. "Day after we're done with this mess, no, that night, I'm finding an IHOP or Waffle House and going to town."

"No pancakes at Waffle House," Bear said. "Made that mistake before. Wasn't let down though."

"Whatever," Spinks said. "I'm having a batter-laden feast right after I tell that old cocksucker to go stick a tree branch up his ass."

"Careful," Bear said. "You saw where that got Calhoun."

"That guy was an idiot who brought it on himself. You'd think he'd have learned after that day in the gym. I mean, Noble over there figured it out."

Jack shook the comment off. He hadn't forgotten or forgiven anything. He wanted to make it through training without further incident. That was all. He wouldn't be able to avoid all encounters, but he had managed to minimize them.

They finished eating, cleaned off their plates, and headed outside. Cribbs and his collection of trainers waited for them. Cribbs had a smile spread across his face.

"Get ready for the toughest goddamn week of your life, dickheads."

Two hours later they wrapped up the most intense PT session yet. Every exercise was to exhaustion, then they did it again. Spinks hurled halfway through. More than once he thanked Noble for convincing him to give up the pancakes. Cribbs caught wind of it once and singled Spinks out.

"Sprint over to that tree and get up on that ropes course," Cribbs said. He ran alongside Spinks and continued to shout at him.

It was a bad idea. The men had been through two grueling hours of bodyweight exercises, pushed to the point of collapse. Spinks would have to fight through that and take on a course that required small, controlled motions performed fifty feet above ground.

Noble and Bear followed Spinks, albeit at a slower pace, using the walk to catch their breath. The other instructors remained behind.

Spinks dug his fingertips into the top of the hunk of two-by-four nailed to the tree. A couple dozen of them created a ladder. The guy looked shaky heading up and he was only ten feet off the ground.

"This isn't a good idea," Noble said.

"Who the hell asked you?" Cribbs said.

"He's exhausted, and he's got no gear on."

"Think you'll have gear on when you're walking through the streets of Somalia, a hundred dudes just waiting for you to say something, anything, so they can justify riddling your ass with bullet holes?"

Noble bit his tongue and turned his attention back to Spinks, who had reached the platform and had his hands on his knees, bent over, catching his breath.

"Get moving," Cribbs yelled.

Spinks glanced down. His face looked pale in the early

morning light. Could've been the workout. Might've been the fact he had no harness on and was about to traverse a hundred-feet of rope while fifty-feet off the ground in front of a team of instructors who'd like nothing more than to see him fall.

"Go now," Cribbs yelled, "or I'm coming up there."

That provided Spinks with the necessary motivation. He hooked his arm around the top rope so it settled into the crook of his elbow, then stepped out onto the bottom rope. Inch-by-inch he made his way forward, glancing down at the ground below.

"Christ," Cribbs muttered. "He's never gonna get through it."

Noble thought back to other times they had been on the course. Had Spinks showed signs of trouble with it before? The guy came from a job where death was a near certainty if you stayed out there long enough, so it wasn't unreasonable to assume he'd faced his share of adversity and terrifying situations before. It wasn't the absence of fear, but how you faced it. That's how the saying went, right? Whatever was going on inside of Spinks' head, he was pushing through it.

"You better get moving, you asshat," Cribbs yelled. "I don't have all day."

"Pipe down and let him get through it at his own pace," Noble said.

Bear groaned. They both knew what was coming. Noble had followed the big man's advice as long as he could, though. This was different. Spinks's life was at risk. If he rushed, he could slip.

"What did you say?" Cribbs glanced back at Noble.

"He's no good to the team injured or dead. Push him too hard, he's gonna fall."

"And what if there's a teammate on the other side of that rope in danger? Then what? Should he take all day getting over there?"

"Maybe in that situation he'd cast aside his doubts and truck through the obstacles."

Cribbs spit out a condescending laugh. "Hey, nitwit," he yelled at Spinks. "Noble is on the other side of that tree dying. Hurry up and save his ass." He turned to face Jack. "Now get up on that other platform."

Noble had a feeling this was only part one of the treatment Cribbs had in mind for him. After Spinks finished his task, Jack would be given something ten times more difficult. That's how it went early on in training, and how it continued to go, even after he had learned to keep his mouth shut.

He sprinted the fifty or so yards to the next makeshift ladder and hustled up the side of the tree. His fingers were numb from the cold. Didn't slow him down. Spinks had barely made it two feet by the time Noble reached the platform.

Cribbs kept yelling from the ground. Much of what he said was lost to the wind, which whipped stronger up at the level of the ropes course.

"Look at me, Spinks," Noble said.

The guy glanced over.

It was the first time Noble had seen a trace of fear on Spinks' face. In the weeks before Spinks had entertained them with stories of operations he'd been a part of. The kind of heavily classified ops that could've been derived by the best Hollywood imaginations. Where did this fear come from?

"You got this, man," Noble said. "Come on, after everything you've been through? This is nothing. Just put one foot in front of the other and hang on tight."

Was it working? He couldn't tell. Spinks still looked panicked, but the guy was moving. Maybe his pace had picked up a notch from banana slug to two-toed sloth.

Movement on the ground caught Noble's attention. He grabbed a strap tied to the tree and leaned forward to get a better look. Bray had moved into position between Bear and Cribbs and it looked like he had a pistol in his hand. What did the crazy bastard have in mind now?

Two seconds later, Noble found out.

The sound of his .45 shredded the silence of the woods. Might as well have been cannon blast. The few remaining birds took off, their squawks barely audible over the echoing gunshot.

And it was a hell of a shot. The bottom rope hung in the air for a moment and then split in the middle. It fell to the ground in slow motion. Noble followed it down, catching the looks on the men below. Even Cribbs appeared shocked.

Spinks dangled from the top rope, one arm hooked over, the other flailing in an attempt to reach up and grab it. He shrieked in pain. It all happened so quickly. Noble replayed the images in his mind. The bottom rope had split near Spinks. Had the bullet hit him?

Spinks answered that question. "I'm shot."

"Just hang on right there." Noble grabbed the remaining rope and started out like a kid crossing the monkey bars.

Spinks was losing his grip. His arms were shaking. A red stain had spread on his sweatpants below the knee. Noble was ten feet away when the other man lost his grip on the line and plummeted fifty feet to the ground.

# CHAPTER TWELVE

A sullen final week of training was capped off with news from Cribbs that Spinks had suffered a severed spinal cord, leaving him paralyzed from the waist down. Noble had assumed as much. By the time he reached the ground, Spinks had started to regain consciousness but couldn't move any of his extremities. So perhaps it was good news he would only be a paraplegic.

For his part, Bray had been led away by the other instructors and detained in Cribbs's cabin until a car from Langley arrived. During their debriefing, Cribbs said Bray would no longer be working for the Agency in any capacity. Requests from the other trainers for more information were denied. Noble hoped the man was free to leave Langley so one day they might run into one another. But Cribbs cast water on that idea. He said Bray had snapped from the stress. It'd been a long time coming. His jacket indicated he'd suffered from PTSD from his last few times in the field. They thought working with trainees under Cribbs might do him well.

Noble and Bear sat alone in the mess hall shoulder-to-shoulder, facing the front door. Temperatures had risen toward the end of the week. It was a balmy sixty-degrees out. A mild wind blew in through the screen door, rattling it against the frame. Noble lifted his mug to his face and inhaled the scent of bad coffee.

"First thing I'm doing on the outside is getting a decent cup," he said.

"It's all piss water to me," Bear said. "Does the trick, though."

"What do you think's next?"

"Beats the hell out of me, man. You got any thoughts?"

"I'm assuming we'll head to Langley, go through a more formal round of training there."

"After that?"

"Hopefully a couple weeks off. A chance to go home for a bit. Your guess is as good as mine from that point on."

Bear pushed his plate across the table and leaned back in his chair. "I think first thing we need to do is find that IHOP or Waffle House and have a bite to eat in honor of Spinks."

Noble nodded in silence. They hadn't spoken about the man after the incident. Seemed like it would inspire some bad juju, which there had been plenty of while at the camp. How much of it would be reported to Cribbs' superior? Or that person's boss? Did anyone know what really went on at the camp? After everything he saw and experienced, Noble half-wanted to blow the whistle. The other half of him was proud to have survived. Odds were against Bear and him completing the training, yet they had. Two green, wet-behind-the-ears, FNGs outlasted the other trainees in spite of everything Cribbs and his lackeys hurled at them.

The screen door creaked open and Cribbs stepped through. He had a softness to his face they hadn't seen before. He dropped a canvas bag on the floor and dragged a chair from the corner of the room and sat down in front of Noble and Bear.

"Morning," Noble said.

Cribbs nodded. "That it is."

A long silence left Noble feeling uncomfortable. Bear, too, it seemed. The big man shuffled his feet under the table, knocking the top with his knees. Coffee crested over the lid of Noble's mug and pooled in a ring around the bottom. He waited for Cribbs to explode over it.

Cribbs stared at the spill for a couple of moments, then shook his head back into focus and looked up at Bear and Noble. "Obviously there won't be any ceremony or anything like that today. You've probably figured out what we're doing down here isn't known to many people. I know we've told you as much in as round about a way as possible. Things got a little out of hand recently. That's not all that uncommon. We're under a lot of stress. And by we, I mean all of us. You, other recruits, my instructors, and me. Remember, I've got a job to do, and that's to get douchebags like you ready to go out and defend our nation in the most unorthodox of ways. I can't send you out there unprepared. What you saw here over the past few months will be nothing compared to what you come across in places like Iraq, Somalia, Syria, and so on."

"Understood," Bear said.

Was the big man really ready to sweep it all under the rug?

"As much as it pains me to say this, you two made it. You passed. You're about as ready as I can get you. Gotta be honest, you surprised the hell out of me. Never figured two green-ass recruits fresh from Parris Island could have made it, besting not only more qualified recruits, but also my handpicked men. But you two did it."

"That must hurt," Noble said.

Cribbs shook his head. "That mouth is gonna get you killed, son. It almost did here. You'd be wise to realize you're better off cutting out your tongue than to keep talking."

"Only messing with you, Cribbs."

The older man sat there for a few minutes, stone-faced, silent. Finally, he continued. "Get something straight, you and I will never be equals. We'll never be partners. We'll never be friends. You will never earn the right or respect to be in a position where you can mess with me."

Noble gripped his mug tight and leaned back. The ceramic mug was as hot as the coffee. The pain in his fingers helped him bite his tongue.

"Anyway, you're probably wondering what's next?" Cribbs glanced between the two.

Bear leaned forward. "Langley?"

Cribbs folded his arms over his chest. His rolled sleeves pulled up past his elbows, revealing thick forearms. "There's one more test for you two to complete."

Noble glanced past Cribbs through the screen door. What more could they have for them to do at the camp? They'd drilled incessantly on the basics of the job. When they weren't drilling, they were running or doing pushups or shooting. Their skills had been tested non-stop over the past week. They were ready.

Bear said, "We've passed everything you've thrown at us, can't see this as being any different."

Cribbs pushed away from the table, rose and snatched the canvas bag off the floor. He tossed it on the table in front of Bear.

"What's that?" Bear asked, twisting his head to get a look inside.

Cribbs sat back down. "Your final test is also your first mission. In three hours you'll head out to catch the train to D.C. Sleeping arrangements have already been made. You'll be contacted at the hotel by an asset who will provide you with the tools you'll need for the job."

"Who's the target?" Noble asked. If it had been any other

destination, he figured there might be something else to the job. But D.C. meant one thing.

An assassination.

Cribbs nodded, smiled, glanced at Noble out of the corner of his eye. "You figured it out."

"Doesn't take a genius."

"No, I suppose it doesn't. But for the record, that's not going to be your only function. But we need to make sure you can handle anything we throw at you. Killing a man, a citizen of this country, who you don't know, for reasons you aren't entirely sure of, is one of the hardest things you can do. It's an unfortunate aspect of the job, but a necessary one."

"So who is this guy and what did he do?" Noble said.

Cribbs laughed. "I'm liking you a little more now, Noble. I can't tell you all of that. You'll find out enough about the guy from the information in that bag. And you'll have to trust us that he did something heinous enough to warrant his execution."

"You know what that is?" Bear asked.

Cribbs shook his head. "Sure don't. And I don't wanna know, because it doesn't make a damn bit of difference to me. One of our bosses determined he needs to die. It's our job to carry out that wish."

"What if we fail?" Bear asked.

"Well, asking that question is planning to fail."

"Just curious is all. Anything is a possibility, right?"

"I suppose," Cribbs said. "The Agency will deny any knowledge of you, the assignment, and this program. You'll go to jail, and at some point, a couple of guys from Langley wearing black suits will show up and dose you up with something that'll make your heart explode within a few seconds. It doesn't bother me to tell you that your personnel records have been rewritten. Your entire life story has been rewritten. Maybe your family will start asking questions. It'd be a stupid thing for them to do. The Agency will come after them with everything to discredit them."

Bear and Noble sat in silence.

"So, short answer is this: don't screw this up. Do the job quickly and cleanly and get the hell out of there before anyone has a chance to stop you."

# PART II

# CHAPTER THIRTEEN

Two minutes ago, a man Jack Noble had never met stuffed his mouth with lobster risotto and flushed it down, half-chewed, with a glass of water after fanning his mouth in an attempt to dispel the heat of the meal. The man had no reason to suspect that Noble's partner, Riley "Bear" Logan, had infiltrated the kitchen staff of his favorite restaurant. Nor had he suspected that Bear would layer his risotto with poison. Not enough to kill the man, but to cause a certain amount of intestinal distress.

Keith Witherspoon pushed his chair back into the patron behind him and worked his forty-eight-inch waist free from the table. He clutched his gut, mumbling something about the damn medicine his doctor had put him on. He spotted the concerned-looking chef, a rather large man, peering out from between the stainless shelves in the kitchen.

Noble watched the scene unfold on the five-inch black and white screen. The moment Witherspoon hit the restroom hallway, Noble ditched the monitor in the trash and flipped the lock on the bathroom door. He spun on his heel, cut the water on and placed his hands in the cold stream.

The door whipped open, clipping Noble's heel in the process.

"You all right, fella?" Jack made eye contact with Witherspoon in the mirror.

Witherspoon wiped his damp forehead with his sleeve as he made a line for the first stall. Noble had anticipated this and had rigged the door so it would not open until someone slid underneath it. Not a concern with Witherspoon and his girth. The second stall was much wider, allowing Noble more room to operate. After the target slipped out of sight, Noble opened the restroom door to allow Bear inside. The guy almost had to duck to clear the doorframe, and his wide shoulders brushed against the jambs. The big man locked the door and turned to Jack.

"Ready?" Bear said.

Noble thought for a second. He hadn't been so sure how he'd react in this moment. They'd trained on the farm in West Virginia for ten weeks. They'd been pushed to the edge of their physical and mental limits and taught to be elite killers. Both men possessed some moral and ethical flexibility that made the act of killing more art than crime. Combined with an intense desire to serve, they were perfect for the CIA-sponsored program for which they had been selected without their consent.

So when it came down to it, faced with the prospect of taking the life of a man they knew little about, Noble felt no remorse. He and Bear wouldn't be there if Witherspoon hadn't screwed up by protecting some bad people at the expense of innocent lives. They saw the files. Read what he had done. Most recently a family of four, two young children aged three and five, gunned down without consequences. When Jack looked at Witherspoon, all he saw were the faces of the men who had killed his sister, Molly, when he was a boy.

Noble wiped a layer of sweat off his brow and looked up at his partner. "Yeah, let's do this."

"Cribbs said it has to look like a gang killing," Bear said, referring to the man who had made their lives hell for close to two months on the Farm.

The old bastard had told them this could not look like a professional job. No problem, Jack thought. It was their first time. It was bound to look sloppy.

Noble produced an H&K 9mm pistol and threaded a suppressor on the end of it. It wouldn't silence the shot to the sound of a nun's fart, but it'd reduce the noise enough to prevent the restaurant's patrons from hearing, like a pebble in a tin can. He questioned the use of the Heckler and Koch, though. Would it be a gangbanger's weapon of choice?

Bear pushed the stall door open with his foot. In Witherspoon's haste, he had failed to secure the lock. The sight before them looked like something out of a drug awareness campaign. Witherspoon's forehead rested on the toilet tank. His glasses were on the floor surrounded by a lake of blood-tinged vomit. The guy's face had turned beet-red.

Witherspoon noticed the men behind him. He wiped his face with his sleeve and lifted off the toilet seat. His gaze shifted to the pistol in Noble's hand.

"Who are you?" Witherspoon said. "What do you want?"

"I think you know the answer to that," Noble said.

"I-I-I'll pay you anything," he said reaching for his pocket. "Let me offer you—"

Noble squeezed the trigger. The bullet entered Witherspoon's forehead and tore through his brain. It exited at an angle, shattering a wall tile. He gestured toward the lifeless body. Bear stepped forward and delivered a couple of blows to Witherspoon's torso and face to make it look like he'd been roughed up first.

"Good enough," Noble said. "Let's move to phase two."

Bear heaved through a couple of breaths. He was taking it harder than Noble. "Should we move him?"

Noble considered this for a moment. Would it better if they perched him on the seat? "It won't match up if we do. Splatter will be all wrong, plus we'll get his blood all over us. Right now we're pretty clean. Out through the back and no one will ever know we had anything to do with this."

"All right, leave him where he is." Bear pulled the stall door closed and managed to get it to catch and stay.

Noble broke down his H&K, pocketed the suppressor and holstered the pistol.

A rap on the door echoed through the restroom. The two men looked at each other. Bear held up a finger, pointed for Noble to move to the hinge-side of the door, out of view.

Bear opened the door about six inches, enough for his face to press through. His large frame blocked the opening. "Can't come in. There's been an accident in here. You can use the bathroom upstairs." He paused a few seconds, then shut the door. "That was too close. Let's get the hell out of here."

Noble pulled out the plans for the building. Their escape route was marked in blue highlighter. "Storage room is to the right, then left at the end of the hallway. The exit will be in the back corner."

Bear held the door open for Noble to exit. After Jack had passed, Bear pulled a small wooden wedge from his pocket. He pulled the door closed until it held the wedge in place. One final yank ensured it would be some time before anyone managed to open it. Wouldn't be long until someone started looking for Witherspoon. It'd take a while for them to get to the dead man though.

They moved at a hastened clip, down the hall, to the left, through the door labeled with a small black plaque that read ST

*RAGE.* The O had been marked out with magic marker. It was in the room that the building showed its true age. The brick walls hadn't been reconditioned to simply look weathered. They were covered with the dirt and grime of a century or more of various uses. Mildew hung in the air. Mold stained the ceilings. Jack scrunched his nose at the smell as he pushed through. Light seeped in through small windows near the ceiling, but it failed to provide enough illumination. A fan droned on while cold air billowed down on them through an open vent.

"Watch your step," Noble said to Bear as he stepped over a ladder perched sideways on the floor.

A disheveled stack of cardboard boxes blocked their path to the exit. They began tossing them over their shoulders. Noble's fingertips slid into the wet cardboard. It felt like picking up rotted corpses.

"The hell is this?" Bear yanked the final few boxes out of the way and slapped the brick wall with his open hand. "Jack, you sure it was this corner?"

Noble pulled out the plans and verified they were in the right spot. "This is it, man."

"Why are we staring at a solid goddamn brick wall?"

The constant mechanical whirr in the room gave way to the sound of sirens. In a matter of seconds they rose to a peak before silencing amid squealing brakes. It was too soon for an ambulance to arrive for Witherspoon. Hell, it was too soon for anyone to have arrived. Noble shook his head as he caught Bear's eye. His stomach felt as though it had flipped and twisted and been severed in two.

"They set us up."

# CHAPTER FOURTEEN

The mountain of discarded boxes they'd tossed behind them provided the first obstacle on Noble and Bear's path to escape. Jack took large steps, crunching the cardboard down. Bear opted for a more direct route and barreled through.

*See escape, get to escape.*

"What's at the other end of that hallway?" Bear yelled over his shoulder as he grabbed the door handle and yanked it open.

Noble recalled the building plans. "The office."

"Should be a window in there." The big man pulled the door all the way open and dashed into the hallway. Seconds had passed since they heard the sirens. Enough time for the police to have breached the restaurant and determine what had happened?

Jack turned his head as he ran through the intersection. Four people crowded the restroom door, including a hysterical woman saying something about her husband being followed on his way home last night.

*Mrs. Witherspoon, if only you knew the truth.*

Someone yelled at Noble to stop.

Not a chance.

Bear drove his shoulder into the office door. It broke clear off its hinges. Jack caught sight of the door sign and noted that the first *F* in *OFFICE* had been crossed out and changed to *RI*. Clever. And fitting. If they didn't get out of the building now, they'd be taking it up one of their orifices in short order.

"What are you doing in here?" A woman in her early forties shoved away from her desk, knocking over a mug filled with pens. They scattered and fell on the uneven floor and rolled toward the opposite wall. She aimed her computer mouse at Bear.

Noble pulled the H&K from its holster and drew a bead on her. Her face slackened as she threw her hands in the air. "Please, don't shoot. I've got a boy at home." Her eyes darted between him and the wall behind him. He took a quick glance and spotted the camera mounted in the corner.

Noble didn't want additional casualties, and he especially didn't want any recorded. "Get that window open yet?"

Bear worked the window free from years of dirt buildup on the sill that had cemented it in place. He pushed the black screen out and stuck his leg through. The rest of him followed.

Noble looked back at the woman. "Get home to that little boy." Outside, he looked around, adjusting to the sunlight and gathering his bearings. He'd gone over the aerial images a dozen times that day alone. "You remember the area?"

Bear nodded. "I got it."

Jack pointed down the alley. "You go left. I'm heading around this building." He pointed at the weathered grey stone structure on the other side of the asphalt. "We'll meet on Q Street. Got it?"

They had decided earlier if things went sideways and the authorities closed in, they would split up to reduce the risk of both of them being caught.

Bear took off without a word. The man moved faster than you'd think given his height and muscle.

The empty loading dock provided shaded cover as he put distance between himself and the restaurant. Sirens wailed, drowning out the sound of his footfalls as his boots slapped the concrete. Any cops inside were assessing the scene at this point. It would be another few minutes before they made it through the office, and another five before they started venturing out beyond the building's walls.

They would have additional units coming to create a web around the area. To get out, Noble had to avoid the chokepoints.

He turned left at the next alley, a slick, wet stretch of street lined with dumpsters and grease traps. He covered his mouth and nose with his sweaty shirt. The smell was worse than where they used to pile up the shells and sand they collected while dredging the sea in Florida. His mother loved taking them there when they were kids.

*"Oh, look, another sandollar!"*

Blue and red lights brightened the shadows as a squad car raced past. They were gone in an instant. Noble rested against the wall for a moment and slurped down a few deep breaths. He'd sprinted the entire four minutes since leaving the loading dock. Another squad car raced past. This wasn't the place to linger. After catching his breath, he continued on to 29th Street.

He was half a mile from his rendezvous point with Bear. He cut down a side street and continued to work his way over.

Bear's route had been more direct. All the big man had to do was head due north for the most part. The first few intersections were the most treacherous where he'd be out in the open for longer stretches. Bear had proven himself intelligent while on the farm. Jack had little doubt the guy would be waiting for him.

It was hot for mid-November in D.C. The temperatures had

peaked at eighty earlier that day, and hadn't given in much since. Humidity was high in advance of an approaching tropical storm. Noble didn't know the name. He'd been kept from such things for the better part of two months now. They were only told about the storm because Cribbs didn't want them to get caught up in it.

Get the job done and get the hell out.

Cribbs had made it clear they would have a very limited window to get out of the city. But Noble saw through it all now, starting with the walled-in escape route. He knew there'd be no car waiting for them at the rendezvous point.

A chill raced down his spine. They were making the wrong move and he had no way to warn Bear. The big man might not suspect whoever waited for them there. Someone armed with an identical H&K 9mm with a suppressor threaded on the end.

Noble paused for a moment, took a few deep breaths. He had to get there before the big man. He broke into an all-out sprint, dodging pedestrians and bikers. He paid no attention to traffic signals. Cars honked at every intersection. Drivers probably flipped him off. He didn't bother to look. A few narrowly avoided colliding with him. Crunching metal indicated he'd caused at least one accident.

He made it a half-mile before his burning lungs and thighs could no longer keep up. He collapsed against the side of a building and sucked in air so thick it might as well have been steam. Sweat dripped off the ends of his hair. Noble glanced up at the street signs and found them on his mental map of the area. The rendezvous point was only one block away.

Two men and a woman all dressed casually in jeans and sweaters walked past. Where the hell were they from that they were cold today? Jack filed in behind them. He stayed close to the woman and kept his head down. Every few seconds he tossed a glance at the upcoming corner.

Bear wasn't there.

He'd figured it out.

Noble exhaled in relief.

"What are you doing?" The woman stared at him like he was an overgrown mosquito trying to bite her. "Get away."

Both men stepped between Noble and the woman.

He threw both hands up in front of his chest and backed off to avoid a scene. Lucky for the men he had bigger things to worry about. This was not ideal though. He had hoped to cross the street with the group. He glanced around for another option and found it in the form of an open door.

The fan above the doorway blasted him with frigid air. In a few seconds he'd gone from overheated to slightly chilled as his sweat-soaked skin devoured the AC.

An Asian man holding a cleaver next to a meat cooler stared him down. He didn't ask if Jack needed anything. Why would he? Noble looked so out of place in the shop the man behind the counter probably figured he was there to rob the store.

"I'll be on my way in a moment," Noble said. "Hot as balls out there."

The guy brought the cleaver down on an unsuspecting duck carcass. He tossed the head into a bowl and pushed the rest of the body aside. His stare never wavered off of Jack.

"Dammit," Jack muttered. He spotted Bear at the opposite corner. The big man towered above a group of school kids wearing blue plaid uniforms.

The light turned. The kids went and so did Bear, keeping a couple yards of separation between them. Noble heard the engine rev before he saw the unmarked sedan. It skidded to a stop in the middle of the intersection. Jack reached under his shirt and put his hand on the H&K while he waited for the sedan's occupants to exit the vehicle.

He feared they were a couple of spooks from Langley, there on Cribbs's orders. It made sense. If Noble and Bear were dumb enough to head to the rendezvous point after what had happened in the restaurant, they deserved to die. Lesson failed. No retest given.

The entire time they had been staring at that map before leaving for the job, Jack kept thinking they needed an alternate place to meet up. One where they wouldn't be found. But Cribbs's men hadn't given them a chance to wipe their asses alone. Forget about time to create their own plan. This mission was about following orders and proving they could get the job done.

He'd thought so, at least.

Two male police officers hopped out of the sedan, guns drawn. They shouted at Bear, ordering him down.

The big man backpedaled with his hands in the air, yelling, "Don't shoot! I'm a federal agent."

This led to more shouting over one another by the cops.

Noble grabbed a large brim hat off a coatrack as he slipped out of the shop. The butcher yelled something at him, but Jack ignored it. A crowd of people stood by and watched the scene unfolding in the intersection. The cops were so embroiled in their situation with Bear, they hadn't noticed Jack coming up behind them.

Bear had though.

The big man locked eyes with Noble for a second. The confidence in his look was all Jack needed to see. It wasn't lost on him that he was about to commit a felony for a guy he couldn't stand a few short months ago. Not only that, Noble had grown up with a strong sense of right and wrong. It was pounded into him by his father. The waters began to muddy after his sister's murder, but he still had a moral compass that guided his decisions. He wondered if he ever would again after this. He pulled his pistol from his belt, spun it in his palm. A woman shouted, "Behind you!" to the cop. The officer ignored her.

Big mistake.

Jack cracked the guy over the back of the head with the H&K. The officer stumbled, fell to his knees and mumbled something. His partner must've been a rookie. He turned his back on Bear to see what had happened behind him. Before the cop could make sense of the situation, he leveled his Glock 17 at Jack and opened fire.

Noble had seen it coming and dove behind the sedan before the first shot rang out. The rounds ricocheted off the asphalt. A man screamed out in pain. A red blossom spread across the midsection of his white tank top.

The officer lurched forward and collided with the ground a few feet from Noble. The street had torn half the skin off his cheek. Bear was on the guy's back. He looked over at Jack, grinned.

"Get in the car," Bear said.

Jack scrambled to his feet and pulled the passenger door open. A second later, Bear slammed into the seat next to him. The vehicle was running. Bear dropped it into reverse and slammed the skinny pedal to the floor. The tires spun before gaining traction on the asphalt. He whipped the car around in a tight semi-circle, threw it into drive and sped off with the lights on and the siren blaring. Cars and pedestrians hustled to get out of their way on the busy D.C. streets.

Bear slammed his hands on the wheel. "I gotta get me one of these, man." Adrenaline was a powerful thing, and right now, it had a grip on Bear.

Jack took a deep breath and wiped his face. Against all odds, they had made it. He couldn't believe it. A chuckle escaped his mouth. He closed his eyes and enjoyed the chilled air billowing out of the vents.

He felt something buzzing against his thigh. He pulled out the thick portable phone Cribbs had given him earlier that day.

"That him?" Bear said.

"I hope so." He pressed the button to answer the call.

"Noble," a woman said. "If you want to get out of the city alive, then listen carefully to every word I say."

# CHAPTER FIFTEEN

Bear pulled the sedan to a stop a hundred feet from a beat up dark-green Jeep Wrangler. He had cut the lights and sirens following the phone call. The woman never identified herself to Noble. She said her purpose was to help them escape the city. The moment Jack asked her a question, she hung up. That had been after she gave them directions to the Jeep.

"What you think, man?" Bear asked.

Noble scanned the area, studying windows and doorways looking for shadows or a protruding barrel. He gripped the warm bezel of the side mirror and angled it, giving him a view of the escape vehicle. A minute later he popped open his door. "I think if we stay in this unmarked, we're done for. Let's go check it out."

Noble lifted his shirt and tucked it behind the H&K's grip. The easier the access, the better. Bear remained a few steps behind. He grunted every few steps. Must've picked up an injury along the way. When Jack reached the Wrangler, he placed his hand on the rough hood. It felt cool. There was no lingering smell of gas and oil. It had been parked there for a while.

The top was down and the doors were off. Bear reached under the driver's seat and found the keys right where the woman had said they would be.

"She's two for two," Bear said.

"Let's see if the rest is true." Jack reached into the map pocket behind the passenger seat. He paused, wondering if there was an exposed blade or razor or needle concealed in there. He nudged the thought aside and felt around until he found the notebook.

The jeep dipped toward the driver's side. Bear cranked the engine. It started after a long choking pause. He looked over his seat. "Got it?"

Jack held up his find, a hardbound notebook stuffed with extras. He climbed into the passenger seat and leafed through the contents.

"We good?" Bear said.

"Yeah, get us out of here and we'll pull over and check it out once we're clear of the city." He tucked the notebook under his left thigh. "I don't like the idea of hanging around here much longer."

Bear shifted into first and pulled away from the curb.

"Wait."

The Jeep came to a halt. "What is it?"

Noble reached into his pocket and pulled out the cell phone. He jumped to the ground, placed the device underneath the thirty-five inch all-terrain tire. He hopped up in his seat and smiled at Bear.

"Now you can go."

The Jeep lurched away from the curb with a satisfying crunch as the cell phone crumbled under the weight. It took Bear a few minutes to get the hang of the clutch. After a couple lights and stop signs, he was good to go.

Noble kept his gaze fixed on the side view mirror. The woman had led them to the vehicle. That meant she was in place or had someone close by to verify that Jack and Bear took the Jeep. A tail following them was the next logical step.

Of the dozen or so cars on the road behind them, a black Lincoln sedan stood out. It looked like a government vehicle. He squinted to see inside, but the sun reflected off the windshield. He couldn't get a view of the vehicle's occupants.

"See that car back there?" Noble said. "The Lincoln?"

Bear glanced up at the rearview. "Think we're being followed?"

They weren't in the most evasive vehicle. The Wrangler's high center of gravity, especially on the large tires and lift, made it susceptible to rolling should they take a turn too fast. And it didn't have a lot of punch to it. But there was one place it would shine.

Noble poured over the maps tucked inside the notebook. The highlighted route took them west on I-66. He compared it with the topographic maps and spotted a forest service road they could utilize. There would be few obstacles that would slow the Wrangler down. The terrain alone would prevent the Lincoln from giving chase.

Redirecting his attention to the traffic behind them, Noble noted the change of vehicles. Three of the originals remained, including the Lincoln. "I think there's a good chance he's on us. Let's see what happens after we get on the highway."

Bear merged onto the interstate and leveled the speedometer out at sixty-five. The knobby tires sounded like train wheels. The wind roared, slapping them in the face. The Lincoln had to wait for a tractor trailer to pass before merging. Noble lost sight of the sedan. He made adjustments to see around the big rig. It was of no use.

"Here he comes." Bear pointed at his side mirror.

The Lincoln emerged from the other side of the tractor trailer, doing upwards of ninety miles per hour. It closed the gap between the vehicles in a matter of seconds. Noble held his H&K between his legs. He imagined a scene with the Lincoln slowing to match their speed, the passenger window rolling down and a shotgun poking out at them. A couple rounds of buckshot would do some damage at highway speeds. They had no doors to protect them either.

But the Lincoln never slowed. It raced forward, weaving through traffic until it slipped out of sight in the myriad of vehicles ahead.

It took a few minutes for Jack's pulse to recover. His fight or flight mechanism had kicked in and he was raring to go.

"High anxiety?" Bear said.

"No kidding. The hell was that?" Noble still wasn't convinced the vehicle had nothing to do with them. Perhaps the woman wanted to see they followed the initial instructions. She knew where Noble and Bear were headed. She could watch from various waypoints.

"The maps," Bear said with a quick finger gesture. "They're leading us back to the farm, right?"

Noble nodded. "Best guess based on the terrain? I'd say yeah."

"So who do you think this woman is?"

Noble ran through mental images of all the people they had seen while on the Farm. For several weeks they had dealt with Cribbs and his collection of instructors. Noble had a feeling that whoever ran the new program wanted guys like him and Bear. Wet behind the ears, they could be molded into what Cribbs wanted in his operatives without their previous training getting in the way. Despite this, it was fact Cribbs hated them. How else could they explain what had happened today? Cribbs saw a way to get them out of the program, and he took it.

"I don't know who she is, Bear. Didn't see a single woman the whole time we were on the farm. Maybe she's got a beef with

Cribbs. Maybe he planned on us not making it out of this alive, or at least without being detained. She knew this, and now she's leading us to him so we can get our revenge."

The thought settled in. He hadn't had enough time to think about how he'd deal with Cribbs the next time he saw the older man. The two had come to an understanding early in training when they went one-on-one on the mat. Noble had kicked the guy's ass, but in the end the instructors took care of Noble. It was a tough lesson to learn. After that day, Cribbs eased off a bit. Perhaps the guy realized Noble could've killed him on that mat. Instead of being gracious, Cribbs took advantage. Ever since that moment, Noble knew he had to act the same.

Bear glanced over. "She wants us to take him out."

"And if that's the case," Noble said, "then she's leading us there without him knowing. We're going to take that bastard down."

# CHAPTER SIXTEEN

The dense canopy blocked most of the moonlight from filtering through except in those spots where the road widened enough to part the leaves overhead. The temperature had started dropping around six and continued its downward trajectory after Bear and Noble entered the mountainous terrain of West Virginia. It might've been fifty out, but with no top and near-highway speeds, it felt like mid-January. Things improved when they got off the main roads.

Jack held a small flashlight in one hand, the maps in the other. Bear only ran the Jeep's fog lights, which cast a small cone of light in front of the vehicle. Ample enough to crawl forward on the deserted dirt road. Soon he'd cut the lights completely.

Ten miles to go to the farm. To their showdown with Cribbs. Noble tensed at the thought of placing the man in his sights, watching him crumble as he stared down the barrel of Jack's H&K.

They never spotted the Lincoln again. They checked each rest stop, and even pulled off at a couple of exits for gas and water. Bear got under the Jeep and inspected under the hood at the first stop for any kind of transponder that might be used to track them. He found nothing.

They stopped and cut the engine a few times in the past fifteen minutes to listen for the sound of crunching ground. Out here someone could stay out of sight, but would find it impossible to go undetected.

"Smell that?" Noble said.

Bear tipped his head back and inhaled. "Woodsmoke."

"Yeah, someone's here."

Bear pointed past Jack's window, away from the Farm. "Or there. Face it, man, we really don't know who all is out here. Could be a dozen houses or cabins on the other side of the valley."

The farm occupied a few hundred acres, at least. The government probably owned a ring of land around it as well. But Bear was right. Noble had no idea who else lived out here. These people kept to themselves and heeded the warning signs posted along the six-foot high chain-link fence topped with barbed wire.

Bear pulled the Jeep off the rutted dirt road and squeezed between a couple of pines. It had to be the easiest vehicle to parallel park. The whole vehicle fit deep enough into the clearing that it was hidden from the road. A three-mile hike lay ahead of them. After the long day, both men wanted to crash. But the desire to confront Cribbs consumed them. There would be no stopping tonight. They pushed on in silence and completed the final leg of the journey in forty minutes.

The half-moon hovered over the road now, providing enough illumination to see a hundred yards ahead. They stuck to the shadows at the wood's edge with the road to their right. The fence lingered on their left, a reminder of how they'd been prisoners to Cribbs's regimen the whole seven weeks they were in training. That wasn't entirely true. They could've quit, but neither man understood the meaning of the word.

They reached the entrance to the Farm. A wooden sign etched and painted in red named it the *Tradecraft Farm and Orchard*. Noble hadn't spotted a single fruit tree the entire time they were there. There were, however, crops, cows, and some goats and chickens.

Bear took the lead and walked over to the gate. The thick chain that bound the two sections together was gone. He pushed the left side open far enough for the two men to enter, then he closed it again. They spotted the chain and padlock on the side of the dirt and gravel driveway about fifty yards further.

"What do you make of that?" Bear said.

"After today?" Noble said. "I'd rather not even try to figure it out."

Bear chuckled. "I think you're gonna go far in this business."

*This business.* What the hell was this business? Go out, kill some fat slob who pissed off enough politicians to earn a price on his head, then take the fall?

They approached the gym first. The barn-door style steel sliders stood open. Noble shone his flashlight inside the building. The mats were rolled up and placed against the wall near the free-weights and machines, which were arranged in a neat line, not spread out like they had been. The men entered, but the heavy odor of bleach made it impossible to remain inside for long.

"Somebody's been cleaning up." Bear's words echoed around the steel chamber.

What were they hiding? Noble's blood? Cribbs's? Something worse? Had the men who quit really gone home?

It took three minutes to reach the barracks from the gym. The surrounding woods stifled the breeze. The ever-present red glow in the windows from the emergency lights was gone. They were black now. It had taken a few nights for Noble to adjust to always-on lighting. Even after he had, he never felt as though he managed a solid night of sleep. Although that could've had something to do with the trainers banging pans together every few hours.

Noble pushed the door open and swept his light across the barracks. Bear followed him in and sighed at the empty room. Even the beds were gone. They checked out the head, where the smell of bleach intensified.

"It's like they tried to scrub every shred of evidence we were here," Bear said. "Why?"

"Fear of the hit being linked back to the program, I suppose."

"You come from a military family," Bear said. "Dad high-ranking in the Army. He ever talk about stuff like this? These clandestine operations? I mean, I can't imagine many people in the government even know what's going on out here. Probably some by-line on a billing statement that some dude sitting in a cushy office in the Pentagon signs off on."

"Why don't we go find Cribbs and ask him?"

The mess hall was located in the same clearing as the barracks. They entered and found it stripped down to the basics. The kitchen had been left in place. The refrigerator was unplugged and emptied. Bear turned the cold water on in the sink. Nothing came out of the faucet.

"Maybe everything went sideways today," Bear said. "And they had nothing to do with it. So they shut this place down in advance."

Noble nodded and said nothing. He wasn't sure what to make of any of it. He exited the building and stared up at the sky. Wispy clouds raced past. The lingering smell of bleach made it impossible to take in the clean air surrounding them.

Cribbs's cabin stood two miles from the barracks. They'd seen it twice during their time on the farm. Both times had come after they were given freedom to complete their twelve-mile runs without instructors present. The first time they found Cribbs's place by accident. They spotted the older man sitting on his porch, sucking on a cigar and holding a bottle of beer. Pabst. Cheap garbage. And at that moment, both men would have killed for a pull on the bottle.

The second time, they went back to see if they were being followed while on their run. A black sedan had been parked in front of the house. From fifty yards out they heard Cribbs in a shouting match with another man. They didn't linger long enough to see who it had been, but figured it had to have been someone from Langley. If Cribbs ran the training program, it only made sense someone else was in charge of operations.

They reached the Cabin in less than fifteen minutes. A single light illuminated the front windows. The porch light was off. Noble watched for signs of movement inside, while Bear crept along the wood's edge. The big man moved deftly for a guy his size. He'd grown up in western North Carolina, spent a lot of time in the woods. He enjoyed tracking wildlife and the occasional hiker, seeing how long he could stay with them before they noticed his presence. According to Bear, they never did. When Noble had asked if any of those hikers had turned up missing, Bear only offered a shrug in response.

Noble didn't notice Bear had returned from patrol until the guy spoke.

"Perimeter's clear."

Jack hid his surprise at Bear standing a few feet from him. "Let's make our move."

"You didn't know I was there, did you?" Bear clamped his hand on Jack's shoulder. "It's all right, man. You can admit it."

"Screw you," Noble said. "Let's go deal with this prick."

They dashed across the grounds to the corner of the house. Noble crept to the first window and eased around the edge. He peered in through the sheer drapes. They created a haze but otherwise did not distort his view inside.

"Empty," he said.

Bear moved past him to the porch. He grabbed the rail, pulled himself up, and stepped over the railing. He passed the front door and checked another window. A few seconds ticked by and he gave Noble the all-clear signal.

Jack climbed onto the porch and pulled his H&K. An empty front room meant nothing. Cribbs could be anywhere inside the cabin. Noble tapped the doorknob with the back of his hand to make sure it wasn't hot. Grabbing anything with live power ensured a death sentence. There was no way to pry your fingers free once the electricity caused the muscles to lock down. He turned the knob and pushed the door open with his foot.

Bear hovered behind. "I got your back."

Noble stepped inside with his new partner not far behind. They cleared the three-room cabin.

"Where do you think he is?" Bear said.

"Langley," Jack said, taking a stab at how the afternoon had played out for Cribbs. "Can't imagine he'd be anywhere else. What went down has to be explained. He's at the forefront of it as far as they're concerned."

"So did they turn on us and feed us false intel about the building, or were *they* set up?"

"It's crossed my mind." Jack noted the humming of the refrigerator and pulled the door open. Half the shelves were empty. The others were stacked with hot dogs and beer. He pulled two cans out and set them on the counter. Before he could open them, the front door crashed open.

# CHAPTER SEVENTEEN

Cribbs stood in the doorway, a crooked smile across his weathered face. He chomped down on a thin cigar on one side of his mouth. His labored breathing didn't seem to bother him. Maybe he'd sprinted to the house. Perhaps he felt a tinge of anxiety over the face-off. He had an advantage over his two trainees, though, as he aimed his M4 in Noble and Bear's direction.

Jack reached for his firearm, but came up with air. He hadn't re-holstered the H&K after setting it down. He glanced toward the fridge and saw it on the counter next to a sweating can of Pabst.

*Putrid beer.*

"So you two mutts managed to find your way back home? Like a couple of lost puppies." Cribbs shook his head. Floorboards creaked as he moved toward the kitchen. His eyebrows raised into his forehead as he blew out a large breath. "Guess we're gonna have to burn the place down now. Question is, do I need to tie you guys to the posts while it falls?"

"Eat me, old man." Bear took a step forward. This was met

with a single round fired over his shoulder. He flinched at the sound of the gunshot. The bullet slammed into the wall, sending splinters in all directions. Bear remained in place. He didn't back down. Didn't raise his hands. His fists were at his side, balled and ready for action. The scowl on his face intensified, but he said nothing else.

"You crazy bastard." Noble worked his jaw and tugged at his earlobe in an attempt to diffuse the ringing in his ears. "Just do it already. Quit dragging this out."

Cribbs's shoulders heaved as he laughed, sparking concern there might be another discharge of his weapon. "If I wanted you dead, you never would've made it out of D.C. Don't you get that?"

"We almost didn't make it out of the restaurant," Jack said. "Cops were there so damn fast, only logical explanation is they must've been called in advance."

Cribbs shrugged. "Possibly. You got out though, right?"

Neither man replied.

"And once outside, confronted with capture by a larger force, you knew it was better if only one of you were taken, so you split up with a rendezvous point already determined." He took a step forward, lowering the barrel of his weapon toward the floor as he moved. "One of you was caught. The other could've kept going. Now, I know how it goes out there. Each man has to make this determination based on the situation at hand. Could've been it was in your best interest to run, or maybe you thought doing so put something greater than your life, or even the mission, at risk. Now, I don't necessarily agree with the chance you took with the cops, Noble, but it worked. Can't argue with results. Most of the time, at least. You and your partner got out and were smart enough to ditch the cruiser."

"That wasn't our doing," Noble said. "Someone led us to the Jeep."

"I did." The screen door scratched open and a tall brunette stepped in. Her hair was pulled back in a loose pony tail with strands draped over her right shoulder. Slight traces of makeup remained on her attractive face. She looked to be in her early thirties. Her tank top revealed toned arms and shoulders adorned with a small amount of ink. Might've been the tips of angel's wings. Noble couldn't tell from the current angle.

"It was you on the phone." It started to crystallize in Jack's head.

She nodded once. There was no smile or other sign that she did it for any reason other than it was part of the job.

"Gentlemen, allow me to introduce you to Alexa Steele. For reasons unknown, she selected and recommended you two scumbags for my program."

Steele stepped forward. "Let it be known I did not agree with how the events of today were handled. And it is *not* your program, Cribbs. You oversee training. That is all."

Cribbs pulled the cigar out of his mouth and spat a few loose pieces of tobacco toward the floor. His cheeks burned red, while his lip twitched.

"We were told the mark was—"

Steele held up her hand and cut Bear off while shooting a look at Cribbs. "Witherspoon was everything you heard, and more. My boss verified all of it. My problem does not lie with the job, but how Cribbs handled you two. It's funny how someone who criticized his handlers for years could be so horrible at the job."

"They made it out alive," he said. "Passed the final test."

Something about the smug look on the old instructor's hardened face combined with the knowledge they were deliberately set up as a means for a test triggered a reaction in Noble. He lunged forward, fist drawn back. He didn't care about the consequences for what he was about to do. But he didn't make it that far. Bear hooked his elbow and spun him around.

"Stand down, man." He grabbed Jack by the shoulders. "This isn't the time or place."

Noble stared into Bear's intense eyes for a moment. The rage subsided.

Cribbs laughed, but the fresh sheen of sweat on his forehead told a different story. He knew what Noble and Bear were capable of, and the last thing he wanted was their anger directed at him.

"This was nothing different than we've done in the past." Cribbs held up a finger to silence Steele as she started to speak. "You and I can discuss this alone, *Miss* Steele."

Steele's mouth drew tight and her nostrils flared. She took offense at the way Cribbs emphasized *Miss*. Made it sound like he didn't regard her as an equal in any way.

"Guys, you passed." Cribbs reached into his pocket and tossed them a set of keys. "You're part of the team now, God help us. Take my car, head down to the barracks and get rinsed off and changed. There'll be a meal waiting for you after."

# CHAPTER EIGHTEEN

Alexa Steele sat at the table across from her uncle. She frowned at the man as he chugged half a can of beer. He slammed it down in the sweat ring on the table and drew his bare arm across his mouth. The wetness matted down his graying arm hair.

She'd known Cribbs as long as she could remember. He'd known her longer. In fact, he'd been there at her birth. Not all that uncommon, considering her mother was his sister. She grew up in awe of the man. A spy for the CIA. He always told her she could never tell any of her friends his secret. They could both get in trouble. He had spent years in Eastern Europe following the Vietnam War. Cribbs had ingrained himself amongst top KGB agents. He was responsible for collecting hundreds of secrets over the course of four years before outing himself when he took down a corrupt general in the early eighties. It wasn't planned, but he couldn't let the opportunity pass.

Steele knew from a young age she wanted to be like her uncle. She dedicated herself to martial arts, running track and cross country, and her studies. She was so devoted to school that she graduated a year early. She didn't have many friends at that time, but it didn't bother her. Dating and partying were for those without life plans. She'd been fortunate enough to have adopted one before turning eleven years old, a time when the other girls were starting to lose their minds over boys.

Cribbs had been a good uncle to her, even after her father passed away and her mother remarried when Steele was only eight years old. She took her new father's last name and followed his advice regarding her future. If she really wanted to make a difference, he told her, then she needed to pursue her law degree before opting for the Agency. Then she could be placed in a position where her work would affect millions at any given moment. This strategy had served him well in D.C., as he spent years inside the White House serving both Democrat and Republican presidents.

Steele's journey led her to Georgetown for her undergrad and law school. She had the grades and extracurriculars to go anywhere. Graduating top of her class while running track at the collegiate level was impressive, even to the board at Harvard. But D.C. was where she wanted to be. It pulled at her. It was home.

Cribbs tried his damnedest to talk her out of joining the Agency. A man with plenty of dirt on others, he pulled every bureaucratic string he could find. This resulted in numerous interviews for Alexa with some of the nation's top law firms. Steele obliged and interviewed. And she turned down every job she had been offered. She wanted the CIA.

She wanted this, she supposed.

"Alexa, I know you don't agree with my methods."

Steele cut Cribbs off. "I don't agree with the plate of bacon you eat for breakfast every morning, Douglas. This is an entirely different matter. Those boys could have been detained or could have even died today."

"Could've, could've." He leaned back in his chair. "Those *boys,* as you call them, are killers now. And I set that job up the way it had to go. We're not gonna be there for them when they're standing in the back of a Baghdad brothel trying to find a way out of the city because they were made by some terrorist's girlfriend."

"You wouldn't have done this if they were any of the other recruits. All of whom, I might add, washed out. And now, we've got felony assault of police officers to deal with. This won't go over well."

"You can take care of that." Cribbs lifted his bottle of beer to his lips and took a sip.

"I know I can take care of it. But I shouldn't have to. That's the point." She pointed at her chest. "It's only because they're my guys you did this. I told you'd they'd make it through the first week when you were whining about them being unfit for the program, and they made it. I warned you about pushing Noble too far and you almost got your old ass beaten by him. Every step of the way, you fought me on them, told me to pull them, and they showed you up."

Cribbs's eyes narrowed.

Randall McKenzie stuck his narrow frame into the room. He offered a smile to his associates. "Am I interrupting something?"

Steele waved him off. "You got a beef with me, you take it up with McKenzie, or go over his head to the director. But you risked two lives today and it didn't have to be that way."

"What do you know?" Cribbs slapped the table with his palm, knocking over his drink. "You got your damn law degree and you sit there in Langley without a clue how things work in the real world."

"I know exactly how they work. We put our agents in the best possible position to succeed. That's the support they'll get from us when they go over to do their jobs. Now you've set Noble and

Logan up to distrust us from the moment they're part of the team. How does that help anybody?"

Cribbs knocked his chair over as he rose to his feet. He aimed a stubby finger at his niece. "You listen to me, girl."

"Girl?" Steele's chair toppled back as she leapt up to meet him. They stood chest to chest. "I haven't been a girl in—"

Cribbs moved his head to the side to get away from her sharp fingernail. "When everything goes wrong, it won't be you heading out there to fix it. You understand? If I'm gonna have to work with these guys, trust them out in the field, I need to know they can survive. They don't have the pedigree of everyone else on the team."

"You mean all those guys who were outed as operatives and are sitting on their thumbs in Nice while waiting for a boat out?"

Cribbs took a deep breath. She'd cut him on that one. She knew her uncle prided himself on the work he had done, and the training he used to build up his recruits. They were an elite team who moved in and out of hostile countries at will. Whatever the job called for, they did it. One simple breach, and all that work meant nothing. It was ruined until they learned how far the information had been disseminated.

"If I might be so bold as to interject," McKenzie said, splitting the pair apart with his arm and redirecting them to their turned-over seats. "Noble and Logan are the perfect pair to send over. There's no tape on them, so to speak. They have no background in any force aside from half of Recruit Training on Parris Island, and as you know, the guys we're up against have managed to gather intelligence on many of our operatives."

"That's been my point all along," Steele said.

"No one could have predicted this situation," Cribbs said.

"Regardless," McKenzie said, "Alexa is right. So I move that we put behind us what happened today and move forward with preparing those two for what they are about to face."

"They're prepared." Cribbs folded his arms over his chest. He worked his jaw, shook his head. "I didn't think they'd get out of that situation today, but they did."

Steele stifled a smile. She knew how hard this was for her uncle. No good could come from reveling in it to his face.

McKenzie leaned forward. "We don't have much time, Cribbs. Every hour that passes places our asset in more danger. We need a team on the ground capable of infiltrating and rescuing her. Are Noble and Logan our guys? Because if they are, I want Alexa to escort them to Langley tonight, get them processed and read in, and outfitted for their trip. We need them overseas by this time tomorrow."

Cribbs stared at the bottle in front of him for several seconds. He worked the corner of the label free and pulled it off. It rolled up tight, like a joint.

*If only,* Steele thought.

"They're our guys." Cribbs refused to make eye contact. "I hope."

# CHAPTER NINETEEN

The plane touched down in Istanbul mid-day, capping off an intense twenty-four-hour period that saw Bear and Noble finish their first assignment, face betrayal from their handlers, and officially become unofficial contractors for the CIA. Outside of a small circle at the Agency and Pentagon, anyone who accessed their personnel files would see that they were Marine Scout Snipers, which was usually enough to put an end to any further prying.

When Noble asked Steele how small of a circle knew the truth beyond her and Cribbs and the ATRIA team, she replied, "Three people, and the President is not one of them." He doubted the President didn't know of the team's existence. Later that night they met a man named McKenzie and fit him into the puzzle as Cribbs and Steele's boss. Their interaction with him was minimal, consisting of a quick introduction and wishes of good luck.

Steele whisked them around the installment while filling their heads with more information than they should have been able to retain in such a short amount of time. Noble powered through with increased focus and managed to keep about eighty percent of it fresh. He figured between him and Bear, they should have no issues recalling the most important details.

Both men were required to memorize three series of twelve-digit numbers linked to bank accounts and safe deposits in Switzerland, Grand Cayman, and Singapore. The accounts had accessible balances in the six-figures. A warning followed that if they drained them, the Agency would make sure they would have no chance to enjoy the money. In the safe deposits they would find small bills in multiple currencies, firearms, and alternate identities. Noble thought it was something out of a *Bourne* novel and wondered if the accounts truly existed, or were they mentioned solely to give Bear and him the feel-goods. The hour that Steele made them review the dossiers of their false identities was enough to convince him the accounts did in fact exist.

They left the facility the next morning with little more on their backs than they had entered with, but equipped with enough knowledge to survive for months on their own. Prior to boarding the Gulfstream bound for New York, they were briefed on the task ahead.

Mary Margaret O'Neil was a thirty-six-year-old, fourteen-year veteran of the Agency. She had been responsible for extracting intelligence from a well-placed foreign official that had led to the downfall of Nicolae Ceausescu and his wife Elana in Romania. Extracting information was her specialty, it seemed. When she began her career as a young woman fresh out of Trinity College, she had aspirations of becoming an analyst. Psychological testing indicated she was better suited for another path. Training revealed she had far more ability than she ever realized. She took to the job of being a spy like she had been born across enemy lines.

Two weeks ago, O'Neil's small team had been infiltrated by a man they believed was a solid informant. Two of her men were captured and taken to Syria. The terrorists who abducted them made no effort to hide this from anyone. One man was killed shortly after arriving at their fortified facility. They tortured the other until he gave up the names of every man and woman in their group, effectively neutering the Agency's Middle East clandestine operations.

By the time O'Neil realized the extent of the damage, they abducted her in broad daylight with a corrupt police chief's blessing. He even provided them with an escort out of Istanbul.

The Agency moved quickly against the chief, detaining him and taking him to an undisclosed location in a non-neighboring country. To date, they had not been able to extract any information from him. He tried to pass it off on a colleague. This turned out to be false, as expected. Clearly his terrorist ties were stronger than those to his job.

Steele ended their briefing with one final piece of advice.

If you have the option of choosing between death or capture, take death.

They traveled from New York to Paris, switched planes, and flew to Istanbul's Ataturk Airport.

Noble and Bear waited until the plane cleared out before exiting. The vessel whistled at them as they trudged down the deserted aisle. It was easier this way. No one bumping into them. No chance of their carry-ons being knocked loose or stolen.

They were dressed in jeans and flannels. The goal was to make them look like American tourists starting a journey across Europe in Istanbul. With their ragged beards, the look was convincing.

One step into the exhausting jetway, both realized they needed a change of clothing. The heat and humidity were as intense as late August on Parris Island.

They cleared customs with little scrutiny, found their checked luggage, and stepped out into the heat. Smog choked the horizon, diffusing the shimmering sunlight. Traffic in front of the terminal was unlike anything Noble had seen before. There were taxis everywhere, parked however the hell they wanted. The smell of exhaust was unbearable. Bearded men yelled at them in a language neither understood. The smart ones quickly switched to English.

"Give you a ride, buddy?"

"I know the best place in town for two Americans like you."

"Come with me, I know special spot."

They ignored them all. Bear led the way down the crowded sidewalk to the predetermined meeting place. A man named Serkan was to meet them. They hadn't been told anything else about him. Wise, Jack figured, in case they were detained by officials at the airport. The less they knew, the less they had to lie about, and there was already plenty.

A man with close-cropped hair and a short beard stood at the end of the long walkway holding a piece of paper in his hand. He glanced between it and Noble and Bear. With a quick nod, he opened the rear door, grabbed their bags and dropped them in the trunk, and then hopped in on the front driver's side without waiting for Noble or Bear to climb in.

"Guess that's our ride," Bear said.

Noble looked over his shoulder. Were they being watched by anyone? What if Steele's transmission had been intercepted by the group who took O'Neil? They could have already dealt with Serkan and sent an imposter in his place. No picture of the guy had been provided to them.

Bear placed his hand on the door and leaned inside. Noble saw the driver pull something from his shirt pocket and twist in his seat to show Bear.

"I think he's legit." Bear stepped back and made room for Noble to see.

Jack stopped. "One day on the job and all of a sudden you can read people in a foreign country like you've got twenty years' experience profiling?"

"Don't know about all that," Bear said. "But he's got a shield that matches what we saw earlier."

"Yeah, can't fake that." Noble shook his head. For the first time he wondered if they were in over their heads.

The guy leaned over and rolled down the passenger side window. "Gentlemen, you can continue to stand on the sidewalk all day if you wish. But if you see that car up there, inside it are two men who would like nothing more than to detain you two and find out why you are here. So I suggest, if you want to move forward, get inside of the car."

"Jack, even if he's armed, look at him. The two of us can take him."

Noble craned his neck and looked back once more. "It's not him I'm worried about."

Bear slid across the backseat, leaving Noble no choice but to join him unless he had a deep-seated desire to fend for himself in a foreign city where he hadn't made arrangements. It wasn't his first time overseas. Just his first where the possibility of not making it home was real.

Noble took a seat next to his partner and stared out the window at the throng of people and taxis and security guards. His mind drifted back to Crystal River, Florida. Home. He'd only been allowed a couple of phone calls since leaving for Parris Island. It had been a tough sell keeping the Colonel and his mother away when they thought Jack was graduating Recruit Training. Brigadier General Keller, the commanding officer of Parris Island, had to call Jack's old man and tell him that due to scheduling conflicts, Noble would not graduate with his class. He had to advance to Scout Sniper school a day early.

Jack's brother Sean was headed to law school soon. Molly's

murder had driven them in different directions. Jack had felt powerless to do something to stop the men. An intense desire to never allow that to happen again burned. He wanted to prevail over evil men who lived to hurt others. That feeling led him to the Corps, and now to the program. His brother, however, felt that justice needed a voice. As a lawyer, he could provide it.

They had been close as kids, but drifted in those final years under the same roof following Molly's death.

Noble pictured the small hill in the cemetery where Molly's headstone stood out like a lost soul, out of place on the mostly empty plot where the Colonel had decided to purchase five grave sites. One for each of them. Noble often wondered if his father had anticipated they'd all perish at the same time in a car or plane crash. Certainly no one expected Molly to be the first and only to find her place underground.

Bear slapped Noble's shoulder and pointed at a café. "I heard they got the best *manti* in town."

"You heard?" Jack said, welcoming the distraction. "You got family in the tour guide industry?"

"When you dozed off back at Langley. Steele told me about it."

Jack stared at the café. "So she's been here?"

Bear shrugged. "How should I know?"

Jack imagined himself back in the drab grey room they shared for part of the night and morning. Were there cameras in there? Had it been bugged? Steele had said the room was used as an informal meeting room. By who?

"Maybe she was trying to tell you something," Noble said.

"About what?"

"That I don't know. Just odd she'd point it out to you, and Serkan here drove us by it." He caught the driver's eye in the rearview as the man offered a slight nod. Noble paused a moment.

"Let's make sure we check it out after we get our feet back under us."

A few miles later Serkan pulled to the side of the road. Horns blared as two other vehicles swerved to avoid hitting them in the rear.

"We are almost there, gentlemen. Before we proceed, I do need to ask you to reach into the pockets on the back of the seats and put on the black hoods you find there."

# CHAPTER TWENTY

"The hell you talking about?" Bear yanked back on the seat so hard it jerked back a few notches. "Hoods?"

Noble reached for his door handle but stopped when he found himself staring down the barrel of a pistol. "Bear, I think we need to do what he says."

"Screw that, man."

"Look out your window." Noble gestured toward the man holding a submachine gun a few feet from Bear's door. He glanced at the rearview and spotted a third man behind them, positioned in front of a parked car. The guy didn't look like the locals. He had sandy blond hair and a matching beard covering his fair skin. When Bear reached for the door handle, Jack grabbed his arm. "I don't think that's a good idea."

They were surrounded by a team of highly-trained killers.

"It's just a formality," Serkan said.

"They're with the Agency?" Jack said.

Serkan's head bobbed once. "Put on the hoods and we proceed

to the safe house. They'll verify you once we are there, and then you'll have access to everything you need."

Bear leaned back in his seat, elbow on the window. He wiped his hand down his face and tugged on the beard he'd grown since leaving South Carolina. "I don't know about this, Jack."

"If the plan is to kill us, we're dead one way or another." Noble stretched the hood open. "But if Serkan is telling us the truth, then we'll live if we do as they ask."

The world went black as Noble slipped the hood over his head. The smell reminded him of a pizza place he'd tried once in Miami after a game. Heavy on the garlic.

Serkan rolled down his window and said something to the man closest to him. Jack heard the guy reply back with a "Ten-four," in a solid south-Georgia drawl. He'd run into plenty of guys from the area while camping in the north Florida woods.

Hearing a guy from the States put him at ease. He was either a contractor or part of the Agency. Either way, he was on their side.

Presumably.

The car pulled away from the curb and sped and slowed and stopped and went. They turned right and left and completely around so many times that the map Noble tried to keep track of in his mind's eye looked more like a plate of multi-colored spaghetti than an actual route. He gave up trying to keep it going after ten minutes.

When the vehicle finally came to a complete stop and Serkan cut the engine, Noble didn't bother to move. He expected they'd take off again any moment. When Serkan told them they could remove their hoods, he didn't hesitate.

A dim light illuminated the space surrounding the car. They were in a garage with bare walls and a low ceiling. A string hung down from the single overhead light. There were a few feet of space in front and on the sides. The back of the car almost touched the roll-up door.

Serkan opened his door. Warm air fragranced with used cat litter filled the cabin. "Come on, let's not hang out in here too long."

Jack pushed his door open and stepped out, forcing his tight calf muscles to stretch all the way. Too much sitting over the course of the past day.

Serkan stood at the top of four stairs in front of an oil-and-grease stained door. He left it open after exiting the garage. Bear followed right behind. Noble took his time, listening for conversation or any other distinctive sounds. The whirr of a fan overhead in the attic was all he heard.

He caught a whiff of seared meat as he entered the house. Lamb, probably. They were in Turkey, after all. He glanced around the kitchen and took note of the bamboo knife block. Every blade in its place. The fridge was small and old and mint green with a chipped chrome handle and a badge on the freezer door to match. The open shelving housed a half-dozen plates and bowls and cups and mugs. The safe house received few visitors.

Serkan ushered them into the dining room and told them to sit on one side of the rectangular table. It showed its age, like everything else in the place. A sanding and a fresh coat of stain would do wonders for the table.

The sandy-blond guy entered the room. "Name's Schofield."

"Noble," Jack said. "The big guy's Bear."

Scofield nodded and took a sip from a white mug with streaks of dried coffee running down it. "Get you guys some coffee?"

"None for me," Bear said.

"Extra strength," Noble said.

"Serkan, can you take care of that?"

Serkan exited and left the three men alone.

"I've verified you two with Langley," Schofield said. "And I'm guessing you guys have figured out who I am by now."

"You run this safe house," Noble said. "The other two guys stay here with you to protect visitors that need protecting. Other than the safe house, you manage a few local informants and assets, and keep tabs on who comes and goes from within your community and its associates."

"*Our* community, friend." Schofield leaned over his arm resting on the table. "And enemies. Never forget about our enemies. They are many, and we are few. Can't even trust some of our allies these days. They're always trying to pick through our intel, and the bastards never reciprocate. More than ever I feel like I'm fighting everyone off."

"Who stays here?" Bear asked. "I mean, how often do you get visitors?"

Schofield crossed his hairy arms over his chest and shrugged. "It's not like there's a schedule people follow. Sometimes we know a day or two ahead of time. Other times, we get an hour's notice. Occasionally one or two of us will have to go out and recover someone, bring them back here."

"Dead?"

"Not usually. Stranded, mostly." He leaned back in his chair and tipped it a couple inches and looked up at the ceiling. "We're in a funny place here. The cusp of hostility, I like to call it. Not many people in this section of the world like us. Istanbul lets us get about as far as we can before they—the generic they—start getting suspicious. You'd never find me at a safe house in Mosul, that's for sure. Got guys that look more like Sarken to run those."

"Right, make them fit in so they draw less attention," Noble said. "Dad always talked about SEALs being the masters of disguising their looks to fit in wherever they operated. They could take someone who looked just like you and have him pass for an Iraqi."

Schofield lit a cigarette. "We've got guys like that, too. From what I gather, you two are gonna fill a similar role."

Neither of the men spoke. It'd been drilled into their heads not to offer more information than necessary, especially with Agency personnel. The full extent of their job had never been outlined by Cribbs and Steele. They knew enough to know officially the job did not exist.

Schofield smashed out his smoke on a plate that still had some of that morning's breakfast on it. A few pieces of egg and crumbs remained. "Let me show you around the mansion."

The level they were on consisted of one more room that spanned the width of the structure, a living area with two couches, a chair and a television.

They hiked up a set of solid stairs that didn't bow even a millimeter under their weight. Upstairs, Schofield pointed out his and his men's rooms, then showed Noble and Bear to theirs. The room was a ten by ten box with three bunk beds, one against each wall that didn't have a door. There was no closet in the room. The carpet was sea-foam green and stunk like a three-day old bag of stale Fritos. There were two black bags on two of the bunks. They were not the bags the men had flown with, which still remained in the trunk of the car.

"That's everything you should need here," Schofield said. "If you think something's missing, let me know. I'm your point of contact from here out." He picked something out from between his teeth and flicked it on the carpet. "But let me make something clear to you. I am not your handler. I don't want to know why you're here. I don't want to know any details before or after your job. I might see something on the news I think is related. I am not gonna talk to you about it. The less I know, the better the chance is I get to go home and procreate one day."

"Plausible deniability," Noble said. A concept his father had drilled into him. Perhaps he realized early on how much trouble Jack would get into later in life.

"You could say that. But I'll tell you, these pukes out here, they don't play by normal rules. They get ahold of you, say goodbye to your fingernails. Get ready for three days of having alcohol poured on those festering wounds. Then, when you think you can't take it, or your blood's about to boil because infection is gonna set in due to the open wounds and nasty conditions you're being held in, they'll just start lopping off digits." He held up five fingers and closed them one by one.

Noble held the man's gaze for a second and spotted a slight smile on Bear's lips.

"Now, I'm a man who's been through enough training I can handle most things. But once they start cutting digits off, I'm gonna sing. So the less I know, the better."

Had the guy said that? Jack blew it off as dramatics, but made a note not to trust Schofield with anything.

Ever.

"I'll give you guys a few minutes to go through your gear. Lunch'll be served soon. Got a nice lamb roasting. Only good thing about this country. The meat is fresh and off the chain." He pulled the door shut and stopped an inch short. "Oh, and the whores are damn cheap."

# CHAPTER TWENTY-ONE

Noble inspected the bag on his bunk. The tough exterior looked like it was made from a ballistic material. He gave it a yank at the seams. It didn't tear. The zipper glided on its track. The smell of fresh lubricating oil greeted him. The 9mm H&K resembled the one he'd used throughout training. He'd become intimately familiar with the pistol over those ten weeks.

He stripped the sidearm and inspected it. Satisfied it had been well taken care of, Noble reassembled it and inserted a full magazine into the hilt. He chambered a round and set the pistol off to the side in a location where only he could access it.

He found various items of clothing and a flak vest. Underneath a divider was a satellite phone with a string of coded numbers and letters taped to the back. He instantly recognized the code as one Cribbs had taught them in the final week of training. It must've been a universal code for the team to use. That explained why Cribbs had waited until the end after the other trainees had washed out. The final week had pushed them, but not like the previous ones. It was about ironing out the kinks rather than building up the armor.

Also in the bag were short range comms units, presumably meant for Noble and Bear to communicate. The small square packs were attached to tiny ear pieces with wires.

At the bottom of the bag was a folder. Noble glanced across the room and watched as Bear finished inspecting his duffle.

"You get one of these?" Jack held up the folder.

Bear nodded as he produced a red folder that matched Jack's. "Guess they figured one of us might not make it here."

"Let's see." Noble slid off the bed to the floor and stretched his legs out. He placed the folder on his lap and opened it.

Bear joined him and did the same.

The first item in each folder was a black and white photo of an attractive woman with short blonde hair and dark eyes.

"Mary Margaret O'Neil." Bear traced the angle of her jaw with his thick forefinger. "She doesn't look like a killer."

"Not everyone in the Agency is a killer," Noble said.

"You really believe that, man?" Bear looked him dead in the eye. "Whether they pull the trigger, spot a target, or dig through someone else's mail and trash for that single nugget of intel that leads the field guys to an encampment, they're all killers. They got us here, right? What do you think we're gonna do at the end of this job? Play patty cakes with the guys that took her?"

The big man lived with a healthy dose of cynicism. Noble knew it'd be good for some of that to rub off on him. The world wasn't as black and white as he wanted it to be.

Bear flipped to the following photograph, an image taken at the time of abduction. Two men with their faces wrapped in black accosted O'Neil on the sidewalk. One had her by the arms while the other was swinging his fist toward her stomach.

"Bastards," Noble said. "Who do you suppose took that photo?"

"Good question. Maybe from security footage?" Bear flipped to the next page. They studied the satellite imagery of a ten square block area. "Must be where they think she is."

"All well and good," Noble said. "But if we don't know where that is, we're not gonna get very far. See what's next."

Someone had placed the images out of order. The next showed the entire city of Aleppo, approximately twenty-five miles past the Syrian border.

"Well, this should be fun," Bear said.

"They didn't hire us to bake Girl Scout cookies."

"You buy them in front of Lowe's, man. Who the hell would bake them?"

Noble waved him off and shuffled back to the previous image. He held them side by side.

"Where do you suppose that is?" Bear said.

"Look at the large circle in the bottom corner," Jack said. "And that bare strip of land next to it. That looks like this on the large map, doesn't it?"

Bear held the two photos in front of his face and studied them. "What is that at the top of the strip? A mosque?"

"Hell if I know. Could be a park. A market. Doesn't matter right now, but it might in a day or two. For now, I think we've got our area nailed down."

"Yeah, but there's gotta be at least fifteen thousand people living in that section. Maybe more."

"I'd bet on more."

"Right, so how are we gonna find a woman no one wants found?"

"Why do you say it like that?"

Bear set the images down on his thighs. "Like what?"

"No one wants found. We want her found, don't we? Our employers want her found. That's why we're here."

"I meant those who have her in their possession. No one's gonna advertise she's sleeping in their building."

"We need to know more about this area." Noble read through the next few pages, which contained more personal information about O'Neil, as well as a list of her contacts in Istanbul.

"What about the police chief?" Bear said. "I don't see anything here about that. Think they'd let us bust his balls?"

"They've got people who are better trained for that than us. Plus, I'm betting they want us to stay as far away from the local authorities as possible."

"Why's that?"

"For one, they did nothing to prevent O'Neil from being abducted, despite knowing what her fate would be. I think that makes it pretty clear they hate us. Not necessarily the American us, but the Agency us. We're either meddling in their affairs, or we're screwing with people who don't want to be screwed with. And when they are screwed with, they are more apt to come after the government who harbored the screwers since these terrorists don't have the fire or man power to take on the U.S."

Bear leaned his head back and laughed.

"What?" Noble said.

"You are overthinking things too damn much, man."

It was true, though not always the case. This was a time for analyzing and planning. Once they strapped on their boots and hit the street, Noble would turn into a raging bull. The ponderous owl would disappear. He figured Bear didn't get his nickname only because of his size. He'd seen how forceful the guy could be up close, having been on the receiving end of a few blows from the big man just a few short months ago while in Recruit Training.

"The point is," Noble said, "if we talk to too many of the

wrong people, we aren't leaving here alive. Let's check in with one or two of O'Neil's recent contacts. See if they can point us to any specific investigations or developments, and then we'll find our way into Syria."

"You ever watch the news?" Bear said.

"I tried not to. The Colonel made sure I kept up with world events."

"So you know who we might end up dealing with."

"Hezbollah, or those who are affiliated with or support them in some way."

"And you know what they'll do with us if we're captured."

Images of torture flashed through Noble's mind. "Schofield gave us a run down. That's why we won't get captured."

"Well if you see them dragging me off," Bear said, "and you don't think you stand a chance against them, shoot me."

# CHAPTER TWENTY-TWO

Later that afternoon Noble and Bear ventured into the city in a vehicle Schofield had lent them. The men were cramped with their knees against the dash, and shoulders rubbing against each other in the small two-door. Excellent gas mileage, though, according to the safe house caretaker.

They'd located one of the men on the list. A guy named Taavi Macar. He ran a small restaurant in the Bakirkoy section of the city. It was a twenty-minute drive from the house. By the time they arrived, the back of Noble's shirt was drenched. His nose was lined with smog. He wasn't sure he'd ever get rid of the smell.

They parked around the back of the building that housed not only the restaurant, but a package store, pet supply store, and a doctor's office. Interesting combination, Noble thought. In some ways he felt like they were driving around an ethnic neighborhood in a large U.S. city. But the looks they received from many of the people they passed reminded him that he and Bear were the outsiders here.

Bear adjusted his holstered weapon under his tan button up

shirt. "What do you suppose happens if you get caught with a weapon here?"

Noble shrugged. "Hadn't crossed my mind. Don't plan on getting caught."

"So you'll just shoot your way out if you do?"

"Maybe."

"What's your other option?"

"Not sure."

"Can't come up with anything?"

Noble stopped and turned to face his partner. "I'm not going to bother trying. It's an exercise in futility at this point. The situation hasn't occurred, and probably won't. I can waste good brain cells on some made-up scenario, or I can focus on what's ahead of me."

"So what you're saying is you never plan ahead."

"I didn't say that, Bear. If we talk to this guy, and he gives us some solid intel, something we can really sink our teeth into and form a plan with, then I'll start branching out to different possible scenarios and how I'll deal with them. I'm not trying to play checkers when the game is chess. Got me?"

Bear shook his head. "Not really, man. I'm always thinking ahead. Take that woman over there."

"The one pushing a baby?"

"No, she's pushing a stroller. We don't know what's inside the stroller. Could be a kid, her prized bowling ball, or a bomb."

"That's the most asinine thing I've heard come out of your mouth in five weeks."

Bear glanced over at Jack. "What was the most before then?"

"I can't remember. But I'm pretty sure it was something even stupider than what you just said."

"You know, I was just starting to actually like you."

Jack grinned. It had been a while since he had someone

around he could rip on. It seemed Bear just might have the ability to dish it back.

"Let's get serious now," Bear said. "We gotta deal with this guy."

They exited the narrow alley running between the two old buildings. A fine powder coated the ground. Noble thought it was sand at first, but then realized it was remnants of concrete that had fallen from the buildings' facade and had been worn down to dust over the years.

They walked past the restaurant's entrance. Bear stayed to the curb. He tossed his finger in the opposite direction and suggested they go eat at a different place. Noble stopped next to the front door, where the menu was posted. He covered his brow in an effort to shield his eyes. To the casual observer, Jack was a tourist, trying to decide if he wanted to part with his money at the establishment. He took five seconds to scan inside and take note of the restaurant's patrons.

An older couple seated near the entry were of no concern. Across the room were two men seated across from each other at a table. Their girth prohibited them from squeezing into one of the booths. They were mid- to late-forties, if Jack had to guess. They looked rough, like they had been through some dark days. They might pose a problem, especially if Taavi was concerned for his safety following O'Neil's abduction. He could have hired the guys, believing them to be well-qualified thugs.

The only other patrons were a man, woman, and three kids who appeared to be on the dessert phase of their meal. They were seated at a corner booth, out of the way.

Bear leaned back against the window and pulled out a pack of cigarettes.

"Didn't know you smoked," Noble said.

"I don't," Bear said. "But I'll be damned if everyone else in this city does. Might fit in better."

"Suit yourself." Noble waved away the cloud of smoke after Bear lit the cigarette. "Actually, that's an improvement over the smog."

"You think our guy's in there?" Bear said.

"I think so. Maybe in the kitchen. It's not a big place. I figure the owner handles some of the cooking."

"What about the guest list?"

"Only one table we should be concerned about. I'm thinking you should go in there heavy on them. See how they react."

"How many?" Bear tried to grab a casual glance. The reflection made it difficult to see inside.

"Two. Probably weigh as much as you, but they're less than six foot tall."

"Easy peasy." Bear flicked the lit smoke into the road and walked past Jack. Bells dinged as he whipped the door open. The two large men at the table turned their attention to him. This wasn't the most touristy part of the city. A six-foot-six mountain of an American man was going to draw some attention.

But when one of the guys scooted his chair back and put only one hand on the table while keeping the other concealed, Jack felt the hairs on the back of his neck stand. It wasn't a feeling he had often. It hadn't happened the other day in D.C. There hadn't been time for it. The job had gone from finished to sideways in two seconds flat, putting Noble in react mode.

The guy at the table didn't notice as Noble entered the restaurant behind Bear. The big man commanded all his attention. The guy grabbed his napkin, wiped his mouth. Bear tugged at his shirt, bringing the bottom over the handle of his pistol, which was holstered in the four o'clock position, out of sight from the guys at the table.

The man planted his heavy hand on the table and forced himself up. Noble tensed and reached for his H&K. This was not an ideal time or place to draw or use it. Too many witnesses. Not enough friends. They'd never make it back to the safe house, not in that piece of crap tin can Schofield had sent them off in.

The guy at the table brought his other hand into view and planted the cane he held on the floor. He extended his other hand out as a smile formed on his broad face.

"Welcome, friends. Welcome."

Bear adjusted his shirt again to conceal his pistol. He reached for the other guy's hand and went into car salesman mode. "We heard you guys have the best lamb in town. I gotta level with you. I'm not even sure where the hell we are now, but we're flying out tomorrow and I gotta try it before going back to the hotel."

Noble let go of the H&K. He studied the restaurant steward as he walked up and reached for his hand. The guy had a receding hairline, thin wisps of gray at the peak. His forehead and sides of his eyes were weathered and lined.

Noble offered a fake name to the guy. "Richard Clarkson."

"Taavi Macar." The guy's smile diminished as he studied Jack's face. He couldn't have recognized him. But maybe he understood who Noble was and why he was there. "Should we go back to my office to talk?"

Noble gestured to the other guy at the table. "He stays."

The man pushed back in his chair, grating against the tile floor. Taavi waved him back.

"It's okay. They are friends of a friend." He narrowed his eyes. "Right?"

"That's right," Jack said. "Friends of a friend, and we're very concerned about her."

Taavi planted his cane in the ground and spun. "Then follow me and I'll tell you what I know."

# CHAPTER TWENTY-THREE

Noble and Bear followed Taavi through a dirty swinging door into the kitchen. Jack glanced back at the other man, who had remained seated at the table. How did he fit in here? Noble gave the kitchen a once over, locating the rear exit and its proximity to the office door. He spotted an empty knife rack mounted to a cooler next to the flattop. The knives were scattered across three cutting boards. The cook showed little interest in the Americans, instead watching a broadcast on a small black and white television. Soccer, perhaps?

Taavi stopped in front of the office door and reached into his pocket. He produced a set of keys, unlocked the door, and opened it for his guests. Noble entered the cramped office first. Papers taped to the upper cabinets rustled as he walked past. He found a spot in the rear corner and leaned back against the dull yellow wall in a way that left his H&K accessible.

Bear glanced over his shoulder toward the dining room. The big man paused for a moment. Had he seen something? The cook coming around the line? Maybe the other guy at the table had pushed through the door? Bear wiped his mouth with the back of his hand and stepped into the office. The two men occupied half the available space.

Taavi squeezed past Bear and took a seat at his chair. He stared up at the two Americans without a trace of fear on his face. A loud computer fan drowned out the sound of their breathing. The three of them remained quiet, each side waiting for the other to begin.

"So what can you tell us?" Noble said.

"First, I need to see—"

"This?" Noble lifted his shirt and showed his sidearm. "Yeah, we're armed."

Taavi shook his head while tapping his chest. "No, not your weapons. Show me you are not wired."

The guy didn't want anyone outside the office to hear what he had to say. What did he have to share? Noble and Bear obliged and confirmed they were not recording the meeting. Taavi appeared satisfied.

He worked a pen around his knuckles. "She knew something was going down."

"How do you figure?" Bear said.

"I last saw her, let me think." Taavi looked up at the ceiling. "Seventeen days ago. She brought me a package."

"Where is it?" Noble said.

Taavi held up his hand and waved Noble off. "It is gone. She instructed me where to drop it, and so I did."

"Who picked it up?"

"I do not know because it is not my business to know. She gave me an order and I followed it."

"And this was the last time you saw her, right?"

Taavi nodded, said nothing.

"You mentioned she knew something was going down. How so? Did she say that, or was it a gut feeling?"

"Gut feeling. First, she requested to meet me in a small café for breakfast in Levent."

Noble recognized the neighborhood name as one of the main business districts in the city.

"What's wrong with that?" Bear said.

"She wanted the protection being in public could provide to both me and her."

"She figured no one would make a move in such a populated area," Noble said.

"Exactly." Taavi twisted in his chair and pulled open a drawer. There were scraps of paper and pens strewn about. He rifled through the contents. "There it is."

Noble watched as the guy unfolded a worn map. Taavi traced his finger along a series of streets and tapped his finger on a final location.

"We were there."

Bear and Noble leaned over the guy to study the map. The man smelled like fry grease.

"Anything significant about that location?" Noble asked. "Close to public transportation? Easy to get to the airport?"

Taavi looked up at him. "You think she might have fled after I spoke with her?"

"She might have planned on it. Obviously something kept her around for a little bit longer." Noble straightened up, arched his back. "When and where was the drop?"

"Later that day." Taavi shook his head. "I can't tell you how nervous it made me, holding onto that package."

"And you never snuck a peek at it?" Bear said. "I mean, everyone likes to sneak a peek."

"Never." Taavi's eyes narrowed as he stared the big man down. "I have honor."

Bear leaned away from the guy. "Fair enough. Where was the drop?"

"Ataturk Park."

"Ataturk," Noble repeated. "That's near the airport?"

"Yes, to the northeast. But I doubt you will find anything there. I left the package in the designated drop location—"

"Which is where?" Bear placed his hand on Taavi's shoulder and leaned over the map. "Show me on here which section of the park."

Taavi picked up a pencil and marked as close to the spot as he could. "There's a row of benches there. This one is at the top on the right side of the walkway. Sit on the right end and feel underneath it and you'll find that the bottom curves toward the back. It's a false bottom."

"You think that spot is monitored?" Noble said.

Taavi looked over his shoulder and shrugged. "It is not a place where I spend much time. I'd gone there for her twice before in the past three months."

"Had she ever sent you elsewhere?"

"I think she had other associates for different drop locations. She felt it best to limit our involvement should something...happen."

"As it did." Bear walked to the door and leaned against it. "Anything else you can tell us about her behavior that day?"

"She kept checking our surroundings, almost non-stop. Ever been around someone high on cocaine?" Taavi held his hands in the air, wiggling his fingers at high speed. "Well, that's how she was acting."

"That wasn't her typical mannerism?" Noble said.

"Not at all. She was, how you Americans say, cool as a cucumber. One cool customer. Ice running through her veins. All those things wrapped up in one. But not that day. If I had to guess, she knew someone was watching us. I started to fear she felt I had betrayed her. And also, when she removed her sunglasses at the end of our meeting, her eyes were red."

"Like she was high?" Bear said.

"Like she had been crying," Taavi said.

Bear glanced at Noble. They had a picture of the woman that ran contrary to the way Taavi described her. Something had spooked her, but why hadn't she gone to her bosses with it?

"She felt like someone was watching you," Bear said. "Have you noticed anyone following you since that day?"

He shook his head. "No, but I'm not confident they won't show up. That is why I have Uri out there. He's former Israeli Special Forces. Best in the business."

Noble felt a pang in his stomach at having underestimated the other man. "Why didn't he do anything when we came in?"

"It was easy to peg you guys as with the Agency. Believe me, if he had any concern, we wouldn't be back here."

"She had other contacts," Bear said. "Can you tell us about a guy named—"

Taavi waved both hands in front of his chest. "No names, please. I do not need to know any more than I do. You give me other names, it opens me up to scrutiny from people I do not want to be scrutinized by." He tapped a button on his desk three times. "I think this meeting is over."

A few seconds later the door opened and Uri stood there. Noble had misjudged the man more than he realized. The guy wasn't heavy. Not in the least bit. He was thick in the same way as Bear, heavily muscled. He had a quiet confidence. He stood in a way that let you know he was ready for anything you could throw at him.

The guy beckoned Noble and Bear with two fingers. "It's time to go."

Bear gave Noble a slight nod and they followed Uri out.

They stood outside the restaurant for a few minutes. Street lights brightened the sidewalk. The air had chilled since they had gone inside. Noble stared up into the light-washed sky and couldn't make out a single star. The air was thick with flavor and he wished they had grabbed a bite to eat while in the restaurant.

"Back to the house?" Bear said.

"I think we should drive by the place they met, and then head over to that park."

Bear glanced over his shoulder. Jack followed his gaze to the two men inside watching them. They had unsettled Taavi and Uri.

"You know we're gonna be followed," Bear said. "Think that dude's as badass as Taavi says he is?"

"If he's Israeli Mossad, then I have no doubt. My dad introduced me to a guy who'd spent twenty years in the Kidon unit, the Mossad's counter-terrorist unit. He moved to the States and did private security. Used to come out every week or two, taught me Krav Maga."

"What's that?" Bear said.

Jack studied their surroundings. There were two separate groups of young men who looked like they didn't appreciate the Americans hanging out in their neighborhood.

"I got a feeling if we don't get out of here soon," Noble said, "you're gonna witness it firsthand."

# CHAPTER TWENTY-FOUR

Alexa Steele set the phone in the cradle and took one last look at the notes she had scribbled on the pad during the call. She had to commit the information to memory. No one else could ever see it. She tore the sheet in half, then fed it through her shredder. After the device finished, she pulled the stainless-steel container from the machine and lit and dropped a match in it. A handheld fan sucked up the smoke. The smell of a mini bonfire lingered for a few moments afterward.

"Are you going to give me an update, or should I start taking guesses?" Randall McKenzie said.

She offered a slight smile to her boss. The man had taken her under his wing the moment she had submitted her application. He coached her through the interview process. He offered her inside tips on dealing with the rigorous training. And he talked her out of the more dangerous path of field work and convinced her to start as an analyst. This was advice she had heard from several of the men who influenced her. McKenzie had convinced her with her intelligence, it wouldn't take long for Steele to advance.

And it hadn't.

Others questioned how she had risen so quickly. And some didn't bother questioning. They assumed Steele had taken advantage of the man who was closer in age to her father than her. In fact, McKenzie had been one of her father's best friends, and he was close to her step-father as well.

She let the whispers wash off her. At the end of the day, Steele was on the fast track to running the show, while the gossipers would do their thirty and go on to collect their pension. She went to bed each night knowing she had the respect of men like McKenzie and other decision makers throughout the Agency and the Pentagon.

Steele watched the final embers in the container fade to black. Thin wisps of smoke rose and were sucked into the fan.

"Alexa?" McKenzie tapped on her laminate desktop. "Are you going to fill me in?"

She refocused her attention. "Sorry. Yes, I am. They arrived without any problems. Survived the shakedown on the way to the safe house. No issues there. They took the list of O'Neil's contacts and distilled it down to who we wanted them to start with. They were verified going in and taking a meeting with Taavi Macar."

"And who is that?"

Steele shook her head. "You don't need to concern yourself much with him. He's good at moving money and selling stolen art, believe it or not. His bodyguard is Uri Cohen, a veteran of the Mossad."

"An individual linked with O'Neil who has a bodyguard like that might be someone we need to keep a closer eye on. Maybe he's in on this?"

Steele pulled open a drawer and retrieved a folder. Arguing with McKenzie was pointless. He wanted the facts laid out. She set the folder in front of McKenzie. "You can read all about him here."

McKenzie placed his hand flat on the file and slid it back across the desk. "I trust you. But tell me, what's special about this guy?"

"As far as we know, he's the last one to have contact with O'Neil. Perhaps she told him something relevant that will help us determine who took her."

"I thought we had that narrowed down."

"Narrowed, yes. But in the sense that you can narrow down where you are going to eat a month from now. There's plenty of choices and none makes a compelling enough argument to say, 'That's the one.'"

McKenzie smiled. "Is your guy gonna stick with Noble and Logan the rest of the night?"

"That's the plan. It's hard to tell with these two. They're still wildcards."

"Losing faith in your handpicked men?"

"It's not that at all." Steele leaned back in her chair. She laced her hands behind her head and looked up at a water stain on the ceiling. "I'm concerned they didn't get the proper training. My uncle had it out for them the moment they arrived. He did everything in his power to get them to wash out."

McKenzie chewed on his cheek for a moment. He tapped the desktop with the tip of his index finger. "They survived that snafu in the city."

Steele let her chair bring her forward. "Don't get me started on that. I still think you need to come down on him—"

"Your uncle has a job to do. Not only that, he has accumulated the time and bonus points to run that place the way he sees fit."

Steele felt her cheeks start to burn. She let her face go slack.

McKenzie continued. "Against all good advice, including my

own, you chose two never-done-nothing recruits with attitude problems straight off of Parris Island and placed them in this program. Up until now, we've always brought in experienced Spec Ops from all branches. They have the time in, and are battle proven."

Steele thought back to the week she spent observing at Parris Island. None of the recruits had any idea why she was there, if they even noticed her at all. Judging by Noble and Logan's response to her, she hadn't made enough of an impression to register in their memories. But they had left a lasting mark on her. She'd never seen two new recruits with so much potential for their program.

"Now place yourself in Cribbs's shoes," McKenzie said. "Your uncle gets these two young guys, and he doesn't know if they can even wipe their asses correctly. He had no choice but to come down hard on them."

"He comes down hard on everyone. But with these guys, he wanted them to quit."

McKenzie chuckled. He knew the man well enough to realize there wasn't a soul who Cribbs didn't get under their skin. "That may be, but he had to make sure these two could stand up to his idea of tough. I don't think I need to remind you what we are doing here would cause a hell of a stink if certain people found out. Hell, could you imagine the outcry if this program went public? We can't just throw a couple of guys out there without knowing they have a chance of withstanding some pretty brutal stuff."

"Everyone gives in." Steele pointed at him. "You told me that when you convinced me to come work for you inside. We've seen it with plenty of our own people. It's all a matter of how much they divulge."

"A man can only take so much, Alexa. A woman too, I suppose."

She thought of O'Neil and what the woman might be enduring at this moment. The toughest could go months before revealing any information. Their interrogators knew that. Many cracked far before then, doling out just enough to keep themselves alive. Every day they provided one more piece of the puzzle. That was a lot of pain and trauma to endure when the captive had no idea whether help was coming. They were taught to believe they'd never be rescued.

But everyone held out hope.

O'Neil had planned to leave the field soon. With a young child at home, it was growing more difficult to do her job. It probably factored into how she was handling her current situation.

"We have to get to her now," Steele said.

"I agree," McKenzie said.

"So that means we need to throw as much support to those two guys as we can."

"Maybe we should meet with—"

"Don't say it."

"—your uncle." McKenzie smiled. "Or we can give it a couple days and see if his training paid off."

"I think that's the more sound decision." She had no desire to see Cribbs at the moment. Anything to push it off for a day or two was fine by her.

The red light on her phone flashed. Steele slid the phone so McKenzie wouldn't notice her ignoring her uncle's call.

# CHAPTER TWENTY-FIVE

Noble spotted the tail a half-mile into their trek across the city. The other driver seemed to make it obvious they were following. Bear turned at random, always returning to the same main road. The vehicle behind did the same.

"Someone from the safe house?" Bear said.

"Could be," Noble said. "Or it could be Taavi's guy, Uri, seeing what our next move is. Not sure I want to run into him at our next stop. But I doubt it's him."

"Do they really think he'll find out following us so close?"

Cribbs held driving classes the second to last week in school. They traveled to an abandoned raceway and had at it in a couple of Ford Crown Victorias equipped with police intercepter engines. The training lasted three days. Probably the most fun three days of the entire ordeal, even with Cribbs yelling at them most of the time. But it was there they discovered the three of them shared a similar passion.

Speed.

Too bad the little car they were in now had none.

"I think I can shake this guy," Bear said.

Noble studied the map for a moment. "Wait until we pass the place where O'Neil and Taavi met before her abduction."

"That could be giving a lot away."

Noble nodded. It was worth the risk to see how the tail reacted. He thought about the setup in D.C., and wondered if something similar were happening here. What if it all were an elaborate hoax, and it was O'Neil following them? It sounded crazy in his head, so he didn't bother testing the theory out on Bear. At least not until he had an idea how the tail would proceed.

Bear kept the throttle steady for the next ten minutes, stopping only when traffic signals dictated he do so. The roads were uncrowded. Didn't make a difference. The last thing they needed was to welcome a local cop into their lives. If everything had gone down with O'Neil the way they had been told, they knew some of the local police would not be sympathetic to their cause.

"That's the place. Same place we saw earlier with Serkan." Jack pointed at the glass-lined bottom floor of a ten-story building. An unlit open sign hung next to the front door. The lights were off inside and the only illumination came from the street lamps. "Pull over up here."

Bear pulled to the curb and left the car in gear and his foot on the brake. The tail slowed to a stop as well. Its turn signals blinked in unison for a few seconds before the other vehicle lurched forward. Tires squealed as they attempted to grip the asphalt. As the maroon coupe raced past, its driver held up a bag or briefcase, covering his face. A thick layer of dirt and grime made it impossible to read the license plate.

"Don't suppose we'll figure out who that was anytime soon." Bear balanced the clutch and gas pedal. The tiny engine revved in response.

"Let's go," Noble said. "We can come back later to scout it out."

Bear reversed to the previous intersection, then drove off to the left. Both men stared into the mirrors and scrutinized each passing car in search of the maroon coupe. None fit the bill.

"Think it's a good idea to head to the park?" Bear said.

"You scared of the dark now?" Noble said.

"What if that other car is there?"

"Then we'll get out and ask them what they're doing following us around town."

"Think ahead, man. That the best move?"

"Probably not, but it's the most direct. Sometimes that's the right play. Screw all this setting up of the pawns. My queen's got a direct line to the king, and she's taking that arrogant bastard down."

"Let the record state that I disagree."

"Over what?" Noble turned to him. "A hypothetical situation? Because that's all we got at this point. Yes, someone was following us. When met with a potential confrontation, they drove off, hiding their face. You know what that tells me? They were only there to fact check. Nothing more. Now, if we get to the park and they are there, we can resume this conversation."

"I think my first instinct was right," Bear said.

"About what?"

"You."

"And what was that instinct saying?"

"That you're a damn mess, Noble. And I'd be better off staying away from you."

Jack patted his heart. "You cut me man. Deep."

"Shut up." Bear sped up to beat a red light. He was a second late, but went anyway. He watched the rearview for a half-block in search of police lights. "How much further?"

"Two miles. Let's circle around a couple of times before we get there. Maybe check out the airport perimeter, too. Place is so busy, it'd be easy to hide in plain sight there."

Bear followed the signs for the departure terminal and drove through. The crowds were less dense than they had been when the two men had arrived. Maybe a few dozen taxis hung around waiting for fares. They exited at the opposite end and drove the large loop south to west to north. The air billowing in through the open windows thickened with salt. They were near the coast. When it was all said and done, Noble hoped he would have an opportunity to visit it.

They hit the north end of the airport loop and veered west. Bear slowed the vehicle as they neared the park. Large shade trees surrounded it, while walkways intersected and led to multiple entrances and exits. It appeared well lit within.

"Drive around a couple times." Noble studied the park from the car. He could only see so far through the trees. He wanted to know every inch of the outer perimeter before they ever set foot there so he could determine the best path to their destination.

Bear bypassed the small parking lot and found a spot on the street a half-block away. They waited there for a minute before exiting. People entered and exited what appeared to be a nightclub close by. The women were dressed up and most men had on dress slacks and button up shirts. Nice place, probably. The kind that wouldn't welcome Noble and Bear.

"What're you thinking?" Bear said. "Get in, get out, get going?"

"More circumventing. Let's get on the other side of the trees and see what it's like. I'm guessing some people from there,"—he gestured toward the night club—"are bound to wind up at the park. Plus kids from the college over there. If so, we'll have to be a bit more subtle."

"While you're being subtle, I'll check for security."

"Good idea. We need to be aware of any cameras."

Technological advances had made spycraft a different game from when Cribbs had been out in the field. He'd seen it grow and change, and taught the guys as much as he could, but they knew it would continue to evolve. The best they could do in any situation was be cognizant and assume they were being watched at all times. "Live paranoid", as Cribbs had put it. Bear said that came naturally to him. He lived at a higher level of anxiety than most, and it served him well to be so in tune with his surroundings, whether in the woods, a biker bar off a deserted stretch of highway in the middle of the desert, or walking around the big city.

The park lights cast cones of orange along the pathways. The grounds were manicured with multiple flowerbeds that fragranced the air. It had continued to cool down to the point where a light jacket would be comfortable, but not necessary.

The men split up. Bear moved from light post to light post. He slowed or stopped at each and investigated them while Noble located the landmarks provided by Taavi and isolated the bench where the drop had occurred. It was unoccupied. A couple sat on the one across from it, their lips intertwined. Not good. He couldn't have anyone see him check underneath the bench.

It didn't look like the lovers were going to leave anytime soon. They needed motivation. Noble knew he could provide it. There were five benches on either side of the walkway. He took the next in line and coughed loudly as he sat down. The man and woman stopped kissing for a moment, and glanced over at him. The guy's entire face was a frown.

"Sorry," Noble said. "Carry on." But before they could, he spoke again. "Either of you have a cigarette?"

"No," the man said. "But there is a store across the street where you can buy them."

"Gotcha." Noble crossed his legs and leaned over the arm rail. "Problem is, I got mugged earlier today. Guy got away with all my stuff, including my passport and cash. Can you spare a little so I can get a bite to eat?"

"What do we look like?" the guy said. "Why don't you go panhandle where the rest of the bums do and leave us alone?"

"Guess that's a no, then."

"Oh for Christ's sake," the woman said, pushing her man away. "I have a cigarette right here. Will you go to the other side of the park if I give it to you?"

Noble stood up. He hadn't expected it to get this far, figuring they'd leave once he started begging them. The woman retrieved a pack of smokes from her pocketbook and pulled one out for him.

"Got a lighter?"

"Want me to smoke it for you, too?" she said.

In fact, he did. He'd avoided smoking most of his life, only lighting up a couple times as a teenager. He sucked on the stick and nearly choked as the smoke grabbed his throat and stifled his lungs. He exploded into a coughing fit.

"What is wrong with you, man?" The guy lurched up and shoved Noble in the chest.

Jack took a few steps back, held up his hands, apologized. "I'm not sure what happened."

The man shoved him again.

Bear lingered in the background. Noble shot him a quick look intended to tell the big man to stand down. He had this.

"All right, guy," Noble said. "I get your point. Keep your hands to yourself."

"Or what?" The guy shoved him a third time.

Noble looked over at the woman, winked. "Or else your girl there might decide I'm the man she needs to go home with."

The guy snarled, took a swing. It was horrible. He telegraphed it the whole way, balling his fist by his side and whipping his arm out too high and too far.

Noble didn't bother to deflect it. He leaned back and watched the glint of the man's ring as it flew three inches past his face. A simple nudge was all it took to topple the off-balance man.

The woman hopped off the bench and knelt by her boyfriend's side. When the guy made to come at Jack again, she pulled him back. At least she was smart enough to realize what kind of man Noble was. The boyfriend hadn't quite figured that out.

"I see you again," the guy yelled out, "you're a dead man."

"No, I'm not." Noble watched them leave, then took a seat on the target bench.

Bear emerged from the shadows and walked over. "This is you being subtle?"

"I'm a work in progress," Noble said.

"What if you were caught on camera doing that?"

"Was I?"

"The park's clean."

"Then I guess it doesn't matter." He shook his head at the big man. "You and your damn what ifs."

Bear looked over his shoulder at a couple walking along the outer rim. "It's never gonna be quiet here. Just check it out."

Noble leaned forward and reached his hand underneath the bench. He knocked on the panel. It sounded hollow. Taavi had told them the truth. A few moments later he had it open and reached his hand inside. He felt around until his fingers brushed against something flexible far in the back. It took a few seconds, but he managed to trap the edge of it between his middle and ring fingers and pulled it close enough to get a solid grip on it. He pulled out a plain brown envelope and tucked it under his shirt.

He followed Bear's gaze around the park, noting several faces in the shadows.

"We better get out of here."

# CHAPTER TWENTY-SIX

"I still can't believe you took the package." Bear sat with his arm teetering on the windowsill. Cool air rushed into the cabin. They were in the middle of the city, and enjoying all the smells associated with that. It was a cross between the pound and the dump.

Noble held the envelope with both hands. He hadn't decided whether to open it. Bear had insisted they put it back under the bench. They had no idea who might be watching the drop. Any number of spy agencies or terrorists could have been onto O'Neil's operation. Why else was it still there?

He turned the envelope over and worked the corner of the flap. "What's in here might lead us to O'Neil."

"What's in there—," Bear swatted at the enveloped, "—might get us killed for no good reason." The big man stared up at the rearview for a second too long.

"Watch the light." Noble braced his left hand against the dash.

The little car drifted into the next lane as the tires failed to grip the asphalt.

"See, it's already causing adverse effects." Bear slapped and gripped the wheel. Noble was surprised it hadn't broken.

"Look, this is part of our job now—"

"We're supposed to be a team, Jack. You and me, a team. We gotta decide these things together. If one of us strongly voices a contrary opinion, then the other should take a step back and consider what's being argued. We still might've walked out of that park with the package. But you didn't bother to listen to me."

Noble leaned back in his seat and stared out his window.

"I get what we signed up for here," Bear said. "We're not guaranteed a tomorrow ever again. But hell if I'm going to die because of your stupidity."

"You want out, I know right where the airport is."

The light flashed green. Bear pressed the accelerator to the floor. An old lady with a walker could've taken off faster than the tiny vehicle.

"Let's go pay Taavi another visit," Noble said.

"I think it's better to get back to the safe house, figure out if we need to call this in to Steele."

Jack wondered if Steele knew about the drop, or much about any of O'Neil's network in the city. "If she knew of its existence, there's no way it would be sitting there two weeks later. This had to be something O'Neil did on her own."

"Taavi's dates put it that she was abducted two days after," Bear said.

"That's right."

"If you were in his shoes, wouldn't you have—"

"Gone back to check for it?" Jack thought it over.

"Yeah."

"Maybe he feared the drop had something to do with her being taken. Figured the park was being watched. Wouldn't be hard, right? You got the university on one side. The airport on another.

Buildings behind it. Easy enough to slip an agent into any of those places and have them sit on the location. He's got Uri to watch his back, but then again, Uri might've been the one to call it off."

Bear pulled into a neighborhood and stopped at a curb a few blocks from the safe house. "If that's the case, then we were spotted."

"Guess we'll have to deal with it when the time comes."

"How can you be that nonchalant about it?"

"They snap a couple of pictures of us, so what? Who the hell are we? It's not like we're sitting in a bunch of spy databases, our life histories waiting to be read."

Bear continued on to the house. The garage door lifted as they pulled into the driveway. Neither man questioned how. Could've been something wired into the car. Or maybe Schofield was watching for them. Bear eased the car to a stop and cut the engine. It rattled and ticked for several seconds. The room smelled like exhaust and oil. Noble's foot slipped on the smooth floor as he stepped out.

At the top of the steps they heard chatter from within. Bear rapped on the door and stepped back. Schofield cracked it open and poked his Beretta 9mm out.

"Easy, chief," Bear said. "Just us."

The guy smiled and opened the door wider. "Just in time for dinner."

"You guys eat late," Noble said.

"No, we eat a lot." He headed toward the table. "Come join us."

Noble adjusted his pants and shirt to hide the outline of the envelope. They had decided before approaching the house it was best to keep the package's existence a secret. After all, Schofield had instructed them not to tell him anything about their investigation. They had suspicions he knew more than he let on, and that he was the one who compiled their list of O'Neil's local associates. How close was he to this? They figured his interaction with them after returning would speak volumes. The more questions he asked, the more involved he was.

Bear went straight to the table and grabbed two pita shells. He loaded them with sour cream, lamb, fresh blood-red tomatoes, and a pile of onions. He devoured half of one in a single bite before Noble had pulled a seat out.

"See food, eat food," Schofield said with a laugh.

Bear swallowed hard, wiped a fine layer of sour cream off his lips and surrounding beard. "See moron, beat moron."

Schofield leaned back in his chair, the same smile spread across his broad face. "Look at you. Think you're such a badass because you made it home after your first night out in the field? Sitting there, disrespecting me and my fifteen years of doing this."

How'd he know it was their first night? Who was feeding him info about them?

Bear took another large bite and nodded. "Pretty much." He made no attempt to hide his mouthful of food.

Schofield kept smiling. "I'm the only friend you got out here. You understand that? Things can go from bad to worse in a few seconds in this part of the world. Something goes wrong, I'm the one who has to arrange to bail you sorry schmucks out. You really think it's wise to crap on me like that?"

Noble gave Bear a look telling him to back off. The last thing they needed was for Schofield to kick them out and turn his back on them. They needed the guy's full support, no matter how much of a jackass he was. After it was all over they could deal with him how they wanted.

Bear chewed his food, swallowed, and sat there for a minute. It was a stare off between him and Schofield, one that the other guy had to win.

For Noble, it was another insight into his new partner. He'd seen this side of the guy come out, but only with him. During all the mind games the instructors and Cribbs played on them, Bear had never reacted in this way. Maybe he understood that Cribbs's intention was to push his buttons. Why didn't he see it now? It was the kind of behavior that could get them into trouble one day.

Schofield and his two underlings grabbed their plates and left the table. Apparently he'd had enough. He told Noble to leave the hallway light on and refrain from using any communications devices until morning. A bit of an odd request, but there had to be a reason for it. Could the reason be that Schofield wouldn't be able to monitor their calls while he was sleeping?

Later that night Noble tossed aside his sheets and stepped out of bed. Dull light knifed through the slits in the blinds. After a few minutes of lying there, it had lit up the room. Bear snored in his own bunk across from him. From the moment Jack had met the guy, the big man had no issues with getting to sleep.

See pillow, get sleep.

Or something like that.

For Noble, it had never been that easy. Some nights he replayed events from the day or previous week over and over, trying to figure out what he could have done differently. And then there were the dark nights. When he thought of his sister Molly. Watching her body hit the ground. Her soul whisked away in the blackness of night. And he'd been powerless to do anything. He imagined a hundred ways it could have played out if only he could have taken another step. She might be alive. He might be dead, but that was no big deal. While not his first choice, he prepared himself for the eventuality of his own demise, as well as that of his father, mother, and brother.

Tonight his thoughts centered on the envelope and its contents. What had O'Neil wanted dropped by Taavi that night? And for who? Why hadn't the intended recipient shown up? In the course of questioning himself, Noble realized perhaps the other party had shown. The package he and Bear had found was a response to O'Neil from them. Was it wise to use the same drop location? Perhaps not. But what if they had? O'Neil had been abducted shortly after Taavi made the initial delivery. She received the message a response had been left, but never got the opportunity to collect it. But why wouldn't the other party have reclaimed it?

Noble came up with two possible reasons. One, they feared the park was being watched. In that case, returning could have detrimental consequences. And two, they didn't know O'Neil had been taken. The first option was cut and dry. But the second led Jack down another rabbit hole. How could they not know? Perhaps they were no longer around, and he had a pretty good idea why.

He tucked the envelope under his mattress and left the room. The old house felt alive as he crept down the stairs. It breathed in and out with the hum of the fan. It moaned with every step he took. What was its history? Who had lived here before? How long had the CIA had control of it? Who knew it was now a safe house for spies?

Noble stepped through the back door into the chilly air. The rear porch was twenty feet wide and ten feet deep. The trees shielded it from the street lights that penetrated his bedroom and cast a large shadow across the space.

A bright orange glow grabbed Noble's attention. His heart skipped a beat. How had he missed the other man?

"Can't sleep?" Schofield said.

Jack sucked in a deep breath and nodded. "Most nights. You?"

"Most nights, lately." He took a drag on his cigarette, got up, and walked over. A trail of smoke rose into the light wash behind him. "What's on your mind?"

Noble placed both hands on the rail and stared into the backyard. "Just adjusting, I suppose."

Schofield nodded. "This way of life can take some time to get used to. Lord knows, it took me a couple of years."

"Always been in the field?"

"Only place I wanted to be."

"You like running this house."

Schofield turned and leaned his hip against the railing, crossed his arms over his chest. "What do you think?"

"I'm guessing no."

He nodded, said nothing.

"Then why are you here?"

The guy watched Noble for several seconds as though he was determining whether to reveal any more of himself. "Let's just say, being here allowed me to keep watch over some special assets."

"Allowed?" Noble turned his head toward the guy. "The special assets aren't around anymore?"

Schofield smiled slightly. He'd slipped up. "Not at the moment."

"How long had you been seeing O'Neil?" It was a stab in the dark, but Noble figured it was best to be direct.

"It was an on and off thing. Mostly off lately."

"Why's that?"

"Son, one thing you're gonna find is that being a field operator doesn't go all that well with dating."

Noble recalled the little he knew about O'Neil's life, about her wanting to spend more time at home with her kid, but decided not to push him further about their relationship. What Schofield had told him gave him plenty to think about. He decided to ask one more question.

"Did she say anything to you before she was abducted that might help us find her?"

"She hadn't spoken to me in a month. Maybe more." He flicked his cigarette into the darkness and walked to the door. Before heading inside, he turned back to Noble. "This is the last time we'll speak of her. And when you give your update to Langley, don't tell them about her and me. They'll come down hard on her when she's back safe in the States if they knew she was seeing me."

Noble remained outside for another fifteen minutes, rehashing the conversation. Not much had been said, but what slipped past Schofield's lips had been powerful. He now climbed to the top of Noble's suspect list, though he wasn't quite sure what the guy might've done. It sounded as though there was some resentment, but possibly also vengeance behind the guy's words. Noble decided he would talk it over with Bear for a second opinion after they were away from the house.

He went back inside, grabbed a glass of water and headed upstairs. The quiet house felt different as he climbed each step. All eyes were upon him. Was someone waiting up there? Had Schofield realized he'd said too much and now wanted to correct his mistake?

Noble tightened his grip around his H&K as he hit the second-floor landing. Slowly he eased past the wall. The hallway stood empty. Shaking his head, he took a deep breath.

Back in the room he pulled the envelope from beneath the mattress and slid his finger underneath the back flap. The adhesive pulled free without tearing. He reached inside and felt a single sheet of paper. Using the light from the window, he stared at a face he'd never seen before. The close cut black hair, dark skin, heavy eyebrows and wide face had the look of a banker. Or a killer. If it weren't for the fact the image was inside a package at a dead drop it might have been impossible to tell. He flipped the picture over. One word was inscribed there.

*AVOID.*

This was the guy who'd lead them to O'Neil.

# CHAPTER TWENTY-SEVEN

Schofield flat out refused to even look at the picture at first, even though the man had promised to lend support in any way he could. He was their only contact in the region. They had nowhere else to turn. Noble understood it had to be tough for the guy, but he wondered what the driving forces were. After all, the man had admitted to an affair with O'Neil, and in the same conversation, had also said they hadn't spoken in at least a month.

It begged the question: Did he want her found?

Noble looked at the man in a different light. But he figured the guy deserved another chance before he went to Steele. In the end, Noble managed to appeal to Schofield's sense of duty to country.

Schofield fed the photo through a fax machine connected to a computer. Noble assumed it was connected to a database maintained back home. Perhaps a few of the geeks at Langley would go to work looking for a match. Maybe the computers did it all these days. There was much he didn't know, and wasn't sure he cared to yet.

"If this comes back on me, man," Schofield said while they

waited for a hit. A cursor on the computer monitor went from blinking to spitting out hundreds of lines of gibberish. Code of some sort.

"You're doing the right thing," Noble said.

"What the hell do you know about the right thing?" Schofield said. "You're a kid. A never-been-nowhere kid. You ain't seen the mayhem out there. Ain't been in the shit. Don't talk to me about the right thing when you gotta make a decision between taking out a nine-year-old walking down the street with explosives strapped to him, and you can look in his eyes and know those bastards convinced him it was his time to die, and that *he* was doing the right thing."

Noble said nothing. The world wasn't black and white, and that fact would be cemented day after day in this new life.

The men passed a few silent minutes staring at the monitor. Schofield seemed pretty intent on finding something in the lines of code. What? Noble figured it was just the language of the computers sending data back and forth. Was there something in there? Or was Schofield too pissed to even look at him right now?

Bear entered the room carrying a carafe and three mugs. He filled each with coffee and positioned himself on Noble's outside shoulder. He'd been there for the argument that led to Schofield looking at the photo and agreeing to assist.

"Anything yet?" Bear asked.

Noble shook his head. "Guess we're waiting on someone, or something, back home to make a match."

Schofield snorted and shook his head.

"We're all ears if you wanna tell us what's going on now," Noble said.

Schofield stared at the monitor without replying.

"What'd you do?" Bear nudged Noble with his shoulder.

Jack shrugged. "Just my nature, I guess."

Schofield leaned in toward the monitor. The lines of code had stopped and the green cursor blinked on an empty line in the middle of the screen. Noble shifted position to get a better look at the last line. The random string of letters and numbers made no sense to him, but the other man seemed pretty intent on deciphering the message there.

"What is it?" Bear said.

Schofield held up a finger. Several long seconds passed with no action on the screen. The house fan droned on in the background. Bear sipped on his coffee. Schofield sniffled a couple of times even though a box of tissues sat on the desk. The shrill tones from the fax machine cut through the calm in the room.

"Looks like we got ourselves a match," Schofield said.

All eyes landed on the fax machine. It appeared to be an advanced piece of kit, not that Noble was an expert on office machines. His family had one in his father's study, though, and it was nothing like this.

The fax spit out three sheets of paper, which Schofield collected. After the machine had finished he carried them over to the square table in the middle of the room and laid them out in sequential order. Bear and Noble joined him. On the first page was a shrunken picture of the same man, but in a different pose.

"This is your guy," Schofield said. "Imman Khoury, member of Hezbollah, wanted in five countries for committing acts of terrorism. Last known location was Aleppo."

Bear and Noble were familiar with the city from the intelligence that had been waiting with their gear when they arrived.

"I thought Hezbollah kept to Lebanon," Bear said.

"They're active in this region," Schofield said. "Influential in the Syrian war for sure."

"What connections does he have here?" Noble said.

"Asking the wrong guy," Schofield said. "I can read what's on here, and that's about it. I've never come across this man or heard of him before."

The rest of the documents told of Khoury's history. Born to a wealthy family. Secondary and post-secondary education in New York. Returned to Lebanon to pursue a law degree. Then he went off the deep end. Got involved with Hezbollah before he finished school. It didn't stop him from completing it, but the track he took afterward had been severely altered. None of the intel indicated he actually practiced law in Lebanon, or any other country. He was a rising star in the organization, and had been accused of planning several small terrorist attacks.

"Avoid," Bear muttered.

"What's that?" Schofield asked.

"The photo we found of this guy, the back had 'AVOID' scrawled on it. But what we're seeing here is this man isn't a front-line soldier. He's sitting in an office somewhere, organizing activities."

"Maybe he had reached out to O'Neil?" Schofield stared at the picture of the guy. "He could have come at her with the front of wanting to turn himself in for immunity from his crimes, something like that. We don't necessarily need to know why, as much as he knew of and about her. That's not a good thing."

Noble said, "The drop indicates someone knew of his plan and was trying to warn her."

"But she never saw it," Bear said.

"But it wasn't Khoury who kidnapped her," Noble said. "Maybe she refused to help him, so he resorted to having her taken?"

"Wish I had an answer for you guys," Schofield said. "She kept everything she was working on away from me."

"Where did she live?" Noble asked.

Schofield shook his head. "Won't find anything there. First

thing they did was lock that place down, go through the contents inside, then purge everything, even her Cosmos."

"It's empty now?"

Schofield nodded. "Don't repeat this, but I went over there last week after I was sure they weren't watching the apartment anymore. There was nothing left. They even found the cutout she had in her closet wall and took her emergency cash."

Noble was left with no choice but to trust the man. Maybe he or Bear would spot something there, but would it be worth the time it would take to learn the location and get access inside? Khoury's dossier combined with the intelligence they'd gone over the previous day pointed to Aleppo being their destination.

"I think we're ready to make our move," Noble said.

Bear nodded while staring at the picture on the table. "Agreed."

"I'd say this combined with the other intel gives you guys a solid place to start," Schofield said.

"I thought you didn't want to get involved with what guys like us were working on," Noble said.

Schofield shrugged. "Most of the time, no. This is personal to me. If I could, I'd go along with you guys."

Noble wasn't sure he would accept that offer, but kept his mouth shut. No point in getting into an argument over hypotheticals.

Schofield tore off a piece of paper from a yellow legal pad and scrawled a name and number on it. He folded it, then handed it to Bear. "That's a contact of mine. Trust them with my life. You make it to Aleppo, you give them a call. They can provide you with everything you need."

Bear tucked the paper in his shirt pocket without opening it. Noble had doubts about reaching out to the person before having them vetted.

Schofield picked up on this. "You can't out them, either."

"Not sure you're making a compelling case," Noble said.

In that moment Schofield's expression changed, softened, and Noble could see the fear in his eyes. Not for himself, or for his contact, but for O'Neil. The guy was only trying to help.

"I know you don't have any reason to do so, but trust me, guys. The contact is legit. They have their ear on the heartbeat of the city. They'll get you where you need to go. The rest'll be up to you."

The meeting ended a few minutes later. Bear and Noble went through their gear and packed the items they deemed most necessary for a two- to three-day stay in a city that didn't want them there.

Serkan arrived at noon to drive them to the border. It was a long, quiet trip during which Noble realized there was no going back now. Whether the job had chosen him, or his actions had led him to it, he was locked.

# PART III

# CHAPTER TWENTY-EIGHT

The clock on the dash read three-forty a.m. The orange-tinged sky ahead wasn't due to an early sunrise. The border was approaching, and twenty miles beyond that lay their destination. Noble had never considered how long it would take to drive from Istanbul, Turkey to Aleppo, Syria. Dots on a map. That's all the cities had ever been. And not ones he'd paid much attention to.

They'd been in the car since noon the day before. It wasn't the most pleasant-smelling interior when they got in, and was downright unbearable now. The only way they managed was keeping the windows cracked.

Bear stretched out across the back seat. He'd been out since their last stop five hours ago. Good for him. Noble found his anxiety increased with every passing mile they drove east. This was happening. This was real. Not that D.C. wasn't. But they were home then. No matter what occurred, they were in a familiar place, with familiar faces all around. Despite the situation, Noble found that helped him to think clearly.

What would happen once inside the Syrian city?

The turn signal's blinking green dash light illuminated Serkan's face. He glanced up into the rearview and pulled onto the off ramp. At the bottom, they merged onto a deserted stretch of single-lane blacktop. Beyond the highway there were no street-lights. Couldn't even see the light wash from the border. The world around them was illuminated solely by the moon.

They had gone over the plan several times. The exit was one of the last before the border crossing. Though the credentials they had would allow them to pass without issue, issues could and often did arise. Any delay meant O'Neil's chances of survival lessened. And it would be better that their faces were not seen and recorded entering the country. So it had been determined they would cross on foot about five miles north of the highway.

Bear stretched his arms overhead and leaned forward, twisting at the waist. He grabbed the edge of Jack's seat and pulled himself upright. "I miss anything?"

"A carload of strippers in burkas," Noble said.

Bear chuckled as he cocked his head left, then right, soliciting loud pops. "Probably better I was asleep then." He leaned closer to the dash, craning to get a better look at the sky out the windshield. "Guessing we're off the highway."

Serkan lifted his index finger off the wheel and aimed it into the vehicle's light wash. "Close to the drop-off point. Another mile or so."

Bear wiped his hand down his face and scratched his beard as he leaned back into his seat. It was real. It was happening. No turning back now. Noble could see the thoughts as they raced through his partner's head.

Serkan slowed as he diverted his attention from the road to the shoulder. The path they would take to the border was unmarked, unpaved, and unpatrolled. His eyes narrowed at a stretch of land ahead. The car slowed to a crawl. Instinctively, Noble's gaze drifted to the side mirror and what was happening behind them. What if someone was behind them, following them? He saw nothing but blackness in the reflection.

With only the parking lights on, the sedan rolled along the uneven ground at low speed. A cone of orange spread out in front of them, illuminating enough of the terrain for Serkan to navigate. Noble gripped the *"oh crap"* handle overhead to keep himself from bouncing against the door.

The vehicle came to a stop. Serkan cut the lights and engine. The three of them remained silent for a few moments. Noble's eyes adjusted to the dim light outside. He scanned the horizon for obstacles. How long until sunrise? He figured they had another hour of total darkness. Enough to get across the border?

"Follow this path roughly a half-mile," Serkan said, interrupting the calm silence. He unfolded a map and shone a small pen light at it. "You'll reach the river, which you'll stick to across the border. It's not well-defined in this area, and you won't necessarily know when you've crossed over. Proceed with caution because you never know where the patrol is. You'll stick close to this road for a short while, and pass this one." His slid his finger a few centimeters, roughly a quarter-mile of distance on the map. "When you reach this second road, take it north. You'll reach the outer edges of what will look like slums to you. Open the glove box, Jack."

Noble pulled the latch and eased the door down. Inside he found a set of keys.

"Just inside the area you will reach a gas station. Parked in the lot there is a red two-door. That's your transportation. Inside the car you'll find maps and the instructions on how to find your way in Aleppo."

"What if the car's gone?" Bear said.

"I received word at our last stop that it is there and ready for your use."

"So someone's been watching?"

"I didn't say that."

Bear took a deep breath and exhaled slowly. "It is what it is, I guess."

Serkan pulled the keys from the ignition and opened his door. "We should get moving."

Noble and Bear met at the trunk and collected their gear. There wasn't much, and most of what was there would be useless when it came time to fulfill the duties of the job. If stopped by the authorities, the jeans and flannels in their bags might buy them a few extra seconds to catch the cops or soldiers apprehending them off guard. Both men retrieved their pistols and tucked them into concealed holsters.

"You have an hour until first light," Serkan said, staring off into the distance. "You should make it before then. You need to make it there before then. Once eyes are opened, you two will stick out in this area."

They strapped on their backpacks, shook Serkan's hand after he gave each a flashlight, then headed off into the darkness. The orange glow from the parking lights faded as Serkan reversed and turned around. It felt strange standing there in the darkness in an unfamiliar land. Noble had never been to Mississippi, but if he'd been dropped off there in the middle of the night, he was sure he could find someplace safe. Here his confidence wavered.

"Let's get moving." Bear didn't wait for Noble to respond. The big man bounded across the landscape with his dimmed flashlight covering the ground in front of him.

Noble sprinted to catch up before matching Bear's pace until they reached the river. The border was close, meaning it was time to tighten up. Lights off. Proceed with extreme caution.

The path veered southeast and then turned sharp to the north. It was at this point they crossed the border into Syria. The experience was anti-climactic. There was no fence to stop them. No patrol of soldiers waiting there with AK-47s at the ready.

Headlights approached from the distance. Both men hunkered down a mere twenty feet from the road that skirted alongside the river for a stretch. There weren't many places for them to hide, so they lay flat in the dirt until the vehicle passed. Afterward, they resumed their trek, moving a bit quicker to get away from the road. A short jaunt through open fields brought them to the first road crossing.

Two light posts stood at either end of the bridge, casting a dull haze over the road, which split off into two branches on the north side. A small square structure with dark windows offered a place to wait and watch. It didn't appear to be a house. There was no vehicle out front, and no garage to park one. A low mechanical hum could be heard and felt through the exterior walls.

"Looks like it's a dam," Bear said. "Look at how wide the river is on the other side."

"Too busy looking for someone watching for us," Noble said, scanning the road in both directions. He stepped away from the building. "Let's not linger here too long."

They dashed across the road and found cover in the trees along the bank of the flooded river. The landscape was strange here. Unnatural. Even in the dark, Noble could tell everything from farm fields to the trees had been planted in rows. Nature was chaotic. This was planned.

The river quickly narrowed to a creek as the trees along the bank thinned and disappeared. Light rose in the sky to the north and east. They traveled a quarter-mile and found the next road. The final stretch on foot.

"Let's stay off the pavement," Bear said. "Those shrubs don't offer much, but it's better than being out in the open."

Noble agreed. They kept the road twenty feet to their right until they reached the first structure, leaving them no choice but to venture into the open. The shanty-town seemed peaceful under the fading night sky. Aside from a few barking dogs, there was no activity. All but a few windows were darkened. Street lights were sparse, and where they existed, offered little illumination beyond a small pool surrounding them.

They walked along the side of the road at a quickened clip. Noble pointed ahead at the gas station. Bear nodded. They hadn't spoken a word since entering the town.

The red coupe was parked in the far corner next to a white truck outfitted with a hoist on the bed. A makeshift tow truck, Noble presumed. When their boots hit the parking lot, the truck's headlights switched on, dull at first, then full-on high-beams.

# CHAPTER TWENTY-NINE

Noble froze in place as the truck's engine roared to life. He brought his hand up to shield his eyes from the blinding light. It already had the effect of overpowering his night vision. He was blind where he stood. His other senses went into overdrive. The smell from the gas pumps filled the air. Sweat on his neck chilled in the early morning air. The sleepy town now came to life in the background. Instinctively his hand went to his pistol. He looked away and blinked the high-beams out of his field of vision.

Bear already had his pistol out and concealed from view by his side. "We're in a bad spot, man. No good place to retreat."

Open road and a wide building lay behind them. They could sprint. The truck could drive faster. The driver could blare the horn, drawing attention to the two white guys in the road.

"Let's keep walking." Noble patted Bear on the back, shook his head and put one foot in front of the other. If they seemed casual enough, whoever sat behind the wheel of the truck might pay no attention to them.

But what if they'd been there all night, waiting for Noble and Bear to arrive to claim the red coupe?

Noble turned his collar up and kept his head down. He watched the truck out of the corner of his eye once they were past the high-beams's intense cone. The vehicle eased out of its spot and rolled across the parking lot.

"Nothing to worry about," he said. "A guy going to work is all."

The truck made a sharp turn in their direction. Its speed remained steady at a slow crawl. Noble resisted the urge to look back. Bear didn't. The brakes squealed and the frame groaned as the truck came to a stop. Noble saw his shadow stretch across the ground.

Bear had already spun around, keeping his pistol behind his back. Noble joined him. The flashlight wasn't as intense as the high-beams, but came in at a distant second.

The door creaked open on rusted hinges. The light dipped toward the ground between them. Skinny legs poking out from khaki cargo shorts slipped into view.

Noble's grip on his pistol tightened. He fought the urge to bring his arm around and level the H&K at the person presenting in front of them. There was enough light in the parking lot to make out his features. Wrinkled forehead. Mostly dark beard cropped close. Receding hairline. He was definitely from the area.

"Help you?" Bear said.

The other man waved his light across the ground. With a heavy accent, he said, "You two lost?"

"Guess that depends on where we are." Bear offered a hint of a smile.

The guy looked toward the shack where people paid for gas and cigarettes and who knew what else. "You shouldn't be here."

"Thirty miles to cover today." Bear glanced down and lifted one leg, showing his hiking boot. "Figured we'd get an early start.

Were told to follow the river. Saw the lights at an intersection and thought maybe we could get a bite to eat here."

Noble stood back and let the scene play out. He hadn't initially figured Bear for much of a talker. The pressure was on and the big man took center stage.

The man stretched a bony finger and aimed it past Bear and Noble while shaking his head. "Don't head that way. Go back south, then west after you're clear of town. Get back to Turkey. There's nothing but trouble here for two guys like you."

"Understood."

He switched off his light, slipped it into the cargo pocket on his shorts, and hopped back into the truck. Orange lights flashed on the roof, circling the area, amid an expanding wave of gas vapor. The truck pulled out of the lot and turned left, north, easing down the road.

Noble turned to watch the taillights fade. "That was too much of a coincidence."

"Odd, to say the least." Bear slapped Noble's shoulder. "Let's get moving."

A few seconds later the big man was on the ground investigating the underside of the red coupe. Noble reached in through the open window and popped the hood and trunk. The former checked out while the latter was empty aside from a spare that would fit on a bicycle and a tire iron that he placed on the backseat. Never know. Might come in handy.

The car filled up fast as the six-two Noble and six-six Bear took their seats. Jack was behind the wheel. Bear had to spread his knees to open the glovebox. He retrieved the keys, a street map, and a small yellow legal pad.

"Got a name and number on there?" Noble asked.

Bear handed him the keys. "Not that I can tell."

Noble pressed the clutch and cut the engine on. "What's it say?"

Bear read over the chicken-scratch while Noble reviewed the map.

"Only two turns to reach the main road that leads into Aleppo," Noble said. "Maybe half an hour of drive time."

"Let's get going." Bear pointed out his window at the first tinges of red in the sky. "Sun's coming up soon."

"You got a contact on there?"

Bear shook his head. "Just another destination. Figure that's the safe house. Guess we'll learn more there. Maybe Schofield's contact is who they want us to use."

It was dark enough outside to make it less obvious two white males were driving the stretch of highway leading into Aleppo, an area known to be less than receptive toward Americans, let alone two CIA operatives. When they reached the outer fringes of the city, the sun crested the horizon. They shared the road with dozens of vehicles. The traffic pattern was insane. Noble's gaze bounced from mirror to mirror, keeping track of every car around them.

Like many old cities that grew outward from a central location, Aleppo's Great Mosque served as the nail that once held the city in place. The densely populated Old Quarter section of town might be the most dangerous of all. Today's journey would not lead them far, though.

Noble hopped off the highway and merged onto a city road that cut through the heart of town. A few miles later they cruised past the large oval they spotted on the satellite images they received in the safe house. It was a stadium amid a collection of sports facilities and fields. An interesting backdrop to the dozens of acres they had to sift through to find O'Neil.

Rows upon rows of houses and buildings, some damaged by

previous artillery strikes from the Syrian War, passed by in a blur. Every block looked the same here. Would they ever manage to know their way around by sight alone? Noble hoped not. He had no desire to remain in the city any longer than required.

"Our road is coming up," Bear said.

"You sure?"

The big man lowered the map to chest level. "Can't read a damn thing on here. Keeping track of each intersection." He pointed ahead. "This one's ours."

Noble turned left in front of a barrage of oncoming vehicles whose headlights stood out against the paling sky and grey-washed buildings.

Bear concentrated on the houses on the right, counting ahead. "Slow down."

Noble eased off the gas and let the car cruise along at fifteen kilometers per hour.

Bear tapped his window with the notepad. "I think that's it. Says here green trim around the doors and windows. That's the only house I've seen like that."

Noble sped up. "Let's make absolute sure. I'm gonna take us around the block."

It was too early for folks to be out and about. Noble knew they were unlikely to draw much attention. And it wasn't like an extra five minutes would cause a problem in the long run. But if they went to the wrong door, who knew what kind of manhunt that would set off.

With the tour of the block complete, Noble eased up to the curb and parked behind a similar vehicle painted blue. "We got a key in there?"

"Series of numbers. A code." Bear squinted at the house. "Yup. A lock box. Key's in there."

"Let's grab our gear and head up."

The less time they spent outside, the better. Doors opening and closing drew attention. No point in running back out to the vehicle.

Noble watched the windows of the safe house, and of those surrounding it. He still hadn't gotten over the feeling the tow truck incident was more than coincidence. Was someone watching them at each step? Another prove-it mission arranged by Cribbs and Steele?

"You coming?" Bear backed into the shadows under the porch overhang.

Noble cast one last glance up, and then over his shoulder at the houses across the street. Everything looked calm, in place. Looks could never be trusted, though.

Bear punched in the code on the lockbox, pulled the cover off, and retrieved the key. It slid into the door lock and turned with no resistance. "Easy, eh?" He grabbed the knob and pushed the door open.

The shrill sound that came next could've woken the dead.

And most definitely the neighbors.

# CHAPTER THIRTY

B ear lifted the security system's cover and stared at the instructions written in a foreign language. Unfortunately, it was one he hadn't learned. A bright red button stood out in the green glow. He jabbed his thumb into it several times. The alarm continued to blare.

At least one neighbor had stepped outside. Noble pushed past Bear and shoved him toward the wall as he slammed the door shut. A puff of morning air whiffed past them before the smell of left-over Chinese food overtook their new environment.

"This friggin thing." Bear made a fist and pounded the security panel twice. The foyer went silent. Bear's shoulders rose and fell as he chuckled almost silently.

"Nice work," Noble said, redirecting the big man away from the door so he could engage the security lock. "Why don't you go find the source of that odor and deal with it now."

"Eat me."

Noble gestured toward the short hallway leading to the kitchen. "I'm afraid that's what is on the menu in there."

Bear grabbed hold of the back of Noble's shirt and dragged him along for the walk. Noble broke free, retrieved his H&K pistol. They'd been given an address, nothing more. No assurances the place was empty, unused, unknown to anyone else.

A small window over the ceramic sink allowed the lingering orange glow of an alley light to seep into the kitchen. The counters were bare except for an old coffee maker and toaster. A stainless sheet covered the two-burner stovetop. Noble opened the fridge, which stood about five-feet high. It was empty. The cabinets were minimally stocked. A fine layer of undisturbed dust covered every surface. It had been a while since anyone had been there.

They proceeded through the rest of the house with the same level of caution, stopping at every window front and back, checking to see if the inadvertent alarm had drawn the attention of the local authorities.

Or anyone else.

"Feel good about the place?" Bear asked, throwing back a white sheet that hid a large stain back over a twin mattress.

Noble shrugged. "Not much choice in the matter, is there?"

"Incentive to get this done quickly, I guess."

"Speaking of...." Noble exited the bedroom and went downstairs. Where was the contact's information? Was that the point of the alarm? To let the contact know they were there?

Bear plodded down the steps almost like he was falling, the tips of his large feet barely making contact before sliding off the carpeted edges. They searched the downstairs again for anything that would tell them the next step. Every drawer and cabinet was rechecked. Noble climbed under the square dining table and overturned the chairs. They did the same with all the living room furniture, even going so far as to eject the tape inside the VCR.

Noble figured that cassette titled *Ghostlusters* had little to do with the person they were to meet. He tossed the tape to Bear, who snatched it out of the air, glanced down at the title and accompanying background image of four naked women and a green ghost, and let out a quick laugh.

"Bedrooms again?" Noble said.

"There was nothing..." Bear lowered the tape and turned to the front door.

"What is it?"

The big man brushed past Noble and stopped in front of the alarm panel. He peeled it back, shook his head.

"What do you have there?" Noble walked up beside the man, but couldn't see past his thick arm.

"That's why the alarm went off," Bear said.

"To alert them?"

Bear shook his head as he yanked the cover free from the wall. "Look at that."

"Farah Nazari."

Bear read the string of numbers following the name. "That's our contact. Same one Schofield wrote down."

Two hours later they sat in the back of a crowded cafe across from a woman who could have come straight from a photoshoot for a lingerie catalogue. She wasn't a local, but she could fit in based on appearances. Noble pegged her at mid- to late-twenties. She wore her hair pulled back into a high pony tail. Her face needed no makeup to accentuate her attractive features. She had on a blue sweater, faded jeans, and black boots. Gold bracelets surrounded her wrists. She carried herself as though she didn't care what any of the men in town thought.

She read through the information Noble provided her, stopping to study the aerial photographs and the primary suspect. O'Neil's photo meant nothing to the woman. She took a quick glance and flipped it over without much thought.

Noble studied Farah's face for a moment, looking for signs of concern or distress. "Know her?"

She looked him in the eye for a couple of seconds. "Never seen her before." Her accent was as neutral as any he'd heard from a foreigner.

He decided to take her response as in invitation to pry further. "How do you know Schofield?"

Farah ignored the question and diverted her attention back to the file. "You're sure this is the area?"

"We don't analyze all the intelligence," Bear said. "The ones that do provided us with those shots."

"That's a condensed area," she said. "Gotta be at least fifteen thousand people living there. Maybe more. Then you have everyone coming and going for work and so forth. This might take some time."

"That's something we don't have," Noble said.

"I'm not some kind of miracle worker, despite what you may have heard."

"We haven't heard anything. And, frankly, there's no room for excuses here. We've given you everything we've got. We need you to take that and see if you can narrow down our search perimeter."

She leaned back and crossed her arms over her chest. "How am I supposed to do that?"

"How the hell should I know?" Noble said. "Don't have a damn clue who you are, who you work for, what you do here. I'm guessing you have contacts here. Maybe you should show that picture to them, see what you can find out."

She snatched the photo off the table and held it up to Noble's face. "I show this to the wrong person, and it's my head. Do you have a damn clue how that works out here?"

Bear covered his mouth in a failed attempt to stifle a chuckle.

"What are you laughing at, you oaf?" She shifted her cross

stare from Noble to Bear. "You two are so obviously a couple of FNGs, I'm not sure I want any part in this. If you made one mistake, one simple slip-up, I could pay for it. In this town, that's a death sentence. Get me?"

"Are you refusing to help?" Bear asked.

She leaned back, dropped her hand below the table, and cocked her head to the side. "What if I am?"

Noble studied her for the slightest twitch, anything to signal she was retrieving a concealed weapon. She had already been seated when they had arrived. Hadn't bothered to get up to greet them. That left them with no chance to look for an obvious, or not so obvious, bump along her waistline.

"You know who gave us your information," Bear said. The unnatural way his lips moved, sort of frozen open, indicated Bear wasn't comfortable threatening the beautiful woman across from him. "You know why we're here. Do you want it relayed to our bosses that you refused to help?"

Her lips thinned to bloodless lines. The color shifted to her cheeks, which even with her dark complexion burned red.

Bear hunched forward a little more. "You know where they work, right?"

She remained silent.

"Do I gotta spell it out?" Bear leaned over his thick forearm perched on the table. "Come on, this is a serious situation."

"I know it's a serious situation." She matched his posture and leaned in until they were face to face. "So help me, if I run into either of you after this, you're as good as dead. You're right. I know exactly who you are, and who you work for. I even know the woman in the photo. But here's something for you two idiots to contemplate. You don't know me."

# CHAPTER THIRTY-ONE

Noble sat in a rusted iron chair on the back porch watching the final traces of sunlight slip into the night sky. A silvery slice of the moon hovered over the roof of the house behind theirs. The air smelled like a restaurant's dumpster when the adjacent grease trap was overflowing. It killed the serenity of the moment.

Bear had turned in earlier. Not for the night. The big man made that clear. He needed a little shut eye. They decided they would alternate watch. The earlier meeting with Farah had left both men uneasy. They left with the feeling she'd just as soon gut them as their enemies. How much did she know? Did she know where they were staying?

The meeting had ended with an agreement to meet at the same location twenty-four hours later. The idea didn't sit well with Noble. What if she had been followed? What if the people they were there to rescue O'Neil from were watching Farah?

*"You'll drive yourself crazy with the what-ifs..."* He heard his old man's voice as clear as if the Colonel stood right behind him.

There was wisdom in his words, but Noble also figured there were times you had to contemplate the actions of your enemies. His father would agree, and he knew it. Right now, Noble and Bear were closer than they had ever been to a set of enemies who would relish the chance to torture them for every ounce of intelligence they could squeeze through their broken limbs before beheading them and sharing the footage with news outlets around the globe. God forbid they earn their notoriety in such a manner.

He grabbed a sweating glass bottle off the side table and took a long pull of malted liquor. The bitter taste lingered on his tongue like spoiled olives. He swallowed hard, then took another drink, stopping mid-sip after a series of bangs on the front door.

"Who the hell?" he muttered, wondering if a prying neighbor had spotted the two Americans and wanted to get a closer look.

Four more knocks rang out in quick succession.

Noble rose and twisted at the waist to see down the hallway. What he wouldn't have given for a window cut in the door or placed next to it. He set the bottle on the table and stepped inside. The air outside had managed to cool enough that it now felt warmer in the house. He slid a dining chair in front of the back door to keep it open. Might be useful if he had to make a quick escape. Of course, Bear wouldn't have much of a chance. He stopped by the stairs and considered heading up to wake the big man.

The visitor knocked again, louder and longer than before. If Bear and Noble hadn't managed to draw attention to the safe house, the person outside surely had by now. With one hand he lifted the lid covering the security system panel. The other flipped the three door locks, then turned the knob.

"About time you opened up." Farah wedged a black boot inside and pushed against the door with her shoulder. Noble didn't give in so easily. She backed off. "Hey, I can just go and let you two knuckleheads figure this out on your own."

"Let her in, Jack."

Noble looked back and saw Bear standing on the bottom step. He hadn't heard the big man leave the bedroom, let alone descend a dozen rickety stairs. "How the hell did you do that?"

Farah pushed hard against the door, driving it into Noble's nose.

"Yeah, sure, come on in," he said, pinching his nostrils together to see if she'd broken anything. The door creaked open wide. A group of kids stood on the opposite side of the street. Probably had been playing soccer before Farah pulled up in her car. "Thought the plan was to—"

"Plans are made to be broken." She walked down the narrow hallway to the rear of the house. Noble and Bear followed into the unlit kitchen. Bear reached for the switch. Uncovered fluorescent tubes flickered on. Farah looked different under the unnatural light. It didn't work all that well with her skin tone.

"Assuming you've brought us good news?" Noble said.

"There's nothing of the sort in this town," she said. "I hope to God this gets me transferred back to Europe."

"Tired of dealing with the terrorists?"

"Tired of not seeing my daughter. It's been fourteen months." She slipped the bag off her shoulder and unzipped it. There were folders, a thick laptop, and what looked like a change of clothes inside. She reached for the folders and set them on the counter, opened the top one, turning it so the images inside faced Noble and Bear.

Bear tapped the top image. "That's the search area, right?"

She nodded. "Only a little more close up."

"We think that's where O'Neil is?"

Farah slid the top photo to the right, uncovering the next. A gaunt man with a high forehead stared back at them. "I did some digging around with my network, asking about any unusual activity. People here know things, know about some of the more unsavory characters running about. Seventy-five percent of my contacts fingered this guy, Wahid Samara, as being particularly active the past week."

"What's that mean?" Noble said. "Particularly active? He's been visiting Wal-Mart more often than normal?"

Farah took a deep breath. "You're worse than dealing with my child. It's not only him, but his group. And I dug further. While no one admitted to seeing O'Neil, or a white woman matching her description, they did place the man you had intel on with Samara."

Noble placed both hands on the tile counter and stared down at the image. The swirling pattern on the tiles blurred and danced off to the sides. "So this is our guy, then. What do we know about Wahid?"

Farah showed them the next image, which was really six smaller pictures lined up in a two-by-three grid. The photos were of buildings that could only be differentiated by the cracks in the facade.

"He either owns an interest or regularly visits each of these locations."

"Do we know which he's been most active at recently?" Noble asked.

She shook her head. "And we can't just send in a team. For one, there's no way any agency could get enough men in Aleppo to raid all locations simultaneously without drawing serious scrutiny and setting off a diplomatic train wreck. You can't just hit one location, either. If Samara is as tied into each of these as I think, and the purpose of each building is what I assume, then invading the wrong one will result in the swift termination of your agent."

"And probably us, too," Bear said.

Farah glanced down at the photos strewn across the counter. "Yes, you, too." She pulled out a map and laid it on top of the folder. "The six locations are marked on here. You'll be able to figure which is which by the photos."

"Any idea which is the most likely?" Noble asked.

"That's not my job." Farah snatched her bag and zipped it up, then slipped her arm through the strap and slung it over her shoulder. "I can continue looking for sources if you want, but my recommendation at this point is that I go dark. We've already stirred things up. If we go too far, Samara might grow suspicious and start watching his back. Or bring in others to do it for him."

"What kind of presence do they have here?"

"That's for some analyst to know, not me. I fade into the background. Look at me." She hiked up her sleeves and held her arms out. "I look like I belong here. Or any other number of cities in this dank corner of the world."

"If we need to contact you...?" Noble glanced at the hallway leading to the front door and security panel. He had a hunch the number written on the inside of the cover was no longer in service.

Farah reached into her bag and pulled out an empty envelope. She scrawled something on it in black ink, folded it twice, and handed it to Jack. "Only call if there is a dire emergency, or you've found her. We can't have contact otherwise."

It was concerning that she was ready to cut off contact right then and there. But that was her job. She provided the intel they needed to do theirs.

"I'll see myself out," she said.

Jack turned to watch her leave, but Bear had followed her to the door and blocked the view. The big man stood in front of the open door for a few seconds, presumably waiting until Farah was safely in her car. He walked back down the hallway and stopped at the opening.

"What do you think?" Bear said.

"I think we've got a long couple of days ahead of us watching buildings."

# CHAPTER THIRTY-TWO

I t didn't take long for Noble and Bear to realize how much they stuck out in Aleppo. They had trouble finding places to watch the first building with any sort of anonymity. A bustling café had to do. It was not lost on the majority of the business's patrons that two young Americans were seated at a table near the window. And then there were the people who returned three hours after their morning order for lunch. To them, Noble and Bear were quite a curiosity.

The guys covered the table with notebooks and sketchbooks, several pencils, and an architecture textbook they found in a used bookstore on the walk over. If anyone asked, they were students in their final year of studies. It helped that Bear had an artistic eye. He recreated scenes from across the street, while Noble doodled, impressed at the big man's ability.

During those hours, nothing happened across the street outside of an old couple exiting the main entrance, both equipped with walkers. They strolled from one end of the street to the other, oblivious to the world surrounding them, while younger pedestrians heading in and back out of the corner drug store lapped them.

"Maybe we should move on," Bear said during a lull in activity in the cafe. "Wouldn't expect the only people we've seen to be that old couple if something was going on here."

Noble shuffled and stacked the loose papers on his side of the table and placed them inside a folder. There were so many that they stuck out a little on the side. He twisted at the waist to retrieve his bag slung over the chair back.

"Whoa, whoa," Bear said. "Let's hold on a second."

Noble turned back to see Bear holding the large mug up to his face. Between the cup and his large hands supporting it, all Jack could see were the man's eyes, which were fixated on something across the street. He followed Bear's gaze to the two men at the entrance. One stood inside, shielded by the shadows. The other man was on the sidewalk with his back to them. He had dark hair. Wore black pants and a dark grey shirt and tactical boots. There was a noticeable bulge on his rear right hip.

"That could be our guy." Bear's head turned toward the opening door. Noble was already on it. The teenaged girl would not normally pose a threat, but under the circumstances, anything was possible. "I can't make out who that is inside, though."

"Me either." Noble watched the girl saunter up to the counter. She slid her bag off her shoulder and set it on the floor. He kept his gaze fixed on her hands.

"Everything OK over there?" Bear said.

"Think so. Keep watching across the street."

Ten seconds dragged on and felt like ten minutes. The words exchanged between the girl and barista were even more distorted than they had been at real speed in the peoples' native tongue. Noble felt as though he were underwater, listening to people shouting on dry land.

Bear slapped the table. Noble snapped his head toward the window.

"That's our guy," Bear said.

Noble didn't have to think twice. The image of Wahid Samara burned in his mind matched that of the guy walking across the street in their direction.

"Take him now?" Bear slid back, his chair scraped along the tile floor. The girl at the counter looked back at him. Her eyes grew wide as she stared at the large American.

"We do that, we might never get to her," Noble said, referring to O'Neil. They knew of six locations, and only one so far had been confirmed. "Best bet is to follow him."

"We'll be spotted if we do."

Samara walked right up to them. His eyes were focused on a space above their heads. Perhaps he was checking his reflection in the mirror. His hand went to his face, brushed back the hair hanging in his forehead. He planted one boot on the sidewalk, pivoted, and turned to his left. Noble and Bear hadn't been a blip on his radar. Maybe they could get away with following him.

Bear was on his feet and making his way toward the door. He knocked a few tables out of the way. He had his hand on the door handle when Noble yelled at him to stop. Bear looked at him, mouth open, eyes narrowed.

Noble shifted his gaze from the big man to the young woman standing in front of the counter. "Do you speak English?"

She turned away.

"This is important," Noble said. "Do you?"

She nodded once while staring at the floor between them.

Noble pulled a wad of cash out of his bag. It was half their allotted money to use while in the city. "All of this is yours, if you can follow that man who just walked past. Come back here with the address of his next destination."

Shaking her head, she backed up until her rear hit the counter.

"Look, I know it sounds odd. But he won't ever suspect you. And if it feels unsafe at any time, just come back."

She glanced at the large stack of money Noble had set on the table next to him. "All of that is mine?" Her English was perfect, if heavily accented.

"All of it," Noble said. "But you have to hurry. He's going to be out of sight soon."

Her head bobbed up and down as she took a couple of quick, deep breaths. She grabbed her backpack off the ground and rushed toward the door, pushing Bear out of the way. Bells jingled as she emerged onto the sidewalk. A rush of cool air filled the space she had passed through.

Bear let the door fall shut. He held it in place for a few moments so no one else could get in. The barista stood behind the counter, staring at them. Bear tossed her a quick glance, but it was as though he didn't see her standing there.

"You think that was smart?"

"I think she was our best bet in this situation." Noble pressed his head against the glass, watching the woman for as long as he could.

Bear clenched the fist on his free hand while the other white knuckled the handle. "We could've just gone to the next logical location and waited."

"And waited and waited until he came out again, if he came out again, because we might be waiting at the wrong spot." Noble turned toward Bear. "It's not going to be long before word gets back to Samara and Khoury that two Americans are poking around for information and hanging out in front of their haunts. We don't have a lot of time."

Bear stepped outside and paced the stretch of sidewalk in front of the cafe. He stopped frequently to stare off in the direction that Samara and the girl had traveled. Noble reconsidered the decision he'd made in a flash. He figured he'd been fifty-fifty on such decisions in his life. None mattered as much as this one, though. There was a difference between deciding whether to throw twenty yards to a covered receiver or take off running, and putting a teenage girl's life on the line. He stared at the cash still on the table and cursed at himself. He should have gone. That was his job. Not hers.

The door whipped open and the exhaust fumes entered ahead of Bear. He gestured with his head. "She's coming."

"Alone?"

"I didn't see anyone following, but who knows?"

Noble freed his pistol from its holster and did his best to conceal it and his hand in his front pocket. The grip stuck out. What did it matter? They were the only ones in there at the moment aside from the barista, and she wasn't paying much attention.

Bear pulled the door open for the girl, who wasted no time entering.

"Well?" Noble wiped his forehead with the back of his thumb.

She spat out an address. "He stopped there and talked with another man. As I walked past, they went inside. I glanced over and saw two more men standing inside the doorway. They were holding guns, machine guns. I heard what sounded like a woman screaming."

# CHAPTER THIRTY-THREE

A lexa Steele closed the laptop's lid and turned her attention to the hallway leading to the front door. A black mark and gouge in the paint near the edge of the wall had been there since one of the guys moving in her new furniture had tripped over his own shoelace. It could have been worse. They could have punched a hole in the wall. For three months, the store had been blowing her off about getting the spot repainted. She could have done it herself, but it was the principal of the matter.

And she really didn't care. She spent so little time in her place during the day that the spot went largely unnoticed. Except at moments like this. Times when she wanted to ignore the knock at the door and just enjoy a few moments off.

The visitor laid on the doorbell, exhausting the chimes before they could complete the full melody. Alexa grabbed her laptop, stuffed it in its bag, and shuffled across the plush rug, feeling the long strands rub between her toes, to the entry foyer.

Her uncle's distorted figure hovered behind the decorative glass. He pounded on the door again.

"I see you in there. C'mon, girl, open up."

She disarmed her security system, unlatched three deadbolts and a security chain, and pulled the door open an inch. "What are you doing up here?"

He took off his camouflage hat and covered his heart with it. "Can I come in?"

"Has someone died?" She eyed him, wondering what his angle was. Why was he appearing so timid and meek after pounding on the door hard enough to snap it off its hinges?

"No, not yet, at least."

"Then what are you doing here, and not at the farm with the latest batch of recruits?"

"My guys got that under control. Besides, it's their first *off* day."

She pulled the door open, but remained in place, blocking entry. "There's never an off day with you, Cribbs."

"Alexa, let me in. We need to talk."

She studied his face for a few moments. There was a softness she hadn't seen present since she was a girl. Maybe he had a reason to be there unannounced. She relented, turned her back to him and walked to the kitchen where she took a seat on a stool at the island. He sat down next to her a few moments later, plunking his elbows on the countertop and holding his chin in his hand. He ran his thumb and forefinger across the short stubble that had collected on his cheeks.

"What is it?" She said, breaking the silence.

"I got the latest update on our boys this morning."

"They're in Aleppo, made contact with the asset, and have a plan."

Cribbs nodded in response to this.

"And?" She spun a quarter turn on her stool and faced him. "What's wrong?"

"I'm worried we sent them in there too soon."

She nearly had to pick her chin up off her lap. "You're worried about them? The two recruits you couldn't stand because they were so green? What do you care if they die out there?"

"You know I had to be tough on them, girl."

"I'm not a girl anymore, and frankly, I'm tired of telling you that. You need to start showing me the same respect you show McKenzie, because one day it's gonna be me running—"

"I know, I know." He conceded victory to her. "You picked them, and you did a good job. But this job has the chance of going so sideways it'll send them into a spin."

Alexa hopped off her stool and walked around to the other side of the island. She grabbed the coffee pot, rinsed it out, and refilled it with fresh water. What was Cribbs talking about? He was normally so arrogant that he was sure any recruit he had trained would rise to the top no matter the circumstances. After filling the machine with grounds, she started it and turned back to her uncle.

"What aren't you telling me?" she asked.

"The caretaker," he said. "Of the safe house."

"Schofield."

"Right, that idiot. I got a message last night that he was involved with O'Neil in the past."

"Who sent the message?"

Cribbs said nothing, an indication it was someone they both knew, which meant someone from the team.

Someone who knew O'Neil.

"You deem the information credible?"

He nodded, still said nothing.

"And your concern is that...?"

"How do we know he wasn't involved in her kidnapping?"

"Vengeance?"

"Possibly. That asset in Aleppo, he fished her out, right?"

Alexa nodded. It was her turn to say nothing. Scenarios unfolded in her mind.

"So what if this guy sent our boys into a hornet's nest? How long would it take to get them some backup?"

"Too long."

## CHAPTER THIRTY-FOUR

Noble left the cash behind and bolted for the door. He was lucky he didn't get caught up in Bear's wash. The big man was halfway down the block by the time Jack stepped into the early afternoon heatwave. The crowds had thickened during the lunch rush, but were back to normal levels now. Several vehicles drove past at low speeds with their windows down, filling the air with a mix of talk, pop, and traditional music. Heavy exhaust smoke poured out of tailpipes.

Five minutes later they reached the destination block. The building was the third one on the right. From where they stood, they could only see an awning stretching out five feet over the sidewalk. Every face was a potential enemy. It wasn't until now that Noble considered they could have spotted the girl. She had walked past them twice. Unusual? Only to someone looking for it.

"Split up?" Bear asked.

"Don't think that's a good idea." Noble paused and watched as a man stopped underneath the awning. The guy reached into his pocket. For what? A key? A gun? He pulled out a pack of cigarettes and worked one out with his meaty fingers.

"Let's cut around back, then," Bear said.

"You sure there's an around back here?"

The big man looked up at nothing, nodded. "I remember from the photos."

The side street was narrower by a full lane. It didn't seem wide enough to allow two cars to pass. And as small as it was, the alley was even more cramped. Both men nearly brushed buildings while walking shoulder to shoulder. It was shaded and hot and smelled like a thousand soiled diapers had been left to rot back there for three weeks.

"Christ," Bear said. "Dunno if I'm gonna make it halfway down."

Noble nudged Bear to shut him up. Anyone could be watching. They had to figure everyone was. He glanced up at the high walls surrounding them. There was no easy escape. It would only take two armed men, one at each end of the corridor, to make life difficult.

"What was that?" Bear stopped and threw his arm out in front of Noble.

Jack cocked his head and listened.

"You hear it?" Bear said.

"You must have some kinda super hearing, 'cause I don't hear anything."

"It's a woman." Bear took a step forward, turned to his right, then left. He aimed a finger upward at the center building, the building they were investigating. "Up there."

Noble followed his gaze to a cracked window on the top floor. He honed in best he could. Maybe he did hear something. It was high pitched, not constant, rising and falling instead. Could it be a woman? Maybe. He couldn't tell. There was a way to find out.

They pushed forward, sticking close to the facade. Noble brushed up against the building and felt a warm, wet substance coat his arm. It stunk like sewage but showed no immediate signs of irritating his skin.

A gap of two feet separated the buildings from each other. The small walkway led to the main road, with what appeared to be a tall gate or fence blocking entrance from the sidewalk. The narrow passage was even darker than the alley. If there were someone hiding there, they couldn't be seen. And neither could any doors or windows on the sides of the buildings. It was a good place to get trapped with less of a chance of survival than where they stood.

Bear pointed to a rear door and hurried toward it. Noble stayed behind, covering him. He looked up and down the facade across the alley. Six stories of rugged concrete, empty spaces where windows should be, rebar poking out in some spots. Abandoned mid-construction. Why? What was the history here?

A quick whistle drew his attention back to his partner. Bear stood in front of the doorway, his fist wrapped around the handle. He held his other arm up, counted down from five to one, leaving his middle finger standing out against his grey shirt. Noble lifted his pistol and drew aim at the expanding swath of dull light emanating from the opening as Bear pulled the door toward him. His heart pounded in time with each of the ten steps he took to the landing. The stairs leading up shifted under his weight. How secure were they? He decided a quick escape would require avoiding them completely, hopping the five feet to the asphalt, or whatever made up the ally floor.

Noble stuck his pistol into the opening and eased around. For a few tense seconds he was exposed. The area was small and confined, leading to a metal stairwell. Black paint chips clung to the handrail. He started up with Bear in tow. They moved slowly and deliberately in an effort to make as little noise as possible. If the building was what they thought, and O'Neil was there, there would be lookouts.

Bear tugged at the back of Noble's shirt, stopping him two steps before the next landing. The overhead light hung from a string. It swung a few centimeters left and right. The big man pointed up at it while Noble watched his shadow move back and forth. Someone had been through and had disrupted the light. Had they gone up for reinforcements when the door opened?

Noble mouthed, "Wait?" to Bear.

Bear's nostrils widened as he pulled in a deep breath and held it. He shook his head, then jutted upward with his chin.

Noble wiped the sweat off his palm and re-gripped his pistol. He was starting to feel as though they weren't armed well enough for the job. The plan had been to return after finding the right location. Things hadn't worked out that way, though. Should they go back and get the rifles and submachine guns? It was too late for that. They'd already entered, and the tenants were possibly aware.

He stepped up on the landing and whipped around to face the next set of stairs with his pistol aimed at an angle. No one was there, but he could see the top of the door beyond the next landing, and it stood a few inches open.

Bear stopped next to him, noticed the same thing. He whispered, "They playing a game with us?"

"Bad hinges, maybe? Airflow, perhaps?"

They'd climbed three floors and this was the first door they'd come across. The building was only four or five stories. The main area might've been set up like a warehouse, high ceilings, lots of crap stacked on shelves, or some other setup. Didn't matter, though. They'd start here and work their way down if necessary.

"Should we call for backup?" Bear asked.

"Not sure that's an option, big man. Let's check it out. We're here already, right?"

Bear took the lead and climbed to the next landing. Near the top step, he backed up to the wall and inched his way toward the door. His eyes swept right to left and back.

Noble had faith in his partner to get it right. What other choice was there?

"See anything?"

"It's open," Bear whispered in between heavy breaths. "But a couple doors on the wall, too."

Noble moved past Bear and took in the room head on. It was large and square with doors on the right, as Bear had said. There was a rectangular table in the middle with boxes stacked three high on the far end. Closer to them there were rows of bags laid out. He took cover behind the door and fished the suppressor out of his pocket and threaded it onto the barrel of his H&K. It wouldn't eliminate the sound of his gun firing, but it'd reduce it enough to not alert others if they weren't in the room.

"Going?" Bear said.

"Cover me." Noble whipped around the edge and entered the room with his pistol at the ready. Loud enough for Bear to hear, he said, "Clear." He heard Bear fall into position behind him as he headed for the table. He dropped to a knee and checked the underside for cameras, sensors, or explosives. All bets were off at this point. If they got a tip Noble and Bear were coming, they could've rigged the place to blow after leading them there.

"Anything?" Bear said.

"Nah."

"What's on the table?"

Jack hopped up and grabbed one of the clear bags. It was filled with an off-color powder. He pulled off the tie and let the bag unwind, then took a sniff.

"What is that?" Bear said.

"Heroin, I think," Noble said.

Before Bear could make another remark, the furthest door opened and a man stepped out, his face buried in a paperback. He took two steps into the room and lifted his gaze. His brows knitted while he tried to figure out why there were two Americans in the room with him.

"Don't move," Noble said.

Either the guy didn't understand English, or he didn't care enough to stay put. He retreated a few steps. The book fell to the floor with a smack. The guy reached behind his back and pulled out a MAC-10. He planted a foot on the paperback, and as he whipped the gun around, his leg slipped forward, causing his knee to buckle and his finger to squeeze down on the trigger. A hail of bullets tore through the ceiling. Chunks of plaster and asbestos rained down on the table.

Noble fired two shots. Both hit dead center. The man flinched backward, fell to his right onto his chest. His gun fell to the floor. His legs and arms twitched for a few seconds. Bear rushed over and grabbed the MAC-10 and searched the guy's pockets, coming up empty aside from a pack of cigarettes.

Shouts echoed behind the open door. Footsteps clanged up metal stairs. Sounded like they were coming from both directions.

Bear hustled around Noble and flipped the table over. Heroin wrapped in bags spilled out onto the floor and rolled across the room. The boxes toppled over, ripped open, revealing several more packages within.

"Get back here, Jack."

They angled the table so they had a cover from both ends of the room. It sounded as though they were in for a shootout. Question was, how bad were the odds stacked against them?

# CHAPTER THIRTY-FIVE

"I got that door." Bear took aim at the opening where the dead man had come from.

The shouting had stopped. The clanging of boots against metal stairs had subsided. Were they formulating a plan? Waiting for more men? Noble strained to hear anything other than Bear's and his breathing, fast and ragged. They'd been in a few situations, but nothing so perilous as this. The chance that they wouldn't make it through the situation was real. At the very least, a serious injury could befall one of them.

"I don't like sitting here waiting," Noble said.

Bear jutted his chin to the door they had come through. "We know what's back there. We can retreat to the alley. But if they're waiting back there, penning us in, we're done. Up here, we have a natural chokepoint. Gives us a chance."

"How much of one?"

Bear's gaze slid off Noble. He said nothing.

For thirty seconds the men knelt behind the table. An occasional creak or bang interrupted the silence. The heavy air was overtaken with a foul smell. Gas? Were they leaking it into the building?

Noble turned to Bear, ready to whisper something about it. But Bear had something else in mind. He pointed to the opening they had entered the room through. The black tip of a rifle barrel cut into the dull white background. Both men aimed at the doorway, about chest high, ready to fire. The barrel poked into the room. It aimed toward the wall of doors at first, continued to turn toward them. Noble was about to fire at it, hoping for a ricochet into the man wielding the weapon.

They fired first. Ten wild shots slammed into the floor, wall, ceiling, and the table Noble and Bear used for cover. The bullets had no problem punching holes through.

Silence followed. Bear tapped Noble on the shoulder, pointed at the wall next to the doorway. He slid over there without making a sound. Noble glanced at the other entrance point. They couldn't remain too focused in this case. Someone could be coming up the other way.

"You don't have to die," someone outside the room said. "Step to the middle, hands up, and you'll be free to leave."

Noble grabbed the nearest baggie of drugs and launched it through the opening.

"There are many of us here, and one or two of you. You will not live."

Noble looked at Bear, who shook his head. They wouldn't live if they gave themselves up, either. The men exchanged a nod. It was going down now. Jack moved to the back of the room, made his way to the opposite side and started toward the front until he had sight of part of a torso. He drew aim on the guy and unleashed a muffled shot. It hit the man on his shoulder. The guy's rifle dipped toward the floor as he screamed in pain. His body lurched out of sight, perhaps pulled back by someone.

This is when the other men would make a mistake.

Grey-gloved fingers grabbed the door jamb and propelled the next man into the opening. He fired blindly, over Noble's head. Jack made sure he paid for it with three shots starting at the man's chest and ending in the center of his throat.

Three distinct voices rose and fell. They were coordinating their next attack.

Bear pointed at the far door. Noble fell back but hesitated going through. He wanted the men to see him as he did so.

The first man to appear did not wait to shoot. That also meant he did a horrible job of aiming. The rounds he fired tore through wall and left behind a cloud of dust.

Noble returned fire, hitting the man in the leg, before backing through the opening and taking cover behind the wall. Stairs descended just past the doorway. Noble took them backwards far enough to glance below at a dimly lit garage with six yellow hydraulic lifts, three of which were in use. There was no movement down there. He returned his attention to the room he had left moments ago.

Two men stood outside the doorway. They didn't appear to notice Noble in the shadows. He held his fire, waiting to see what they would do. Once they crossed the threshold, they became better targets with less chance to escape.

The first man made it through and traveled five steps before glancing over his shoulder. Bear unloaded on the guy, and at least a half-dozen rounds from the MAC-10 cut him down.

The second man had one foot in the room. He froze for a second before swinging around the doorway with his submachine gun in Bear's direction. The big man didn't have time to recover, so he dove to the floor, rolling on his shoulder and lunging for the table, not that it'd stop the onslaught of fire.

It all happened so fast, and by the time Noble had the guy lined up in his sights, the man had emptied his magazine and reached around his back for another.

Noble fired twice, hitting the guy in both shoulders. He wanted him alive if possible. The guy stumbled backward into the wall. Noble climbed the stairs. A door whipped open on the ground floor below him. He glanced down. Sunlight flooded the concrete floor.

Two men escaped through the front of the building. Noble cursed and turned back toward the wounded man. He was no longer there, though.

"Bear," Jack shouted.

The big man stood up and kicked the table out of his way.

"Come on," Noble said, already across the room and heading for the other stairwell. A trail of blood about shoulder-height created a diagonal line along the wall. "He's down there somewhere."

Bear caught up. The two hit the landing and rounded it for the next set of stairs. Gunfire erupted the moment Jack cleared the railing. Bear grabbed hold of Noble's shirt and pulled him back as the rounds punched holes in the concrete.

Noble sucked in two deep breaths, held up his hand, counted down from three. The two men exploded around the corner, ready to unload on the guy. He was gone. A puddle of blood remained. The sound of his staggered footsteps echoed through the chamber.

"We need to get him before he gets outside."

The door at the bottom grated open, slammed into the wall with a loud bang. Two shots rang out, someone hit the ground. The stairwell grew quiet after the echoes dissipated.

Noble gestured toward the next landing and they climbed

down, taking extra care to minimize the sound of their footsteps. He leaned forward, saw a shadow stretched out below them. He also saw the feet of whoever lay on the ground.

The shadow disappeared as the door slammed shut again. A hooded figure appeared. Who was down there, hovering over the dead man?

# CHAPTER THIRTY-SIX

"Noble? Bear?"

The woman ascended the stairs toward them.

"Farah?" Noble replied as he made his way down two steps at a time.

They met on the next landing. She pulled the hood off her head and tucked wayward strands of dark hair behind her ears.

"The hell happened here?" she said.

"Ambushed," Bear said. "Had to shoot our way out of it."

"This isn't the place," Noble said. "There's drugs, but no torture chamber I can tell."

"Yeah, no shit it's the wrong place," Farah said. "Did anyone see you and escape?"

Bear shook his head. "We got 'em all."

"No, we didn't." Noble wiped the sweat from his face, looked at it glistening on his palm. "Two guys in the garage got out. They saw me."

"That means they're going to wherever Samara and Khoury are now," she said. "And I'd assume O'Neil, too."

"You've got the pulse of this city," Noble said to her. "You know the people here, the good and bad players. Where do we need to go?"

"I don't know." Farah retreated back a step. "It is not my job to know. I got you the intelligence you needed. That's it. I'm done."

"Then what are you doing here?" Bear asked.

She looked away and said nothing.

"You were following us." Noble inched his pistol up. "Why?"

She said nothing. Noble made it obvious with the pistol. She stared down the barrel with no fear in her eyes. "I was told to."

"By who? Cribbs?"

"Who?" She shook her head. "I don't know names. I was asked to keep tabs on you two to make sure this all goes down without a problem."

"That's not your job though, is it?" Noble threw her words back in her face.

She took a deep breath and surrendered. "We've got one shot at this. I can guarantee the men you saw in the garage are on their way to tell Samara that the Americans are here. He will not hesitate to extract whatever last bit of information he can from O'Neil, and then he'll kill her."

"So take us to the most likely location." Bear's impatience shone through in his tone.

She turned for the door without a word.

Noble braced himself for what might be waiting for them outside. The small alley offered little protection. They were already low on ammunition. A shootout behind the building might leave them empty. Farah pulled the door open. Daylight flooded in, but did little to brighten the space. He followed her outside. If anyone was out there, she didn't fear them, which would mean the woman they knew little about was working against them the entire time.

He surveyed the stretch from one end to the other. It looked and sounded the same as when they had entered. There was no concern over what had happened inside. Maybe the locals were used to it and just didn't care. Better to ignore it and stay alive than put yourself in the middle. Everything was corrupt here. Call the cops, and they'd let the bad guys know where you lived.

"I'm down at that end." She pointed the direction they had come from.

"We need to go by the house first," Noble said.

"Why?"

"We're not equipped for this. I got a damn nine-mil with six rounds left. If what happened in there is any indication, we're in for a shootout."

"It's going to add ten minutes," she said. "Do we have that kind of time?"

"We don't," Bear said. He ran back inside.

Noble and Farah waited in the shadows for the big man to return. A long sixty seconds passed before his lumbering steps echoed through the open doorway. He emerged carrying two submachine guns, and three pistols.

"This should do us." He handed Noble two pistols and a KGP-9 submachine gun, keeping the MAC-10 and a pistol for himself.

"What about me?" Farah said.

"Hell with that," Bear said. "Get us there, and get us out of the way."

"You'll need a ride out."

"We'll get in touch with you." He wasn't backing down on this point. She hadn't been through anything with them. Neither man wanted to break her in now.

She reached in her pocket and pulled out a notebook, which she scribbled a series of numbers on. "This is the best way to reach me."

They hurried down the alley, with Noble and Bear waiting at the end while Farah retrieved her vehicle and reversed to where they stood. The inside was clean, but cramped. Noble took the backseat. It didn't look like Bear would fit.

"This other building," she said, "I'm somewhat familiar. It's likely set up like many apartment buildings in this area with a wide hallway down the middle. There's no corners or other cover. You'll be exposed from the moment you walk in if they have surveillance set up."

"Chances are they do," Noble said. "We'll need to check the back to disable it."

"Allow me," Farah said.

Bear glanced back at Noble.

"It's what I used to do," she said. "In the military."

The two men nodded.

"All right," Bear said. "You do that, then you get the hell out."

She wanted to drop them off a block away on a side street. It wouldn't work. They couldn't walk around in broad daylight with guns strapped to their chests and bulging out of their pockets. And neither man was comfortable with her heading into the alley alone. They'd go with her. If something went down back there, so be it.

They ditched the car on the curb. Twenty meters separated them from the confines of the alley. It wasn't as bad here. The buildings on either side weren't as tall, and there was more space between them. Back here, Noble and Bear made no effort to conceal their weapons. The KGP-9 and MAC-10 were strapped across their chests. They walked with pistols held at the ready as though they were in an urban battle zone.

"That panel," Farah said. "Most likely controls their comms. Cover me while I check it out."

Bear remained where he stood. His position offered him a view of the back of the building, and part of the side. He scanned the facade. Like a shark in the water, his eyes never rested, never stopped, always on the prowl.

Noble accompanied Farah, relying on Bear to notify him if trouble was about to strike. He took note of the lock on the panel as Farah tugged on it.

"Step aside." He didn't wait for her to move far before freeing the submachine gun from his body and slamming the buttstock down on the point where the lock held the two pieces of metal together. One blow was all it took to snap it clear off.

Farah stepped up and pulled the top panel off, revealing a rat's nest of wiring.

"You know what all that is?" Noble asked.

She shot him a sideways glance and rolled her eyes as her hands went to work separating the telephone wires from the rest. Once that was done she pulled out a pair of metal scissors. "We'll leave them with dial tone and take out the rest. That way they won't be too suspicious when the feed dies."

"That's not gonna shock you, is it?"

She shrugged. "A few volts at worse. No amps. That's what kills you. You could take a million volts through your entire body, but if the amps aren't there, you'll just feel a little like Keith Richards."

Noble chuckled. His mother loved the Stones. He used to watch her and Molly dancing to song after song when he was little.

It took less than ten seconds for Farah to do the damage. "It's up to you guys now. Call me as soon as you're out."

She and Bear nodded at each other as they crossed paths, him coming toward Noble, her walking away. Her pace quickened to a run. By now someone inside noted that their security feed had gone to snow. They'd check the phone, still have dial tone. Maybe they'd panic a little less. But in a few seconds they'd get up, find

Samara and Khoury. With everything else that had happened today, the men might be spooked enough to end O'Neil's interrogation.

Permanently.

# CHAPTER THIRTY-SEVEN

The first floor of the decrepit building was dark, and the hot, stale air smelled like Cribbs's gym back in West Virginia. It clung to them as they made their way down the darkened hallway with only the light filtering in through the window cut into the exterior door.

Noble couldn't hear much over the swooshing of his heartbeat. Had to be going at a touch over a hundred beats per minute. It would be higher when they found O'Neil.

They pushed through the door into the stairwell where yellow incandescents hung behind sconces mounted to the wall, one at the beginning and end of each flight. At the second floor, they waited by the door and listened. A five-by-five-inch pane of glass offered a view of blackness. No chance they were down there. Bear cracked the door open anyway to get a better listen.

A fast breeze whistled into the stairwell. More hot air, but at least it didn't stink as bad.

The third floor was also the top floor. The stairs ended at the landing. A series of rusted bars poked out from the wall, leading to a square cutout in the ceiling, with an attached handle. Roof access. Noble wondered what waited up there, hoping they wouldn't have to find out.

The door separating them from the hallway was the same as the one on the second floor. Through the small window they saw a long, carpeted hallway with eight doors on either side. The same sconces clung to the walls.

Bear checked the door and frame quickly in search of a trip-wire. Nothing on their side. They had to take their chances with the other. Noble glanced up at the roof again. Was there another access somewhere else? Bear pulled the door open. The same rush of air blew past. Difference now was it smelled like dinner. Someone was up here. How many someones was the question.

"Ready?" Bear whispered.

Noble nodded, and the two of them stepped into the hallway. Noble was on the left. Bear to the right. They stopped at the first set of doors and waited. Mounted above the door on Noble's side was a black camera aimed at the stairwell. Every muscle in his upper body tensed. What if the camera system hadn't been disabled? What if Farah was wrong?

He'd figured he'd find out right about now. The pistol's handle felt hot against his palm. He pointed the barrel straight ahead with his finger on the trigger. Dangerous, should a regular person step out of their apartment, on their way to pick up the kids.

There was no one like that here.

"Someone's in here," Bear whispered.

Noble turned toward the room and waited for Bear to check the handle. It gave without resistance. The big man pushed the door open and got out of the way so Noble could enter.

He stepped in and made his way through the small apartment to find a bald man with a heavy beard asleep on the couch. An almost bare coffee table was in the middle of the room. On it, a roll of duct tape. At the far end of the couch, leaning against the wall, was an AK-47. Noble lifted his left hand and gestured for Bear to enter, then he pointed at the roll of tape. Bear wasted no time stripping a piece off and then wrapping it around the guy's face, covering his mouth.

The man bolted upright. He didn't remain in the position long. Bear drove him back down, then planted his wide fist in the guy's gut. The man's rigid body went limp. Bear secured his ankles and wrists with enough tape to hold a car upside down to the ceiling of a garage.

Noble grabbed the rifle and checked the magazine. Thirty 7.62×39mm rounds ready for use.

"Put him in the bathroom for now," Noble said. "We might need him later."

Bear hefted the guy over his shoulder and dropped him in the oval tub, then shut the bathroom door.

They exited the room, ready to check the next set of doors, when a scream erupted from further down the hallway. It was high and shrill and sounded like someone had just had a limb snapped off. A second scream from the same person spurred them into action. They hurried down the hallway and stopped in front of a door where they heard a man yelling in a foreign tongue.

Noble looked up and down the hallway. All of the doors were evenly spaced. Unless someone had done some interior remodeling, they were about to step into a room roughly the same size as the first. That wouldn't leave much space for anyone to work, so chances were they'd face two, possibly three other men in there.

Bear reached for the knob. "Locked."

"Guess we better be quick to decide who's a bad guy," Noble said, then gestured toward the door while dropping to a knee.

Bear took a step back and drove the sole of his boot into the door near the latch. He might as well have been kicking a stick.

The door buckled and caved in. Noble moved first, driving his shoulder into the swinging hunk of hollow-core wood and getting it out of the way. It slammed against the wall and remained there.

The room in front of him was nothing like the first they had entered. It was more of a foyer, with a hallway on either side. Someone had renovated, and they'd created what was probably a torture chamber.

The woman screamed again.

A man emerged from the right corridor. Dumbass had his pistol pointed at the floor. He might've had a chance had he been ready with it. Instead, Noble squeezed the trigger of the AK and a thunderous round slammed into the man's chest an inch to the left of his sternum, piercing his heart and taking his life. After he fell, blood and seared cloth clung to the wall.

Any benefit of surprise was erased in that moment. Not that there was much choice. Him or them. Noble would choose them in any such situation.

A door slammed shut down from deep within the hallway. Did they have another way out? All those doors lining the main corridor had to open up to something.

Noble entered the hall with the AK leading the way. He wouldn't think twice if anyone appeared. Chances were he wasn't going to encounter any families here. Anyone stupid enough to step out into the open deserved to die.

But what if they pushed O'Neil out?

He could only hope her distinct look would stifle his instincts.

Bear fell in line behind him, sounded out of breath. "Checked the hallway. No activity."

"Better watch our backs anyway."

"On it, bro."

Noble heard crying from behind a closed door. He turned the handle and pushed at it slowly while easing the barrel into the expanding opening. O'Neil dangled a foot off the ground, suspended by her wrists. The thick cord was wrapped tight. Her tear-stained cheeks met dark red circles under her eyes. It looked like they had cut her hair short with a knife. She had on a dirty and bloodied white tank top and dark panties. She looked down at him and her eyes grew wide. Noble held a finger to his mouth. She glanced to her right. Her nostrils flared. Her mouth opened, but nothing came out.

Someone was there, waiting for Noble. He took a step back, kicked the door into the guy. Six holes punched through as the man unloaded his pistol. Slivers of wood sprayed across the room. Noble waited until the firing stopped, then put the barrel of his pistol up to the door and returned his own fire through the bullet-ridden hunk of wood. The man called out, stumbled forward, fell to his knees. The exit wounds in his lower back told Noble his shot had done significant damage.

"Turn around!" Noble yelled. He kept a little distance between himself and the man.

The guy looked back. Noble knew him instantly. Khoury. The guy in the photo they found in the package underneath the park bench. *AVOID*. He shot a glance to O'Neil, who now sobbed heavily. Fresh tears ran down her face.

"How we looking, Bear?" Noble asked.

"Nothing doing," Bear replied.

"You two are dead," the guy said. He held his hands to the hole in his stomach. Blood seeped through his clenched fingers.

"Think you got that wrong, friend." Noble pulled the trigger again.

The bullet tore through the man's left eye and blew out the back portion of his skull. He rocked back and fell over his heels, coming to rest against the wall.

"Let's get you down," Noble said to O'Neil.

She stopped crying long enough to say something. "Samara."

"What about him?"

Her head shook violently. "We can't let him get away."

"He's here?"

She made her best attempt at gesturing with her chin toward a closed door. "In there."

# CHAPTER THIRTY-EIGHT

How many minutes had passed since Samara had left Khoury and O'Neil behind? Was the next room a dead end, or did it connect to another? O'Neil couldn't tell them. She'd gone back to sobbing, perhaps overwhelmed by what she had endured and the fact it was almost over. Her training would kick in, and the hardened operative would return. But for now, she was about as useful as a Jell-o mold.

There wasn't time to waste. Noble headed for the next room. He looked back at Bear. "Get her down."

Before reaching the door he fired six rounds through it, chest height. The fractured door only required a tap from his foot to open it. The room was small and adorned with a bed and wide chest. The mattress butted up against the wall underneath a closed window. Red curtains parted an inch or two. A bright slice of sunlight cut down the middle of the floor.

"He in there?" Bear called out.

"Empty," Noble said. "But there's another door. I'm going through."

He held off on wasting any more ammunition and entered the next room the old-fashioned way. It smelled like garlic and cinnamon. He took a quick glance around. It was empty except for a step ladder in the middle. He glanced up. Roof access. The panel had been moved over an inch or two.

Noble glanced back through the opening. Bear had O'Neil resting on one shoulder, hefting her up, while hacking at the cord with a knife.

He climbed the ladder, placed both hands on the opening and pushed it up and to the right. A steady wind billowed down on him. Warmth spread over his head and shoulders. The rooftop was empty. He gripped the edges and pulled himself through. Gravel bit into his knees. It skated as he shuffled the first few feet, taking in his surroundings. Noble walked the perimeter and found the escape route. Iron rails curved over the low wall that ran along the edge.

The sun reflected off windows on nearby buildings. Anyone could be watching and Noble wouldn't have a clue. He was an easy target. He slowed his pace the final steps and leaned over the edge. A man clung to the ladder with about a story left to descend.

Noble aimed the rifle straight down.

The tussle of black hair dipped back as the man looked up. Samara. Even at this distance Noble had no trouble recognizing him. Samara glanced over his shoulder, let go of the rails and dropped the final ten feet or so to the ground. He hit it hard, spilled onto his side. He scrambled to his knees, crawled for cover.

Noble didn't let him get far. He squeezed off five rounds with the AK-47. Four of them connected with Samara. Were they fatal? Hard to tell from on the roof, but Samara collapsed on the ground, his arms splayed wide.

Noble took a step back, lowered his head. The warm air spread through his body. It was too soon to relax. They still had to get O'Neil out of the country.

When he reached the roof access, he saw Bear in the room below, ripping drawers out of the chest. Noble dropped through the opening.

"The hell are you doing?"

Bear dumped a bunch of clothes on the ground. "She had a satellite phone when they abducted her. Thinks they kept it in here."

"We've got one, too. Back at the house."

"We can't go back there, man."

Noble took a step back to get out of his partner's way. Then he lifted the mattress off the frame, revealing a black box about a foot long and eight inches wide. "Check that out."

Bear grabbed the box, unlatched it. Both men exhaled when he opened it and revealed a phone. "Let's get this bad boy powered up and call Farah."

Noble took the satellite phone from Bear so the big man could carry O'Neil.

"Any major injuries?" Noble asked.

"She's pretty beat up. Pretty sure nothing's broken, though. Nothing major, anyway. They kept her in decent shape."

Noble looked down at the woman who sat against the wall, her knees to her chest, her head folded over them. "She must've sang for them."

She looked up at him. The shadows cast over her face made her look like a walk-on for a zombie flick.

"Any signal yet?" Bear asked.

Jack checked the device. "Not yet. We need to get outside."

Noble led the way through the building. They couldn't assume it was clear, but once they hit the stairs, it was a sprint to the bottom. They exited through the rear so they could check on

Samara. He blinked a few times against the intense sunlight. The ground came into focus.

Samara was gone.

Noble froze in place, blocking the doorway.

"What is it?" Bear said, pushing Noble forward a foot.

"He's not here."

Bear eased around him, stared down at the ground. "Hell of a lot of blood for the guy to get up and walk away."

Noble vaulted over the railing, landed near the spot where Samara had collapsed. There was a hell of a lot of blood. And it was confined to this one place.

"He didn't get up," Noble said. "At least not on his own. Someone picked him up from here." He walked ten feet down the alley, then ten feet the other way. "And they didn't carry him. There'd be splatter somewhere."

"They drove him out?" Bear said.

"That or he straight up ascended into the heavens."

"You shot him. Was he dead?"

"He took four rounds to the back. If he's not, he's in pretty bad shape. Don't see him lasting through the hour without some serious medical attention."

"Don't feel good hanging out back here," Bear said. "How's that phone?"

Noble checked the readout. "Good to go." He dialed the number Farah had given them. She picked up before the second ring and told them where to meet her.

They hustled down the alley, taking the first left they came to, which was nothing more than a simple walkway. The shadows eased Noble's mind. He slowed the pace, allowing him to pay better attention to their surroundings and the ambient sounds of the city.

There were trashcans lining the walkway. All were full. It smelled like a landfill without the airflow to ease the burn.

After a hundred feet, the walkway widened, yawning into the sidewalk of a busier street. It was there Farah was to meet them. Good thing, too. They'd be too far out in the open to get away with Noble carrying a loaded AK-47 and Bear carrying a half-naked and bloodied woman over his shoulder.

"Wait here." Noble pointed to a concrete bump out along the side of the building to their right. It was wide enough to conceal Bear. The big man took up position there with his pistol dangling from his hand.

Noble continued toward the end of the walkway. It brightened with every step. He lowered the rifle, tucked it behind his hip. Felt the warm barrel against his leg through his pants. Would he have to use the weapon again today? He'd find out in a second.

Farah's small car screeched to a stop at the curb. Bad move. It drew the attention of everyone around. She exited the car and dashed toward him.

"Where is she?"

Noble leaned past the side of the building that offered him cover and looked both ways down the street. There were dozens of people out, strolling along the sidewalk, standing in front of store windows.

"You're alone?" he said.

"Of course," she said. "Where is she?"

He jutted his chin toward the bump out. "Go get those doors open. We can't be out in the open long."

She backtracked to the car. Noble watched as she opened the rear door and took note of the cramped backseat he had occupied earlier. It was going to be a tight fit with O'Neil back there with him. She didn't smell as bad as the alley, but clearly they hadn't offered her a shower in recent days.

236

He called out to Bear. "Let's go."

The big man emerged with his arm around O'Neil. She had progressed to the point of being able to walk on her own. That would make things a little less conspicuous. But not much. They could shield her from view. Partly, at least.

Noble threaded his arm around her sweat-soaked back. She squinted up at the sun and stopped walking.

"This ain't the place to stop, darlin'," Bear said, pulling her along, out of Noble's grasp.

The open sidewalk separated them from the vehicle. Noble pushed ahead, scanned the street again. It didn't really matter if someone looked out of place. They only needed the few moments it would require to shove O'Neil in the backseat and take off.

He nodded at Farah. She slipped into the driver's seat. He hustled across the sidewalk, pulled the door open wide, looked back and gestured for Bear to move.

Bear stepped out from the shadows, his left arm moving ahead and outward as though he were swimming. He slid his other hand up O'Neil's back, onto her neck, and ducked her head for her. She went into the backseat on her left knee. Noble entered behind her, helping her across to the other side. By the time he closed his door, Bear was buckling up and Farah had her foot on the gas.

She bolted forward, wove around a city bus, and cruised into an intersection. "We made it."

Not quite.

Noble saw the other vehicle out of the corner of his eye, coming right at them.

## CHAPTER THIRTY-NINE

The van was white. Its hood rusted. Two men with heavy beards sat up front. The passenger was armed. The driver gripped the steering wheel with both hands and had a look on his face like he was ready to enter the next realm of existence.

Noble gleaned all of this with a sideways glance in a fraction of a second. Another moment or two and the men would be much closer to him after the van smashed into the side of the small car.

"Dammit!" Farah jerked the wheel and the car lurched to the left.

Noble and O'Neil whipped hard left then right. His head smacked against the window. Pain radiated across his face, through his jaw. He forced his eyes open, expecting to see the glass shattered. It wasn't. And the van that was moments away from impact was now braking hard in the middle of the intersection. Farah's defensive move had worked. Noble turned to get a better look. Momentum carried the van all the way across. The driver was reversing.

O'Neil turned to see what was going on. "They're after us."

"Observant," Noble said, then added. "I got Samara outside. Four rounds to the back. Khoury was taken care of inside. Another man in the hallway. How many more were there?"

Though O'Neil had glanced at him before, this felt like the first time she truly made eye contact. Her pupils were large, and Noble wondered what they had been drugging her with.

"Need you to think about this, O'Neil," he said. "How many others?"

"It's all a blur," she said, shaking her head. "I just...I can't think...I don't know."

"She's probably got a lot of a benzodiazepine coursing through her," Farah said. "It's gonna take an hour or maybe more before she's coherent."

"Looks coherent to me," Noble said. He turned his attention to the van following them. "Think you can lose them?"

He hadn't finished the question before a burst of automatic fire erupted from the van. The rounds slammed into their car. He grabbed the back of O'Neil's head and pulled her down below the seat. The rear window shattered, spraying them with shards of glass. Noble reached for the rifle on the floorboard.

It wasn't easy maneuvering the AK-47 in the back of the vehicle. He managed to poke Farah in the neck with the barrel, and almost smacked O'Neil in the face.

Noble swung the barrel over the top of the seat and popped up and took aim at the van. He emptied the magazine. Rounds hit the windshield, took out a headlight, tore through the grill and damaged the radiator. He couldn't tell if he got the driver, but the van whipped left violently. It rolled over and skidded on its side past the sidewalk into a building. Sparks rose, igniting a trail of gasoline. Somehow the van managed to miss nearby pedestrians, who were now scrambling away from the scene.

"Get us out of here," he yelled at Farah, who cursed at him in response. He stole a glance at the dash. She had pushed the car well past a hundred kilometers per hour.

O'Neil looked at him from between her hands, which were wrapped over her forehead. "Are we safe?"

"Define safe," Noble said.

"Think those guys had a way of communicating with others?" Bear said to Farah.

"Anything's possible, I suppose. We need to watch our six the rest of the way out."

"Where to next?" Noble said.

"South and west, about thirty miles," she said.

"What's there?"

"A friend who can help us get across the border."

"Us?"

She met his gaze in the rearview. "I'm done here. I'm coming in with you guys."

It wasn't a bad idea. She had the chops to get through this situation. Made her a good asset. Someone who they could use as they made the long trek back to Istanbul.

"And you trust this friend?" Noble asked.

"With my life," she said.

"Yeah, well, what about with my life?"

"I can stop here and let you sort it out."

"My father says stuff like that. He's an ass. Don't be an ass."

The dense city gave way to sparsely populated roads where traffic was nonexistent. They had driven to the east, gone south around Aleppo, and now headed west. Noble found it impossible to relax. He spent his time alternating between trying to stoke O'Neil's memory, and scanning their surroundings.

The van had been the only trouble they had encountered. How had those men known the exact moment they'd travel through the intersection? Someone had to be watching from nearby. That explained how Samara's body had been picked up in the span of three minutes.

Samara had to be deceased by now, though they wouldn't know any time soon. His people would keep it under wraps as long as they could. The information would leak at some point, and the analysts would confirm.

Farah turned off the paved road and navigated down a dirt trail for a mile. The house came into view as they crested a low hill. It looked like a multi-building compound, surrounded by a fence topped with razor wire.

"Who's he trying to keep out?" Bear said.

"You sure they're not trying to keep someone in?" Farah shot back. "And who says it's a he?" She stopped in front of the gate, rolled down her window. A pole stuck out of the ground, about four feet high. Farah reached for the touchpad, entered a code. The gate peeled back from the middle. She drove them through and parked behind a sand-colored Jeep Wrangler, similar to the one Noble and Bear had escaped D.C. in.

The front door opened and a tall, attractive dark-haired woman in her late thirties emerged from the shadows. She looked back, said something, then the door shut.

Farah exited the car. "Wait here a moment."

Noble felt chills race down his spine. Positioned between three separate structures, they were sitting ducks should this mystery woman decide to have them terminated. Wouldn't it be something to make it through the day they had in Aleppo, and end up dead out here in the middle of nowhere?

Farah turned back and waved them out of the vehicle. Bear was first to hit the ground. He jogged around the back of the car and opened O'Neil's door.

Noble walked up to the mystery woman. Farah introduced him, but never mentioned the other woman's name. He didn't pry.

She was sticking her neck out for them. If she chose not to reveal anything else about herself, fine by him.

"Does she need to wash up?" the woman asked as Bear assisted O'Neil.

"That'd be a good thing," Noble said.

"Follow me." The woman spun on her heel and walked toward the house. The door opened before she got there.

As Noble entered the shaded front porch, his eyes adjusted to the dim lighting inside. Two armed men dressed all in black stood in the foyer. They glanced over him before returning their gazes to the woman.

"You know your way around, Farah," the woman said. "Take her back to the guest quarters so she can clean herself. There should be something in the closet that fits her."

Farah and O'Neil disappeared down the hallway.

The woman turned to Noble and Bear. "Where is it you need to get to?"

"Istanbul," Bear said.

Her gaze drifted over their heads while she nodded with her finger pressed to her lip. "How quickly?"

"As quickly as you can," Noble said. "And with as little chance of us being stopped."

"I'm assuming you work for the Agency," she said. "Can't they help?"

"No support while in-country. Can't risk it. We need to get her back to Istanbul."

"Walk with me."

They followed her down a long hallway that opened up into a sunroom with floor-to-ceiling windows. Cold air billowed down from a large overhead vent. Noble waited under it for a few moments before stepping fully into the room. He followed the woman's outstretched finger and spotted the plane.

"You have your own air strip?" Bear said. "Is that your plane, too?"

She nodded.

Noble watched his partner for a moment. He had learned the big guy didn't care much for air travel. How would he handle being cooped up in a ten-seater?

"Pilot's on the way," she said. "He'll get you close to Istanbul. You'll have about forty miles to go on your own, but it's much safer on that side of the country than near Syria. If you'll agree to do me a favor to be named at a later date, I'll have a car waiting when you land."

The two men shared a glance. Bear said, "We can work with that."

Noble agreed.

The woman retreated to the end of the room where she pulled a bottle of whisky down from the cabinet. She filled three glasses half-way, carried two of them back to Noble and Bear.

"Might as well relax for a few," she said.

Again, Noble agreed. He threw his drink back and asked for another. She obliged.

Thirty minutes later, Farah and O'Neil returned. The agent looked like a new woman, dressed in a clean pair of khaki pants and a white shirt. Her hair looked darker when wet. It was brushed back, held in place with clips.

They filled the women in on the plan. Noble thought Farah didn't seem all that surprised that they were flying out.

Less than half an hour later they were thrust back in their plush leather seats as the ten-seater lifted off, destined for the other side of Turkey.

# CHAPTER FORTY

They arrived at the safe house later that afternoon when the sun hung low and the buildings cast long shadows across the highway and the smog gave the sky an alien appearance.

Serkan had met them at the private airstrip two hours out of town. Not forty minutes, as the woman had said. They climbed into a mini-van and settled in. Noble noted Serkan and Farah were on a first-name basis, but no conversation developed between them despite them both being seated up front. He took the middle row next to O'Neil. Bear had calmed down somewhat by mid-flight, and slept on the rear seat for the duration of the car ride.

The garage opened as they hit the driveway, as it always did. It was empty. Serkan pulled into the middle, cut the engine, and exited without a word. Was that because everyone present was familiar with the house?

Schofield met them in the kitchen. He stared at O'Neil for several seconds. She avoided his gaze and slipped past him, retreating to the table where Serkan sat leafing through a newspaper. Schofield turned his attention to Noble.

"They want you to call in." He handed Jack a slip of paper and the telephone. "Follow the prompts and no one will be able to trace the call back here."

Noble headed upstairs and placed the call.

"Jack?" the woman answered.

"Yeah. Is this Steele?"

"It is." There was a brief pause. "Everything went OK?"

"We're here, safe, alive. O'Neil's gonna need a hell of a lot of counseling after this, but as far as I can tell, there's no major injury to her."

"To her," Steele said. "But to our intelligence community...."

"That's what I figured. The only way they kept her for two weeks and did so little damage is—"

"She gave them everything." Steele sighed into the phone. "Did Schofield leave?"

"No, he's here now. Greeted us when we entered."

"Damn him."

"What's up?"

"There's a relationship between him and O'Neil."

"Was."

"What do you mean, was?"

"Schofield told me the night before we left for Aleppo that she called it off a while ago. Hadn't spoken to him since. Was over a month."

"He was instructed to leave."

Noble traced the barrel of his H&K next to him on the mattress. "I can remove him."

"The damage is done, he's there now. Keep a close eye on him and if you notice him pressuring O'Neil, get in the middle of it. You have to get through tonight. Tomorrow you'll receive transport to Germany."

"What's in Germany?"

"A safer place."

"Flying?"

"Not initially. They'll play it by ear." The line went silent for a few moments. "Hey, Jack?"

"Yeah, Steele?"

"Good job."

She ended the call. Noble went through the duffel bag on his bed, grabbed a change of clothes, and took a hot shower. Red-tinted water circled the drain. When he thought back on it, he wasn't sure how they'd managed to survive the day. What were the odds? They had better training, sure. But to take on so many and come out unscathed? For the first time in his life, Noble realized he was living on borrowed time, more so than the common stiff.

After his shower, he made his way back downstairs and took O'Neil to the side.

"Schofield had been instructed to leave," he said. "You want me to get him out of here?"

Her listless eyes fell upon Schofield, who stood in front of the stove. The room was filled with the smell of searing lamb. "I'm OK with him here."

Noble nodded and walked past her. She reached out and grabbed his arm. He stopped and looked down at her. "What is it?"

"Taavi," she said. "I'm assuming since you found me, you found him, too."

Noble nodded, recalling his initial meeting with the man in his restaurant.

She continued. "I'd like to apologize to him, for getting him in this mess. And thank him, too."

"I can't let you leave here," Noble said.

She cast her gaze downward and sighed. "I really—"

"You've been through so much, but the ordeal isn't over. They found you here once, they can do it again. The safest place for you is in this house with four trained men watching over you."

"With you and your partner there's six."

"Not for a couple of hours."

"What do you mean?"

"Go grab a pen and pad of paper. Write down whatever you want to tell Taavi. Bear and I will deliver it to him."

For the first time, O'Neil smiled. It wasn't the beautiful smile he'd seen in her dossier. There was a sadness behind it, as though she realized she'd never see Taavi again. The man meant something to her beyond being an informant. A lover? Father figure? Both?

Noble and Bear skipped out on dinner to head into town. Farah followed them into the garage.

"Leaving?" she asked.

"Running an errand," Noble said.

"Be gone long?"

Noble shrugged. "Not sure."

"I'm taking off shortly. Flight out departs tonight."

"Where're you headed?"

She shrugged, smiled, said, "Not sure."

"Well, wherever it is, hope you get a fresh start. Sorry things went the way they did."

"I'm not. I never got into this line of work to stay settled in one place. At least now I can go somewhere I'll enjoy."

Noble wondered where that might be. She had a look that would allow her to assimilate in the Middle East, Africa, Central and South America, and even back home in the States.

Farah gave each man a hug, then climbed the stairs into the house.

Thirty minutes later Noble and Bear entered the small restaurant. Uri sat in the back corner, giving him a view of the street and entrance. The swinging door separating the dining room and kitchen whipped open. Taavi emerged, waved Uri off, and hurried up to the two men.

"You have news? Is she safe?"

Noble took the man's outstretched hand. "She's alive. Not too damaged, at least physically. She's safe, awaiting transport home."

Taavi wept, drawing the attention of the restaurant's patrons. Even Uri cocked an eyebrow at the outburst. After he composed himself, he led Noble and Bear to the back. They piled into his cramped office. Uri caught the closing door, blocking their escape. He eyed Bear reaching for his concealed pistol.

"No need for that," Uri said. "We are all friends here."

"Uri," Taavi said. "Go wait for me in the dining room. As you said, we are all friends here. I'd rather you keep an eye on things out there."

Uri hesitated a moment, his gaze flipping between Noble and Bear. Finally, he nodded, said, "Yessir," and left.

The door fell shut and Taavi wiped the lingering tears from his cheeks. "Where is she?"

"Somewhere safe," Bear said. "She starts her journey home tomorrow."

"Can you bring me to see her?"

"No." Noble reached into his pocket and pulled out the note O'Neil had written. "She wanted me to give you this."

"What's it say?"

"Dunno. Didn't look."

Taavi eyed him for several seconds before taking the slip of paper from Noble's hands. He started to unfold it, but thought better of it, instead tucking it under his keyboard.

"Taavi," Noble said. "I want to ask you something."

"Sure, go ahead."

"Did you leave anything out last time we spoke? Or has anything new come to mind since then?"

He stared at the wall between the two men. His head shook a few centimeters to either side like it was stuck in a loop. "I told you everything exactly as it had happened."

"And the name Khoury means nothing to you?"

"I've never had dealings with him. As far as anything coming to me since we spoke, there's really nothing. I wasn't as involved in her dealings as you might think."

"What about Wahid Samara?" Bear asked. He stretched his arm across the room after Taavi glanced at the door. "What do you know about him?"

"I recognize that name." He straightened in his chair. "I've seen it in the news."

"Don't screw with us." Bear leaned forward. "And keep your hands where we can see them for a second here. Tell us what you know about Samara?"

Taavi licked his lips as he folded his hands in his lap. His eyes darted to the call button on his desk. "She had mentioned Samara in passing at lunch that day."

"As someone she was investigating?" Noble asked. "Or someone she feared?"

Taavi shook his head. "It's all so jumbled now. Was it before we were spotted or right after? I can't put it together anymore."

"Did she mention any reason why Samara would want to have her kidnapped?"

Tears welled in Taavi's eyes again. The mention of O'Neil's ordeal likely played out a scene in his mind of her being beaten by a handful of men. "I don't know what would have happened if you two didn't find her."

"She'd be dead," Bear said. "Come on, Jack. We're done with him for now."

They cut through the kitchen toward the front of the house. As they pushed through the doorway, they found Uri standing there, waiting for them in the empty dining room with both hands behind his back.

# CHAPTER FORTY-ONE

"Y ou ever know a guy by the name of Alex Kairis?" Noble asked. "Served in the Mossad, back in the eighties."

Uri nodded once. "Good man. How do you know him?"

"Friends with my father. Used to come tutor me in Krav Maga."

Uri narrowed his eyes as though he were sizing Noble up. "You can fight."

Not a question, an observation. "Little bit."

Bear chuckled. "Don't believe him. He let an old man beat him up during training."

Uri fished a stack of cards out of his pocket. He peeled off the top two, handed one to each man. "Call me if I can be of service."

"Thanks, but we're heading out soon."

Uri smiled, said, "Is there not an airport a few miles from here? My skills go far beyond protecting a little restaurant in Istanbul."

They both pocketed Uri's card and left through the front door. The city was cast in an orange haze of streetlights lining the sidewalks.

"Wanna go check that park out again?" Noble said.

"Get outta here," Bear said.

They drove back to the safe house. Half the lights on the street were out. But not their destination. Every window burst with light. Bear pulled into the driveway and waited there for a moment.

"What's up with that?" He pointed at the garage door. "Every other time it's opened up."

"Guess they're not watching the security camera feed." Noble rolled down his window and stuck his head out for a moment. He leaned back in, said, "Cut the engine."

Bear did, and the motor knocked for a few seconds then choked into retreat. The still night was interrupted by the occasional motorist passing on the nearby highway.

"What's going on?" Bear said. "You spooked?"

"Dunno." Noble opened his door and swung his leg out. "Let's go in."

They walked up to the garage door to inspect the camera mounted on the corner. A small red dot indicated it was recording. Bear stood underneath and waved his arms, then tapped the garage door. It didn't budge. They crossed the front walkway to the entrance.

Bear said, "Door's cracked."

Noble retrieved his H&K. He glanced back at the street, scanning for faces in the shadows. Satisfied they weren't being watched by anyone in plain view, he crouched and stuck the barrel into the opening and pushed the door. Inch-by-inch, it creaked and groaned, then thudded to a stop. Jack pushed on the door. It didn't move. He put his shoulder into it and got a little more out of it. Something heavy waited on the other side, but they weren't doing anything to counter him.

It was dead weight.

Bear leaned in and offered a hand. The door opened up a few more feet.

"Sweet Jesus," Bear said.

Noble followed his gaze to the smeared blood at their feet. He pushed through the doorway and cleared the entry foyer. There laying behind the door face up was Serkan. His glazed over eyes stared up at the ceiling. His mouth twisted open in an eternal silent scream.

Bear came in, cursed, and said, "We need to clear the house. They might still be here."

"No, they're not."

"How do you know?"

"See how sticky that blood is by the door? How ashen his skin already is? This happened shortly after we left."

"Come on, let's do this together."

The house felt alive in that moment, pulsing with energy. What the hell had happened here? Serkan had been shot in the back because he was trying to get away. He'd made it to the door, turned the knob, started opening it. The shooter put an end to that.

Noble turned to the staircase. There were several bloody handprints on the wall. They'd check that out in a minute. First, they moved into the living room. The slider behind the couch, in front of the dining table, was open a couple feet. The patio light burned bright, illuminating the deck. Noble craned his head, saw nobody out there.

Bear moved past him. "No one on the furniture or floor over here."

Noble started toward the kitchen and stopped at the sight of blue jeans-clad legs poking out from behind the island. One black combat boot was missing. The other was untied, the laces loose. He side-stepped slowly to his left in an attempt to get a view of the door leading to the garage. It looked secure.

As his gaze swept back, he noted the jagged lines of blood along the wall. Closer inspection revealed there were three, and sometimes four, individual lines about the width of a fingertip. Blood tracked on the floor into the kitchen.

Whoever lay dead in there had been shot elsewhere.

Bear was at the backdoor, peering out into the darkness. He flipped the switch off and continued to stare.

"Anything?" Noble asked.

"A little blood. No bodies. No one out here."

"I'm gonna go check out this situation in the kitchen."

"What situation?" But Bear didn't need to ask. His downward gaze as he turned around indicated he knew. He held up his pistol to cover the garage door for his partner.

Noble moved in and found the man on his stomach. There were several wounds on his back. His right arm, hand, and fingers were coated in crimson. He felt the guy's neck for a pulse. There was none. Noble didn't need to turn him over to identify him. His blond hair gave him away.

"Who is it?" Bear asked.

"Schofield."

"This the work of Samara?"

"Couldn't begin to surmise who did this." He stood up and met the gaze of his partner across the island. He recalled the handprints in the stairwell. An imaginary fist pummeled his stomach. There were more bodies waiting. "Let's check upstairs."

They traveled back to the entry foyer. Bear stopped to secure the door, then followed Noble upstairs. The crime scene worsened as they reached the landing. Just past the corner was one of Schofield's men. A chef's knife stuck out of his back. His throat had been slit ear to ear. Most of his blood had seeped into the carpet.

Further down the hallway, a bedroom door held on by one

hinge. Noble led the way. In the room he found Schofield's other guy on the bed, a single gunshot wound to his forehead.

"Lucky bastard must've slept through it," Bear said.

Noble felt the imaginary fist latch onto to his gut and twist. "O'Neil."

"They were putting her up in the room next to ours."

"And Farah," Noble added. "She was supposed to leave tonight. Presumably Serkan was to take her to the airport."

"We don't know that. He might've dropped her off, came back, and walked into this mess. Come on, let's check O'Neil's room."

They crossed to the other end of the hallway. Their bedroom door was smashed in the center and rested against the wall. Their duffel bags were overturned, the contents strewn about the room. What was missing?

Noble glanced down at the bloody footprints on the carpet. They traveled in every direction, in and out of their room, back down the hallway, and right up to O'Neil's door, where Bear had stopped and knocked the way a timid five-year-old knocks on his parents' door six o'clock on a Saturday morning.

"The hell, man," Noble said, shoving his partner in the back. "Open it."

Neither man had the benefit of seeing the contents of the room prior to that moment. They had no idea if the stripped-down bed, bare walls, and single dresser were the norm.

Bear was the first to enter. He went straight for the closet and opened it.

"Nothing," he said.

Noble squatted at the threshold and studied the carpet. The last bloody footstep was on the outside of the room. Inside, it was pristine.

"Check the dresser," Noble said.

Bear pulled each drawer out, tossing a couple onto the bed. "All empty."

Noble entered the room, dropped to a knee and looked underneath the bed, then lifted the mattress.

"Think you're gonna find her under there?" Bear said.

"Doubtful," Noble said, not feeling like returning the sarcasm. He found in such cases it was best to ignore it all together. Make the sarcastic one feel like an ass. "But none of her stuff is in here."

"How much stuff did she have?"

"Serkan went out, bought her a bag, some toiletries, couple changes of clothes. All of that's gone."

"They found her? They came in here, shot everyone up, and took her again?"

"And took all her stuff, too? I don't think so." Noble turned toward the hallway and left the room. "You saw the condition she was in when we found her in Aleppo. Think they care if she has enough toothpaste or a clean bra to wear?"

Bear grabbed the back of his head and exhaled. "You don't think...?"

Noble stopped, looked back. "O'Neil did this."

# PART IV

# CHAPTER FORTY-TWO

Noble stared up at the popcorn ceiling. It had a yellow tint to it he figured developed from the time it was built up through the late '90s, before they banned smoking in the building. The mattress he rested on was firm. Almost too much so. He might as well have been on his back in the street. Rest evaded him despite a greater than twenty-four-hour stretch without sleep.

Steele ushered them out of Istanbul on a private transport to Germany within minutes of receiving the call about the safe house slaughter. Noble filled them in on the losses at the house and O'Neil's disappearance. Steele asked no questions.

From Germany they were flown straight to Fort Meade in Maryland, a few scant miles from D.C. Steele and four men Noble had never seen and who were wearing dark suits met them. Noble and Bear were separated on the tarmac, each hustled into different vehicles. Noble's rode behind Bear's and never did it leave his sight until after they had arrived at Langley.

He was led to the small efficiency and told to make himself comfortable. It had all the comforts of hell, including the rock-hard mattress. At least there was a microwave, two-burner stove, and a fridge stocked with eggs and jugged water. One door led out and it was locked from the other side with four deadbolts.

Up to this point he hadn't been asked a single question about what had happened. The men who drove him to Langley weren't all that talkative. Steele rode alone in her personal vehicle. At least he thought she was alone. He never got a good view as she pulled the door open, and the tinted windows made it impossible to see inside.

A rap on the door jostled Noble from his thoughts. He swung one leg over the side of the bed and sat up and stopped himself from walking to the door. Not like he could open it. The locks were on the other side. His visitor had access if they wanted it.

The knock was a courtesy.

"Yeah," he called out.

"Are you decent?" Steele asked.

Noble looked down at himself. The shorts covered everything she didn't want to see. "Sure, come on in."

Four deadbolts unlocked with slides and clicks, the door pushed open. A whirl of distilled air slipped into the room. How had they managed to keep the hallway so cool, yet his room felt like Florida in April? Not too bad, but still a bit too warm.

"Hell of a week, huh?" Steele forced a smile.

Noble saw the woman in a new light. His first time meeting her had been following the Witherspoon incident in D.C. It all had happened so fast, he hadn't had time to process it. Now he understood who Steele was. What she was capable of.

"You two exceeded all expectations," she said.

"Good to know."

"I'm serious. That was not an easy job. The odds were at best fifty-fifty."

"Why would you waste all that time and money training us, only to send us over there to be butchered?"

"I'm not an optimist, Jack. Fifty percent is as close to perfect odds as I'll lay."

"How's Bear holding up?"

"Logan? He's fine. Had a nice talk with him." She glanced back at the blue vinyl chair nestled in the corner and sat down, crossing her legs and resting her hands in her lap. "Now I need to speak with you."

"About what?"

"What happened?"

Noble took a few moments to collect his thoughts. Since leaving Istanbul, the entire trip played over and over in his mind at a rapid clip. He brain-dumped, starting with his first interactions with Schofield, Taavi, the park bench.

For her part, Steele never interjected and kept a steady gaze on him. If she thought anything of what he told her, she kept it to herself. Never gave a single tell. Must be a hell of a poker player, Noble thought as he regurgitated his story.

"When we met Farah, I didn't know what to think. Her contact info was on the inside of the security system cover. Matched what Schofield had given us. She did her part, isolated a couple of locations. I was concerned that she might be working against us, but when we needed her, she pulled through without prompting."

Steele finally spoke up. "You didn't place a call or anything to her?"

"Yes and no. She showed up at the first location, took out a hostile. After rescuing O'Neil, we had the satellite phone, called her. She was still nearby." He thought about reaching the alley, and Samara's bullet-ridden body missing.

"What is it?" Steele asked.

"I filled that prick Samara with four out of five rounds from an AK-47 at the top of the building. But when we got down there he was gone. I figured they drove him out, but recalling the location now, I can't see how anyone could have fit a vehicle down there."

"Was he dead?"

"On his way."

"You're sure?"

"As sure as I can be from fifty-plus vertical feet."

"Maybe they carried him out?"

"No blood trail."

"You're sure he couldn't have walked out?"

"Again, no blood trail." They stared at each other for a few moments. Noble clenched his eyelids and lowered his chin to his chest and shook his head.

"What is it?"

"Body armor."

"Body armor?"

"I aimed dead center. From that distance with that rifle it gave me the best chance to terminate him. Bastard was ready for it. Ready for us. He's still alive."

Steele pulled a small blue spiral bound notebook from her pocket and jotted something down, presumably a reminder to have analysts start looking for signs Samara was still alive. She closed the notebook with the pen inside, but didn't put it back in her pocket.

"Tell me what happened next," she said.

"We loaded up in Farah's car, almost got splattered by a van who tried to give chase afterward, then made it out to Farah's contact's house. She gave us transport to Turkey."

"Did you catch the woman's name?"

Noble shook his head.

"Remember anything about her?"

He shrugged.

"Think you can pick out on a map where she lived?"

"What's this about? You think she's involved?"

Steele said nothing.

"The woman got us out of the country. Makes her an asset in my book." He paused. "Speaking of assets, is Farah on the payroll here? I never could figure that out."

Steele shifted the notebook to her other hand. "I won't confirm that we've ever paid her, but she is not our employee or contractor."

"So she was Schofield's contact."

"She's a lot of people's contact. Tell me about how she acted at the safe house."

Noble thought about this. He didn't have much interaction with Farah once they arrived in Istanbul. "We got there. I cleaned up, changed, and told O'Neil I'd deliver a message to Taavi. Farah stopped me on the way out. She said she would be gone before we got back. And when we got back, she wasn't there."

"Neither was O'Neil."

"Right."

Steele opened her notebook and clicked the tip of her pen. She started to write something, but stopped and looked up at Noble. "Did Farah ever give you any indication that she knew of O'Neil prior to this?"

"No, and neither did O'Neil of her. O'Neil was out of it until around the time we landed in Turkey. Whatever they sedated her with, it did the trick." He watched as she wrote something down. "What's going on here, Steele? What aren't you telling me?"

Steele looked up at him with a cold stare. The woman gave nothing away. "I'm simply gathering facts, Jack. At this point, I have no idea what is going on here. If you want me level with you—"

"I do."

"Well, then, let me continue without interruption." She raised an eyebrow and went silent for a few moments. Satisfied Noble wasn't going to say anything else, she continued. "O'Neil obviously had enemies outside the Agency. But there may have been some within. She might have had motivation to kill Schofield, too, based on their past relationship. But to wipe out his entire team?"

Noble waited a couple of seconds, then said, "No witnesses that way."

"Back to Samara. If the line of thinking is that he didn't die, and wasn't injured, is correct, could he have led the attack? Considering what they were able to arrange with O'Neil's broad daylight abduction, that isn't out of the question."

"That was my first thought," he said. "Not Samara, because at the time he was dead to me, but someone in his group...the people in the van, or contacts they had in Istanbul. But here's the thing."

She leaned forward, notebook wide open in one hand, pen in the other, ready to scribble on the page.

"All of O'Neil's stuff was missing. It wasn't much, but clothing, toiletries, a couple books. All gone."

"What kind of terrorist takes that into consideration?" Steele said more to herself than Noble.

"Right, that's exactly what I thought."

Steele rose and paced across the room with the notebook folded in her hand. She gnawed on the end of the pen, almost like she was smoking a cigar. She was an athletic woman, trim and toned, with healthy skin. Practically wrinkle free. Noble doubted she had smoked a day in her life. Maybe hadn't ever taken a drink.

"Could the whole thing have been set up?" Steele said.

"Finding her?" Noble asked.

"Abducting her." Steele stopped in front of him. "Think about it. Broad daylight. Never mind that the police turned a blind eye.

She allowed herself to be caught in that situation. This woman was one of the best. Better than Cribbs on her worst day. She was that good. This never should have happened. Never sat right with me or Cribbs or McKenzie that it had happened."

"They beat her, though. You saw the pictures."

Steele found her way back to the chair. "I know what you saw, and I know how you must feel about it. But believe me, we've seen far worse done to our people. She was in captivity for two weeks. Not a broken bone on her? No fingernails taken? No fingertips taken, for that matter. Why?"

"Simple. She sang."

"Did she? Are we sure of that? Did she tell you that? Are you qualified to interrogate her in a way that feels friendly to get that information out of her?"

Noble sat there, said nothing. He felt like his mother was lecturing him over eating her fresh chocolate chip cookies before dinner when he'd been instructed not to.

"I'm just throwing questions out there, Jack. Something doesn't add up here. We've got a team processing the house right now. What they come back with might clear up a few things."

"Such as?"

"How many shooters. Doesn't sit well with me that only one person did all that. Not with the men inside that house. Even Serkan, a driver, had enough training to make the odds severely not in her favor, four versus one." Steele rose and walked to the door. She stopped there and looked back at him. "Get dressed. I'll see you and Bear at my office in thirty."

# CHAPTER FORTY-THREE

Noble and Bear were led through a maze of corridors to a windowless office in a building near the edge of the facility. Beyond it was a stretch of forest. The man escorting them opened the door and stepped away. The room was bigger than Noble had expected. Steele sat at a desk in the center of the room. An older man dressed in a grey suit and tie was seated opposite her. McKenzie nodded at the men, then turned his gaze on Steele

They entered and heard a gruff Chicago accent from the right. "You boys did a helluva job over there."

Noble felt an iron press down on his chest and went rigid. Bear glanced over at Cribbs and nodded.

Cribbs stepped around the big man and faced them both. He stood there for a long moment, eyes set on Noble, who did his best to avoid looking at the man. He focused on his breath, in and out, cool and warm.

Cribbs extended his hand. After a few seconds of it dangling in front of Noble, Cribbs said, "Don't be a damned fool, take it. You won't get this opportunity that often with me."

"I don't deserve it," Noble said, looking at Steele instead of Cribbs. "We didn't bring her home."

"But you got her out of Aleppo, and might've stumbled on something far worse than an agent in captivity."

"Why don't you guys take a seat?" Steele rose and gestured at the empty chairs in front of her desk.

Noble glanced at Steele once again. She looked away for a moment, but that was all it took. They'd unearthed something else, and when taken with what Noble and Bear had gone through, it led them to an even more dire discovery.

After they were all seated, Noble spoke first. "I've been thinking about our conversation, Steele. I'm still trying to put these pieces together. But the thing that sticks out is this possibility that Samara had on body armor."

"Body armor?" Bear said.

Noble nodded. "When I looked back on the scene, there was no way a car got to him. Not down that alley. And if anyone had carried him, there should've been blood everywhere, but we hardly found any."

"There was plenty on the ground where he'd collapsed."

"True, but we don't know that was his, or that it came from a fatal wound. Maybe I got him in the arm with a round. Doesn't matter. He got up and walked away. Do you think he walked around with protective gear on all the time? It's doubtful. Someone tipped him off."

"Then how come we found Khoury unprepared? He wasn't wearing a vest."

"No, he wasn't. Perhaps there was tension between them. What if Samara let Khoury die there?" Noble twisted in his seat and faced Bear. "Doesn't it seem odd how little resistance we faced before finding O'Neil? I mean, how many guards did we encounter in that building? They're holding an American operative, and we only have to go through a couple guys to reach her?"

"It was a setup," Bear said.

Steele cleared her throat, drawing the attention of all four men. "I'm beginning to agree with you, and things only get worse from here."

"What is it?" Bear asked.

"Either of you speak Romanian?" McKenzie said.

"Romanian? What?"

"Spanish, French, Russian," Bear said. "That's it."

Noble said, "What did you want to be when you grew up?"

"This is serious," McKenzie said. "O'Neil had eight direct reports. When the abduction went down, they split into two groups. Two men came home. Checked in within five minutes of wheels down." He took a sip from his mug. "Two were dead. The other four went to Bucharest, Romania. They left a trail, whether knowingly or not. We never heard from them, though, and only recently located them hiding out at an apartment rented in a fictitious name."

"Have you made contact?" Noble asked.

"Yes," McKenzie said.

"Could they offer any insight into O'Neil's dealings?"

"No," McKenzie said.

"What'd they say?"

"Nothing."

"Why not? Couldn't extract anything out of them?"

"They were all dead."

Noble leaned back in his chair, paused, asked, "Any idea who did it?"

"We have a few suspects," Steele said.

"The two men that came back Stateside," Noble said. "How long's it been since you've spoken with them?"

"They were put on leave," Steele said. "We have it set up to alert if they attempt to travel outside of the country."

"Have they?" Bear asked.

Steele directed her gaze at him. "Not that we are aware."

"If they travelled back," Bear said. "They could have been in place near that apartment, waiting for O'Neil's return."

"There's no way she took all those men out at the house in Istanbul," Cribbs said. "Too much ground to cover against highly-trained agents. She's as good as any I've ever seen, but even then, there's just no way. And then, presuming she's the shooter in Bucharest, to terminate four men from her own team? We're talking about men *I* had a hand in training. She had help."

"*If* it was her," McKenzie said. "We have to remain a little paranoid, but let's not jump to conclusions without the intelligence to back it up."

"What does the intelligence say?" Noble asked.

McKenzie took a few moments to collect himself before answering. "It doesn't say a damn thing."

The room went silent after that. McKenzie was the first to leave, followed by Cribbs, who offered his hand to Noble and Bear again and told them he was proud of their actions.

"I'd fight alongside either of you," he said as he left Steele's office.

Noble and Bear returned to their seats opposite Steele. She had poured three cups of coffee. Noble refused creamer and sugar. He always did. Coffee was a pick-me-up and nothing else. He didn't want to become addicted to the stuff like his old man, and figured if he drank it black, he'd never enjoy the taste. He took a swig and battled the bitter aftertaste.

"What's next for us?" he asked Steele.

"You're flying out on a private jet in a few hours," she said. "Taking you there myself. It's not as tough to get you into Romania, but we're going to limit the amount of time you have to spend standing in line."

"You think O'Neil will be watching?" Bear asked.

Steele tapped her pen on a desk calendar in a chaotic fashion. "I think if she went through the trouble to set up her own safe house under a fictitious name, she's probably corralled a few assets to work for her. The airport would be a good spot to have an informant."

"Why Romania, though?"

"Easy to blend in for her." Steele closed her eyes and leaned back in her high-back leather chair. Tension drained from her face. She came to, said, "I can't figure out the end game here. She can't be working with Samara. I just don't see it."

"Then who?" Noble said. "I can't see any other scenario."

"No offense, Jack, but you haven't been around this business long enough to develop those kind of instincts. Trust the people we have sifting through the data. What they uncover, combined with what you find on the ground, will bring everything into light."

A silent lull offered Steele the chance to spin in her chair and grab two packets off the credenza. She set one in front of each man.

"What's this?" Bear asked.

"Creds, IDs, cash, credit cards," she said. "Everything you'll need."

"Will we have a contact when we arrive?" Noble asked.

Steele shook her head. "On your own. The apartment address is noted in there. We've got a place for you to stay across the street. Surveillance should be simple."

As she had said, Noble hadn't been around all that long, but even he knew nothing should be taken for granted as simple.

Steele reached into her pocket and pulled out a pill bottle, set it down in front of Bear.

He held it up, shook it, gave her a quizzical look.

"Take two now," she said, "and you'll be out before the plane races down the runway."

"How...?"

"I know more about you two than your own mothers."

# CHAPTER FORTY-FOUR

Bucharest was blanketed in a late-afternoon orange haze as Noble and Bear pulled up to the curb behind the apartment building. The cab driver collected his fare, then drove off. The two men didn't linger on the frozen sidewalk long. They hustled around to the side entrance, unlocked the door, and stepped in from the cold.

A young woman with a baby strapped to her chest stood in front of a long bank of mail slots, rifling through a stack of envelopes. Her long blond hair was pulled back in a loose ponytail. She glanced back. Dark circles hung under her eyes. Her gaze lingered on Bear for a few extra seconds while a crease formed over her eyebrows.

He'd learned three phrases in Romanian before he passed out on the plane. A greeting, a goodbye, and directions to the bathroom. He spoke all three of them to the woman. She looked away without responding.

In the hallway, Noble nudged the big man. "Good job in there. Gonna have the police at our door within the first hour."

"Shut up."

"That all you got?"

"Still groggy from whatever Steele gave me."

"Valium, probably."

"Whatever it was, had some vivid dreams on the way over."

"You'll have to write them down for me. Need something to read on the toilet."

"Ass."

Noble checked that the hallway was clear, withdrew his pistol—flying private had its privileges—and opened the door to their new temporary home in Bucharest.

The place looked like it was decorated thirty years ago. The furniture had visible dust on it. The kitchen table might've been in an episode of *Happy Days*. Bear went straight to the olive-green refrigerator and opened it up.

"Anything in there?"

"A black apple."

"Guess we're calling for take-out. Get back into that phrasebook you found."

Noble pulled back the drapes and raised the blinds on each of the four windows looking across the street. He counted three up from the ground, and two over to the right.

"That the place?" Bear said from next to him, startling Noble.

"When'd you get there?"

"Like a cheetah, bro."

"Puma," Noble said. "You're like a puma."

"Whatever."

"Yeah, that's the place. Can't see anything with the sunset reflecting off the windows, though."

"Really expect to see anything? I mean, is someone gonna come back there after four of our agents were found dead?"

"Have you thought about that?" Noble turned to the side and

leaned against the window. "Why would they go into hiding, only for O'Neil to kill them?"

"We can go to the morgue and ask."

"Don't think that's gonna get us far."

"Right, so let the people back at Langley do their jobs, and we'll do ours."

"Which is?"

"Watch that building non-stop and take note of who goes in and out."

"Sounds exciting."

"I got plenty of sleep on the plane," Bear said. "I'll take first shift. Why don't you go rest?"

"I'll grab us some food first."

Bear patted his stomach. "Chinese?"

"Sure, man, whatever you say."

Noble grabbed his coat and a scarf and headed back out into the cold, passing the woman by the mailboxes again. He kept his stare from lingering too long. Was she a lookout? Or just someone who had far too many letters to mail? Maybe a pen pal for half the Romanian army?

The sun had slipped behind the city skyline, sending the temperature plunging further. Noble doubted he'd ever get used to anything below fifty degrees. Not after spending the majority of his life in Florida. The icy sidewalk proved a challenge for the first thirty seconds until he got his legs under him. From there, he managed a brisk walk, passing the occasional person or couple crazy enough to be outside. Of course, to them the weather was nothing new.

He continued on for three blocks, passing six bars, three sit-down restaurants, and two coffee shops. The aroma of fresh-ground beans sliced through the frigid air. He was shocked that the smell enticed him. He didn't stop for a cup though. That'd keep him awake and a few hours of rest was much needed.

The sign for a *Chinese Garden* lit up in wondrous neon red and green. Noble chuckled at the sight of it. He entered the deserted dining room and walked up to the counter. The menu on the wall was written in Romanian, so he ordered based on pictures, two meals for him, and two for Bear. Within ten minutes and one downed Coke, he was on his way back to the apartment.

The cold bothered him a little less as he trudged down the sidewalk. Hopefully it wouldn't chill the food too much. He couldn't recall a microwave in the apartment. Noble slowed his pace, looked around, took in his surroundings.

Had the slaughtered men walked this same stretch?

He tried to imagine what their final days were like.

It all started with O'Neil's abduction. The remainder of her team fled, presumably on her orders should something happen to her. Their destinations were predetermined. Two back home, four here to a safe house off the books. How long ago had she set it up? And for what purpose? The questions could only be answered if the initial presumption was correct. Noble hadn't considered until now that O'Neil's team might have been acting without her knowledge. They could have set her up to take the fall in Istanbul, not expecting she'd be rescued. So when she returned, more psychologically damaged than physically, they acted quickly and took her out. *They* being the two men who returned Stateside. If that was the case, then it led Noble to believe that O'Neil had a hand in the unknown safe house. The other four men were waiting for her, only to be killed by the Stateside agents.

So who were these two men? Were they still operating with the nation's best interest in mind? He needed more info on them, some background history. Would Steele be willing to offer that up? It was clear they still thought of Noble and Bear as newbies, and rightly so. They had trusted the men to do more than play lookout and be the ones to rush in, guns drawn, to take out the bad guys in Aleppo. Why not here?

He saw a flash of orange up ahead. The flame died, leaving behind the small glow of the cherry of a cigarette. Noble continued toward the man who was wearing a dark trench coat, leaning back against a brick wall. The man nodded when Noble was within a few feet.

"Evening," Noble said.

"Evening," the guy said back.

Noble slowed for a step, eyeing the man who'd spoke to him with an American accent. Was it unusual? Hell if he knew, he'd never been to Romania before. But the fact the guy seemed like an older version of himself and had a stare that looked through him as though he were absorbing the surroundings and playing out an attack in his mind moments before he carried it out. Reminded him of the look always present in Schofield's eyes. An experienced, hardened view of the world.

The guy looked away as he drew his cigarette to his lips. Noble glanced in the same direction, saw someone across the street wearing a jacket with a fur-lined hood turn away. He watched as the person entered a building that appeared as though it might connect to the one he and Bear were staying in.

Scanning the facade, he tried to pinpoint the apartment that could be theirs. Was Bear watching? What was going on behind him now?

Noble had to do something.

And he did.

# CHAPTER FORTY-FIVE

The level of activity in such a condensed area was lower than Noble would have expected. Perhaps due to the hour, or the weather conditions. The first snowflakes settled on top of the iced sidewalk as he passed the man with the cigarette. He caught a glint three stories up. Bear signaling him, he supposed. Over the hum of distant traffic and far off pedestrians, Noble heard the distinct *chunk-chunk* of the man racking his pistol's slide.

Years as a quarterback had taught Noble how to take a fall. He never would have survived his freshman year with a deficient offensive line without the skill. This would be trickier though. He had to fumble the items he clutched in his arms.

He planted his right foot awkwardly in the ice so it slid out. At the same time, he released his right hand's grip on the bottom of the take-out bag. He spun around and got a view of the man as he flicked his cigarette into the street. It arced high and sparks flew like fireworks as it collided with the asphalt. The guy had a smirk on his face, which faded.

*Not as easy of a target now, eh?*

Noble had pulled his pistol mid-way through his twist and covered it with the second takeout bag. Maybe that's why the guy's eyes widened twice their normal size when the thunderous shots rang out.

The first bullet missed and slammed into the building a foot away from the guy's torso. The second one was less off-target. The guy fell back against the wall, still on his feet, dropping his pistol as he clutched his stomach.

Noble was on the ground now. He scrambled to his feet on the ice and found it much more difficult to get up than it was to fall without cracking his skull open.

The other man staggered away with his back to Noble. The entrance to the building whipped open before the guy got there. He fell in, his feet hung out on the sidewalk. Someone dragged him inside.

Noble was up, half-walking and half-skating toward the door.

"Look out, Jack!" Bear's voice boomed from overhead. The echo traveled down the street for a mile at least.

He spun to see another man dressed similarly and wielding a submachine gun coming toward him. Three rounds exploded. This time Noble didn't try to hit the ground gracefully. He dove and slid along, trying to get behind a parked car. Two more rounds slammed into the ice beside him, chunks pelting his face.

He rolled over onto his back and fired without aiming. Dangerous, considering the environment. But it had to be done. The other guy retreated to where he had emerged.

Noble saw the muzzle blast and heard the rifle round from three stories up at the same time. A few seconds later the man who had shot at him stumbled toward the sidewalk and collapsed. By the time Jack reached him, a pool of blood surrounded the man's torso. Noble turned him over. There was still life in his eyes.

"Who are you?" he said to the guy.

The man coughed. Blood plumed from his mouth, settled around his lips, dripped toward the sidewalk in thin strands. His breathing was shallow, rapid, noisy. Bear's shot had likely torn through his lungs and done a ton of additional damage along the way. He wasn't going to make it.

Noble went through the man's pockets, finding a wallet and an envelope. He shoved both in his coat and turned around. The first man's shoe had come off while he was being dragged inside. It acted as a wedge. The door hadn't shut.

———

Bear shrugged off the Barrett's recoil and watched as Noble stepped away from the man Bear had shot a few seconds ago. Noble stared down at something. A piece of paper? An envelope? Whatever it was, his partner shoved it in his pocket and turned away.

"What're you doing, Jack?" Bear muttered as he watched Noble head for the cracked door. "No, come back up here."

What the hell was Noble thinking? He'd been attacked by two men and was going into a strange building uncovered. How many more were in there?

Bear grabbed the phone and dialed the number he'd memorized. It asked for his access code, and then required him to enter the next phone number. The line rang through.

"This is Steele."

"We got a situation here." Bear went on to explain what had just happened.

"She's gotta be in there, and there's not going to be any time to waste. Get moving. I'll mobilize the closest team I can find."

They ended the call. Bear hid the rifle where he'd found it, armed himself with an H&K MP5, a .40 caliber pistol, and two extra magazines for each. Enough to take on the entire building.

And that's just what he feared lay in wait across the street.

———

The hall lights flickered in random intervals, staying off for as long as ten seconds at a time. The corridor ran a hundred feet and turned right at the end. There were five doors on either side, but Noble didn't bother with any of them. The blood trail on the carpet continued all the way to the end.

His adrenaline had subsided enough that he could think again. Two men outside. One wounded. One deceased. At least one of them had an American accent. That could account for O'Neil's two agents who returned Stateside. A third individual pulled the first wounded man inside. Could that have been O'Neil?

As he retrieved the dead man's wallet, he recalled the person across the street wearing the jacket with the fur-lined hood. He never got a good look at their face. But the build seemed slighter. Perhaps a woman?

*Could that have been O'Neil?*

He paused near the end of the hallway underneath the one light that hadn't cut out. The ID in the wallet was a fake, but the picture was legit. Even if the wounded man and his accomplice managed to escape tonight, he could fax the picture back to Langley to get a positive identification. He couldn't tell in the dim lighting outside, but now there was no doubt. The implications created a rock that sat in his stomach.

But what about the wounded man? Noble had a better look at the guy yet couldn't place him.

The entrance door whipped open. Noble spun, pistol drawn.

He figured he was about to scare the piss out of some guy coming home with dinner.

Bear's tall frame blocked the doorway. The big man took in the hall, taking note of the blood on the floor. "That yours?" he asked as he closed the distance between them.

"I came out of it unharmed," Noble said. "Thanks for saving my ass out there."

"Any time."

"Yeah, well, let's try not to make too much of a habit out of it." He paused. "This all went down a little too quickly, don't you think?"

"They definitely had eyes on the street."

"Think we were set up like in D.C.?"

Bear shook his head. "Spoke to Steele. She's locating a team to help."

"Help who?"

"I know it don't sit right at the moment, man, but we gotta put some trust in her."

"Let's see if we can end it here." Noble continued toward the end of the hallway.

They reached the corner. The blood trail didn't stop there. They followed it, noting smears along the wall. Someone was hurrying, and someone was trying to keep up. Noble thought it might lead to one of the doors ahead, but no such luck. They stopped outside of each for a moment to listen. Families, televisions, radios, all the trappings of life seeped into the morbid hallway, but none indicated the people they were hunting were inside.

The trail led to the door at the end of the hall. They stopped there for a moment.

"I think there was someone else," Noble said.

"Where?"

"Outside."

"I didn't see anyone."

"You wouldn't." He pointed toward the front of the building. "They were on the other side of the street."

"What'd they look like?"

"Never got a view of the face. Jacket had a hood that obstructed the view. I get the feeling it was a woman."

"O'Neil?"

"The way my brain is working, I hate to make a statement like that and get off-track. We start thinking she's elsewhere, we'll miss the signs that she's standing in front of us."

"Whatever happens at the end of this trail," Bear said, "let's make sure we keep someone alive so we can make the bastard talk."

They stepped through the doorway into a grey stairwell.

"We visited Norfolk when I was a kid," Noble said, placing his hand on the concrete wall. "Reminds me of the carrier we toured."

"Which one?"

"The Nimitz."

"Good ship," Bear said.

"What do you know?"

"Watched a lot of History Channel while recovering from a broken leg."

"Didn't know that'd happened to you."

"Why would you?"

"Good point."

Bear pointed at the bloody doorknob on the door leading to the next floor. "I think this is our stop."

Noble glanced through the dirty pane of glass and saw a body on the floor.

# CHAPTER FORTY-SIX

The wounded man sat propped up against a door. He held his stomach with both hands. Blood seeped through, stained his shirt, pants, and the floor. He took a short breath every few seconds like a guppy sitting on the counter next to its bowl.

Noble knelt in front of the guy while Bear watched his back. He didn't recognize the man from the photos they'd been shown at Langley. His face was covered in patchy stubble. A scar on his left cheek stopped a centimeter short of blinding him. The guy's unfocused eyes looked through Noble. He didn't have much time left.

"Who are you?" Noble asked.

The guy looked like he just realized someone crouched in front of him. He swallowed hard, opened his mouth, but said nothing.

Noble poked him in the abdomen with his pistol's muzzle. The guy clenched his eyelids and teeth and groaned.

"If you can make that noise, you can talk."

A soft chuckle escaped the man. "What's it matter?"

"You can put an end to this," Noble said.

"To what?" His voice was gravely and weak.

"Tell me who you are."

"I'm dead whether I do or not."

"At least you can die with a clear conscience."

"Haven't had one of those in two decades."

Noble jabbed him again. The man made to grab his pistol, but his reaction time was too slow. It gave Noble reason to inch back from him.

"Where's O'Neil?" he asked.

The guy stared at Noble and said nothing.

"Was she the one who dragged you in here?"

He gave a slight shake of his head.

"Who was it then?"

He took a deep, gurgling breath, coughed. Blood trickled through the hair on his chin. "You're asking the wrong questions."

Bear said, "We gotta get out of here, man. Cops are already outside."

Noble waved him off. "What should I be asking?"

"When you find O'Neil, ask her how high up the chain it goes."

"How high what goes? Where is she?"

The guy shifted against the wall. His pained expression gave way to a morbid, bloody smile. "She was right across the street when you passed me."

Noble felt an icy chill race up his spine. "Where would she head next?"

But the man didn't answer. He couldn't. A ragged exhale was the last sound he made.

Noble went through his pants and vest pockets. There was no wallet, but he did find a key with a tag attached. Written on the tag was a three-digit number: 324.

"Come on, let's check this out before the cops get up here."

Bear looked back at the stairwell door. "We need to come back later. This is too risky. Might get ourselves pinned in."

"I noticed fire escapes on the side of the building. Probably have them on the back, too."

Bear hesitated while Noble started toward the other end of the hall.

"Every second we wait," Noble said. "O'Neil is going to get that much further away. This starts and ends with her."

Bear caught up and they found the stairwell on the opposite end of the building. The entered slowly while listening for sounds of someone climbing up toward them. A whistle of wind was the only thing Noble heard. Could be coming from above or below.

They hustled to the third floor. The stairwell door was a solid piece of metal that did not offer them a view of the corridor it protected.

"Allow me." Bear grabbed the handle and pulled it open a crack. The whistle subsided. After a few seconds, he stepped into the hallway with a gesture for Noble to follow.

Apartment 324 was the second one on the left side of the building, facing the rear alley. Bear stopped short. Noble ducked below the peephole and continued to the other side. He inspected the knob as he passed. There was no blood on it, or the surrounding frame. That didn't mean anything, though. The person who dragged the other man to the second floor might've been wearing gloves and had taken them off.

He stuck the key into the lock and turned it. It stuck for a moment before giving way with a slight click. Noble looked up at Bear and nodded, then gripped the MP5 Bear had given him with both hands. The big man stretched his arm over, grabbed the knob, and pushed the door open.

Noble pivoted on a knee and swept the open room with the submachine gun. "Clear."

Bear entered and moved quickly to the side wall, giving him a view of the hallway. He nodded without saying anything.

Shutting the door with his foot as he passed, Noble stepped into the room. The curtains were drawn. A cold stream of air blew at him from the hallway. He gestured for Bear to follow him.

There were three doors at the end. The one in the middle was open and led to a bathroom. Noble ignored it and kicked open the door on the left. A mattress on the floor had a red sheet draped across it. It was the only thing in the room.

"Other side," he said. By the time he'd turned around, Bear had the door open.

The big man holstered his pistol as he crossed the room toward the window. The drapes whipped in the wind. Bear stuck his head out.

"What's out there?" Noble said.

"Fire escape. No one's on it."

"Keep an eye on it. I'm gonna do a once over and see if I can find anything."

He hurried through the small apartment, going through drawers and cabinets in search of any evidence of who was here and where they were going next. The drawers were empty. The cabinets contained a few plates and glasses, but nothing else.

"How's it going out there?" Bear called from the hallway.

Noble walked toward him. "Nothing out there."

"Hear those sirens?" He pointed toward the open window where blue strobes reflected off the end of the building behind them. "We need to go now."

Noble started to follow his partner through the window. He stopped before sticking his foot through.

Bear looked back. "What?"

"I'll be right back." He rushed into the hallway and reached inside the bathroom for the light switch. The room brightened.

White and black tiles alternated on the floor and walls, disorienting and dizzying him for a second. He focused on his reflection in the mirror, taking note of the blood smeared on his right cheek. He wiped it with his sleeve, then pulled the medicine cabinet open.

"Jackpot."

Shouts from the hallway beyond the apartment startled him. They were closing in already. How?

Someone had tipped them off.

*O'Neil.*

Noble grabbed the six pill bottles and a small memo notebook.

The yelling drew closer. They were outside the apartment door. Had he locked it? No, he'd kicked it shut. There was nothing to stop them from entering.

He shoved everything in his pocket.

The door slammed into the wall as they broke it down.

Noble exited the bathroom with the MP5 aimed down the hallway. He squeezed the trigger twice. Six rounds slammed into the far wall. Probably penetrated into the next apartment. Would it be enough to hold the cops at bay? He didn't wait around long enough to find out.

Bear was already on the asphalt below, staring up at the window. The big man bounced from foot to foot. He knew they were closing in on them.

Noble used the rails to support him as he half-jumped, half-fell down each flight, tapping one stair in the middle of each. When he reached the bottom, he spotted Bear across the alley. He'd found a way into the other building. The two men entered and pulled the door shut.

"They're already in the apartment," Noble said. "Fired a couple of rounds. Must've kept them back long enough."

"Almost got yourself caught." Bear cracked the door and

looked upward. He cast a quick glance at his partner. "Was it worth it?"

Noble leafed through the pages of the memo book. The lines were filled with numbers. The sequence was random and made no sense.

At least not until he reached the final page.

# CHAPTER FORTY-SEVEN

A lexa Steele wafted the rising steam from the pot on the stove and inhaled the simmering Alfredo sauce. Any other day, her thoughts would cease to exist at that exact moment as the cream and cheese and garlic combined for the most heavenly of smells.

No such luck today. She'd been up for forty hours straight, which explained why she was making dinner at noon. The anxiety ran high in not only her, but McKenzie and Cribbs as well. This was the longest her uncle had remained within twenty miles of Langley in thirty years.

He watched her from the couch, throwing an occasional glance at CNN playing on the television. Nothing had been said about O'Neil or the slaughter at the safe house.

"How's the sauce coming along?" Cribbs asked.

Steele licked her finger and dipped into the pot. She pulled it out, covered in Alfredo, and stuck it in her mouth. The sauce burned her tongue for a second or two. She swallowed slowly, reached for the cabinet.

"Needs more garlic," she said, shaking powder into the mix.

"Don't go ruining it with too much."

"You can never have too much."

Her smile faded, and she turned toward her uncle when her phone began ringing. Cribbs started to get up.

She held up her right hand to indicate she had it, then reached for the phone. "This is Steele."

"It's Logan."

Steele nodded at her uncle. "Is your partner with you?"

"Jack's here." His voice sounded strained.

"What's going on? You can speak freely, this line is secure."

Bear exhaled and the tension left his voice. "This is a mess."

"The two missing agents?" Steele felt a lump rise in her throat faster than Cribbs hopped off the couch at that same moment. He leaned against the wall in front of her, his forehead brushing against hers. She tilted the receiver so he could hear the conversation.

"Yeah, well, the guy I took out. We're not sure about the other guy. Someone pulled him back in the building."

"O'Neil?" Cribbs said.

"That's Cribbs," Steele said.

"No, the worst of it is Noble saw her across the street but didn't realize it. We're thinking that the guy who dragged the man into the building was Stateside operative number two."

"You're sure about the deceased man though?" Steele asked.

"Jack pulled an ID off the guy. Picture matched the one you showed us."

"What happened after that?"

"We followed the blood trail into the building. Found the guy on the second floor, gulping down his last few minutes of life. Didn't get much out of him other than the info on O'Neil. He didn't have anything on his person other than a key for an apartment on the third floor."

"Did you search it?"

"We did. Place was empty. But we found a bunch of pill bottles and a notebook in the bathroom."

"Anything of interest?"

"Bunch of numbers." Bear paused and she could hear the rustling of turning pages. "Pages and pages of them for about three-quarters of the pad. Then nothing until the final page."

"What's there?"

"An address in Budapest."

"What is it?"

Bear cleared his throat. "You need to level with us, Steele, 'cause we're a bit confused by events here today."

"I'm not following." She stared her uncle in the eye. "What events?"

"We're not in town two hours and someone's watching out for us. How's that possible?"

"I don't know."

"You sure about that?"

Cribbs grabbed the phone from Steele. She held on just enough to hear. "Listen here you little bastard—"

"I'm not your damn trainee anymore," Bear said. "We got enough reason to doubt everyone on this, especially after what happened in D.C."

"We told you that was for your training," Cribbs said. "Without that, I don't know if we can trust you to wipe your own ass."

Steele ripped the phone free from her uncle's hands. "Get back." She put the receiver to her ear again. "Riley, I can assure you we are not responsible for what happened today. We figured they'd have fled the area by now, maybe sending a single man to check it out. I have no idea why they were waiting for you. But I still need you to work with me here. Where in Budapest?"

"First tell me what's in Budapest. Who do we have there?"

"We? Our team? No one. We hardly touch Hungary."

"What about the Agency at large?"

"I'm sure it's a possibility we've got a few people in place."

"Where are they? Tell me the addresses."

"Bear, I can't just..."

"Yeah, you can. I'll call back in twenty."

The line went dead. Steele and Cribbs stared at each other from across the room. His cheeks were red, jaw clenched. She raised a finger at him.

"Don't you start. We've got to get their trust back, not hamper it anymore."

He walked past her and stopped in front of the cabinet where she kept liquor. He reached up, pulled down a bottle of Jack Daniels and poured two fingers into a tumbler. She offered him some ice, but he refused. He downed the whisky in one large gulp. Didn't even exhale to stifle the burn.

"What are you thinking?" she asked.

"I need to get over there."

"Me too, then."

"Not a chance in hell. I need you here coordinating."

She filled a tumbler with ice, then grabbed the bottle from her uncle. "What are you planning?"

He stared at the bottle with his mouth agape, as though he was eight and she'd stolen his favorite baseball card.

"Cribbs?" She held the bottle at an angle but hadn't poured a drop yet. "What is your reason for going over there? It better not be to hurt our guys. They're the only shot we have at catching up to O'Neil."

He blinked away whatever thoughts were racing through his

mind and frowned with his lips and eyebrows at her. "No, of course not." He reached for the bottle after she finished pouring her drink and refilled his own glass. "Alexa, something stinks to high hell here. I'm gonna join them and we'll figure this damn thing out."

"I can get you on a plane there in the morning."

He tipped his head back and emptied the contents of his glass into his mouth. Shaking his head, he bit back a grimace. "No, I'll fly out tonight. Commercial."

"You'll be unarmed."

"Don't worry. I got a guy over there."

"Why am I not surprised?"

"Because unlike most, I busted my hump the last thirty years and people around the world respect me. It's only at home everyone treats me like I'm an asshole."

"You are an asshole." She smiled, and so did he. She reached out and hugged him. "Stay safe."

"Get those boys there safely. Don't tell them about me until they've landed in Hungary." With that, he set his glass on the counter, grabbed his tan jacket off the back of the couch and left Steele's place.

She hadn't managed a full breath before her phone rang again. She grabbed it after the second ring. "This is Steele."

"Well? Are you on our side?"

"Jack?"

"Yeah."

"Of course. I want you to go back to the airport. Wait at the arrivals terminal. Someone will approach and they'll give you the following access number: four, two, two, eight, one, nine, four. You'll reply with: six, eight, eight, five, three, seven. Got that?"

Noble repeated both numbers.

"A private jet will take you to Budapest. I'll make sure you skip customs." She eyed her empty glass. "There'll be a car waiting for you. No driver. It's yours. From that point on, I won't know where you are unless you tell me."

"It should go without saying that if this is a double cross, Steele—"

"Full disclosure," she interrupted. "My uncle is on his way over there right now. He says he's going to help you two, but...."

"You have your doubts."

She nodded, even though Noble couldn't see. "Yeah, that's putting it mildly."

"I'll be in touch after we land."

She hung up the phone and walked over the window looking out over her backyard. At one time, she lived in a place where her view had been of downtown D.C. The bustle of the city had contributed too much to general anxiety, something that went hand in hand with her position.

Staring into the woods, she couldn't help feeling that something was off. The ease with which O'Neil had been kidnapped, the lack of apparent torture, the men at the safe house executed, and O'Neil knowing that Noble and Bear were in Bucharest. It had all the trappings of an inside job.

Steele hurried to the front door and ran outside into the cold air. Her breath fogged in front of her face. It was too late. Cribbs was already gone.

And she couldn't help but feel she had signed Noble and Bear's death warrants when she let him leave her house.

# CHAPTER FORTY-EIGHT

N oble found a bank of pay phones stretched along the faded blue exterior wall of a drug store. He lifted the receiver, dropped in a few coins, and placed an international call to Istanbul, Turkey. Bear was nearby. The lookout. Noble turned his back to the phone booth anyway. The silver cord stretched across his chest. He stared down one end of the artificially-illuminated street and then the other while the beep-beep tones carried on for what felt like an eternity.

"*Selam?*"

"Is this Uri?" Noble asked.

"Who is this?"

"Is this line secure?"

"That depends on who this is."

"Noble. We met at the—"

"Restaurant. Yes, I gave you my card. You must be calling for a reason, so what can I do for you?"

"You still have friends in the intelligence business?"

"You could say that, though I would classify none as friends."

He paused a beat. Noble heard a door click shut on the other end of the line. "What is it that you need?"

"Did you or Taavi hear about the safe house?"

"I can't speak for him. But I have not. What should I have heard?"

"It was shot up while me and my partner were visiting Taavi."

Uri said nothing in response to the news.

Noble said, "Every man in the place died. O'Neil was gone, along with all her stuff."

"Who would kill the men, abduct her, and let her bring her things?"

"My question exactly."

"I can't answer that."

Noble grinned at the simple thought processes of the man. "No, I didn't expect you could. Can you do this one thing though?"

"Anything. Just ask."

"I need you to see what you can dig up on two names: Farah Nazari and Wahid Samara. Their relationships with each other, with O'Neil, and what they might have to do with the cities of Bucharest and Budapest."

"Bucharest and Budapest...which are you in, and which are you traveling to?"

"Thank you, Uri. I owe you big time. I'll call you back within three hours." He spun free from the silver cord and hung the phone up.

Bear gave him a slight nod. He was clear to proceed. Noble picked up the receiver once more and placed a call for a taxi.

Ten minutes later the transport arrived. The driver asked for their destination and didn't say another word until it was time to collect the fare. They headed into the airport with nothing more than the clothes on their back. An old man vacuuming the carpet glanced up at them with no interest in his eyes. The arrivals gate was deserted. Three out of every four lights over the luggage carousel were switched off. Rows of chairs were empty. Bear headed that way and took a seat that offered a wide view of the terminal.

Noble joined him. "How you feel about this?"

Bear shrugged, then scratched at the scruff on his face. "Not a lot of choice in the matter, I suppose. Gotta trust that Steele got us this far, she can get us the rest of the way."

Noble looked around the empty terminal. In twelve hours it would be a bastion of activity. People coming, going, working. Thousands of faces that no one would remember. He'd feel more comfortable in that setting. Right now they were the proverbial sitting ducks. At least the lights were dimmed. Made them less obvious from both inside and outside.

A guy in a black overcoat, dress slacks, and black wingtips entered arrivals through the same door Bear and Noble had. He glanced left at the row of car rental kiosks, then right. After a few seconds, his gaze fell upon Noble and Bear. He nodded and started toward them. He looked like a powerful businessman coming from a cocktail party or straight off the cover of GQ. He held his shoulders back, walked tall and confident. The smile on his face was both genuine and told a story of a man who got what he wanted whenever he wanted it.

"Gentlemen," he said with a decidedly English accent. He spouted off the access code. Noble replied. The man said, "I believe our mutual friend arranged our meeting here."

Bear eyed the guy and said nothing.

Noble stood and nodded. "Budapest."

"Budapest," the guy said. "Let's go."

He led them back to the entrance, but this time turned to the right away from the bank of entrance and exit doors. They wound through the airport to an unmarked exit door that led down a set of concrete stairs and out onto the tarmac where a Gulfstream was waiting with the joyous high-pitched squeal of a jet ready to get back into the air.

A set of metal stairs led up to the open door. A woman wearing black slacks and a long-sleeved white button-up stood at the top. The wind whipped her dark hair to the side. The man went first, nodded at the woman, and disappeared inside the plane.

Noble went next.

Bear third.

After they were inside the cabin, the woman pulled the door shut and opened the door to the cockpit, said something Noble couldn't make out, then walked up to them.

"Anything to drink?" she asked.

"Nothing," Bear said.

"Coffee," Noble said.

"Cream? Sugar?"

"Black."

"Make that two," Bear said.

"Three," the man said. "Though add some Bailey's to mine."

"What were you doing in Bucharest?" Bear asked the guy.

He smiled and glanced down at his knees, then back up at Bear. "I'm happy to share if you'd like to go first."

Bear chuckled. "Think I'll pass on that."

The man studied them while waiting for the coffee.

He said, "This jet is equipped with a decent bathroom if either of you'd like to clean up first."

A hint? Suggestion? Demand?

"Just gonna get dirty again," Bear said.

"Fair enough," the guy said.

Noble rose and headed to the bathroom and splashed some

water on his face, then returned to his seat next to Bear as the Gulfstream began taxiing into position.

"Did you know this plane has a shower?"

Bear shrugged. He eyed the man's mixed coffee. "How long is this flight?"

"Not even ninety minutes," the guy said.

"Just grip the armrest, big man," Noble said. "Can't have you drinking up there. Not on this flight."

Bear retreated into his seaside retreat or wherever he went when the flight anxiety kicked in. He'd flown almost a hundred times. It never got any better.

Noble leaned his seat back. He covered his eyes with a blanket. Sleep set in before the jet leveled off at thirty-thousand feet or so. Seconds later he felt a tap on his arm. Felt like seconds at least. He pulled the blanket down and stared into the eyes of the attractive dark-haired woman who stood at the top of the stairs. She'd loosened a few of the buttons on her shirt. He found it hard not to look.

"We are beginning our descent, sir." She took the half-full mug of coffee from the armrest and walked away.

"This plane yours?" Noble asked the guy who had his nose buried in a book.

He looked up and nodded.

"Well, technically it belongs to my company. But since I own the company, the plane's mine to use as I see fit."

They touched down fifteen minutes later on a snowy runway at the airport on the outskirts of Budapest. The plane rolled along the runway and settled at the end of the terminal. It was dwarfed by the commercial jets on either side of it.

The woman opened the door, stepped out onto the metal platform that some guy in a yellow cart had pushed up. She waited there, eyes clenched shut while snow billowed in on a fast and frigid gust of wind. It infiltrated the cabin. The men shuddered against it.

Noble shook the man's hand and thanked him. The guy palmed his business card to Noble and told him anytime. Then he patted Bear on the back and said, "Congratulations on surviving the flight. The moment you step off my plane, your chances of dying will have gone up over a thousand fold."

That was no consolation to Bear.

Another man dressed in grey overalls sitting in a luggage transport cart waited at the bottom of the stairs.

"He'll take you to your car," the woman said.

Before they exited the man told them to wait. He hurried to the back of his plane and came back with two hard-sided briefcases.

"What's this?" Noble asked when the guy handed one to him and the other to Bear.

"Don't open them until you are alone." He winked then turned toward the cockpit, no doubt to tell the pilot where to take him next.

*What a life,* Noble thought. *Go anywhere, anytime, all on the company dime.*

They rode on the open-top cart while the wind and the snow pelted them with the force of tiny pebbles fired from a high-powered turbine. They were traveling away from the airport on a small road that Noble hoped wasn't a runway. It wasn't. He knew that. Too narrow. The man drove alongside a tall fence topped with razor wire and came to a stop near a high pole with a dim light affixed to the end. He got out, unlocked the fence, and stood there with the gate open.

"Guess this is our stop," Bear said.

They hopped off, carrying their briefcases, and followed the man's outstretched arm to the black four-door parked on the curb.

A set of keys dangled from the man's hand. Noble grabbed them and walked to the driver's side.

Bear got in the passenger seat. Opened the glove box. He pulled out a map book and flipped through it until he found the index. He ran his large fingertip down the lines until he pinpointed their destination street.

Noble fired up the engine. Cold air billowed out of the vents. He pushed the little lever on the dash from blue to red and the air remained cold.

"Find it?" Noble said.

"Yep," Bear said.

"Ready?"

"Yep."

"Then let's roll."

# CHAPTER FORTY-NINE

The house was located on a quiet street three blocks off a thoroughfare outside the city perimeter as established by the M0. The neighborhood had everything you needed: shopping, dining, banking. The sprawling city of Budapest, like most major European cities, started from one central point and spiraled outward. For folks out here, going into town would only be reserved for special trips. Families in the neighborhood could live the quiet life and avoid the bustle.

Noble and Bear watched the cottage from inside their car with the windows cracked. They dealt with the cold. Otherwise the windows fogged. A single exterior light lit up the front porch of the little house. Darkened windows revealed nothing of what was going on inside.

They opened the briefcases the businessman had given them. Each contained a single Heckler & Koch MP5 and two fully loaded magazines. Nice parting gift, thought Noble. Too bad all airlines weren't so gracious.

Bear leaned back and napped for three hours. Noble

watched and waited. It was after two in the morning. He hadn't seen a car pass by since Bear had fallen asleep. After a few hours, the big man got up and Noble leaned back and took a nap of his own. This was the way to do it, he thought as he drifted off. A couple hours at a time. He could make up for a full night's rest that way.

When he woke, Bear was stretching his long legs out his open door. The sky was a pale pink. A deep breath cleansed his palate. The woodsmoke smelled new again.

Noble rubbed his thighs, a little concerned he couldn't feel them. "Anything happen while I was out?"

"Nope."

"What time is it?"

"A little after five-thirty."

"I gotta stretch out." He opened his door and stepped into the street. He crossed it and cinched his hood tight over his head and face. Anyone watching would see part of two eyes, a nose, and the center of his short beard. Hardly enough to make a positive ID.

Bear fired up the ignition to circulate some hot air through the cabin. He'd done it at random intervals overnight. It helped keep the coldest air at bay.

Noble returned to the car and sat in the reclined seat. He yawned away any lingering sleep. An urge for coffee surfaced. When the hell did that start?

"Don't look now," Bear said.

Noble looked, said nothing.

"I think we're about to get a little activity."

The front door opened and out stepped a man in a dark green jacket that covered him from his neck to his knees. He had on blue jeans underneath. Snow boots covered the bottom half. Fur peaked out from the top of the boots. The guy turned from sideways and looking away to facing them as he pulled the door shut.

And before he lifted the hood over his head, Noble saw enough of his face to know who he was.

"That's the other Stateside agent," he said.

"You sure?" Bear said.

"I don't forget a face. He's got a beard, but it's him. I bet he was the one who fled apartment 324. He met O'Neil, and they boarded a plane or hopped on a train and came here."

"You want him? Or should I go?"

Noble shed his jacket and threaded his MP5's strap over his head and under one arm. "I got him." He stepped out of the car and shrugged his jacket on and crossed the street.

The man had a half-block lead. Seemed the right amount of distance that early in the morning. A dog on a leash would have been better. But he had to work with what was available. The man reached the end of the block and turned toward the cloudy sunrise. Noble turned the same direction. The man headed toward the road with the shops and restaurants and banks. Noble thought maybe he was heading for coffee.

No.

He hoped the guy was heading for coffee.

Then he wondered if the guy had seen him in Bucharest. The two men who had died had. O'Neil probably had.

But what about *this* guy?

The guy stopped and reached inside his pocket. Noble fought his own instincts to freeze in place. Not a good idea. Keep marching. There was enough distance that it shouldn't matter.

The guy turned sideways and lifted a cigarette to his mouth. Perched it between his lips. A flame burst inside his cupped hands. He took a deep drag, exhaled. Didn't look any different from any other breath he'd taken. Maybe a little thicker. Grayer. After a few feet it was lost in the looming clouds.

Noble continued behind the man. Twenty steps later he

sucked in a nose-full of discarded secondhand smoke. Nearly coughed it out.

The guy reached the corner of the main road and stopped. He looked over his shoulder. His gaze swept past Noble. It never stopped on him. But Noble knew that didn't matter. This man had been trained the same as him. Maybe better than him, since he came out of the ranks of Special Forces. Nothing would have been lost on the guy, including a six-two man hiding his face while following behind him.

"Shit," Noble muttered into the cold air.

The guy disappeared around a brick wall.

Noble picked up the pace.

A truck rumbled past. Brake lights lit up far short of the next intersection.

Noble's right arm wasn't poking out of the limp sleeve. It was tucked underneath the coat. The MP5 grip rested against his palm. He unzipped the coat. It fell open a couple inches.

The truck's passenger door opened. Boots hit the ground. The person was crouching. Noble couldn't see their head. He readied himself for a gunfight out in the open with houses blocking them in. All shots had to be dead center. An errant round could kill an innocent bystander.

He tossed a glance to the end of the street, expecting to see the Stateside agent. No one was there. The truck pulled ahead.

The MP5's muzzle poked through the draped opening.

Noble pulled it back.

His would-be-assailant was nothing more than a four-foot-six girl dressed head to toe in a pink snowsuit trotting toward a little blue house.

He took a deep breath, trying to silence the rush in his head and the whoosh of his rapid heart rate. After he made it home—*if he made it home*—he decided he'd take up meditation. Cribbs had suggested they learn something to control the mind. Old bastard was right.

Noble continued toward the corner. The sun peeked through a crack in the silvery clouds. He squinted against the brightness. Placed his left hand over his brow. He hadn't zipped his jacket up and wouldn't until he had a view past the corner.

When he reached it, Noble felt like waiting there until the man returned. What if the guy didn't return, though? He might take a different route back to the house. Noble watched the light cycle twice then made the decision to move into the open.

As he did, he came face to face with the man he had followed.

# CHAPTER FIFTY

Momentum carried Noble forward what would have been another three feet. The guy in front of him cut that down to less than twelve inches. They collided, shoulder to chest. Coffee spilled as the man threw his arm out. The guy turned to the side, pushed Jack as he walked past. He uttered a few phrases he probably wouldn't say to his mother. Then again, Noble didn't know the guy's mother. Noble put his head down and walked forward and resisted the urge to say anything back. As far as this guy knew, he was a local. Not an American. Not someone there to take the guy out.

The agent cut around the corner and Noble pressed forward. He couldn't double back. Not now. It'd be too obvious. So he scanned the street ahead and saw the shop where the guy had bought his coffee. Noble went inside. Before he entered, he glanced over his shoulder and saw a deserted sidewalk behind him. Of course. Not like the other agent with his training would make it that obvious. If he had any concern at all.

Noble found the coffee and uncovered his face and sniffed

each carafe. He couldn't make out the placards but the flavor of the roast didn't matter to him. It all tasted like jet fuel anyway. But he wanted the freshest jet fuel. He poured two large styrofoam cups full and covered them with plastic lids, the kind with the peel back tabs that tucked into a little slot. He figured by the time he got back to the car, the coffee would be lukewarm at best.

Hot. Cold. Jet fuel. Didn't matter.

He grabbed a couple pastries from under a warmer. He let his hands linger there for a few extra moments to soak up the heat.

The fair-skinned woman behind the counter smiled in a way that pushed her rosy cheeks up so high her eyes disappeared for that half-second or so. She said something which he assumed was a greeting, so he nodded and pulled out a wad of cash while she rang up his order. She looked back at him and started to tell him the cost but something caught her eye. The semi-smile that had lingered now faded and her eyes disappeared again, but this time due to her brow furrowing. As the door crashed open, her eyes went wide and she threw up her hands.

There were few things that could cause that kind of reaction. An old boyfriend. A giant lizard walking on two feet. Or a man Noble had bumped into on the street corner a few minutes ago now armed and kicking in the door.

Noble swiped his arm across the counter and grabbed the closest cup of coffee. The door was between four and six feet away over his left shoulder. He turned in that direction while dropping to a knee and flinging his right arm in a wide arc. He caught a glimpse of the man as the guy was extending his right arm. The guy fired prematurely. He had no choice. A scalding hot cup of coffee was headed toward his face. The first few drops of liquid had already landed on his cheek.

The bullet passed a foot wide of Noble. It crashed into the

lower display underneath the counter through a bag of cookies, the contents of which exploded into the air.

The woman shrieked. She'd been hit. Noble couldn't see it, but people didn't yell like that for nothing.

The coffee nailed the guy across his nose and cheeks. He pawed at his face with his free hand. He took two more wild shots. The bullets went high into the wall above the clerk where the cigarettes were lined up neatly. The woman screamed again. The guy tried to retreat. He slipped on the puddle of coffee, regained his footing, but then stumbled and collided headfirst into the glass door. He dropped to a knee.

Noble lunged forward, head down, arms wide. He slammed his right shoulder into the guy's gut. The door was set on the hinges so it opened inward. The force of Noble's impact and the weight of the two men broke those hinges and the door opened up backwards and the men spilled out onto the sidewalk. Noble came down on the other guy's knee. Knocked the wind out of him. The guy managed to wriggle free of Noble's grasp.

The agent's face was bright red. He struggled to open his eyes. One was clenched shut. Tears seeped past the corner. The other opened a crack and seemed to settle on Noble. The guy had managed to hang onto his pistol through the scalding and the fall and the collision through the door. He lifted the pistol and fired.

Noble saw it coming. He rolled left. Pain traveled up and down his left arm. He glanced down and saw a tear in his jacket. He figured a decent gash was hidden beneath.

The window behind him shattered as the other guy sent a blind follow-up round. Hard to tell if he was trying to hit Noble at all. The guy rolled and brought one foot up and then the other. He staggered away, stopped, looked back.

Noble didn't wait for the man to fire again. He rushed toward the agent and tackled him to the ground. This time he controlled the pistol on the way down while driving the full force of his weight through his shoulder so when they landed all that weight centered on the middle of the agent's upper spine.

The guy let out a thick gurgle of a groan as they smacked into the concrete. His grip on the pistol released. Noble freed it from under his hand, pushed himself back, rigid and ready. But he didn't stay that way long. Noble took a deep breath, ran a hand across the agent's bare head, grasped his hood and pulled it back over.

The guy wasn't getting up. Not any time soon. Not ever.

He'd smacked into a short silver fire hydrant. Blood smears ran down the side where his face had slid along it. When Noble tackled the guy, the man had managed to stumble a few feet before getting tripped up and collapsing. Noble focused all his force through the man. Head met hydrant. The upper part of the guy's body wanted to stop right there. And it did.

But with Noble's two-hundred-twenty pounds the rest of the man's body kept going.

His neck snapped.

Noble reached his hand around the guy's throat and felt for a pulse. He didn't find one. He pulled a wallet from the guy's pockets and a chunky portable phone with a black nubby antenna. He shoved both in his jacket and pushed up to his feet.

A few people had emerged from darkened doorways and were staring at him.

He cinched his hood tighter. The woman inside the store called for help. Noble ran inside and around the counter. She was bleeding heavily from a gunshot wound to her thigh. Noble found a towel bunched up on a shelf. He shook it out, wrapped it around her leg and tied it tight.

He grabbed a phone off the counter and said, "What's the emergency number?"

She shook her head, confused by the wound or the fact that he spoke English or maybe the whole encounter.

"Police?" Noble said. "What's the number? You don't have much time."

She spat it out, he dialed the number, and handed her the phone.

Behind her on a low shelf he saw a VCR. He hit the stop button then ejected the tape. After pocketing it next to the phone and wallet, he yanked the VCR off the shelf and slammed it on the floor.

Back outside one man had the bravery or stupidity to get close to the dead guy on the sidewalk. He looked up at Noble, but his gaze did not linger long. Noble turned the other way. He didn't get to the next corner before the first siren wailed.

# CHAPTER FIFTY-ONE

B ear stood next to the car with the door open. He towered over the vehicle. Anyone inside the house could see him.

But he wasn't looking at the house. Instead, he had his hand to his brow blocking out the rising sun. He turned left to right.

He was looking for Noble.

Noble picked up the pace again. He slipped every five or six steps but managed to keep his balance enough to not fall. If there was a way to guarantee yourself a concussion, falling headfirst on the ice was at the top of the list.

Bear caught sight of his partner, gestured for him to hurry, then disappeared inside the car. The engine revved as he pushed it. The vehicle lurched forward into the middle of the road.

Noble planted his feet sideways and in front of him about ten feet short of the vehicle. He skated across the ice and slammed into the side, leaving a small dent behind. He pulled the door open and stuck one foot in. Bear took off before the other was off the ground. The backend of the car slid right. Bear got it under control and headed for the end of the street.

"What is it?" Noble said.

"They left, man."

Noble looked back at the house. Noticed the front door wide open.

"Maybe we should head back. Check it out inside."

"They all left." He glanced over at Noble. His gaze lingered on the blood. "Maybe they knew."

"How long ago did they leave?"

"A few minutes before you got here."

Noble thought back to the good Samaritan who had come over to check on the dead guy. Another lookout?

"We need to go by the store again."

"What store? What happened?"

Two police cars sat in the far intersection.

Noble recounted the incident for Bear.

"Jesus, Jack." Bear turned around in the middle of the road. "All right, we can't get there this way."

They pulled over on the next side street. Bear left the engine idling and opened his door.

"Where are you going?"

Bear looked back. "Gonna check this out. No one there saw me."

Noble leaned his seat back and covered his face with one hand. In the other he held the MP5 tight and hoped he wouldn't have to use it on a police officer.

Three long minutes passed. Noble counted every second of it. Bear's door opened and the car dipped to his side as the big man took his position behind the wheel.

"Either they work fast," Bear said. "Or our friends from the house got the body before the cops arrived."

"There was a guy," Noble said. "Crossed the street when I went back into the store to check on the clerk. He must've called them."

"They could be anywhere now."

Noble ran his fingers inside his hood and wiped the sweat off his face and into his beard.

"Let's go back to the house."

"You sure?"

"Do it."

Bear shifted into gear and drove back to the house. They didn't bother to park away from it. He pulled up to the curb out front. There was a driveway, but that would be suicide if someone returned. They'd pin them in and have the luxury of chasing them down on foot.

It was obvious the moment they stepped inside there wouldn't be much if anything to be found. The first room had four plastic chairs, the kind you keep on a patio. Nothing else. The kitchen had a fold-up table in the middle. Nothing else. They probably moved the chairs between the rooms. The cabinets were bare. Styrofoam containers littered the counters.

Noble checked the two bedrooms while Bear investigated the attic. They met back in the kitchen.

"Nothing," Bear said.

"Same," Noble said.

"Let's get out of here. Check with Uri. Call Steele. Figure out our next move."

Noble nodded and followed the big man. He spotted a crumpled napkin on the counter. No big deal. It was amid four other crumpled napkins and a couple of pizza-sauce-stained paper plates.

But it was different from the others.

He grabbed it by the corner between his thumb and forefinger.

"What'd you find?"

He looked back at Bear, shrugged. He unfolded the napkin

and flattened it on the counter. Bear pressed in next to him. His head blocked out the light. Noble slid the napkin forward a couple of inches.

*XVIII. TIMON.*

"The hell does that mean?" Noble said.

Bear pushed off the counter and took a few steps back. He worked his fingers through his beard as he searched the ceiling for an answer.

"The map. Districts. XVIII is a district in Budapest."

Noble turned to face his partner. "Timon must be who they're meeting there."

"There's gotta be a phone book here."

"Where? Place is empty."

"Somewhere."

They ripped open every drawer and cabinet. There wasn't a phone book in the house.

"We need to get going," Noble said. "Let's start making our way into the city. We'll find a phone along the way."

"Need to call Uri, anyway."

Noble pulled the sat phone and wallet from his pocket. "Got these off the guy."

"That a satellite phone?"

"Yeah. Using it will give our position away. I think."

"Better hang onto it." Bear dangled the keys from his hand. "What's in the wallet?"

Noble opened the billfold. "No ID. No credit cards. Just some cash."

"Might come in handy. You're sure about the identity of the guy?"

"No doubt in my mind."

"What's on the cassette?"

"*The Sound of Music.*"

Bear chuckled. "Figured that'd be your type of movie."

"It's the surveillance footage from the store. Had my face on it. Figured it best to remove it."

Bear held out his hand.

Noble started to toss him the tape. Hesitated. Said, "What's wrong with *The Sound of Music* anyway?" Then he threw the tape to Bear.

The big man caught it mid-flight. Snatched it out of the air like a short stop killing a line drive. He cracked it in half, then lit it on fire and dropped it in the stainless sink. "Let's get moving. This place is giving me the creeps."

They walked into the frigid wall of air outside. A siren wailed in the distance. The noise softened by the second. It traveled away with the clerk. The poor woman was in the wrong place at the wrong time. She'd taken Noble's bullet. Maybe he could get Steele to help her out when all was said and done.

The car's engine choked the first few times Bear turned the key before finally coughing to life. Noble checked the map and found a back exit out of the neighborhood.

The drive into town didn't take long. The first wave of morning commuters was hitting the road and heading to work. Living zombies, all of them. Noble hadn't been raised to accept that kind of life.

They found a quiet corner with a phone booth on the outskirts of District XVIII. Bear pulled up to the curb next to a sidewalk nearly narrow enough for Noble to reach out the window and grab the pale blue phonebook dangling from a cord. He stepped out and tossed a quick glance in both directions. Not a person in sight. No one to come yelling at him when he tore the phone book away. It took a couple hard yanks, but he got the job done.

Noble leafed through the thin pages, tearing a couple when his fingers stuck to the corners. "How does anyone read this?"

Bear took a quick glance and offered no reply other than a shrug.

"Might as well be looking at hieroglyphics with some of these names."

"Admire it later. Find that name and get the address."

Noble found the first page of Ts. He flipped through Ta, Tc, Te, reaching Ti after two dozen pages. He traced his finger down the page so his eyes wouldn't stop and linger. Tik. Til. Tim. Finally Timo. His heartbeat quickened. What the hell? He was simply reading a phonebook, not staring down the barrel of a gun.

He dropped the book in his lap and looked at Bear.

"What?"

"There's no Timon."

# CHAPTER FIFTY-TWO

They were on a street with more vowels than consonants, and more dots over the letters than actual letters themselves. Üllöi út. Noble didn't try to pronounce it. The trees lining the street were bare and only slightly hindered the view of the mix of old and new commercial buildings. Bear turned left across an intersection that had train tracks running through the middle of it. The tracks were part of the median, separating both sides of the road.

"Another phone booth," he said, pointing at the blue panels with a bright orange trash can affixed to the right side. "Should probably call Uri back, see if he dug anything up."

Noble inched his coat's zipper up. Didn't matter how high and tight he got it, the cold would impregnate his outerwear.

"Gonna head into that store over there," Bear said. "Meet you back here in five."

Noble nodded, exited the car and walked over to the phone booth. He dug out some change and Uri's number and placed the call. What time was it there? It took a few moments to work out in his head that Istanbul was two hours ahead of Budapest. For some reason, he saw Europe as a mirror image of the United States. He pictured London the same as New York City, and Istanbul to be hours behind, like Los Angeles.

"You find anything for me?" Noble said after Uri answered.

"Difficult to do."

"Why's that?"

"Your friend, Farah."

"Yeah?"

"She's a ghost."

"She's dead?"

"No, I mean she doesn't exist. No birth record. No death record. No credit, possessions, belongings. Can you get me anything else?"

Noble leaned back against the concrete wall and pictured the woman who had helped them in Aleppo. He wasn't surprised they weren't given her real name. And the only person he could think of that would have it was dead. Unless Steele knew more about the asset. What about the woman who had helped them out of Syria. Could he find her again? Could he gain access to her house? What were the chances she'd be there? A woman like that, she probably had informants in every country, one of whom would tip her off.

An orange commuter train pulled to a stop in front of him. A few people got off. A couple more got on. An older woman was semi-jogging down the street, waving her bag, calling after the train.

"With nothing more," Uri said, "I have nothing to go on. As to Samara, he was pretty shaken, but minimally injured in the attack. However, it was enough to force him into hiding. He's holed up somewhere along the border now."

"Any idea what he wanted with O'Neil?"

"Outside of general intelligence, I am unsure. I've asked Taavi to tell me everything he remembers about their last interaction, but he hasn't provided me with much. My contact can find very little about the woman. She was well hidden."

Noble watched the older woman board the orange commuter train as he processed what Uri had told him.

"Is there anything else?" Uri asked.

"See if you can dig deeper on Samara. I'll call back later today."

Noble pressed the switch hook and held the receiver for a few moments while he contemplated calling Steele. The train's brakes squealed as the engineer released them and it began to move again. Slow at first, picking up speed. He watched it travel down the line, coming to a stop a few blocks later. His gaze traveled back to center. To the building across the street. The dull brown three-floor building with glass garage door on the bottom right with large yellow letters spelling *AUTO SZERVIZ*. Next to that, double glass doors with *open* written in red neon. AC units were mounted next to the windows on the upper floors.

And in the middle of it all, in square brown letters, he saw it.

*HOTEL TIMON.*

At once he felt naked and exposed on the opposite side of the street with nothing to shield him from view. He retreated back against the wall, watched the windows for any sign of movement. The rising sun reflected off the glass. It was difficult to make out anything behind them.

The building looked less like a hotel and more like a hostel. Couldn't be that many people staying there. A dozen at full capacity, perhaps. That meant fewer doors to bust down. Didn't make the job any easier. That assumed O'Neil and her people were here. What if they had already concluded their business? They could be halfway to Serbia by now, or wherever their next destination was. Would the game of cat and mouse continue? Who was even the mouse anymore?

Bear pulled up and left the engine idling as he exited the car and walked over to Noble carrying a white paper bag folded over at the top. Noble caught a whiff of fresh-baked bread and garlic.

"What's up?"

"Turn around."

Bear lifted an eyebrow and then turned in the direction of Jack's outstretched arm.

"Gotta be kidding me."

"Too coincidental, right?"

Bear glanced back at him. "Seen anyone?"

"Been quiet the entire time I've been here."

"Think they're staying here? Or visiting someone?"

"Gotta be some sort of safe house setup. A place to re-arm, grab new credentials, make a phone call or two. The train stops right here." Noble pointed to where the older woman had scurried late to the orange commuter train. "They could ditch their car, take the train to the outskirts of the city and pick up another transport to get them out of the country."

Bear went back to the car and cut the engine. He tossed the white paper bag on the front seat. He slammed the door shut.

"Let's go check this out."

Noble crossed the street behind Bear. He checked through the window panes into the single garage bay where a blue VW bus was up on a hoist. The lights were off. No one was inside.

Bear pulled the right side of the double doors open and entered the hotel office. Noble joined him a moment later after scouting the other side of the street for a lookout. Couldn't be too sure. Still couldn't after taking the time to check.

A man in his mid-thirties with a thick mustache that hung over his lips stood behind the counter with his arms crossed. He had sunken eyes made worse by heavy bags underneath them. He smelled like vodka. Could've been the open bottle on the counter.

"We need to ask you a couple questions." Bear placed his thick hands on the counter and leaned forward. He towered over the guy, even after his posture surrendered a few inches.

The man didn't budge. He shifted his gaze from Bear to Noble and back again. "You are American."

"I am."

"I know. That's why I said it."

"OK. There a no Americans policy in this place?"

The guy shrugged and said nothing.

"We're looking for a woman and a couple of guys who might've arrived here within the hour. Americans."

"Why would I tell you anything?"

Bear had incredible reach. It helped that he was six-six. But Noble figured if you put him next to the average six-six guy, Bear would still have four to six inches of extra reach. Not only could he clear the counter and snatch the guy by his collars, he could also slam the man into the pegboard where the keys hung. Any other man, the guy behind the counter might've been able to step to the side, get to the open doorway leading to a backroom. But this guy couldn't. Not with Bear's massive hand closing in and gripping the fabric and bunching it up and tightening it around the guy's neck. He forgot all about trying to get away and went into self-preservation mode, which started with him wrapping his tiny hands around Bear's wrist.

Bear hoisted the guy off his feet and dragged him over the counter and dropped him on the floor between himself and Noble. Then he placed his large foot on the guy's back and pinned him in place.

Noble crouched down next to the guy's head. "What do you

think he weighs? Two-sixty? Two-eighty? More? What if he puts all that weight on the center right there?" Noble tapped the guy at the base of his neck. "How long you think it'll take your spinal cord to snap?"

The guy's face turned dark red. "What do you want?"

"My friend asked you a question," Noble said. "Answer him or we're gonna find out how strong your spine is."

"Yes! I saw them."

"What room are they staying in?"

"They aren't staying here."

"You offer a continental breakfast or something?"

"What?"

"What were they doing here?"

"They went up to 2C."

"How do you know that?"

"It's the only room rented."

Bear took his foot off the guy and leaned over the counter. "No key here for that room."

"In my pocket," the guy said. "Master key. Opens all doors."

Noble reached into the guy's pocket and pulled out a keyring attached to a pocket knife. It had six keys attached. Two were clearly automobile keys. Another went to a master lock. The other three were identical.

"Which one?" he asked.

"The silver one."

Noble held them to the light and isolated the key. "Why don't you secure him?"

Bear lifted the guy by the back of his shirt and pants and carried him into the back room like he was hauling a dead Christmas tree out.

Noble watched through the glass double door as the orange

commuter train pulled up again. No one got off. He figured they had ten minutes before the next arrived.

Bear came out of the room. "He ain't going anywhere."

Noble pulled the stairwell door open. A sharp gust of air sucked into the space. The double glass doors pulled open, then slammed shut. A bell attached to one jingled. He climbed the stairs, stopping short of the second-floor landing long enough to listen and get a good whiff of fresh coffee strong enough to overpower the smell of mildew.

"We can only assume whoever is on the other side of that door intends to kill us if we don't strike first," Noble said.

Bear nodded and said nothing. He had his MP5 ready to go.

"You enter the hall first."

Noble took the last three stairs in one step and backed up to the door. He pulled it open a crack and waited for Bear to give him the signal. Then he opened it the rest of the way and followed the big man into the second-floor hallway.

The doors were painted brown like the lettering on the front of the building. The carpet looked like it had been in place since the seventies. Off-yellow in color, it was matted down through the middle. Years of visitors coming and going combined with a lack of vacuuming. Smelled that way, too. The coffee wasn't coming from this floor, which led Noble to doubt what the man had said about 2C being the only room rented.

Bear stopped a foot short of the room. The C hung crooked. Noble continued past the doorway, butted up to the wall. He took a deep breath and watched as Bear counted down from three to one. After he lowered his index finger to complete a balled-up fist, Bear reared back and drove his foot, the same one he'd threatened to break the man's neck with, through the door. He hit it right at the handle and smashed it inward. It cracked and the door thumped open and collided with the wall and swung back toward them half the speed it had left. Noble caught it with his shoulder as he scanned the room with the MP5.

There wasn't much to the place, not that he looked around to take the room in. He couldn't. His gaze was fixed on the two dead guys lying on the unmade double bed nearest the window.

# CHAPTER FIFTY-THREE

B oth men had been shot in the head in a different part of the room. One was executed by the window, shot from behind. Blood splatter covered the drapes and the wall beneath the window. The other took a bullet to the forehead while seated in a wooden chair with a blue cushion. Blood and brain coated the wall behind the seat in a wide circle. They were then moved. Why? Did someone care that much about them?

"How many people did you see her leave the house with?" Noble asked.

"Two," Bear said.

Noble stood at the foot of the bed and stared at the dead men. "At the safe house in Istanbul we figured she had help taking out Schofield and his men, if for no other reason than none of them escaped."

"Right."

"So here we've got a small room. Couple of beds. Chairs. Bathroom. She shoots one man in the forehead, scares the other. He kneels in hopes that she's only gonna tie him up or maybe get close enough he can do something. It's his only chance, right?"

"Right."

"She executes him. Then she drags both of them from where they died onto the bed."

"Don't think she's capable?"

"I'm sure she's capable, but she's not hoisting them over her shoulder and setting them down gently."

"What do you mean?"

"Look at the sheets. Where's the blood?"

Bear leaned in, scrunching his face against the putrid smell. "Behind their heads."

"Right, behind their heads." Noble stepped back, gestured to the floor and sheets between the wood chair with the blue cushion on and the pillow the guy shot through the forehead rested on. "See blood anywhere else?"

Bear swept his gaze across the space. "A drop here and there."

"But no lines, no smears. No sign of struggle lifting a two-hundred-plus pound man and getting him into position, which is exactly what I would expect to see in this case."

Bear nodded as he got the point. "She had help."

"Possible she was only a witness, but hard to imagine she didn't have a hand in this."

Another voice spoke up from behind them. "There's no doubt she had help with this."

Noble and Bear spun, MP5s in hand, toward the voice. There was no doubt who it was.

Cribbs lowered his pistol and nodded at the men. "I'd suggest you point those things somewhere else."

"How'd you know where to find us?" Noble said.

"I didn't."

"How'd you know we'd be here then?"

"I didn't." He held up his hand to silence Noble before he could ask another question. "I didn't come here looking for you two. Just a happy accident all three of us ended up at this fleabag motel."

Bear had lowered his weapon a couple inches down and left. Noble kept his trained on Cribbs.

"Sorry if I can't put all my trust in you," Noble said, "considering what happened back in D.C."

"I'm not gonna explain myself again." Cribbs entered the room and continued toward them. He took a glance at the dead men on the bed. "That's in the past. You two made it—"

"Stop right there. You set us up once. How can we be sure you're not here to finish the job?"

Cribbs holstered his pistol and held both hands in front of his chest. "Look, if you want to shoot me, make it a clean kill and do it now. Because I can guarantee whoever did this figures someone will be in this room right about now and they're getting ready to tip off the police."

Noble didn't budge. "You know who did this?"

"I have an idea."

"Then why come here?"

"I had to try and stop it. I'd rather these bastards get taken in and serve time for what they've done."

"No, you don't. I can see it on your face, old man. You're here because you wanted to be judge, jury, and executioner."

"Son, this goes higher than you think."

The words resonated and echoed in Noble's mind. He'd heard them before. In Bucharest. In the hallway. The guy's dying words.

*"Ask her how high up this goes."*

Noble said, "How high?"

Right question.

Wrong person.

"I'm afraid to answer that," Cribbs said.

"Why's that?" Bear said.

"I don't want to be right." He reached into his coat pocket.

"Easy," Noble said, adjusting his aim.

"Just a camera." He pulled out a smaller version of a slim camera Noble had seen once before. It could fit in his palm. They moved to the side and allowed Cribbs to photo the two guys on the bed. He tucked the camera away, shook his head.

"Know them?" Noble asked.

"Unfortunately," Cribbs said. "We were part of a different team once upon a time. O'Neil came up through that team. These guys too. When we started ATRIA, they went another direction."

"Who is it you're really here for?" Bear asked.

"How'd you guys get here?" Cribbs said.

"Piece of crap parked across the street," Bear said.

"We need to get going. Won't be long before the cops get here, or someone comes to visit that bum you got tied up down there."

Noble and Bear stood in place.

"God dammit, that's an order. Let's move." Cribbs headed for the door and didn't stop or stall when he reached it.

"What do you think?" Bear said.

"Guess we should go. Keep him covered in the car. We'll stop along the way and call in to Steele."

Halfway down the stairs a gunshot ripped through the chamber. Noble hurried down the remaining steps and burst into the entry room. Cribbs stood by the front door, pistol in hand. Noble stepped around the counter and looked into the rear room. The man who'd been so hard when they walked in now lay dead with a hole in his head and his hands bound behind his back.

"That necessary?" he said to Cribbs as he brushed past him and stepped into the cold.

"Everything I do is for a reason."

They crossed the street single file and ended up shoulder to shoulder when they reached the orange train stopped in the median. Judging by the folks stepping off, it had arrived within the past ninety seconds. The ruckus of the brakes locking up and the five cars coming to a stop was probably loud enough to drown out the sound of Cribbs's gunshot.

There was a crowd of people waiting to get on. Most of them stared up at the side of the car they stood in front of. A couple glanced at the men emerging from behind the train. Noble turned his head away. He blocked the view of the other two men. By the time they reached their vehicle, the passengers had boarded, the doors shut, and the brakes hissed and squealed as they were let off moments before the train started rolling.

"I'm gonna ride shotgun," Cribbs said.

"Like hell you are," Bear said.

Noble held up a hand. "No worries, Bear. I'll ride in back."

Cribbs pulled the passenger seat up a few inches. "Let's head out of town. I got an idea where to go next."

"You know who we're gonna find there?" Bear said.

"Hopefully no one. Hopefully they are taking a roundabout way there and we'll get there first so when they do arrive we can end it without any more loss of life." He lit a cigarette and cracked the window. "Anyone want one?"

Noble and Bear declined.

Cribbs said, "Why don't you two catch me up on what you know?"

Noble spoke up. "It's a mess as far as we can tell. You know about Bucharest. We were close. Apparently she watched it all go down from across the street. I don't know if they knew we were there, or they were expecting the Agency's next move to be to investigate the apartment. Either way, they were ready, just not for us."

"How'd you end up at that motel?"

"How'd you?"

"Dammit, Noble, it is not your job to ask me that. Talk to me and then I'll talk to you."

Noble could've kept arguing, but it felt pointless. He said, "We were watching a house overnight. Had a run-in with one of her guys, your man who returned Stateside, I guess, a couple blocks away. Didn't end well for him."

"Anyone see it?"

"Yeah, but we destroyed the surveillance footage, so not too worried. But I think they had someone close by. That's why O'Neil and the rest were gone by the time I got back to Bear."

Cribbs shifted in his seat and looked back at Noble. He blew a thick stream of smoke in Jack's direction, which Noble fanned away before continuing.

"So we checked out the house. Almost left empty-handed when we spotted a crumpled-up napkin with something written on it."

"The hotel name."

"Yeah, only it said *XVIII. Timon.* Thought we were looking for a person. Found the hotel by accident."

Cribbs smiled. "Happens that way sometimes. Almost like you willed it into existence."

"That what we have to do now?"

"Possibly. Depends, I guess."

"On what?"

"If he'll come peacefully."

Bear said, "If who comes peacefully?"

Cribbs ignored Bear's question, as if he'd said too much, and asked, "You guys hear about Samara?"

Jack leaned forward. A warm wisp of wind blew at him from the front vent. "We heard he's holed up somewhere."

"Who told you that?"

"Wouldn't be right to give up my source when we've only just met him."

Cribbs shook his head after taking a drag off his smoke. "Yeah, well, Samara's dead now."

# CHAPTER FIFTY-FOUR

Noble thought back to his conversation with Uri that took place less than an hour ago. How had Samara gone from hiding along the border to dead so quickly? Was there a deception there? Was Uri somehow involved in this all the way back to O'Neil's disappearance? Or was it a situation where he couldn't fault the man for the information? After all, according to Uri, the intel had come secondhand. Noble didn't know the source. Hell, he didn't know Uri well enough to tell if the guy was feeding him a load of bull. But what reason would he have to do so?

He could only think of one.

Uri was protecting someone.

Cribbs flicked his cigarette out the window and rolled it up. The biting cold faded and the warm flow of air intensified as they digested the fact Samara had been assassinated.

Bear turned left. He said, "Who did it? Was it Agency supported?"

"It was not." Cribbs paused a beat. "You know the killer as Farah Nazari."

Bear and Noble glanced at each other in the rearview.

"My contact said he couldn't find anything on her," Noble said, doubting more and more what Uri had told him. "He called her a ghost."

"That's because she's paid to be a ghost. If we'd have realized she was your contact in Aleppo, you would have been blown out of there faster than a toupee in a hurricane."

Noble watched a line of women standing alongside a building waiting for a store to open as he soaked in Cribbs's words.

"I'm not following," Bear said. "Farah helped us locate Samara."

"Did she?"

"In a roundabout way. And she was there when we needed her. She got us out of Syria."

"Why do you think that is?" Cribbs said.

Because she wanted to help was the wrong answer. Cribbs wouldn't have left the question dangling if so.

"We were close to stumbling onto something," Noble said.

Cribbs nodded, said nothing.

"What?"

"I'm only beginning to realize myself," Cribbs said. "Turn right up here, Bear."

The next several minutes passed in silence. The city turned to suburbs made up of old houses and even older storefronts. Elderly people crowded benches and engaged in animated conversations. A lively crowd considering temperatures were in the mid-thirties. A definite improvement from six o'clock that morning.

Soon they were on a country road where the stretches of forest outpaced the houses.

A phone rang. Not the chirp of a house phone ringer, but more digital in sound. Noble remembered the satellite phone he'd stuffed in his pocket. He pulled it out and checked the blank screen, but the ringing had already stopped.

"Yeah," Cribbs said.

Noble craned forward and saw Cribbs with an identical satellite phone pressed to the side of his face.

"That's what I figured," Cribbs said. "We're headed that way now to check it out." He paused for several seconds. "I just need verification. Pretty sure I know where to go after that."

A shiver raced up and down Noble's spine. The look on Bear's slackened face indicated he felt something similar. What was Cribbs doing with an identical phone to the one Noble had pulled off a dead guy? Were they communicating with each other?

Cribbs turned his head toward Noble. He opened his mouth to speak. His eyes dropped from Noble's to the phone he held chest-high.

"Where'd you get that?" Cribbs asked.

"I could ask the same thing," Noble said.

"Company issue." Cribbs flitted his gaze from the phone to Noble to Noble's other hand, which now rested on the pistol in his coat pocket. "These are standard issue. Don't go getting any ideas."

"Why weren't we given one?"

"It wasn't deemed necessary for your mission."

"You mean an assignment where being in constant contact with Langley would have been beneficial?"

"I mean a job where if you were picked up by government officials and had a satellite phone in your possession they would have realized you were in their country for reasons other than bumming your way across Europe and it would have caused headaches that reached the White House."

Clandestine.

Kept secret, or done secretively.

Noble knew the definition. Knew that Cribbs had a valid point.

"You get that off one of the dead guys?" Cribbs asked.

"Yeah."

"One of our team?"

"One of the two that returned to the US."

Cribbs waved his phone. "These wouldn't have been standard issue for him."

"What about the dead guys back at the Timon."

"Yeah. Probably. I guess."

"Where're we going?" Bear asked.

"Private airstrip," Cribbs said.

"We departing?"

"No."

"Waiting on an arrival?"

"No."

"What then?"

Cribbs tapped the phone on his thigh. "Just need to ask a couple of questions."

They settled into a quiet lull. A welcome one, as far as Noble was concerned. He sat in the middle where the full force of the stream of warm air coming from the vents hit him square in the face. He breathed it in, let it spread through his lungs. This might be the most relaxed he'd be all day. Hell, no might about it. He was sure of it.

"Drive around the fence."

Noble opened his eyes and saw Cribbs pointing at an eight-foot-high chain link fence topped with razor wire. A half-mile in length and a quarter in width. A stretch of blacktop surrounded it. They drove past the entrance. Past the guard shack next to the gate. You could enter the structure from both outside and inside the fence. Noble didn't see anyone inside of it. He wondered how often the airstrip was used and who used it.

Bear completed a lap around the place and followed Cribbs's follow-up instructions to park in front of the guard shack.

"You two wait here." Cribbs got out, slammed the door behind him, and walked up to the small building. He rapped on the door a couple times. Waited a couple seconds. Hit it again, this time a little harder. A window next to the door opened up and a round-faced man poked his head out. Cribbs said something Noble and Bear couldn't hear. The other man took a deep breath, pursed his lips tight, and then nodded twice. The door opened up and Cribbs stepped inside.

"I don't like being out here," Noble said.

"What do you mean?" Bear said.

"In the car while Cribbs is in there. We don't know what's going on. What if he's calling in someone hiding just inside the woods over there."

They both stared at a thick stretch of pines where the sun couldn't penetrate past five feet.

"Think he wants to take care of us?"

Noble glanced at the phone whose twin was inside the guard shack. "Don't know what to think anymore. All I know is every second we sit here, O'Neil is getting that much further away."

"Maybe not. She might be sitting still. Waiting." He wiped his hand over his mouth. "Why don't you call Uri?"

"From this phone?"

"Sure, why not?"

"Someone is watching this line. Guarantee you that. Whether they're at Langley or some other spy headquarters, they're waiting for it to power on and ping a satellite so they can get the location and close in."

Bear leaned into the passenger seat so he could stare up at the window in the building. "What do you think he's looking for in there?"

"Someone arrived here. Someone from back home. Someone he's suspected involved in something we don't know anything about."

"Thanks, Sherlock."

"What do you want me to say? How about we hold him at gunpoint when he comes back and make him talk? Think that'll work out in our favor?"

Both men seemed resigned to their fate after that. They leaned back in their seats and closed their eyes and waited.

All the way up until the first gunshot rang out.

# CHAPTER FIFTY-FIVE

Noble opened his door immediately following the gunshot, but Bear was first to the guard shack. He didn't bother with the knob. Drove his large boot next to it and split the wood in half. It folded inward and the big man entered the space with his MP5 extended. His loud barks echoed around the small room.

The round-faced man sat on his stool, arms up in the air, pudgy fingers pointing skyward. His eyes were wide as saucers. A wet stain grew across his crotch.

Cribbs took a quick glance over his shoulder. "The hell are you doing?"

Noble waited at the entrance. He was stuck there. No room to enter the little shack.

Bear said, "Thought you were in danger."

"You're about to be in danger if you don't get out of here."

"Look," the round-faced man said in a heavy accent. "It's all right here. All the records you need. Take the book. I don't want it."

"Keep your aim on him," Cribbs said to Bear. He yanked the

red three-ring binder out of the guy's hands and leafed through the pages until he reached the current date. "How many people got off this plane?"

"Which one?" the guy said. He wasn't looking in Cribbs's direction. His eyes were locked on Bear.

"The one that arrived yesterday at two-forty-five."

"One man. Older. Sufficiently credentialed. A car waited for him."

"What kind of car?"

"Sedan. Slate in color. A younger man was driving. He got out, opened the door. Looked about his size." The guy aimed one of those pudgy fingers at Noble then stuck it back up in the air again.

"Put your damn hands down," Cribbs said.

The guy complied. And he said, "If you guys will go now, I won't report this."

Cribbs kicked the door with his heel. "How you gonna explain this?"

"Found it that way. Maybe someone left something good in here. A bear wanted it."

"They'll never believe it."

"Then I'll back my car into it. Tell them I passed out at the wheel. I'm diabetic. They'll believe it."

"Let's do it now."

The guy nodded and grabbed his coat and his keys and excused himself as he squeezed past Cribbs and Bear. Cribbs tore a sheet of paper out of the log book. He set the binder on the stool and followed Bear out of the shack.

The guard slid into his small coupe and moved into position. Noble pulled the door shut. The guard backed up, tapping the accelerator when he was a foot or two away. The door cracked open again, maybe split a little bit more. But the back of the car had no damage to it.

"Put it in park," Noble said.

The guy did. The brake lights went from bright to dull red.

Noble grabbed the guard shack door frame on either side, pulled his legs up, and drove them into the right rear corner of the coupe. His boots went through the taillights and dented the back of the car where the trunk lid met it.

"There we go," Noble said. "Looks about right now."

Bear brought their car around. Noble got in the backseat and left his door open while Cribbs approached the guard.

"I'll know if you talk," Cribbs said. "Don't think for a moment I won't. So if you have any inkling of who I am and what I'm capable of, you'll keep that fat mouth of yours shut." He pulled the paper from the log book and held it front of the other man's face. "Because I know who you are."

"Where to, chief?" Bear said after Cribbs joined them.

Cribbs covered his eyes with one hand and balled the other up into a tight fist. He threw a blind punch at the dash, one that left a sizable dent in the cheap plastic. He reached into his pocket and pulled out his pack of cigarettes. Lit three, handed one to each man, ignoring their protests. Bear rolled down his window and stuck his arm out. Noble figured the big man was going to stay that way until the smoke burned all the way down. Noble faked a drag but didn't inhale. That was all the rage in those days, anyway. He pictured the president, up on the stage, smile on his face and twinkle in his eyes not denying but certainly not confirming that he had gotten high.

Cribbs spit out an address.

Bear said, "There's a map book in the glove box."

"We don't need no damn map. I could navigate there from Siberia if I needed to."

"Then tell me where to go."

"Head back the way we came, and you better not tell me you don't remember because I'll cut your nut sack off if you don't."

Bear chuckled, threw it in reverse and slammed on the pedal, coming close to hitting the guard's coupe. The guard looked on from his perch in the shack. The door hung open like a prize fighter's dangling tooth after getting knocked out for the first time.

They wound through the countryside. Small houses dotted the landscape here and there. Passed a couple open fields Noble hadn't paid attention to before. They were wildly manicured and occupied by herds of cattle who didn't care if it was ten degrees or ninety as long as they had food.

They reached the suburbs where the houses were old and the storefronts were even older. Here Cribbs deviated from the previous path. He told Bear to turn left and follow the street halfway around the city proper where they picked up the M1 and drove slightly north of west for an hour and a half until they reached the M15. The M15 became the E75 in Slovakia and flirted with the Danube River all the way to Bratislava. But they didn't linger there. They headed due west on a road that took them into Austria. Apparently it was easier to get into Austria from Slovakia than Hungary, though Noble would have thought the opposite. Maybe it was the fact that Cribbs knew a road that few but locals traveled.

"What's near here?" Bear asked, breaking his hour-long silence.

"Vienna," Cribbs said, his voice rusty. "Thirty miles."

"That where were headed?"

"Sort of."

"Where to then?"

"Not far from Vienna."

Technically Cribbs was their superior, though they reported to Steele now. As best Noble could tell, Cribbs and Steele were on even footing with McKenzie overseeing both of them. So he had little reason to reconsider his deference. Cribbs knew something that they didn't, and whatever he had found at that guard shack at the airstrip had cemented what he thought he knew into fact. But it was time for the man to reveal more than directions.

"What are we doing?" Noble asked.

Cribbs glanced back at him for a moment, held his eye, then turned back toward the windshield. "For twenty years Eastern Europe was my playground. Up until a few years before the Wall fell. The Cold War was good for business. Things are different now, but I'm not. Neither are the others who worked here back then."

"What's that got to do with O'Neil?" Noble asked.

"Nothing. Everything. I don't want to say in case I'm wrong."

"You don't seem like the kind of guy who believes he's ever wrong."

"I don't." Cribbs pulled out another cigarette but didn't light it. He held it between his fingers like a delicate flower. "But this time I want to be."

# CHAPTER FIFTY-SIX

B ear pulled into the woods a quarter-mile down a deserted dirt-and-gravel road. The trees had shed their leaves months ago, but the dense skeleton-like treeline made it difficult to see more than ten yards in any direction. They exited the car and followed the path back to the road where Cribbs stopped and waited behind a thick tree. He closed his eyes and leaned his head back and listened. Noble did the same. Small critters scurried through the underbrush. Distant birds who lingered through winter called to one another. The wind rustled through the treetops, sending the few clinging leaves into the breeze. And the faint smell of a fire sending smoke through a stone chimney wafted past.

"We stay in the shadows," Cribbs said as he made a circling gesture with his finger.

"Who're you expecting to find here?" Noble said.

Cribbs didn't answer. He darted across the street and started on a path. He picked his way through the woods. Noble followed and Bear brought up the rear. Noble glanced back every ten feet or so, saw Bear checking their six. Then Noble didn't look back again. He trusted the big man to have his back no matter what now.

They stopped often. Cribbs would cock his head like an Australian Shepherd waiting for his next command. Then he'd start off again, sometimes straight ahead, other times closer to the road, and other times away from it.

The smell of smoke grew stronger, but Noble didn't know if that meant they were any closer. For all he knew, Cribbs had a couple of graves dug out here and was planning on filling them with him and Bear.

Cribbs lifted his arm, fist clenched. He leaned against a wide oak. He eased to the side to look around it. Noble squatted and took position a few lengths behind the older man. He strained to see through the tangle of trees and shrubs and dead branches. Through it all he made out what could be the shape of a cabin with stone exterior. Cribbs looked back, pointed at him, and directed him to move south, away from the road.

Noble crouched and moved quickly and quietly through the woods. He stopped at a point where the little house was in better view and he could still see Cribbs, who was now moving. Bear was walking alongside him. They got even with Noble and stopped. The three of them watched the house like it was the only job they'd ever been trained to do. Cribbs whistled to get Noble's attention. He wanted him to return to the group.

"Doesn't look like there's a sentry out here," Cribbs said. He wiped sweat off his forehead, watched it settle into the fabric of his glove. "You two are gonna get a little closer, up to the edge of the woods. Stay low. Watch the house."

"What is this place?" Noble asked.

Cribbs ignored him.

"What are you doing?" Bear asked.

"I'm going in to finish this."

"Let us go with you," Noble said.

"Not necessary."

"Like hell it isn't. There's a trail of bodies from Syria to Budapest. You want to be next?"

"It won't come to that." Cribbs held up his Browning 1911 .45 and switched the thumb safety off. "I know them. I can reason with them."

"And if not?"

"Then Mr. .45 here will settle the argument."

"How long should we wait?" Bear said.

Cribbs sighed as he thought it over. There was no keeping Noble and Bear at bay. How much time could he buy? "Three minutes. No sooner."

"This the end of the line?" Noble asked.

Cribbs nodded.

Noble pulled out the sat phone and powered it on.

"What're you doing?" Cribbs said.

"What's your number?"

"What?"

"Give me your number. I'll preprogram it here. You do the same."

Cribbs shook his head and muttered something about it being a bad idea. But he took the phone from Noble, punched in a sequence of numbers and then handed it back after doing the same on his phone.

"Worst case only," Cribbs said. "If this damn thing goes off while I'm settling things inside, it's likely gonna get someone killed. And if that's me, I'll make sure you go down too."

Noble said, "If you hear it ring, start shooting, because it means we're in trouble out here."

Cribbs gave him a look, pocketed his sat phone, and stepped out from the shadows. He walked on a line to the front of the cabin. Along the way he reached into his pocket. Noble thought he saw the glint of a key in the sunlight. A moment later it was confirmed as Cribbs stopped in front of the door, angled his body toward them, and slid the key into the lock.

"Why would he have that?" Bear said.

"Think about it," Noble said. "Cribbs said he spent twenty years out here, right? He didn't have to consult a map to get us from Budapest to Bratislava to here, somewhere in the middle of nowhere near Vienna."

"You think this was his hideout?"

"I do. And I think he let some of his people know about it."

"O'Neil."

"She spent a lot of time on the fringes of Eastern Europe and the Middle East. Makes sense that when she needed time to cool off, she came here."

Bear turned his attention to the opening door and they both watched as Cribbs disappeared into the house.

"Why would she come here now?" he said.

"That's what I'm trying to figure out," Noble said. "It's like she wanted him or us to find her here."

"Don't got a good feeling about this, man." Bear checked over his shoulder. "This feels like a setup. Can we really trust him?"

Noble glanced at the phone, at the screen, the number Cribbs had typed in. Would it ring to the one in Cribbs's pocket? Was it a con?

"Hate not knowing what's on the other side of this place," Noble said.

Bear nodded.

"I get that Cribbs knows the lay of the land," Noble said. "But what if we're leaving here without him?"

"Then we get back to the car and get to Vienna and get Steele to get us the hell out of Austria."

A loud crack from behind got both their attention. Noble pivoted and leaned against a tree as he scanned the woodlands for what had made the noise. Bear glanced between Noble and house.

"Anything out there?" Bear said in a low voice.

Noble shook his head. "Keep your eye on the house. I'm gonna go check it out."

He hadn't made it one foot when a gunshot rang out from behind him.

# CHAPTER FIFTY-SEVEN

Noble stared at the phone in his hand as though he willed it to ring.

It didn't.

Bear was on his feet. He leaned forward. He was ready to rush the house.

"That came from inside," Bear said.

The forest around them surrendered to the blast. All was quiet. For a moment. Then another shot rang out. Noble looked at the phone again. If Cribbs had fired, he would have called by now. Told them to come inside and help him with the mess.

"We need to go in," Bear said.

Noble tucked the phone in his coat pocket, unzipped the jacket and pulled the MP5 out. He held it the same way Bear held his. They crossed the clearing kind of staggered, kind of side by side, Noble on the right, Bear on the left. They covered a hundred and eighty degrees each, checking their six and everywhere in between.

They reached the front of the house, about ten feet from the door. Both men placed their backs on the wall and paused. They listened. They wanted to hear if something was going on inside, but they didn't have a lot of time. Noble resisted the urge to call out to Cribbs. He didn't want to tip anyone else off that they were there. For all anyone inside knew, Cribbs acted alone. Maybe it was wishful thinking, but it kept him from doing the wrong thing.

Bear gave a quick hand signal and he brushed along the stone exterior, twisted at the waist, his MP5 aimed at the door. The door hung open a few inches. Someone inside coughed a couple of times. Someone inside moaned a couple of times. Was it the same someone?

Under normal circumstances one of the guys would wait on the hinge side of the door while the other crouched down on the knob side. The guy on the hinge side would pop the door open. The guy on the knob side would clear the visible area, gaining the upper hand on anyone looking for someone standing outside the door. But with the door partially open, that plan went out the window.

Bear nudged it with the barrel of his MP5. It creaked on old hinges.

"Help us," someone called out.

Not Cribbs. It was a man's voice, so that ruled out O'Neil. An American accent, so not a local trapped inside. And it didn't sound like a young man. Was he sure it wasn't Cribbs? Definitely not. Cribbs had a very distinct staccato Chicago accent. Of course, if he was injured, it might sound different.

Bear counted down with his fingers three to one, ring to index. He went on one. Noble followed him. Bear moved to shield himself from the open and to cover Noble as he moved through the small foyer.

Noble stepped into a room lit through a skylight cut into the vaulted ceiling. A thick wood beam cast a shadow down the middle of the floor. Cribbs lay half in that shadow, half out. He held his hand over his stomach. A blood stain blossomed between his fingers.

"Jesus, Cribbs."

Noble scanned the room and saw another man on the couch. He aimed the MP5 at the guy and it wasn't until the man lowered his hand and Noble got a good look at his face that he realized who it was.

"McKenzie?" Bear said. "The hell?"

McKenzie shifted and revealed a gunshot wound to his left side, just under his ribs.

"Who did this?" Noble said.

"It was O'Neil," McKenzie said.

Noble glanced down at Cribbs for confirmation, but he just lay there, eyes closed, mouth partially open. He breathed in short bursts. His skin was turning grey.

"Where is she now?" he asked.

McKenzie pointed to the far wall. There was a door there. It hung open.

"Who else was with her?" Noble said.

"Only her," McKenzie said. "I think she got rid of everyone else."

"Why are you here?"

"She reached out to me. Wanted to turn herself in. Wanted to do it here, out of view. We were in the middle of her confession." He held up a small recorder. "Then Cribbs barged in. I let my guard down, and she grabbed my gun off the table. She shot Cribbs. Shot me, but I managed to twist and turn and dive to the couch and she didn't get a good a shot off on me. She knew Cribbs wouldn't have come here alone, so she ran."

He struggled to get to his feet. Stepped across the floor to where Cribbs was.

"He should've brought you two in," McKenzie said. "Damn fool, thinks we're still in our thirties, taking on the world."

Bear had dropped to a knee and began working on Cribbs. Before the training in West Virginia, before he enlisted in the Marines, he had trained to become a paramedic. Figured it would come in handy one day. He hadn't made it all the way through his training, but he'd learned enough.

"We're gonna have to get him out of here," Bear said.

"She can't have gotten far," McKenzie said. "We need to bring her in once and for all."

"I'll go after her," Noble said. "Stabilize him, Bear."

Noble took off for the open back door, unsure what waited for him on the other side. Would O'Neil stay? Would she take off to another unknown location? How far could she get? She obviously knew the lay of the land, having used the house before. Probably spent hours wandering the woods in preparation of an event such as this.

He made it ten feet into the clearing before he stopped. They were surrounded by woods. And if she hadn't taken off. If she waited just inside. He was as good as dead. But she would have shot by now. There'd be no point letting Noble get any closer to her. He took a step in the soft ground, stopped, and looked down. He scanned the dirt in front of him, beside him, and behind him. Every step he took left a clear dent in the ground. Proof that he had been there. O'Neil stood about five-foot-eight. Weighed about a buck-fifty, if he was guessing. Her feet wouldn't sink quite as far in the ground as his, but they would leave an impression. Sure, it might rebound, but not within a couple of minutes. The only imprints there belonged to him.

Noble turned, looked up the wall to an open window.

O'Neil never left the house.

She was upstairs.

His right foot slipped in the mud as he tried to run back to the door. His knee hit the ground. Cold wet spread across the joint as his pants absorbed the muck. He regained his footing and lunged for the door. But he didn't make it inside before the next gunshot.

# CHAPTER FIFTY-EIGHT

Noble threaded the MP5 through the doorway and stuck his head in far enough to look for a five-foot-eight, one-hundred-fifty-pound woman with blonde hair holding a pistol.

There was no one like that.

He stepped inside. His boots, still slick from the wet ground, slipped on the linoleum. He kept his hands on the submachine gun instead of reaching to steady himself. Didn't need to, anyway.

One shot. That's all he heard. Had Bear or McKenzie reacted first, taken O'Neil out?

Noble inched forward, shuffle stepping toe to heel. He saw the couch first. McKenzie wasn't there. Cribbs was still on the floor. The shadow from the wooden beam had shifted six inches to the left. The sun bathed Cribbs. He looked worse than a few minutes ago.

Where was Bear?

Noble took two larger steps. Froze.

"Oh, no."

He stared down at his partner, who lay on his side, eyes closed.

Five long seconds passed. The big man's side rose and fell. Noble exhaled. Bear was still alive.

Had O'Neil taken McKenzie hostage?

Noble dropped all pretense of caution and started for the opening. Bear opened his eyes, managed to say, "Jack." And that was all. But there was something in the way he scrunched his face, furrowed his brow, that enhanced the single syllable that escaped his lips. O'Neil was there. She was waiting for him to step out and give her a target she'd have zero chance of missing.

So Noble stopped and went to a knee. He closed his eyes for a second and visualized the woman he'd spent half a day with. The woman he'd rescued from a dingy apartment in Aleppo. The woman he'd shared a private jet with. The woman who'd slaughtered four trained operatives in a safe house in Istanbul.

She would show no mercy to him. Hadn't to Bear or Cribbs. Hadn't finished the job yet, either. Maybe she wanted to prove a point to McKenzie.

She'd be holding McKenzie with her left arm, on her left side. She might have a couple of inches exposed. Noble would have to aim high. He'd get one shot. If he missed, she'd fire her weapon and shove McKenzie forward. That would give her enough to make it through the door. From there, it would be a footrace. Noble figured he was faster. But she knew her way around. Once she made it to the woods, he'd never catch up. And he couldn't give chase for long. Too many people needed medical attention.

He took a deep breath and held it until his heart rate dropped a beat. It wouldn't go down too far. Not with all the adrenaline coursing through him. He rested his fingertip on the trigger, taking out the slack. He opened his eyes and studied Bear for a moment. Bear looked as though he might've passed out. How bad were his wounds? Noble couldn't tell.

A heavy gust of wind blew through, slamming the door behind

him with a loud crack. He almost squeezed the trigger in response. And he knew that was his moment. If it had startled him, it would have startled O'Neil. In the moments following she might let her guard down. Not much. A sliver, if that. But that was enough to increase Noble's odds.

So he whipped around the corner. The MP5 became an extension of him. He held it high and tight to his shoulder. He supported it with his left hand. He kept his face slack. He looked for the five-foot-eight, one-hundred-fifty-pound woman with blonde hair, the one whose life was about to end.

She wasn't there.

McKenzie had one hand on the gunshot wound on his side. In his other he held Cribbs's Browning. A thin smile played on his lips. He didn't bother to say anything.

The roar of the gunshot was met with the anticipation of fire tearing through Noble's chest. He dove to his right, on his shoulder, and rolled through. When he came up, McKenzie was grimacing as he pivoted and realigned his shot.

Noble didn't give him a chance. He threaded his finger through the guard, took out the slack in the trigger, and squeezed. Then he squeezed again. And a third time for good measure. In all, nine rounds punched through McKenzie, starting at his belly-button and working up to an inch below his Adam's apple. He stumbled and staggered. He dropped the Browning 1911 and it hit the floor with a heavy thud. McKenzie dropped like he'd been hanging by a wire from a tree that had just been snipped.

Noble got up and walked over to the man who stared up at him wide eyed, mouth agape. He was dead before he hit the ground.

Noble turned and went to Bear. His partner's eyes fluttered as he looked up smiling.

"Glad to see you're standing."

"Is it bad?"

Bear shrugged. "Don't think so."

"Save your strength." Noble slid over to Cribbs. Felt for a pulse.

Cribbs opened his eyes. "You get him?"

Noble nodded as he reached for his phone. He had to get help. His mind raced through the files in his memory. He had committed the number Steele had given him to memory, but his mind was blank.

"Your phone," Cribbs said.

Noble looked down at him, confused.

"Call the number I put on your phone."

Noble glanced at the screen and punched the send button with his thumb. He held the phone to his head and waited. It rang, once, twice, three times. It kept ringing. He wondered if it was just ringing on the phone Cribbs had brought in.

And then it clicked and there was a pause. "Hello?"

"Steele?"

"Jack, is that you?"

"It is."

Cribbs said, "Tell her we're at the place near Vienna."

Noble did, and he added, "Cribbs and Bear are in bad shape. We need medical transport now."

"What happened?"

"Get on a flight over and I'll tell you when you land."

There was a long pause. He heard her voice rise and fall in the background, though he couldn't make out exactly what she was saying. She came back on the line. "They'll be there within fifteen minutes."

"What about you?"

"I'll be there in seven hours."

He hung up the phone and looked around the place. At Bear,

who held his hand to his chest. At Cribbs, who looked like the life was draining with every passing second. And at McKenzie's corpse. Where was O'Neil?

He stepped over McKenzie and pulled open a small door, revealing a narrow set of stairs. He climbed them into a small attic with an open window overlooking the backyard. Seated on the floor next to it was O'Neil. She had two gunshot wounds to her abdomen and chest.

She licked her lips. She stared at him. She flinched as tears cascaded down her cheeks.

"I didn't mean for this—"

Noble didn't care what she had to say. He pulled the trigger.

Her glazed eyes stared out at nothing. All he was left with were questions, and he didn't figure she could answer them.

Why had McKenzie shot Cribbs?

Why had he shot Bear?

Why not kill them?

# CHAPTER FIFTY-NINE

Noble leaned his head back against the back of the purple vinyl chair in a small waiting room. They'd escorted him from the general waiting area to another smaller one near surgery. He'd been there for six hours, at least.

They had managed to squeeze Bear, Cribbs, and Noble inside the helicopter. Cribbs wanted to talk, but the medics refused to let him. They stuck an oxygen mask on his face and injected some fluid into his arm and he was out. Same with Bear, minus the talking.

Now they were lying on tables, cut open, surgeons attempting to undo the damage McKenzie had done. The physical damage, at least. There were other scars that might not ever heal.

Alexa Steele pushed through the double doors ahead of a red-faced nurse yelling at her in German.

"Jack," she said.

Noble rose and crossed the small room to meet her. The hugged like they were long lost friends or lovers, bodies pressed tight, arms closing and almost squeezing the life out of one another.

"What the hell happened here?" she asked.

"I'd like to know the same thing," he said.

"My uncle didn't do it, right?"

"No, it wasn't him."

She pushed herself back, but didn't let go of Noble's shoulders. Her eyes were wet. Her mouth open a bit, bottom lip trembling. "McKenzie?"

Noble nodded.

Steele let go and found a seat, stumbling back into it. She sank into the cushion. A bewildered look on her face. She must've been searching through files and intelligence and hushed conversations trying to find a link between McKenzie and O'Neil.

"O'Neil?" she asked.

"Dead."

"McKenzie did it?"

"Best I can tell." No point telling her he'd finished the woman off. "She was upstairs in that house, shot multiple times. In the gut. In the chest. Finally, in the forehead." He took a seat next to Steele. "When we found McKenzie, he had been wounded. Gunshot to the abdomen. Looked like a through and through that might've missed all the major organs it could've hit."

"She got him first."

"Possibly. Maybe he got her first, and she fired back, and he hit her again. She retreated upstairs. Got the window open. Was gonna jump. But he got there before she could. In fact, I think that's when he shot her the second time. She knew she was done, so she slumped down the wall and maybe pleaded for her life. She had some money from that thing with Samara."

It was a shot in the dark trying to piece it together.

Steele said, "What thing with Samara?"

"I was hoping you could tell me. It made no sense. Two or three weeks, and he hardly damages her? We got a lot to figure out here, Steele. A lot."

She nodded, said nothing.

"So anyway, she pleads, she negotiates, but in the end, McKenzie knows it's his ass on the line, so he executes her. Then he shoots Cribbs. Not a fatal shot, but close enough. We surprise him before he can finish the job. He gets me out of the picture, disables Bear, knowing I'll come back in."

Steele nodded some more.

Noble continued. "Thinks I'll run into the room where my partner is wounded. Meanwhile, I'm thinking O'Neil is holding him hostage. So he knows one way or another, I'm gonna be shocked by what I find. A damn miracle that .45 round missed me."

"And then you shot him."

"And then I shot him." Noble's gaze trailed down to the floor.

Steele reached over and grabbed his hand in hers. "You did what you had to do. And I think I'm starting to see what happened here."

Noble was curious, but something else was pressing on him. "What can you tell me about Farah Nazari, or whatever her name is?"

"What do you want to know?"

"She on our side, or...?"

"If the price is right."

"She killed Samara."

Steele nodded. "That's correct."

"So the price was high enough."

"We didn't pay her for that."

"She did it on her own?"

"We think so."

Maybe Farah hadn't conspired with O'Neil after all. Maybe she had been on Noble and Bear's side. "Can you tell me her name?"

"Can't do that. But you can ask her yourself if you ever run into her again. You'll find this world of shadows we inhabit is a small one, Jack."

The double doors opened and a small man with wisps of gray hair poking out from underneath his surgical cap walked into the room. Blue eyes hid behind his gold framed glasses. He stopped in front of Steele and Noble.

"How are they?" Steele asked.

"There were a few complications with Mr. Cribbs, but he will survive and should recover without major problems. Mr. Logan is alert and doing well."

"Can we see him?" Noble said.

"Not for a few hours."

"When can they return home?" Steele asked.

"We'll accommodate your requests, ma'am."

"Thank you," she said. "We need to leave as soon as possible."

# CHAPTER SIXTY

L ess than forty-eight hours later they were home. Cribbs was recovering in a private facility. He requested Steele, Noble, and Bear come to meet with him. Alone. They sat around his bed in a small white room that smelled like Lysol and was filled with the beeps and whirrs of medical machinery.

"Keith Witherspoon is the link." Cribbs wiped pasta sauce off his upper lip and then forked more into his mouth.

Noble and Bear shared a glance. "The same Witherspoon from that day in D.C.?"

"That's the guy," Cribbs said between bites. "The order came from McKenzie, which I found not unusual, but surprising that he was requesting I send you two dumbasses—and I say that in the past tense—to do the job. I mean, if you screwed it up, holy hell, what a price there'd be to pay."

"We almost did screw it up. You said you wanted it that way, to test us."

Cribbs smiled. "That might've just been quick thinking on my part, son."

"So you didn't set it up?"

"Look, what matters is that Witherspoon was killed because he was about to talk. He knew secrets that McKenzie didn't want to get out."

"We saw a file, though," Bear said. "Something about letting people die. Pissing off gangsters."

"One hundred percent rubbish," Cribbs said.

"Why is this the first I'm hearing about this?" Steele said.

"I figured it out on the way to Budapest. McKenzie and O'Neil were working with Samara."

"Why?" Steele said.

"Why else? Money." Cribbs swallowed hard, downed half his glass of water. "They were brokering a weapons deal that included a nice cache of surface-to-air missiles. Imagine what Hezbollah would do with that?"

"But he served our country for years?" Steele shook her head, disbelieving what her uncle was telling her.

"McKenzie had debts," Cribbs said. "Ones he couldn't cover."

"So Witherspoon," Noble said.

"Right," Cribbs said. "Witherspoon was close to the truth. McKenzie had to flip the script, so he arranged for O'Neil's capture, but convinced Samara to go easy on her. You guys saw the outcome of that first hand."

"She was shaken," Bear said.

"Or at least acted like she was," Noble said.

"And Samara knew you were coming for him," Cribbs said. "Didn't he?"

Both men nodded and said nothing.

Cribbs said, "It all went down a little too smooth, too. Maybe you didn't pick up on that, it being your first real job. But it did. McKenzie planned to have all three of you killed, but his girl over there, Farah, went against the grain. She bailed your asses out getting you back to Istanbul. Then O'Neil went rogue. You guys got out of that safe house at the right time."

"Clearly," Bear said.

"Then it was just a matter of time. You two flushed her out, dwindled her resources, until McKenzie caught up with her in Austria."

"You knew it was him at the airstrip," Noble said.

"I did," Cribbs said.

"Why didn't you tell us?"

"Because I figured you'd call Alexa here, and she'd call someone, maybe McKenzie himself. It'd get to him somehow, and he'd find a way to wiggle out of it. There's no chance of that happening now."

Noble pictured McKenzie staring up at him with death's gaze.

Steele said, "Tell me again the business McKenzie had with Samara?"

"He was brokering a deal, gonna arm him up, get him access to some devices that would've put Samara and his people at the forefront of the fracas over there. Samara had access to a donor with some deep pockets. McKenzie figured he'd cash out, disappear."

"How do you know all this?" Steele asked.

"I'm a pretty good spy," he said, smiling.

"What about O'Neil?" Noble asked.

"She came to me maybe a year ago, talking about wanting to get out soon. Take care of her son. She was wondering what kind of money they might throw at someone like her to, I don't know, live a normal life. Stay out of the spotlight. I made it clear that wasn't a possibility, and if she was harboring those thoughts, she was good as dead."

"This was her way out," Noble said. "Collect the big payoff, set her son up for life."

Cribbs nodded and said nothing.

"So that's it?" Noble said.

"That's it," Cribbs said.

"So what now?" Bear said. "We get an island vacation or something?"

Cribbs laughed, winced, coughed, and laughed and winced some more. "You're not going anywhere. Chances are within the next forty-eight hours we're shipping you two to Africa or China or somewhere in between."

"Sounds good, Cribbs." Noble caught Bear's eye and offered his partner a smile. "Sounds good."

### THE END

The story continues in Noble Beginnings, Jack Noble #1. Continue reading for an excerpt.

Sign up for L.T. Ryan's new release newsletter and be the first to find out when new Jack Noble novels are published (and usually at a discount for the first 48 hours). To sign up, simply fill out the form on the following page:

http://ltryan.com/newsletter/

As a thank you for signing up, you'll receive a complimentary copy of *The Recruit: A Jack Noble Short Story*.

If you enjoyed reading *The First Deception*, I would appreciate it if you would help others enjoy this book, too. How?

**Lend it.** This e-book is lending-enabled where available, so please, feel free to share it with a friend if your retailer allows.

**Recommend it.** Please help other readers find this book by recommending it to friends, readers' groups and discussion boards.

**Review it.** Please tell other readers why you liked this book by reviewing it at your favorite retailer or social book site. Your opinion goes a long way in helping others decide if a book is for them. Also, a review doesn't have to be a big old report. A few sentences often suffices. If you do write a review, please send me an email at ltryan70@gmail.com so I can thank you with a personal email.

Into The Darkness

**Affliction Z Series**

Affliction Z: Patient Zero

Affliction Z: Abandoned Hope

Affliction Z: Descended in Blood

Affliction Z Book 4 - Spring 2018

# PREVIEW OF NOBLE BEGINNINGS

# CHAPTER ONE

Baghdad, Iraq. March, 2002

I leaned back against a weathered stone wall. Muffled voices slipped through the cracked door. The night air felt cool against my sweat-covered forehead. A light breeze carried with it the smell of raw sewage. Orange tinted smoke from a distant fire rose high into the sky. Wisps of smoke streaked across the full moon ahead of the mass of artificial cloud cover, threatening to block the moonlight I used to keep watch over the sleepy street while the CIA special operations team did their job inside the house. The smart team leaders kept me involved. The dumb ones left me outside to guard the entrance.

Eight years on the job. Best gig I ever had. Then Bin Laden attacked the U.S. Forty-eight hours later everything had changed. Most teams were deployed to Afghanistan. Bear and I were sent to Iraq. We'd spent six months raiding houses just like this one inside and on the outskirts of Baghdad. And just like tonight, we were kept outside the house.

The only connection we had with the Marine Corps was the ten Marines over here with us. We only saw them a couple times a week. I had no idea where the rest of our Marine brethren were, and I didn't care. They didn't consider us Marines any more than we considered them brethren.

"Jack?" Bear said.

Bear had been my partner and best friend since our last day of recruit training. A recruit training experience cut four weeks short.

"Yeah," I said.

"I'm tired of this."

I turned my head, keeping my M16 aimed forward. Bear stared out into the distance. The faint orange glow of the fire cloud reflected off the sheen of sweat across his face.

"They just keep us posted outside," he said. "Ain't never treated us like this."

I shrugged. He was right. But there was nothing we could do about it. Bear and I were on loan to the CIA and had to do whatever we were told. Before 9/11, we were part of the team. But the CIA agents we normally worked with stayed behind in the U.S. and Europe. The teams over here weren't used to having two Marines with them and they weren't receptive to the idea.

"What do you suggest we do?" I said. "Quit?"

Bear shook his head and straightened his six foot six body. He shifted his rifle in his hands and walked toward the end of the house. Beyond his large frame I spotted a group of men. Figured that was why Bear went on high alert.

There were six of them huddled together. They spoke in whispers and appeared to look in our direction. Another three men walked toward the group. From this distance they didn't appear to be armed, but they had the cover of night on their side. Best to assume they were prepared to wreak havoc on our position.

"What do you make of that?" I asked.

374

Bear looked back at me with narrowed eyes and a clenched jaw.

"Trouble."

Trouble lingered everywhere in this damn city. No one trusted us here. Every time I turned a corner I worried someone would be standing there waiting to take me out. The only person I could trust in Iraq was Bear. The CIA spec ops teams we'd been attached to looked down on us. They all seemed to be waiting for the right moment to drop us. Hell, for all I knew, they were inside that house negotiating our arrest.

Bear cleared his throat and then pointed toward the group. The nine men fanned out and began approaching our position. The sound of their voices rose from a murmur to light chatter. I made out distinct sounds. Despite being in Iraq for the past six months, I had a weak grasp on the language.

"What are they saying?" I asked.

Bear held up his hand, fingers outstretched. He cocked his head like he was looking up at the moon. His body crouched into a defensive position. The barrel of the M16 rose to waist level. He reached out with his left hand to steady the rifle. I did the same. The A3 was a much better option for security teams than the Marine standard issue A4. We could drop the entire group of men in under five seconds if we chose to do so.

"Talk to me, Bear," I said.

He took three slow steps back, blocking my view of part of the street. He yelled something in Arabic.

The group stopped their advance. One man stepped forward. His tall, gangly body stood out from the short stocky men in the group. He lifted his arms, a handgun clutched in his right hand. I tensed and tapped my finger against the M16's trigger. The harsh sounds of words spoken in Arabic filled the air. They echoed through the street. Then silence penetrated.

Bear turned to look at me, then smiled, then looked back at the men. He shouted in Arabic again and lifted his M16 to his shoulder.

The tall Iraqi raised his arms once again. He had put his gun away. He turned his back to us, said something to the group of men and started walking away. The mob held their positions for a moment. The tall man pushed past them. He spoke in an authoritative tone, his voice rising to a yell. They turned and followed him. A few looked back over their shoulders in our direction.

I exhaled loudly. Cool, calm and collected when others would panic. Now, however, I felt my hands trembling slightly. A deep breath reset me to normal. It was a typical sequence of events.

"Christ, Bear. What the hell was that about?"

He chuckled. "I think they're on our side, Jack."

"What makes you think that?" I used my sleeve to wipe a layer of cold sweat from my brow.

His smile widened. "They didn't shoot."

"What did you say to them... ah, forget it. You're a crazy SOB. You know that, right?"

He shrugged, ignoring me and scanning darkened windows.

I leaned back against wall, joined him. "You think this is what Keller had in mind when he shipped us off to the CIA?"

I had kept in touch with General Keller since he took us out of recruit training and placed us into the CIA sponsored program some eight years ago. I knew this was not what he had in mind.

Bear said, "Beats what we'd be doing otherwise."

I threw my head back and nodded over my shoulder toward the door. "You sure about that?"

Bear shrugged. His big head shook slightly. He wiped his face and then looked at me.

"I'm not sure of much anymore, Jack. This is what I know. They ship us somewhere. We do our job. Pretty simple."

I nodded. It was pretty simple. Eight years now and we knew the routine. We do our job. Only here, our job had been castrated down to nothing but a security detail while they did the work that would get the glory. Hopefully they'd get it soon and ship us back to the U.S.

We stood in silence. I stared at the orange glow of the cloud that covered half the sky.

"Noble. Logan."

The voice ripped through the air like a mortar arcing over our heads. The door whipped open. Bealle stood in the doorway.

"We need you two inside."

I turned to face Eddie Bealle, fourth man on the totem pole of the four man CIA spec ops team. "We're ready to go, Bealle."

---

We followed Bealle through the narrow doorway and down an even narrower hallway. The smell of burned bread filled the house. I looked over my shoulder and saw Bear shuffling sideways behind me, his broad shoulders too wide to fit square between the thin plaster walls. We turned a corner to another stretch of hall that opened up to a dimly lit room.

"What's the deal here, Bealle?" I asked.

Bealle said nothing. He just kept walking. His rank on the team was too low to justify acting like a prick. I had wanted the opportunity to beat it out of him for weeks now. He stepped through the opening, walked across the room and rejoined his team.

I followed, stopped and stepped to the right. Bear stepped to the left.

Scott Martinez looked over and nodded. He said something in Arabic to the Iraqi man sitting on the floor. The man's arms and legs were bound with the thick plastic ties we carried. Martinez rose from his crouching position and walked toward me. He ran a hand through his sweat soaked short brown hair and wiped blood spatter off his cheek. He stopped a few feet in front of me. Like most spec op guys, he was a good four inches shorter than me and a head shorter than Bear. There were exceptions. My eyes drifted across the room and locked on Aaron Kiser. He stood six foot two and could look me directly in the eye.

I scanned the room, my eyes inching along the yellow stained walls and ceiling. Paintings and family photos hung crooked in obvious spots. The furniture had been pushed to the far end of the room. The captive family huddled together at the other end. The man stared blankly at the floor between his bound feet. His wife sat behind him, her black hair frizzed and disheveled. Blood trickled from the corner of her mouth. Her hands rested in her lap, bound at the wrists. Hiding behind her were two small children, one boy and one girl. Their scared faces peeked over her shoulder. Their eyes were dark with fear and darted between the men holding their family captive.

I hated this part of the job. If we had something on the man, fine. He likely did something to bring us here. But why keep the family held up like this? It seemed to be the MO over here lately, at least when working with Martinez. And I had no choice but to go with it.

"Your job here," Martinez said, as if he had read my mind, "is to provide support. No different than any other day. I give an order, you follow. Understand?"

I shifted my eyes to his and said nothing.

Bear coughed and crossed his arms across his chest.

Martinez dropped his head and shook it. A grin formed on his lips, but his eyes narrowed. We'd butted heads more than once, and I figured he had become as sick of me as I was of him.

"I'm so tired of you two Jarheads."

I looked over at Bear and mouthed the phrase "Jarheads" at him. He laughed.

The bound man on the floor looked up. His glassed over eyes made contact with mine. I felt my smile fade and my lips thinned. The man's eyes burned with hatred and desperation. He took a deep breath, and then looked down at the floor.

"Follow, Noble." Martinez turned and held up his hand while gesturing toward me. He walked across the room and stopped in front of the Iraqi man and then kicked him in the stomach.

The man fell forward into Martinez's legs. His face contorted into a pained expression while he struggled to fill his lungs with air.

"Get this bastard off of me," Martinez said.

Kiser stepped forward, grabbed the Iraqi by the back of his head and dragged him to the middle of the room.

Martinez moved to the middle and crouched down. He looked the Iraqi man in the eyes.

"I want you to see this. See what your failure to give us any information has led to."

Martinez stood and walked over to the man's wife. He reached under her arm and yanked her to her feet. She gasped, and her children cried out. They grabbed at her with their tiny hands. Bealle and Richard Gallo led the woman by her elbows to the wall across from me. Martinez followed. He stood in front of the woman, leaned in and whispered in her ear.

Her eyes scanned the room and met mine. A tear rolled down her thin face. Her mouth opened slightly. Her lips quivered. She bit her bottom lip and then mouthed the word "please" to me. Martinez brought a hand to her cheek, and she started crying.

Martinez moved to his right and looked over his shoulder at the man on the floor.

"Isn't your wife worth it?" His face lit up as he said it, and his eyes grew wide and the corners of his mouth turned upwards in a sadistic grin. I noticed his respirations increased fivefold. The spec ops leader appeared to find the exchange exhilarating.

The Iraqi man said nothing. He held his head high and his shoulders back. He stood defiant on his knees.

Martinez brushed the woman's hair back behind her ears and leaned in toward her again and whispered something to her. She let out a loud sob and then took a deep breath to compose herself. She looked toward her children and said something in Arabic, and then she turned to Martinez and spit in his face.

He stepped back and used the back of his hand to wipe his face. Then he struck her with the same hand. Her head jerked back and hit the wall with a thud. Her body slumped to the floor. Martinez reached out with one hand and grabbed her by the neck and with his other hand he pulled his pistol from its holster, pressing the black gun barrel against the side of her head. His hand slid up from her neck and squeezed her cheeks in. The pressure of his hands against the sides of her face jarred her mouth open. He jammed the barrel of the gun in her mouth.

"Is this what you want?" He paused a moment. "Huh? Want your kids to see your brains blown all over this wall?"

I felt rage build. This was wrong in every sense of the word. I took a step forward. Bear's large hand came down on my shoulder and held me back.

"Get the kids out of the room, Martinez," I said.

Martinez straightened up and cocked his head. His arms dropped to his side, and then he turned to face me. He stared at me for a few seconds and lifted a finger in my direction. The woman slid down the wall and crawled on the floor to her kids.

"Noble," he said. "I told you that you follow my orders. Not the other way around. You got it?"

"Let," I took a step forward, "the kids," another step, "leave the room." I kept moving forward until we met chest to chest and eyes to chin.

I heard weapons drawn around the room and the floor creaking behind me, a sign that Bear was moving into position.

"Gallo," Martinez said.

"Yeah?" Gallo said, stepping out of the shadowy corner he had occupied.

"Move the man to the corner, then the woman," Martinez said.

Gallo did as instructed. The family huddled together in the far corner of the room.

"Now stay here, Gallo," Martinez said. "Rest of you outside. Now."

I felt the barrel of a gun in my back but didn't turn to see who it was.

"You two leave your weapons behind," Martinez said.

We moved back through the narrow hall to the slightly wider doorway. Bear stepped outside first, I went second, and Kiser came out behind me with Bealle and finally Martinez in tow.

The moon now hovered directly above the street, beyond the cover of the orange smoke. I scanned the street and spotted a group of men hanging out a few blocks away. Were they the same men from earlier or perhaps a new group of men not as friendly as the last? Their chatter stopped. They turned to face us. A few of them stepped forward. Were they planning to attack? That wouldn't be a bad thing, of course. It might give us and the CIA spec ops something in common to fight, instead of each other.

"You guys keep an eye on him," Martinez said.

I swung my head around and saw Kiser and Bealle aim their guns on Bear. Like us, they carried Beretta M9 9mm pistols. Weapon of choice, it seemed. I followed Martinez's movements as he paced a five foot area in the middle of the street.

"Noble," Martinez said. "Step on out here."

I looked at Bear, and he nodded in return, and then winked. I crossed the packed dirt yard and stepped into the street.

Martinez lunged at me the moment my foot hit the pavement.

I ducked his blow and followed up by pushing his back. His momentum sent him into the side of the house. He reached out with his arms and came to a grinding halt. He turned, rolled his head. His neck and shoulders cracked and popped.

Kiser and Bealle kept their weapons pointed at Bear, but their eyes were fixed on Martinez.

I made the next move and engaged Martinez. We danced in a tight spiral, trading blows of fist and foot. Every connection sent a cloudburst of sweat and blood into the air. The two of us struck and countered with the precision of two highly trained prize fighters. We were equals now.

Martinez threw a flurry of punches. One landed on the side of my head. The blow knocked me to the ground. I knew his next move would be to kick me in the midsection. I quickly rolled and got to my hands and feet.

Martinez backed up.

I looked to the side. Saw black combat boots less than four feet away. I didn't have to look up to know the boots didn't belong to Bear. He wore brown boots.

Martinez started toward me. I had to time my attack just right. If I struck too soon Martinez would be out of my reach. Too late and he'd be upon me before I would have a chance to react.

I took a deep breath as time slowed down. Martinez's boots hit the packed dirt, heel then toe, left then right. He was ten feet way, then eight, then six.

I launched into the air to the right and twisted my body. Kiser didn't have time to react other than to turn slightly toward me. His outstretched right arm moved too slowly. My body continued to twist to the right, and I whipped my left arm around. My hand wrapped into a fist and struck Kiser's windpipe hard and fast. He let out a loud gasp as the impact caused him to drop his gun. His hands went to his neck as he stumbled backward and fell to the ground. He tried to suck air into his lungs, but his crushed throat wouldn't allow it. His lungs shriveled and his face turned red, then blue, and scrunched up into a contorted look of agony.

Martinez closed the gap between the two of us. It was the right move at the wrong time. What he should have done was pulled his weapon. Again, I ducked and slipped to the side, letting his momentum carry him a good ten feet away from me.

I cast a quick glance toward Bear, who held Bealle's limp body against the building with his left hand while his right delivered punch after furious punch.

With Bealle and Kiser out of commission, I turned to deal with Martinez, who had just scraped himself off the ground and was approaching. I still couldn't figure out why he didn't pull his gun on me. End it quickly. He stepped over Kiser's limp body, coming to a stop a few feet away from me.

I heard a body hit the ground behind me and then Bear appeared next to me.

Martinez lunged forward. I moved to the side and brought a fist down across the bridge of his nose, sending him to the ground, hard. Bear picked him up, and then drove two hard blows to the man's face and then tossed him onto the ground next to Bealle.

We reentered the house with our guns drawn and confronted Gallo. He gave up without a fight.

"You people should leave," I said to the family. "Tonight. Now."

Bear removed the thick plastic ties that bound their arms together.

The family huddled together. Each parent scooped up a kid.

"Follow us out and then go." I grabbed my M16 from its resting spot on the wall and then led the family down the narrow hall. I stopped by the door, took a deep breath and then stuck my head outside. It was deserted. Martinez and his men and even the group of Iraqi men down the street had bailed. I saw flashing lights reflecting off the surrounding buildings as sirens filled the air.

"Bear," I called down the hall. "We need to get out of here."

# CHAPTER TWO

Martinez and the others peeled away in the van we had rode in. That left Bear and I searching for a way back to headquarters. But before that, we had to get away from the house before the police arrived. We managed to slip around the corner before a squad car arrived.

"You pay attention on the ride in?" I asked.

Bear nodded. "I've been out here before."

I scanned the street. Empty, except for a few small cars parked on narrow strips of dirt between the road and houses.

"Take your pick."

He pointed at a blue two door that didn't look like it could fit one of us, let alone both of us. He started toward the car parked a half block away. The sound of driving slowly echoed from behind.

"We better pick it up," I said.

We reached the car. Both of us were ready to smash in the windows. I checked the door handle and found it to be unlocked. We got inside just before white light flooded the street. I looked back and saw a police car at the end of the road with its spotlight pointing in our direction. Bear pulled at the cheap plastic underneath the steering column and ripped it free. He touched the ignition wires together and the little car buzzed to life. He put it in first gear and we rolled to the end of the street. Anticipation and anxiety filled the front of the car. We stopped at the end of the road. The floodlight still illuminated the street. It didn't get closer, didn't fade away.

"Turn left," I said.

"We need to go right."

"I'm sure we can pick it back up, Bear. But let's go left, circle back and see what these guys are doing."

He nodded, eased the car forward and made a left turn. The shift from bright light to darkness messed with our vision and we almost didn't notice the group of men in the road.

Bear hit the brakes. "Really?" He pounded on the horn. Short bursts of high pitched honks filled the air. "Doesn't anybody hang out in a bar in this damn country?"

"Flash your highs and move slow, Bear."

He did.

The group of men split in the middle, just enough for us to pass between the divided group. They leaned over and peered through the window. A few pushed against the small car, rocking it on its chassis.

"I got a bad feeling, Jack."

"Just keep going."

I clutched my Beretta M9 tight against my chest, ready to fire on the first man to punch through the window. The M16s were lying across the back seat. A chill washed over me at the thought of one or two of the men getting into the back of the car and getting their hands on the fully automatic weapons. One squeeze of the trigger and they could take us and half their group out before they realized they had fired.

The car slowed to a stop.

"What the hell, Bear?"

"Want me to run him over?" He flung his arms forward.

I opened my mouth to say yes and turned my head to look out the windshield. A small kid, maybe seven or eight years old, stood directly in our path.

"Put it in reverse."

Bear's eyes darted to the rear-view mirror.

"They're blocking the path."

I turned in my seat to get a look at the gathering of men behind us. Three silhouettes blocked the moonlit view of the street.

"Run them over."

"What?"

"They put themselves there," I said. "They have a choice. That kid didn't."

Bear's hand moved to the shifter. He slid it over then down, into reverse. Hit the gas. Three quick thuds filled the car. Two men fell to the side. The car bounced as we rolled over the third.

The rest of the men separated and we sped backward. They regrouped and huddled around their injured friend. A few turned their attention toward us and then bottles and rocks rained down on the little car.

Bear whipped the car around in a tight circle. Threw it into first then sped away in the opposite direction. I kept my head turned and watched through the back window for nearly five minutes.

"I think we're good."

Bear nodded, checking the rear-view mirror every three to five seconds. "It's getting too hot, Jack."

"I know. I don't like this any more than you."

I leaned back in my undersized seat, rubbed my eyes with my thumbs, then turned my head and stared out the window. We were outside the city, past the suburbs. The barren landscape was a welcome respite from the hordes of roaming vigilantes and anti-American Iraqis we encountered on a daily basis.

"I'll call Abbot and Keller after we get back. See about getting us out of here."

Bear didn't say anything. His big hands wrapped around the steering wheel, his eyes focused on the empty road. We rode in silence the remaining twenty miles back to base.

———

We shared a single room on base. Two single beds, a small kitchenette with a stove, mini-fridge and microwave, and a wooden table with two matching chairs. Frankly, we didn't need much else. We ate, slept, trained on our own and performed missions with the CIA ops teams. Outside of the missions, the operatives had no interaction with us. It wasn't a written rule or anything like that. They didn't want anything to do with us. These guys looked down on the Marines in the program. A stark contrast from the operatives based in the U.S. and Europe. They welcomed the help and our point of view on the missions. Christ, they pulled us eight weeks into recruit training, and we were then put through CIA training. It's not like Bear and I were hard core Marines.

Bear returned to the room carrying a twelve pack of piss warm beer.

"Get anything to eat?" I asked.

He held up the twelve pack. "Figured it's a good night to drink our dinner."

"Only problem with that," I said, "is six beers doesn't make a meal."

He stepped through the doorway and into the room then lifted his other arm. "That's why I got you your own."

I laughed, then grabbed the cardboard box holding my dinner and cracked open a warm one, taking a long pull from the bottle.

"God, this stuff is awful," I said.

Bear chugged three quarters of a bottle then set it down on the table and let out a loud exhale.

"I don't know, Jack. It's not that bad." A loud belch followed.

I finished my beer and pushed back from the table. "And with that, I'm going to get a shower."

I exited the room into the dimly lit hallway. It was quiet. I checked my watch and saw it was only ten p.m. It was too quiet for ten, though. I shook my head to clear the thoughts and shrugged off the anxiety. I entered the bathroom and shower facility at our end of the hall, finding the communal shower room empty. I quickly washed the sweat, dirt and blood off and then moved to the far end of the row of sinks. I looked into the mirror and smiled at the growth of hair on my face. It had been almost two weeks since I had last shaved. I pulled out a can of shaving cream and my razor, but opted to keep the short beard, for now at least. I liked it.

I couldn't help but think of how bad that night had gone. Everything was routine until the group of men showed up a few blocks away from the house. People never approached us unless they meant trouble. And lately we found plenty of trouble. A quarter of our assignments in Iraq ended up with us getting into an external conflict apart from our primary target. And it always ended up being a mistake on the part of the men who engaged us. Not just our group either, this was the standard for all ops teams. The men who tried to take us on had no way of knowing who we were. And they had no chance of living long enough to find out. Despite that, they always engaged us. It was like they had nothing to live for.

Or maybe they had everything to die for.

On this night, though, those men hung back, like they were

waiting for something. Maybe they were playing games with Bear, the false advancement and the tall man yelling at us. That would have been enough to throw us off, make us think that they were a group of regular guys. Of course, they could have just been a group of regular guys. Maybe they were waiting for us to do something. It'd give them a reason, at least.

Then there was Martinez. He was in rare form tonight. Bear and I worked together, but we weren't always assigned to the same CIA team. We floated between four different groups. We'd spent enough time with Martinez to know he was a high strung, high motor midget. His guys weren't any different, either. This incident wasn't the first time that we'd squared off. It had happened three other times, including once on base. But this time he seemed to be daring me to make a move. Every time we got into it, it was because he pushed the limits on acceptable treatment of detainees. He pushed further than ever before with the woman, and in front of her kids, nonetheless. For a moment, I thought he'd pull the trigger. He might've had I not said anything. His guys sure wouldn't stop him. Pussies.

The gauntlet would come down on me over this. I knew that. It was their word against ours. There were four of them and two of us. Their bosses wouldn't bother questioning the family for their account of what happened. My bosses were in the U.S. in the Carolinas. I needed to call Abbot and Keller. Give them my side of the story before anyone else talked to them.

I got dressed, exited the restroom and walked back down the empty hallway to our room.

I pushed the door open and called out to Bear from the hallway.

"What do you say we go grab something to eat?"

No response.

"Bear?"

I stuck my head in the room. The back door stood open. I figured he'd stepped outside for some fresh air and decided I might as well join him. I grabbed a beer and found my jacket. My hand reached inside a pocket, searching for my cell phone. Oddly, it was missing. It had been in that pocket all night long. I hadn't even taken it to check the time.

"Bear, have you seen my phone?"

Still no response.

I stopped moving things around on the table and looked toward the back door and took two steps toward it. I saw Bear standing on the back patio, and he looked at me, but he said nothing.

"Bear?"

He clenched his jaw, but did not respond.

"Jack Noble," a voice said from behind.

I stopped and turned my head and saw two men, both armed, standing in the back of the room. I knew them by face, not by name. They weren't friends of mine. I dropped my beer and clasped my hands together behind my head. I looked at the floor and saw fizzing beer wrapping around the soles of my boots.

Two other men led Bear inside. He looked at me and shook his head. Pretty obvious what he was thinking. Same thing I was.

"What's going on guys?" I said.

"Shut up, Noble," one of them said from behind me.

"You can't just detain us without a reason," I said.

The man laughed. "We're in Iraq, Noble. We can do whatever the hell we want."

They grabbed my hands, forced them down and behind my back. I felt the thick plastic zip ties close around my wrist and draw my arms close together. The hard plastic dug into my skin the more I moved.

"If we want you to disappear," he continued, "there are thousands of miles of deserted land where we can bury you."

"That a promise?" I said.

"Keep talking." He grabbed my wrists and forced them upward. "And it will be."

"Jack," Bear said, his voice was low and trailed off at the end.

I looked at him.

He shook his head and looked down at the floor.

I followed his gaze and saw my cell phone on the floor, crushed.

"You know, I already talked to Col. Abbot about what happened tonight." I paused. "He's sending a team to investigate Martinez."

The four men laughed.

One behind me said, "You think we're worried about Abbot? He has less say here than he does in America." He walked around me, stopped with his face inches from the side of mine. "He doesn't have crap for pull with us. Our chain of command moves up a hell of a lot faster and farther than yours."

I cleared my throat but said nothing. I felt a knot form in the pit of my stomach but didn't let my external expression change.

"Are you getting this, Noble? You're screwed. Nothing is going to get you out of this."

For what, I thought. Kicking that douchebag Martinez's ass? Hell, the other ops teams we worked with all said they couldn't stand him.

"Let's go."

They led us through the front door, down the hallway, and outside to a Humvee parked in front of the building. We climbed in through the back passenger side door. Bear and I sat in the middle. Two men sat in back with us, guarding the door. They held their weapons firmly pressed into our sides.

"Make sure you avoid the potholes," I said.

Bear chuckled. The four men didn't. These guys had no sense of humor.

"Shut the hell up, Noble," the driver said.

I did.

We drove on in silence across the base. Stopped in front of the building we used for detaining persons of interest. Guess that was what Bear and I were now.

**Click here for your copy of Noble Beginnings**.

# ABOUT THE AUTHOR

Lee "L.T." Ryan lives in Charlottesville, VA with his wife, daughters, and three bully breed dogs. He enjoys writing fast-paced suspense thrillers, and post-apocalyptic fiction. When not writing, he enjoys reading, running, hiking, mountain biking, fishing, and spending time with the ladies in his life.

Current and upcoming projects include continuations in the Jack Noble, Mitch Tanner, and Affliction Z series.

Join L.T. Ryan's New Release Newsletter and receive a complimentary Jack Noble short story: http://ltryan.com/newsletter.

To Learn more about L.T. go to http://ltryan.com.

Join L.T. Ryan on Facebook: https://www.facebook.com/JackNobleBooks.

Printed in Great Britain
by Amazon